Matt pried the talisman out of Ellie's fingers, then leaned back just enough to look down at her.

"Damn you, Devereaux. Why do you have to spoil everything? You have no use for the talisman. Why not let me have it? It is all I want. I swear."

His eyes narrowed suddenly. Anger flickered in their brown depths.

"That's all? There's nothing else here that interests you?"

"Nothing," she said, giving him the answer she believed he wanted.

His scowl deepened. "You claim to be a scientist, right? Then are you willing to put your theory to the test?"

"What do you mean?" she asked suspiciously.

"When a woman sneaks into a man's bedchamber at night, she typically has a little more than thievery in mind."

Outraged, she said, "I beg your—!"

Matt's mouth closed over hers, capturing her lips in mid-protest.

ALSO BY KRISTEN KYLE
The Last Warrior

Kristen Kyle

Touched
by Gold

Bantam Books

New York   Toronto   London

Sydney   Auckland

TOUCHED BY GOLD
A Bantam Fanfare Book / January 2001

FANFARE and the portrayal of a boxed "ff" are trademarks
of Bantam Books, a division of Random House, Inc.

ISBN 0-553-57966-5

Published simultaneously in the United States and Canada

Bantam Books are published by Bantam Books, a division of Random
House, Inc. Its trademark, consisting of the words "Bantam Books" and
the portrayal of a rooster, is Registered in U.S. Patent and Trademark
Office and in other countries. Marca Registrada. Bantam Books, 1540
Broadway, New York, New York 10036.

PRINTED IN THE UNITED STATES OF AMERICA

OPM   10   9   8   7   6   5   4   3   2   1

Chapter 1

New Mexico Territory
August 1897

THE SMELL of blood and dirt penetrated the dark shroud over his senses. Pain radiated from his left arm as he regained consciousness.

Matt Devereaux cracked one eye open and stared, un-comprehending, at a blurry brown mass. He lifted his head slightly, bringing into focus the dry Ponderosa pine needles on which he lay. The sight brought back the memory of how he'd been left for buzzard bait.

Bushwhacked. In the Sangre de Cristo Mountains.

He remembered the flash of gunfire, the agonizing burn of a bullet tearing across his upper arm, the fall from his horse. And he remembered the voices as he fell. He'd heard them last at a high stakes poker game in San Miguel, a game he'd won yesterday just before hitting the trail to Santa Fe.

The tumble down a steep slope had no doubt saved his life. If he'd fallen within easy reach, Clive and Sam Hayley and their gang would have finished him off. They probably assumed he was dead. His characteristic luck was holding . . . just barely.

Matt rolled onto his back. A low, rumbling growl drowned out his groan.

In an instant, Matt lost all interest in his pain. A warning chill swept through his body. He shifted his gaze to the rock outcropping six feet over his head.

A cougar sat on the ledge. The predator watched him with golden eyes, motionless except for the end of its long tail, which curled and twitched as if driven by a separate, restless life force.

One easy leap would bring the big cat down on top of him. Matt inched a hand to his right hip. Only the smooth leather edge of an empty holster met his fingertips. He swallowed another groan. His Colt revolver must have slipped free in the fall.

Dammit! He'd survived the nightmare of his youth, not to mention this ambush, only to potentially end up as dinner.

The cougar bared its white fangs, lips drawing back in a flow of muscles that rippled over its head and flattened its ears. It hissed, the sound like the release of steam from a locomotive.

The noise was enough to send any creature into a blind panic. Matt's heart sank, but he'd glared defiantly at death too many times to let fear rule him now.

He sought the Bowie knife at his waist. Finding the carved bone hilt of the knife secure in its sheath offered little comfort, however. The cougar's claws and teeth were equivalent to ten such knives, and the danger was compounded by a speed he couldn't hope to match.

Matt eased up onto his elbows. Minimizing his movements to avoid antagonizing the cat, he looked around for his missing revolver. He spotted it several yards away, slightly downhill, half buried in pine needles.

The cougar stood.

Matt tensed. Instead of stretching out in a deadly leap, the cat began to pace along the ledge. Its thick coat was darker than most he'd seen in the southwest territories, golden brown rather than yellow. The black-tipped tail, a third of the cat's length, swayed with each sleek, restless stride.

Matt inched toward the gun, crawling backward on his elbows, each careful movement a torment of apprehension. The wound in his arm started to bleed again. The scent of fresh blood permeated the air like an open invitation.

Without warning, the cat sprang.

Matt flung himself to the side. He rolled downhill, grabbing the revolver and coming to his feet in a half-crouch.

The cougar landed several feet from Matt's last position, its shoulders absorbing the impact smoothly. Then it continued straight ahead in a relaxed, loping run. As it headed for the trees, Matt trailed its path with the gun, the barrel's sight fixed on the cougar's ribs.

Common sense demanded he pull the trigger. Yet he hesitated.

The cougar's leap could easily have brought it down on top of him. Why had it landed so far off the mark? If nature's perfect hunter had wanted Matt dead, he wouldn't be alive now to wonder about it.

Teachings from Matt's childhood visits with his Navajo grandmother came rushing back, whispering memories of mysticism and animal spirit guides. The appearance of a cougar signified that an attack from an unexpected source would be met successfully if one trusted in the great mystery and the circle of life.

Matt had been bushwhacked and left for dead in the wilderness, only to awaken and find a cougar watching him. Coincidence?

The cougar reappeared at the edge of the trees. Amber eyes shone like twin gold coins. The cat's gaze locked with his. A shiver of awareness rushed down Matt's spine.

He wondered if the loss of blood had gone to his head. No other man who'd survived range wars, Comancheros, and the harsh terrain of New Mexico would have hesitated to pull the trigger.

His grandmother's people believed that cougars possessed mystical qualities, and that wisdom and good medicine came to spiritual seekers who approached with proper reverence. But that part of his life had ended abruptly at age eleven, when his French father and half-breed Indian mother died of typhoid, and Catholic priests took him away to be educated at a mission. The Navajo teachings seemed a distant echo, barely discernible across a span of twenty-two years and a life that could hardly be called spiritual. Yet he still respected the beliefs.

He rubbed his thumb uneasily over the hammer of the gun.

Making an abrupt decision, he uncocked the revolver, spun its barrel down, and slid it into the holster.

"Don't give me a reason to regret this," Matt muttered to the cat.

The cougar didn't move.

He must be crazy. Who was he to deserve a spirit guide? Such blessings were reserved for warriors and spiritual seekers, not hard-bitten cynics who'd experienced the worst side of life.

Oddly, Matt's fear was gone. Nevertheless, the practical side of him intended to watch the animal's every twitch . . . very carefully.

Matt gazed up the steep slope coated with loose shale and matted pine needles. The climb back to the trail promised to be grueling.

A sudden wave of weariness swept over him. He'd lost a lot of blood as he lay unconscious. A sticky mat of red coated his left sleeve from shoulder to cuff.

Hooking two fingers into the bullet hole in the fabric, Matt ripped it larger. He inspected the damage to his upper arm. Although the Hayleys' attempt to kill him had failed, the bullet had gouged a deep groove across the muscle.

He removed his tan neckcloth and knotted it around the wound, pulling it tight with his teeth. Retrieving his brown, broad-brimmed hat, he tugged it low on his brow. Then he started up the slope.

He kicked footholds with the toes of his brown knee-high boots. The knees of his tan wool trousers, where they tucked into the boot tops, scraped the loose soil. Progress was slow and painful. As he reached the top, the cougar bounded onto the trail several feet to his left with enviable ease.

The cougar turned to watch him. Matt studied the cat, noting its sleek form and the delicate lines of its head. It was small, not over a hundred pounds, he estimated. The cougar must be female.

Not surprisingly, an empty trail awaited him at the top of the slope. The Hayleys wouldn't have ridden off and left his belongings behind. Hell, his saddle alone—hand tooled in St. Louis—was the envy of every man in the territory. His money, clothes, the bay stallion he'd raised from a colt, and the custom-engraved Winchester rifle—all were gone.

But most important, the Hayleys had taken his food and water.

Miles of mountainous terrain stretched between here and Santa Fe. On foot, the trip would take two days, even for a man not handicapped by loss of blood and lack of water. The nearest water was miles in either direction.

Matt started resolutely down the trail.

The cougar followed, as steadfast and elusive as a shadow.

After four hours of walking through the dry August heat, a gray mist began to crowd the edges of Matt's vision. He swallowed repeatedly in a futile attempt to ease his thirst.

At regular intervals the cougar circled wide around him, then headed into patches of forest bordering the trail, only to come back again and repeat the pattern. It was almost as if she expected him to . . . Matt shook his head. The very thought was ridiculous. Follow her? Not likely. An innate sense of survival overrode his shaky notion of an animal spirit guide. Hell, what if he'd only been lucky thus far and she had been more curious than hungry?

Matt ignored her. He trudged on, despite a tendency to stumble with increasing frequency. A cougar attack wasn't the only potential death stalking him in these mountains.

Then abruptly his mysterious companion disappeared.

Matt scanned the trees for any sign of tawny hair. The thought of dying sure made a man conscious of being alone.

Fifteen minutes later she returned. Damp fur was plastered to her lower legs. Her muzzle glistened with moisture.

His throat as dry as bone, Matt croaked, "Well, I'll be damned. Okay, *gata,* maybe I should take this idea of a spirit guide more seriously. This time I'll follow."

She led him at a right angle to the trail, through thick stands of aspens, into an area he'd never explored. A passage between two granite peaks opened into a small, idyllic valley. More aspens stretched down from the neighboring mountain slopes onto the valley floor, creating several places for shelter. The breeze brushed across an area of open meadow and rippled across the calf-high grass in rhythmic waves. A crystalline stream snaked down from one mountain crevice and fed into a pristine little lake.

Sunlight reflected like gold off the smooth surface of the water. Four pairs of mallards burst from the reeds bordering the lake as Matt stumbled to its edge. He sank to his knees and drank, listening to the beat of the ducks' wings and the splashes as they settled down on the opposite side. He cleaned his wound and ripped out his shirt sleeves to use as bandages.

As twilight descended, the cougar slipped away. Just before dark she returned, dragging the carcass of a small mule deer, its neck broken.

Matt watched patiently while she feasted. When she'd had her fill, she moved away from the kill and began to clean the red stains from her fur. Matt eased toward the deer with knife in hand. The cougar paused only briefly, then resumed licking her paws. Taking her lack of interest as acceptance, Matt cut a chunk from the deer's untouched haunch. He built a fire, cooked the fresh meat, and satisfied the hunger gnawing at his ribs.

Afterward, he watched in fascination as the cougar dragged her kill beneath the trees. Her paws worked in powerful sweeps to bury the carcass beneath a thick layer of dirt and leaves. Her movements revealed a heaviness around her middle, which he hadn't noticed before. The more Matt watched, the more certain he became.

"Is that why you watch out for me?" he whispered. "Is the instinct for motherhood hitting you early? It looks like those kittens will be coming into the world pretty soon, *gata.*"

Full darkness came quickly. Frogs trilled from the pond while crickets chirped their staccato song. Matt chose a place to sleep with a granite boulder behind him and thick grass to form a bed. He lay down, trying to ignore the pain in his arm. Exhaustion weighed like a millstone on his chest as he listened to the restless movements of the cougar in the darkness. Finally, the big cat settled down for the night in a spot about twenty feet away. Matt's heavy-lidded eyes closed and he slept.

The next morning he wove snares from the long, fibrous reeds around the lake. He avoided using his revolver to hunt breakfast. Not only did he need to save his ammunition, he was loath to damage the mutual respect between himself and the cougar. A silent hour's wait was rewarded by a catch of two ducks. He killed the mallards, then began the tedious task of plucking them.

The cougar eased closer as he worked.

Matt eyed her as she approached, uncertain of all the rules in their strange relationship. She stopped several feet away. Stretching out her front legs, she settled into the grass. She maintained the Sphinx-like posture, watching him with intense amber eyes. Her broad tongue rasped over her jowls.

Matt's mouth spread in a slow smile. The big cat's expression resembled that of a child anticipating a stick of candy. "Do you like duck, *gata?*"

Another sweep of her tongue answered his question. Matt tossed one of the mallards in her direction. The cougar moved swiftly, catching the limp duck in midair. She settled down and, trapping the carcass between her front paws, finished plucking out the down. Feathers clung to her face.

Matt laughed at the comical picture. Then he sobered, thinking about his predicament.

Although he'd recovered most of his strength, Santa Fe was still several days' distance by foot. What he really needed was a horse. It would take him in the wrong direction, but Angus McFee would provide a borrowed mount.

Two years had passed since he'd last stopped by his former partner's mountain cabin. It had been awkward to talk to Angus since a personal loss had driven the old man into isolation twelve years before. The man who'd once given Matt a new start in life and taught him everything about professional gambling now chose to shun people and pursue the lonely life of a prospector.

Matt left the cougar's quiet valley that afternoon. The cat followed, much to his secret pleasure. Since he'd shared the mallard, a new level of trust had grown between them. Although she maintained a wary distance, the cougar frequently ventured within ten feet of Matt.

When they reached Angus's canyon, the cougar's behavior changed dramatically. She froze in the shelter of the forest and refused to step into the clearing. The skin along her back twitched. Her fangs gleamed white, and she hissed in the same warning fashion that had caused Matt's blood to run cold in their first encounter.

He squatted on his heels and studied the scene. Everything seemed peaceful. Angus's log cabin was nestled at the foot of a rock cliff, facing a slender creek that meandered through the sheltered canyon. A thin plume of smoke curled from the cabin's stone chimney. The corral attached to the squat barn stood open, empty of the horses Matt had expected to find. Perhaps Angus was out prospecting. Yet it wasn't like him to leave the house fire unattended.

Matt continued watching for several minutes. Nothing moved. Nevertheless, a deeper instinct made his palms itch. He rose and drew his gun.

He worked his way along the perimeter of the clearing, using the forest as cover. The cougar trailed silently. Her shoulders moved stiffly, the end of her tail twitching.

Reaching the edge of the trees, Matt stepped into the sunlight, alert and watchful. The cat refused to follow. She paced under the trees as he crossed the clearing.

As Matt reached the cabin, he glanced back one more time.

The cougar had vanished.

Disappointment lanced through him. Two days of tenuous respect, patience, and progress toward trust were severed in an instant because of his need to seek out another human being. Since the cougar's survival depended on avoidance of civilization, however, Matt understood her caution.

But he wondered if he'd ever see the big cat again.

Matt eased back the Colt Peacemaker's hammer. He peered through a window. Overturned furniture and torn belongings littered the large single room in a wanton display of destruction.

Shifting his gaze in a constant search for danger, Matt continued around the building. He rounded the corner and drew in a sharp breath.

The crumpled form of Angus McFee was sprawled on the back porch of the cabin.

Matt ran to the old man's side. Bruises marred Angus's broad face. Blood covered the upper half of his dingy white shirt. His breath was faint and irregular. Matt's former partner still lived . . . but not for long. A man didn't survive a chest wound like that.

Matt dropped to his knees on the weathered wood. "Damn." He brushed a lock of gray hair from Angus's forehead. How he hated this feeling of helplessness. Too many important people in his life had died in his arms—his parents, Father Mendoza at the mission, and now Angus.

The old man's eyes fluttered open. "Matthew? That you, boy?"

"Yeah, it's me, you old coot," he said, forcing a teasing tone and a reassuring smile. "Who did this to you, Angus?"

"Damn Hayleys. Tried to force me to reveal my hidey-hole. Shot me when I wouldn't tell. Sons of bitches." Angus tried to sit up, then fell back, moaning.

Fury burned inside Matt. The Hayleys had bushwhacked him, then continued their path of greed by trying to steal from a lonely old prospector. To beat the victim, then lose all patience when he refused to answer, particularly fit Clive's manic style. The Hayley brothers' careers as bullies and thieves had finally crossed over to murder. They would pay for this.

"It's bad, ain't it?" Angus asked hoarsely. A thin sheen of tears covered his gray eyes.

The old man was too savvy to accept a lie. "There's nothing I can do."

"Well, hell." Angus reached up and grabbed a fistful of Matt's shirt. "And just after I found the big one I've been looking for all these years."

"Stop moving, you stubborn mule. You're only making it bleed faster."

Angus sighed. His grip loosened and his arm fell limply to his side. "I'm glad you're here. You always were like a son to me, you know."

Matt's throat tightened.

"Maybe I shouldn't have cut you loose. Maybe you still needed me after I found you in such bad shape. But after my Marla died, I just couldn't face people anymore," he whispered, still mourning the saloon owner who had died so tragically in a gunfight over one of Angus's poker games.

"Don't worry about it, Angus. We were together four years. I was twenty-one, ready to set out on my own."

"I want you to have everything I leave behind, Matthew."

"I can't take it, Angus," he said, stunned. "I'm not family."

"Hell, yes, you are." Angus groaned. "Besides, I've got no one else. Don't waste what time I have left arguing. Bit of gold is under the floorboards. You know the place. But that's not the best thing. Here, unbutton my shirt."

Matt did as he asked.

A stone disk nestled in Angus's bloody chest hair. The carved image of a crouching animal covered the front. In an odd fashion, it resembled Matt's cougar, except for the large spots etched into the body. The design reminded him of Pueblo Indian art, yet it was unlike anything he'd ever seen. If the bullet had struck this stone rather than flesh, Angus wouldn't be dying right now.

"What is this?" Matt asked.

"Don't know, but it . . . fits into the puzzle." Angus strained to get the words out. "You can figure it out. You always were the smart one."

"Puzzle? What are you talking about?"

"On Table Top rock. Up . . . on the summit." Short, wheezing breaths began to punctuate each sentence.

"Don't try to explain, Angus. Save your strength."

"No time. Best damn thing . . . ever did was take you on after you escaped from those Comancheros. Now this . . . this is the best damn thing . . . I ever found. Can't just leave it there. Can't." He dug his fingers into Matt's forearm with a last reserve of strength. "Find the answer for me."

"Angus," Matt said sadly. "How do you know this means anything?"

"Someone went to the . . . trouble to carve this image into the cliff. The stone was there, hidden beneath it. It's my . . . last wish, Matthew. Swear to me."

How could Matt deny this man who'd given him a new start in life? He owed Angus McFee. "I swear, Angus."

In a barely distinguishable murmur, Angus added, "Find the . . . other four markers . . . from the puzzle."

"Where did you find this one, Angus?"

But Matt's question came too late. His onetime partner and mentor was gone.

Using his Bowie knife, Matt cut the leather string holding the stone piece around Angus's neck. He held the stone up into a shaft of late-afternoon sunlight. Turning it slowly, he noted the straight line etched across the width of its otherwise smooth back.

The stone was warm and sticky with his dead friend's blood. An immense, heavy sadness spread throughout Matt.

"I hardly think this was worth your life, Angus, but I swore I'd find your answer, and I will."

Chapter 2

THERE YOU ARE, handsome," Elysia Carlisle whispered with a smile. "Don't be shy now. Come out of hiding."

On her hands and knees, Ellie bent low to the ground in the underground chamber. A beam of morning sunlight slanted in through the access hole high above her head. Using her pick, she scraped at the hard-packed sand outlining a metal object. Ellie had the patience born of long practice and a reverence for antiquity. She worked alone—if one didn't count the 350-year-old skeleton of the Aztec priest stretched out a foot away.

Ellie ignored the bones for now, intent on the burial ornament. She would excavate the skeleton later, with all the care it deserved, for transport to its final resting place in Mexico City's new museum.

Although she much preferred the idea of the artifacts gracing a display in the British Museum, she'd negotiated an agreement with the Mexican government and would abide by it. She was an archaeologist, though men of science in London argued that a woman shouldn't carry the title. She certainly was not a grave robber.

This isolated burial site offered a rewarding find, but it was not the significant discovery she needed. Unearthing the lone grave of an Aztec priest did not solve her dilemma.

"It is so bloody unfair," Ellie muttered. "I should never have agreed to Father's terms."

She lifted her ponytail of straight blond hair, allowing the earth-cooled air to caress her sweaty neck. She sighed, then bent again to the task of freeing the object. The dense sand finally released its grip.

"Ah," Ellie murmured in satisfaction.

She rocked back on her heels and pushed to her feet, the Aztec artifact nestled in her palm. Almost as long as her hand, shaped in a flat representation of a man, it was the largest piece she'd discovered thus far. It would soon join the thirty other gold pieces that had been carefully cataloged and packed away for delivery to President Porfirio Díaz.

Accustomed to working alone, Ellie lifted her brown cotton skirt and began to rub the encrusted dirt of centuries from the object. Air brushed over her bare legs above scuffed leather boots. Petticoats and stockings were hardly practical when it came to clambering over rocks, crawling through underground passages, and digging in the dirt. Her stylish gowns remained packed in her trunk, alongside pants and split riding skirts custom-made for an explorer's needs.

If Father wanted her to be a proper British lady, he shouldn't have dragged her around the world since she was twelve, from one archaeological dig to another. The Earl of Aversham's love for antiquities and exotic destinations had seeped into her blood, shaped her education, and shown her an independence he now regretted teaching her.

Ellie lifted the artifact to the beam of sunlight. The brilliant gold gleamed, unblemished after more than three centuries. Gold and jewels always were the most rewarding finds—not for their monetary value but for the way they survived burial or even the caustic, salty ocean to appear as perfect as the day they were shaped by the artisan's hands.

A shiver swept down Ellie's spine. These tangible links with ancient peoples and unique cultures gave her life interest, purpose, and excitement—unlike dances, fine clothes, and afternoon tea with women engaged in meaningless chatter. Discoveries such as these were a thrill she got from nothing else.

Archaeology was her passion.

Ellie couldn't bear the sobering reality that soon she would be forced to give it up.

Tears burned in her eyes. What idiocy had possessed her to bargain away her freedom for this one last chance at a glorious find?

It might have something to do with Father's threat to cut off her funds if she didn't return home, settle on a wedding date, and fulfill her responsibilities to the family.

Grudgingly, she accepted that money was a requirement in the pursuit of archaeology. She had to pay for travel to foreign lands, employ guides and diggers, buy supplies, and line the pockets of officials who insisted on an incentive to allow her to excavate. Then there were the minor necessities of food and lodging.

A sad, bitter smile twisted Ellie's mouth. She sat on a slab of stone. With her elbows propped on her knees, she settled her chin on closed fists. Winston Carlisle, Earl of Aversham, wanted grandchildren, and he'd had no luck getting his ever-absent son or Ellie's social butterfly of a younger sister to cooperate.

Ellie had been an easy mark; she'd succumbed two years ago to her father's urging to accept an offer of marriage from Peter Wentworth, the son of his oldest friend. She'd known Peter since childhood and saw his blond handsomeness and undeniable charm, but there was no doubt that this was to be a marriage of convenience. After seven-and-twenty years, and a dismal history with men, what logic was there in waiting for something better?

How had two years' engagement passed by so quickly? If only she'd had the chance to make the significant discovery she'd always dreamed of, a find both spectacular and beautiful, something to sustain her in the coming years while she fulfilled her socially acceptable role as Viscountess Haverton. Something to earn the respect of the scientific community as well as the admiration of her father.

Something astonishing like Montezuma's fabled treasure.

Ellie stared at the opposite side of the chamber, enthralled by the curious design carved and painted into the crumbling stone wall. She'd uncovered the map two days before, when a tiny flash of color had caught her eye. It had taken hours to shovel and carefully brush away the dirt. Thankfully she'd immediately taken a rubbing by pressing a chunk of brown wax against paper, for large portions of the fragile map were crumbling away into useless fragments. She studied it for the hundredth time, already relying on memory to complete the damaged design.

Encircling a central drawing were five engravings—Aztec representations of a spotted jaguar, an eagle, a two-headed snake, a monkey, and their war god. The lower half of the map depicted the Great Temple in Tenochtitlán, the ancient Aztec capital over which the Spaniards had built Mexico City. An uneven line stretched up the wall, marking a journey. It ended in a landscape of mountains and mesas. Above the trail's end was a village of stacked huts, eerily similar to the dwellings Professor Bandolier had described a decade before in his study of the Pueblo Indians of New Mexico.

The ancient story of treasure hidden from the invading Spaniards had captivated Ellie as a child. Yet she had considered it little more than a myth . . . until now.

Legend had it that after the Spanish conquistadores had stolen much of the Aztec wealth, the native leaders smuggled what remained of the royal treasury out of Tenochtitlán. More than three hundred bearers, loaded with gold and other precious items, traveled north to an unknown destination. The priest in charge, fearful of the treasure's location being revealed, then ordered all the bearers to be sacrificed to the gods. Continuing war with the conquistadores and devastating epidemics of smallpox decimated the Aztec population, and all knowledge of the treasure's location was lost in obscurity.

Or was this map a last attempt to communicate the treasure's hiding place? Could this grave have belonged to the priest who led the expedition?

Ellie slipped open the top two buttons of her blouse. She pulled out a stone disk that dangled from a white satin ribbon around her neck.

Before discovering the map, she'd uncovered this talisman buried against the skeleton's chest. The piece intrigued her more than the gold the grave yielded. The chiseled front revealed a snake, its tail ending in a second head as detailed as the original. The back of the stone was smooth, except for a straight line cut across its three-inch width.

Ellie stared at the identical image of the snake on the wall map.

What did it all signify? Eagerness to go north and search out more clues built inside Ellie, but she'd sworn to her father she would return home after this dig. The earl would cut off her funds if she didn't adhere to their agreement, of that she had no doubt.

A feeling of despair coiled through Ellie. She rose and slipped the gold ornament into the deep pocket of her skirt. She tucked the stone talisman away and buttoned her blouse, uneasy that she felt an instinctive urge to conceal this particular discovery. She'd shared every other item of her find with Peter since he'd arrived, quite unexpectedly, three days before. Why not the talisman?

Ellie climbed the ladder and emerged into the heat of the midday sun. She bid good day to the soldier who guarded the site. Dust coated her boots and sweat trickled down between her breasts as she walked the short distance to her rented house on the outskirts of Mexico City.

Peter had little patience for archaeology. Ellie readily admitted that the slow, detailed work was not for everyone. At least he had volunteered to stay behind today and protect the pieces she'd discovered thus far from looters.

Ellie pushed open the door to her house.

She stopped dead in the doorway. A fire roared in the fireplace in the main room, filling it with oppressive heat. Two Mexican men—the men Peter had hired to help guard the artifacts—dripped with sweat by the fire. One stoked the flames with a bellows. The other held a metal rod.

Peter worked at her table, in the spot where she cleaned, sketched, and recorded the details of each discovery with loving care. He bent over a metal mold. The fire's light made his blond hair shimmer and highlighted his handsome, aristocratic profile. He poured a thin stream from a ladle into the mold. The unmistakable smooth texture of liquid gold gleamed before Ellie's eyes.

Her fiancé looked up. His expression instantly changed to annoyance.

"What are you doing?" Ellie managed in a harsh whisper, fearing she already knew the answer.

"You're back early, darling," Peter drawled.

"On the contrary. It appears I'm not back early enough." She moved forward stiffly. Close observation confirmed her worst fears. The gold bar cooling in the mold wasn't the first. Twelve slender bars lay side by side on the table. That many ingots required a great deal of . . .

Cold horror spread through her body. She turned to the wooden packing crates stacked in the corner. She'd nailed them shut before leaving at sunrise. Now all were open.

Ellie rushed over and knocked aside the lid of the top crate. Dry straw scratched her skin as she plunged a hand deep into the box, frantically seeking the familiar shape of a gold burial ornament. Her fingers hit something solid, then she curled her fingers around it and withdrew her hand. A rock lay in her palm. She flung it against the wall.

Continued searching only produced more rocks. Ellie stopped, breathing hard, her hands gripping the sides of the crate until her knuckles turned white.

"All of them?" she rasped.

"So sorry, my dear, but the need has arisen to immediately collect on my investment."

She could barely move or think. Peter Wentworth was an English viscount, a gentleman supposedly governed by honor, a lifelong family friend, and the man her father hoped she would marry. He wasn't supposed to be capable of such treachery. But she couldn't deny the evidence she'd seen with her own eyes.

He had melted down every gold artifact she'd discovered. All those beautiful, irreplaceable pieces of history—lost. Her last and best opportunity to prove her worth as an archaeologist was gone as well. Ellie lifted a handful of dry straw, sifting it slowly back into the crate as she tried to come to terms with the enormity of Peter's betrayal.

Then his words registered.

Ellie blinked, suddenly alert. She spun on her heel and looked at him sharply. "Investment? What do you mean?"

"You, of course." He scowled, and his typically handsome, genial face changed into something Ellie didn't recognize. "And our engagement—if you can call it that, since you are forever extending the bloody wedding date and avoiding the altar. This way I no longer need to pretend."

"But . . . you proposed joining me on this dig! You insisted on traveling all the way from England, saying you could no longer bear being apart. You rented a room at the finest hotel near—"

He scoffed. "Do you really think I would submit myself to this squalid country, to this total lack of society, without a purpose?"

Humiliation washed over her. This wasn't the first time a man's interest had been caused by the depth of her father's pockets. Once again, her taste in men proved disastrous, her judgment clearly flawed.

"This is about money, isn't it? All along, you've been after my inheritance."

Peter flushed. "My creditors were dunning me before I left England. I managed to run up some sizable gaming debts on the promise of your dowry. The estates haven't done well in the past few years, and there isn't the blunt to cover the notes. Now I must pay them off before Father finds out."

"You intended to take what I found from the very beginning, didn't you? That's why you came."

"Unfortunately, this paltry amount you discovered is not nearly enough," he said angrily, as if she'd caused him some great inconvenience. "What else of value is left in that grave?"

"Why don't you dig it up and find out for yourself," Ellie snapped, "instead of always letting others do the work for you."

Peter looked her up and down as if she were a grubby street urchin. "And crawl around in the dirt the way you do? I think not. This little hobby of yours is quaint, but not to my taste. Look at you." He shuddered. "No better than a peasant woman."

Ellie lifted her chin. "At least I'm not a spoiled, greedy child." She strode forward, grabbed a gold ingot from the table, and shook it under his nose. "These artifacts belonged to the Mexican people. They were an important part of the country's heritage. Have you no appreciation for the history you destroyed today?"

He laughed. "Actually, no. Why should I care about preserving anything here? My only interest in Mexico is how to leave as quickly as possible. Now, give me that," he snarled, reaching for the ingot.

Ellie jerked it beyond his reach. "I was a fool for ever believing there was something worth admiring in you, Haverton."

He lunged, grabbing her wrist. They struggled for possession of the gold. Finally, Peter pried it from her hand.

Breathing hard, he smoothed back his hair. "When I return to England, I shall find myself a real woman, someone passionate and warm, capable of experiencing desire and pleasing a man. Not someone obsessed with dead things. You are as cold and passionless as the bones and trinkets you dig up, Elysia Carlisle."

His words stung, striking at Ellie's fragile confidence as a woman. Peter wasn't the first man to accuse her of being cold.

Fighting the tears, she wrenched off her engagement ring and slammed it against his chest, palm flat. Peter grunted and staggered back a step. The ring dropped to the floor. He bent and scooped it up.

"Thank you, my dear," he said, dropping the ring in his shirt pocket. "This will contribute nicely to paying my debts."

Ellie took a step toward him, fists clenched.

Peter called abruptly to the two Mexicans. "Lock her up," he ordered.

"You wouldn't dare," Ellie said.

"Surely you don't think I want you announcing this little incident to the world? Besides, I hardly need you any longer, now that you have provided me with this." He lifted a folded sheet of parchment from the table. Ellie's eyes widened. It was the rubbing she'd taken in the tomb—the replication of the map that could possibly lead to the remains of Montezuma's fabled treasure.

"I want to thank you for telling me about the map and its significance, Elysia. Legend or not, it is certainly worth pursuing. If what you describe proves true, I shall not have to worry about my debts . . . ever again."

Ellie reacted instantly, without thinking. She lunged for Peter's smug face with clawed fingers. A sudden grip on each arm brought her up short.

"Hold her, you idiots," Peter snapped at the men who clasped her arms. "Bloody hell, she almost clawed me!"

Ellie struggled in vain.

The men pushed her into a small, windowless storage room and slammed the door shut. She heard a heavy thunk as something was shoved against the door. She pushed against it only to find her one way out barred.

"Peter! You bastard!" Ellie yelled. She pounded on the wooden door until her hands ached. Then she kicked the door for good measure. "Let me out of here. Don't you dare do this to me. Your father will be furious."

There was no response. Ellie pressed her ear to the door. What was he doing out there? She heard a hissing sound as water doused the hot coals of the fire.

Sounds of movement finally gave way to silence.

Ellie pulled the pick from her pocket and eyed the slender tool doubtfully. Could it chop through the heavy door without breaking? Gripping the handle, she stabbed the sharp end into the door, carefully chipping out a small piece of wood.

It took two painstaking hours, but she finally worked a hole large enough to slip her hand through. She pushed away the chair propped against the door.

Peter was gone. Lucky for him. Unfortunately, she discovered as she searched the house, so was everything else—the gold ingots, her supplies, and her entire reserve of money. Only her clothes and tools remained, things her former fiancé obviously considered useless.

No doubt he hoped Ellie would be thrown in jail, or perish without money or the protection of a man. That way, word of his betrayal would never reach their fathers' ears.

Every time she became involved with a man, it proved to be a disaster. Ellie shoved her fists into her pockets in frustration. Her knuckles brushed something hard. The last gold burial ornament. She'd forgotten all about it!

As she pulled the piece from her pocket, a forbidden

thought leaped to mind. She swallowed, trying to dislodge a sudden lump in her throat. Every honest archaeologist abhorred the black market of stolen antiquities and the threat it posed to true science. To sell this artifact violated everything she believed in.

But what choice did she have? Without money, she would be trapped. This precious piece of history must be sacrificed for a higher goal—the recovery of Montezuma's treasure. She would do whatever was necessary to prevent Peter from finding the treasure first, including defying her father and going back on her word for the first time in her life.

Snatching up a small blanket, she concealed the artifact in its colorful red and black folds. Feeling like a criminal, she slipped out and asked directions to Juan Gonzalez, a known black market dealer who'd made a nuisance of himself at the tomb until the soldiers drove him away. Ellie flushed, wondering if Gonzalez would listen to her proposal. She'd been very rude to him just last week.

She was halfway to his house when she heard the thud of horses' hooves. Ellie glanced over her shoulder. Her heart skipped a beat.

Enrique Salazar approached with the half-dozen Mexican soldiers under his command.

Ever since her arrival in Mexico, Ellie had resented the periodic visits from her military watchdogs. President Díaz had assigned Capitán Salazar to keep an eye on her—for protection, they said. Ellie knew better. Salazar's responsibility included making sure that none of the valuable artifacts went missing.

Now the artifacts were not only missing, they were destroyed beyond hope of recovery. In Salazar's eyes she would appear worse than a thief. He had always treated her with the utmost courtesy, but there was no mistaking that he loved his country and took his duties seriously.

Ellie quickened her pace, hoping to avoid the soldiers' notice. She wove her way between squat adobe buildings.

"Señorita Carlisle," Salazar called out, intercepting her with his sharp gaze.

Ellie battled the urge to run. Like the infamous American gamblers in the ten-penny dreadful books she secretly enjoyed, she would have to bluff her way out of this predicament.

There was only one problem—lying was more foreign to her than the many countries she had visited in her life. This time, however, it was either lie or rot in one of the notorious pits known as Mexican jails. Peter may have destroyed the artifacts, but it was she who had guaranteed their delivery to the government. Ultimately the loss was her responsibility.

Ellie turned and forced a smile, though her cheeks suddenly felt as flexible as cold wax.

"Buenas dias, señorita," Capitán Salazar said, dismounting. Large silver spurs jingled as his booted feet hit the ground. He regarded her with light gray eyes, a striking contrast to his black hair and beard. A thin film of dust covered the straight lines of his gray trousers and dark green military jacket. A scar down his left cheek marred his ruggedly attractive face.

Ellie struggled to keep her expression neutral while guilt tangled her stomach into knots. Salazar was no fool. If he sniffed out her distress, he would order a search of her house.

For a moment, she considered telling Salazar of Peter's destruction of the artifacts. How satisfying it would be to send these soldiers after that scoundrel like a pack of hounds. But it would distress her father if she allowed his best friend's son to be arrested. And that would not save her from jail.

"Capitán Salazar. It is always a pleasure to see you."

He took her hand and bowed over it. "You are not working today, señorita?"

"The heat was too much. I was taking a break to buy supplies. We are running rather low."

"A good idea." He glanced up at the sun. "It is almost time for siesta."

"Then you know why I must hurry. I cannot miss my chance to see the merchants before they close shop."

Salazar slanted a curious gaze at the bundle in her arms. "It looks like you are doing the selling, señorita. Are the merchants demanding such high prices that you must barter blankets for supplies? Should I speak to them for you?"

Despite his disarming smile, Ellie sensed Salazar seeking out her weaknesses, probing for half-truths. She swallowed hard. "You are being unfair to tease me so, Capitán. You know I have given clothes and things to the villagers before."

Salazar's gaze drifted to two children playing in the street nearby. Just a month before, those children had scampered about the hot streets in bare feet. Now each wore a pair of soft leather shoes, two of dozens of pairs Ellie had ordered from New Orleans for the children. The captain's expression softened as he watched them.

"Sí, señorita, you have indeed been generous. Gracias."

The sincerity in his tone caught Ellie by surprise. "It is always important to me to give something back to those who have shared their hospitality," Ellie replied, her voice affected by the knowledge that the treasure she'd most wanted to share had been wrenched away by greed.

She should have known—should have seen through Peter's polished mask to his true nature. But exploration had consumed her attention and kept her from England for much of the last few years. She'd made a mistake by assuming that the charming friend of her childhood had remained unchanged. Never again would she wear blinders where men were concerned.

Salazar bowed and bade her farewell. Mounting his sorrel gelding, he quickly gestured for his soldiers to depart.

Ellie turned at the corner of the nearest building. She leaned back against the adobe wall, breathing hard, most of the strength suddenly leeched from her limbs. She'd narrowly averted disaster—this time.

She would have to work quickly to sell the artifact, gather her belongings and a new cache of supplies, and escape while she still had the chance.

Her freedom depended on her being long gone, well on her way to New Mexico territory, before Salazar discovered the debacle she'd left behind. She would have to take the trail on horseback and maintain a grueling pace until she crossed the border at El Paso.

Surely Salazar wouldn't follow her onto American soil.

Chapter 3

Three weeks later
September 1897

THE SPRAWL OF buildings rising from the flat Rio Grande valley must be Albuquerque, Ellie realized with weary relief.

East of town, the cliffs and rock slides of the Sandia Mountains glowed a yellowish silver beneath an azure sky. Patches of evergreen forest were scattered across the slopes. The light was brighter, clearer than any Ellie had experienced elsewhere in the world.

As she drew closer to town, the setting sun bathed the mountains in rose and gold, highlighting every ridge and hollow with crystal clarity. All too quickly, the vivid display gave way to the deepening blue of falling night.

Ellie tried to find her normal measure of enjoyment in such grandeur, but she was too dirty and exhausted to muster enthusiasm for anything less than a glittering golden cache of Aztec treasure.

A few miles to the south, the desert terrain had heralded her arrival with a sandstorm. Although she'd sought shelter, covering herself with a blanket and forming makeshift cloth bags to protect the noses of her pack mule and pinto mare, the battering sand had worked its way into every fiber of her clothes and every pore of her skin. No matter how much water she drank, she couldn't wash down the coating of New Mexico desert at the back of her throat. The merciless grit had even gotten into her bloodshot eyes. Tendrils of blond hair had come loose from her long braid, forming a scraggly halo around her face.

She felt miserable, grumpy, and willing to squander a good portion of her scant remaining funds on first-rate accommodations, a dinner of something other than beans and roasted jackrabbit, and a leisurely bath with mounds of fluffy, scented bubbles.

Ellie sighed longingly at the image, smiling for the first time since she'd fled Mexico City.

The memory of Mexico banished her smile and fueled a resentment that had only grown in the past weeks. Peter had no doubt passed through this city. Had he paused to partake of Albuquerque's amenities, all the while looking down his patrician nose at the rugged Americans? How many days' head start did he have? She would allow herself one day of rest before pressing on to Santa Fe.

Ellie rode up a wide, sandy street labeled Railroad Avenue, marveling at the lack of paved surfaces of any kind. How did this busy city function when it rained? Did the residents slog through the mud?

Many of the buildings were set high, four or five feet above street level, with steps leading to the board sidewalks that ran the length of the street on either side. Saloons were mixed in with more conservative businesses. Ellie counted an amazing four or five saloons to a city block, noticing colorful names such as Sturges, Silver Dollar, St. Elmo, Zeiger's, and the White Elephant. Men with guns at their hips passed through swinging doors into brightly lit, smoke-filled rooms. The warble of accordions and tinny pianos sounded above the raucous laughter, bawdy songs, and striking billiard balls.

Ellie rode wide-eyed and alert down the noisy street. This was the authentic Wild West she'd read about in her ten-penny novels. Here were the saloon keepers, cowboys, outlaws, ladies of ill repute, and the professional gamblers that had captured her imagination.

She asked for a stable and was directed a block over to Copper Avenue and a building with the tall letters W.L. TRIMBLE & CO., LIVERY, FEED & SALES STABLE emblazoned over the wide, open door. A tall blond youth approached her with a loose-hipped stride. A stalk of straw hung from one side of his mouth.

"Yes'm?"

"Do you have space for my horse and mule?"

He chewed harder on the straw, moving it from one side of his mouth to the other. "Sure. It'll cost you fifty cents a day, though."

"Each?"

"Yep."

"That is a rather steep price, but I will accept it under one condition." From long experience, Ellie knew that men felt free to take advantage of lone women travelers where money was concerned. Fighting such inequality had helped significantly in building her sense of independence. "I want my animals to receive the very best of care and the finest grain. I've pushed them hard."

The youth grinned, nodding with new respect. "Sure, ma'am. You can count on it."

Ellie dismounted, wincing when her ill-used joints cracked. "Which hotel is considered Albuquerque's finest?"

The boy shifted the straw in his mouth again. Pointing down the street, he indicated a three-story building made of red brick. Black iron railings stretched around both the first and second floors to form wide verandas. "That'd be the Grand. The best in town, for those what can afford it." He eyed her bedraggled appearance with skepticism.

"Thank you. Can you find someone to deliver my bags to the hotel?" She nodded toward the mule, indicating the small trunk and two carpetbags strapped to its back. "I'll pay extra for the service."

"Yes'm." He smiled. "I'll do it myself."

Ellie squared her shoulders as she walked down the street, embarrassed by her appearance. She thought she looked like she'd been to hell and back. After Peter's betrayal and the rigors of the trail, she very nearly had been.

The lobby of the Grand Hotel was elegant, though far from equal to the plush hostelries of Europe. Gathering her dignity, Ellie lifted her chin and approached the front desk. Although she looked like a desert waif, she was still the daughter of an earl. She belonged here as much as her younger sister, Amber, who thrived on London's endless entertainments and an eager following of besotted men. Ellie found little use for such things—most of all the men—but right now some pampering would revitalize her.

The front desk was made of carved mahogany with a counter of rose-colored marble. A honeycomb of cubbyholes took up the wall behind the desk, each tagged with a tiny brass plate engraved with a room number. Some of the boxes held folded messages. Brass key rings gleamed from the depths of other cubbyholes.

A clerk in a white uniform helped an elegantly dressed elderly couple to check in. Ellie stood back, hoping not to offend anyone with the smell of dust, horses, and leather. The clerk handed a pen to the gray-haired gentleman, who signed a huge, open register. With a smile, the clerk reached into the cubbyhole marked 42 and handed its key to the Grand's newest guests.

"Enjoy your stay, Mr. and Mrs. Obermeyer. The ball begins at nine o'clock over at the San Felipe Hotel." He rang a bell to summon another clerk for the luggage.

The couple turned. The woman spotted Ellie and gasped. She shrank toward her husband, then clutched his arm and hurried him away.

Ellie sighed and shrugged off the snub, taking courage from the knowledge that she could transform herself—if she chose—into a fashionably dressed aristocrat. Once she'd soaked away three weeks' worth of grime, that is.

She stepped to the counter and picked up the pen, prepared to sign the register.

"Good evening," she said to the clerk. "I would like a room."

The young man with slicked-back dark hair plucked the pen from her fingers. "I'm sorry, madam, but the hotel is full."

Ellie looked up, disappointed and astonished by his rudeness. She'd so looked forward to a bath and a soft bed. "Are you quite certain?"

"Yes. I suggest you look for accommodations elsewhere."

His eyes avoided hers. His expression was arrogant and scornful. Ellie scanned the maze of small boxes. At least a half-dozen key rings were visible.

"I believe you must be mistaken, sir. Don't those keys indicate rooms still available?"

A flush shot up the clerk's neck. "Those rooms are reserved for guests who have yet to arrive."

Ellie smelled the lie and saw it in his rigid, defensive

posture. She pressed her palms flat on the cold marble counter. "It is after dark. No person in his or her right mind would travel at this late hour. You can be certain that few, if any, persons will arrive tonight to claim those rooms."

"Nevertheless, madam, we are full."

"I know that to be an untruth, sir. What you really mean is that the hotel is closed to people who look like me—travel-worn and dusty and not dressed in the first state of fashion."

He shrugged, not bothering to deny it.

Rage built inside Ellie, banishing her weariness. "How would you expect me to look after weeks on the road? A little dirt doesn't make me any less of a lady, and a lady I am by birth and education. I'll have you know I am the daughter of an English earl."

Although he was taken aback by her vehemence, the clerk persisted. "Do you have proof of such an outlandish claim?"

Outlandish? Ellie took a step back, leaving steamy handprints on the marble.

She heard footsteps approaching from behind, accompanied by the lilting laughter of women and the deep rumble of a man's chuckle. Ellie continued, determined not to back away from this fight even though an audience meant additional humiliation.

"My calling cards are packed with my belongings," she informed the clerk stiffly, "which are even now being delivered from the Trimble livery."

The clerk smirked. "Until they arrive, madam, I must request that you wait outside."

The last three weeks had been the most miserable of Ellie's life, and now this presumptuous little weasel was attempting to strip away the last of her battered pride. Four years of travel as an independent archaeologist had taught her everything about patronizing attitudes toward women—and even more about conquering obstacles in her path. She opened her mouth to demand a meeting with the hotel manager.

The man behind her intervened before she could speak.

"What's the problem here, Tom?"

The deep, masculine voice reverberated up Ellie's rigid spine and tingled at the base of her skull. She caught her breath and spun around.

"Elegant" was inadequate to describe the man in the black tuxedo who stood before her. Broad shoulders combined with an erect posture to give the impression of powerful, controlled grace. Thick hair the color of fine chocolate was swept back from a handsome, sun-darkened face and brushed the collar of his white shirt. A straight, aristocratic nose emphasized the strength of his square jaw.

He wore the ornaments that typically accompanied a very attractive man: two beautiful women, clinging to his arms like jewels. The ethereal blonde on his left was attired in a peach gown trimmed in ecru lace. The other woman wore sapphire blue and had mounds of auburn hair arranged artfully on her head. The man cradled their gloved hands in the crooks of his elbows. His hands held a black cowboy hat against his chest.

Ellie couldn't look away from his tawny-brown eyes. Their suave self-confidence, not to mention the crinkles of amusement at the corners, reminded her of what little use she had for arrogant men . . . or men of any sort, for that matter. She refused to act like a damsel in distress just so he could play Sir Galahad.

"I appreciate your help, sir, truly I do, but I really can deal with—"

"Matthew, if we don't get to dinner soon we'll be late for the ball." The woman in blue interrupted Ellie as if she didn't exist. Her perfect, carmined lips tilted in a flirtatious pout.

"There's plenty of time, Melanie," he murmured, not taking his gaze from Ellie.

Melanie. Tom. This man seemed to be on a first-name basis with everyone. Including the clerk. "Are you the hotel manager?" she demanded.

"No, ma'am," he replied with a slight smile. "Just a frequent guest. One the Grand Hotel wouldn't wish to displease, now would you, Tom?" he emphasized, casting a deliberate glance over her shoulder.

"No, sir, Mr. Devereaux."

"The lady seems convinced she can afford a room at the Grand, Tom. You'll see she gets whatever she needs, won't you?" One of Matthew Devereaux's hands disappeared into a pocket. He flipped a gold coin to the clerk.

"Certainly, Mr. Devereaux," Tom said brightly, in a tone nothing like the dismissive, snobbish one he'd used with Ellie.

She stiffened, mortified. She hadn't been beholden to a man's intervention for years, not even her father's.

She started to protest.

Devereaux placed his hat on his head, uncovering the front of his coat for the first time.

Ellie froze, her mouth half open.

Nestled in the folds of his white satin cravat, just above the vee of his embroidered black waistcoat, lay a stone talisman identical in size and shape to her own. It hung from a leather string. The carved image was the Aztec jaguar symbol that had burned its way into her memory. Ellie was too stunned to move or speak.

Matthew Devereaux tipped his hat and bade her good night.

She stared at his back as he walked away.

"Madam," the clerk called for the third time.

Ellie turned, excitement building fast inside her. That man had one of the missing talismans from the tomb map! But how had it come into his possession?

The clerk handed her a key and the pen. She signed her name automatically in the register.

The stable boy came through the front door of the hotel as Devereaux and the women exited, Ellie's small trunk perched on his left shoulder. He held both her carpetbags in his right hand.

The clerk's mouth pinched in disapproval. "I shall call a bellhop for your baggage."

"No, thank you. I'd prefer my own man to carry my things to the room."

"But, madam, he's a stable—I can't allow—" the clerk stuttered.

"Why not?" Ellie challenged, completely out of patience with the man. "You should have no objection. This young man is not nearly as dirty as I am."

With that, she strode away, waving for the youth to follow. His eyes widened as he stared at the polished wood paneling, rose marble columns, and brass accents in every detail of the decor.

They climbed a wide, sweeping staircase to the third floor. Ellie unlocked the door to number 53. The youth stepped inside and set her baggage at the foot of a four-poster bed. A plush olive-green and yellow carpet absorbed the sound of Ellie's footsteps as she followed him.

"Thank you," she said, paying him the money she had promised.

He doffed his floppy, broad-brimmed hat, grinning. "Much obliged, ma'am."

"What is your name?"

"Will."

"Will, did you recognize that man in the lobby, the one escorting those two women?"

"Sure. Everyone knows Matt Devereaux. He comes into Albuquerque whenever it suits him. Stables his mount at Trimble's, o' course," Will said proudly, puffing out his narrow chest. Then a crease appeared between his brows. "He used to have this really fine bay stallion, but this time he stabled a gray gelding. Don't know why."

"What, exactly, does Mr. Devereaux do?" Ellie asked carefully.

"He's a gambler, ma'am. Best there is in these parts."

"A professional gambler?" she asked in dismay. If he'd won the talisman in a game of chance, he might not know where it came from. Discovering the origin of the stone could shave days off her hunt by pinpointing a place to begin her search.

"Yes'm."

"Those women mentioned a ball."

"Every year the wealthy folks put on this fancy dance. It's called Montezuma's Ball."

Ellie reached for a bedpost. Her knees suddenly felt as wobbly as a new foal's. Montezuma's Ball? Was the appearance of that name prophetic, or just another coincidence to mock her? On the road north she'd also heard of the Montezuma Hotel, a resort built by the railroad.

The name Montezuma belonged solely to the history of Mexico. Why did it show up here? Her experience in other areas of the world had taught her that a name or tradition could carry down through the generations, until the local culture forgot its original significance. The mysterious Montezuma name in New Mexico gave further credence to her theory of a historical link between the Aztecs and the Pueblo Indians.

A thrill of discovery coursed down Ellie's spine.

"Thank you so much, Will. You've been a great help."

"My pleasure, ma'am. You just come back to Trimble's when you're ready to pick up your horse and mule. We'll take good care of 'em, like I promised."

Ellie nodded as he left. Her brain churned with unanswered questions and the beginnings of a daring plan.

He comes into Albuquerque whenever it suits him.

Will described a nomad, an adventurer, a man capable of leaving town as spontaneously as he arrived. It was essential that she confront Matt Devereaux as soon as possible, before he disappeared. Tonight, in fact. For all she knew, he intended to leave town at first light.

He couldn't possibly understand the stone's significance. And surely, since a gambler's life revolved around money, she need only offer the right price and the jaguar would be hers.

A renewed hope spurred Ellie into action. Dropping to her knees, she quickly opened the trunk. She flung clothes in every direction, digging frantically for one special item, losing all interest in a leisurely evening.

The unexpected appearance of this new clue was a boon, a major leap forward in her quest. She would do everything in her power to get that talisman.

She pulled out a ball gown, a rippling cascade of blue-green silk. She always packed two evening gowns for her travels—out of necessity, not vanity. Local dignitaries near her dig sites were always interrupting to invite her to frivolous events such as dinners and balls. She'd learned to travel prepared rather than risk offending an important political host by refusing an invitation.

She rang for a bath, as well as a maid to press the gown.

Digging out her embossed calling cards, Ellie smiled. She'd heard Americans couldn't resist hobnobbing with the English aristocracy. She would gain entrance to Montezuma's Ball if it killed her.

MATT TOYED WITH his champagne glass and tried not to look bored.

Albuquerque's elite filled the San Felipe Hotel's main ballroom with a profusion of color, clashing perfumes, and voices competing to be heard above the din. Couples twirled beneath Chinese paper lanterns and burgundy velvet fabric draped from the ceiling to create the look of an exotic setting. Incandescent bulbs in the crystal chandeliers illuminated the scene.

The gossip bored Matt. Matchmaking mamas kept him on the move. Melanie's and Jean's constant clinging had annoyed him, so he'd gently hinted they should practice their flirtation elsewhere. He'd agreed to play escort for the night, not suitor.

He fingered the cat stone about his neck, a habit he'd developed since Angus's death. Other than the cabin and the astonishing amount of gold he'd discovered there, the stone was all he had left of his old mentor. Matt now considered the piece his good luck charm, even though he'd run smack into a dead end trying to solve its mystery.

He'd followed Angus's directions to Table Top rock, where he'd discovered the puzzle—whatever good that did, since the thing was obviously incomplete. There was some significance to the line etched across the stone's back, but without the four missing pieces the secret remained intact. Nor had he uncovered any sign of the markers Angus mentioned. Of course, it would help if he had a single damned clue what he was looking for. But he'd sworn to Angus to see this through, and he would continue searching until he exhausted all options, just as he would doggedly hunt down each member of the Hayley gang and see them brought to justice for his friend's murder.

To keep boredom from overwhelming him, Matt practiced what he did best—observing. The skill gave him success at gambling; it enabled him to detect an opponent's bluff. He could read people's facial expressions and body language.

A sudden curiosity took hold of the people near the ballroom's entrance. Women whispered behind their fans. Men stood straighter and smoothed their lapels.

Matt stared, seeking out the reason for their interest.

A blond woman, resplendent in a fashionable blue-green gown, paused at the top of the stairs. Her beauty and poise were evident even across the room.

Matt sipped his champagne, maintaining his best poker face, concealing the wave of heat shooting through him. Who was she? Somehow, she looked familiar. But how? A connoisseur of women such as he never forgot a beautiful face or body.

She surveyed the room, as regal and confident as a queen. Yet a completely self-assured woman didn't feel compelled to toy nervously with her fan. The defiant tilt of her chin struck a chord of memory.

Matt remembered where he'd seen that stubborn pride.

The bedraggled waif who'd caused the scene at the Grand Hotel didn't appear the least bit helpless now.

Quite the contrary. Matt shook his head in amazement, not so much at her transformation but at his inability earlier to spot the beauty beneath the grime.

The graceful bell of her skirt flared out over sleek hips, gathering at the back before cascading down in a short train. The simple style flattered her slender figure. Clear, iridescent beads ran up four sides of the skirt in an iris design, glittering beneath the chandeliers as she descended the stairs. A tight-fitting bodice, also beaded, emphasized a narrow waist. Layers of folded silk formed a modest neckline over full breasts. Capped sleeves covered her shoulders, while elbow-length white gloves concealed much of her arms. What had been a scraggly mouse nest of hair was now miraculously transformed into a glorious sweep of deep burnished gold, gathered high on her head. A few soft wisps of hair framed her face.

Although a few men greeted her, most of the bachelors hung back. Their caution didn't surprise Matt.

Men instinctively recognized her type—the strength in her intelligent eyes and firm mouth, the decisiveness, the quick tongue that could blister the fragile male ego. She was Artemis, goddess of the hunt—and to Matt, who had never found the ordinary appealing, irresistible.

Matt worked his way toward the entrance. The lady also started through the crowd, her gaze shifting constantly as if searching for someone. Initial invitations to dance were met with a polite, smiling refusal. Other men hesitated after that, fearing rejection.

Her discouraging demeanor only offered Matt more of a challenge. He stepped into her path and bowed.

"Ma'am. I believe we've met, though not under the best of circumstances."

She opened her fan, then snapped it closed, holding the delicate ribs in her gloved hand. "Yes, at the hotel."

Her husky voice appealed to him, particularly with its lilting British accent. Sooty eyelashes shaded eyes of a rich, mossy green. Her gaze met Matt's briefly, then dropped to the level of his cravat.

"We missed a proper introduction before. Matt Devereaux, at your service."

"Ellie Carlisle."

Miss Carlisle stared raptly at his chest. Matt was accustomed to women avoiding his eyes, out of genuine shyness or a coy game, but this was different. She'd acted just as oddly at the Grand Hotel, now that he thought of it. A new revelation settled in. Although he wished he could claim credit for her engrossed interest, it was the cat stone that monopolized her attention, not his person.

Annoyance flashed through Matt.

"I assume you just arrived in Albuquerque today?"

"What?" she answered vaguely. "Oh . . . yes, I did."

Matt wasn't accustomed to women finding his company or his conversation less than stimulating. She was either a half-wit, which he seriously doubted, or the stone so distracted her that she was oblivious to her surroundings. And to him.

He decided to test his theory. Taking her hand, he tucked it into the crook of his arm. He said softly, "Why, yes, Miss Carlisle, I would like to dance. Thank you for asking."

Her head jerked up. Her hand briefly clutched his arm, causing Matt's heart to jump despite his cynicism.

"I . . . I apologize, Mr. Devereaux. My thoughts must have drifted. What did you just say?"

He smiled, all innocence. "I was saying I would very much like to dance with you. I hope you don't mind my asking."

"No, I . . . of course not. I would like that," she agreed a little breathlessly.

Matt escorted her onto the floor, pleased to hear the orchestra begin the strains of a waltz. She was tall for a woman. The crown of her head reached the bridge of his nose. His hand lightly clasped her firm, supple waist. He led her into the sweeping turns of the dance. Her graceful movements followed his lead with perfect fluidity.

"Have you settled in at the hotel?" Matt asked. He waited for her to thank him for his intervention with the clerk.

"Yes, I did," she said simply.

If she was grateful, she certainly didn't show it. Matt's brows rose.

She looked at the stone again. Matt battled a sudden urge to pull her hard against him and command her complete attention.

"Is my tie on crooked, ma'am?" he challenged dryly.

She looked up quickly. "I was just noticing that talisman you wear, Mr. Devereaux. I would like to buy it."

"This thing? It's just a piece of carved rock. Why would you be interested?"

She shrugged. "No particular reason. I am merely a collector of Indian art, and that piece seems somewhat . . . unusual."

"Really," he drawled. *Merely* was not a word he would use to describe anything about her. If she hadn't stared at the stone as if it held the key to her salvation, he might have believed her nonchalant attitude now. "Is it valuable?"

She hesitated. "Uh . . . no, I don't believe so. May I examine it?"

At least she lacked the smoothness of an accomplished

liar. "Certainly, but I never take it off. Gamblers take their good luck charms very seriously."

"Oh." Her hand fidgeted in his. "I would like to see it more closely. Would you mind very much if we stopped dancing?"

First she found his company insignificant, and now she was eager to cut their dance short.

Firmly clasping her elbow, Matt steered her off the floor to an area with fewer people, near some tall windows framed with burgundy velvet drapes. Lantern light outside sparkled through the leaded glass in soft flickers of yellow and orange. Under normal circumstances, he would have considered the setting romantic.

The effect was totally lost on the single-minded Miss Carlisle.

Her fingers slid under the talisman. Despite the barriers of his cravat and shirt, a tingle raced through Matt's chest.

He watched her face closely as she examined the carving on the front. Then she turned the stone over and checked the back before releasing it. Her eyes sparkled with excitement.

Matt's suspicion grew.

The mysterious Miss Carlisle understood the significance of the line cut across the back of the stone. How was that possible? Only someone who'd seen the puzzle on Table Top rock would know that the etched line held the key to the solution.

The stone was worth much more to her than she let on.

"Where did you find it?" she asked eagerly.

"In the Sangre de Cristo Mountains, north of here," he offered, interested in seeing if the stone's origins drew a reaction.

"Would an offer of twenty dollars suit you, Mr. Devereaux?"

"Ma'am, I make twenty times that in an average night of gambling."

"Thirty, then."

"I don't think so. I'm rather fond of the piece." Even if he hadn't promised Angus, Matt felt a burning curiosity to discover how much she knew about the purpose of the stone.

"Fifty?"

Matt shook his head.

"It pains me to admit this, sir, but I'm rather short on funds. The best I can offer you is sixty American dollars."

"I'm sorry, Miss Carlisle. The stone is not for sale."

Her green eyes flashed, confirming the temper he'd sensed beneath the surface. Exhilaration coiled through him, an invigorating combination of desire and competition unlike anything he'd experienced before. She was different from any woman he'd ever met—strong, determined, yet fragile in a way he had yet to define.

"That is ridiculous, sir. It's just a rock. Surely you can bear to part with it."

"Nope. As I said, it's not for sale."

A few seconds of silence ticked by. "You are a gambler, correct?"

"That's right."

"A true gambler never turns down a fair wager. Would you be willing to bet the talisman?"

"What did you have in mind?"

"Your untamed frontier has always intrigued me—saloons, gunfights, and the western tradition of poker. I have avidly studied the rules. Will my sixty dollars be enough to join one of your games?"

The corners of his mouth curved upward. This should

prove interesting. The passionate expression on her lovely face was temptingly easy to read. On the next-to-nonexistent chance he would lose, it was still worth the risk. The stone's trail had led him to a dead end. Without fresh information—which he suspected Miss Carlisle could supply—he had no idea where to go next in his search.

"Poker is a game best played with several people."

"By all means, include others. Just as long as the jaguar talisman is wagered only between the two of us."

"Jaguar?"

"The stone's image is an Az—" She stopped abruptly. Clearing her throat, she continued, "An Indian representation of a Central American jaguar. It is very similar to the mountain lion, except its yellow and black spotted coat serves as camouflage for hunting in the jungle."

Matt had heard of jaguars, though he'd never traveled deep enough into Mexico to see one. Now the spotted pattern made sense. "Miss Carlisle, I feel obliged to warn you. Many consider me quite skilled at poker. Are you sure you want to risk your money like this?"

She looked at him steadily. "Is there any other way for me to gain possession of the talisman?"

"No."

"I would rather take the risk than have no chance at all," she stated with gritty determination. "A game of poker it shall be."

Matt admired her spunk. He hated to take her money, but he had the uneasy feeling that if he didn't accept her challenge, she would walk out of his life then and there.

"All right, Miss Carlisle. It's a wager. Whoever comes out ahead in the poker game also takes home the stone. Ask for me at Zeiger's Saloon tomorrow evening at seven o'clock." Reaching into a pocket, he handed her one of his cards.

"What is this for?"

"Show it to the guard at the door, a big fellow built on the dimensions of a barn. His name is Nate."

She eyed him warily. "Why does this saloon need a guard? Is this a particularly disreputable place? I won't be made to look the fool, Mr. Devereaux."

"There's no such thing as a reputable saloon, ma'am," Matt drawled, his smile broadening. "Nate's job is to keep out the worst of the riffraff, the potential troublemakers. In your case, however, his duty is to escort you through a separate entrance to the private rooms. Ladies aren't allowed in the main area of the saloon."

"How unfair. The presence of ladies would bring a little culture and refinement to a saloon."

He winked at her. "I think that's what the men who frequent saloons are afraid of, ma'am."

A rosy blush covered her high cheekbones.

Did his wink cause that blush, or was she just embarrassed at having her naiveté exposed? Matt watched her walk away, already planning when he could ask her to dance again without raising the collective eyebrows of Albuquerque's judgmental elite. He wanted to claim her for every dance, but more than two turns on the floor would raise questions about her reputation and his intentions.

Besides, he'd promised the next dance to Melanie. Matt sought out the woman he'd escorted to the ball. During the dance, her purring attempts at flirtation distracted him just enough to lose track of Miss Carlisle.

Finally, as his patience reached its limit, the music stopped. Matt ushered Melanie to her next eager partner, then picked a vantage point near the door to scan the crowd.

"She's already left, I'm afraid," came a familiar voice from behind.

Matt turned to greet his best friend. Seth Morgan was quite at home in a black suit, even without his badge. His dark blond hair and thick mustache gleamed like bronze beneath the electric lights. Matt braced himself for Seth's teasing as soon as he detected the glint of mischief in the U.S. Marshal's hazel eyes.

"Who's left?" Matt countered with deliberate nonchalance.

"That stunning creature in the blue-green gown, of course."

Only long practice enabled Matt to keep his face completely emotionless. "Miss Carlisle? What makes you think I was looking for her?"

Seth snorted. "I've got eyes in my head, don't I? You're the envy of every bachelor in the room. Some of the married men, too, if truth be told."

Matt smirked in self-mockery. He could have been six inches shorter, balding, with a rounded paunch and cigar-sour breath, and Ellie Carlisle would still have sought him out for the talisman.

"Odd, don't you think?" Seth added. "The lady went to all that trouble to dress for a ball, only to indulge in a single dance. And she chose you for that honor. There's no accounting for taste."

Particularly odd, considering the effort she'd made to transform herself from dirty urchin to siren. Matt smiled, knowing his pleased expression and lack of retort would goad Seth. "You still joining me tomorrow night for poker?"

"Wouldn't miss it."

"Good. I'll see you then." It would serve Seth right if he kept Miss Carlisle's plan a secret until she showed up for the game. A beautiful woman, particularly an undeniable lady, was sure to create a sensation at the table.

The marshal walked away, leaving Matt alone with his conflicting thoughts.

He'd never before ranked second in a woman's attentions, and he didn't like the feeling one damn bit. Yet at the same time it was a challenge that stirred his blood, building a sense of expectation rivaled only by the thrill of a high-stakes game.

Matt grinned in anticipation.

Chapter 4

ELLIE STOOD ON the boardwalk at noon the next day, staring at the small sign in the window of the Western Union office and fighting the urge to turn and run. She chewed on her lower lip, torn between doing the right thing and the terrible risk to all her dreams.

Her family had no idea of her whereabouts. Despite a desperate need to dodge her father's efforts to bring her home, she'd never intended to cause her family undue worry.

No doubt Mexico's *presidente* had telegraphed the earl by now, offering an embellished description of her villainy and demanding recompense for the missing artifacts. Ellie could picture Winston Carlisle sending a scathing reply, rising to his daughter's defense by saying she was incapable of something so dishonorable, then storming about the house afterward in a towering rage because she'd slipped through his fingers once again.

Ellie smiled at the image. In spite of his gruff attitude and ultimatums, she knew her father loved her. Although he sometimes lamented that she wasn't more like her younger sister, Amber, Ellie was the one who shared the earl's passion for archaeology.

She often teased Amber about being frivolous, the only one to choose the social whirl of London over the world of archaeology. Yet, as the self-appointed mother hen of the family, Amber would torment herself with worry for her.

On the other hand, Ellie needn't worry that her brother, Derek, had any idea she was missing. No doubt his yacht, the *Pharaoh's Gold,* lay anchored in some exotic port. With the privilege of his gender and status as heir, Derek never lacked the freedom or money to mount expeditions in remote corners of the world. Ellie sighed with wistfulness and an unsettling degree of envy.

At one time Ellie's family was quite close, even after her mother died, as long as they traveled together on the earl's excavations. But four years ago her father decided to spend more time on his estates—a sedentary life Ellie and Derek couldn't bring themselves to embrace—and they all went in different directions.

A wave of loneliness washed over her.

She cherished her independence, but it came at a price. While archaeology granted her a unique, fulfilling life, when she slowed down enough to reflect on her lack of meaningful companionship, a dark emptiness opened up inside. This path of discovery her father had shown her sabotaged any chance of contentment in a woman's traditional role. The void would only grow worse once she married. Rather than cure her loneliness, a husband would be yet another person to dictate a role she had to fill.

Of what benefit were men? Even if a man possessed broad shoulders, a penetrating gaze with golden-brown eyes, a rapier intelligence, and a physique that made her feel delicate in comparison . . . Well, there you have it. That was exactly her point! Matt Devereaux possessed all those qualities, and he was a serious stumbling block to her progress.

Just a short telegram, that's all she need send home. What could her father do to intercept her? Even if he sent someone to hunt her down, or—dread shivered through her at the thought—he came himself, there was the trek to New Mexico on top of the voyage to Galveston or New Orleans. The travel time alone allowed her a minimum of six weeks.

She could also ask for more money to be deposited in her account, just to tide her over and get her home . . . eventually.

Allowing for the poker game with Devereaux tonight, she had just enough left to buy supplies for the next two weeks. Ellie didn't hold out much hope for additional funds from her father. But in her present situation, with limited options and a huge source of frustration named Matt Devereaux, anything was worth a try.

THE DOOR TO the private room opened. Music and bawdy laughter from the main floor of Zeiger's Saloon invaded the room.

Matt's adrenaline rushed as he heard the noise. When a red-haired saloon girl wearing a green dress entered the room instead of a certain beautiful, statuesque blond, the tension slipped out of his shoulders.

Sophie carried in a tray of drinks and began delivering them to the four men seated at the round table. Matt pulled out his pocket watch and flipped open the embossed gold cover.

Ten minutes late. Maybe she'd chickened out after all.

Matt scowled at the odd measure of disappointment that lanced through him. Seth and the other players were eager to get the game under way. They had grown tired of his mysterious delay.

Maybe Nate was in one of his bad moods tonight and refused to escort her up. It wouldn't take much for Miss Carlisle to put the guard's nose out of joint. She had a straightforward manner that could rub a lot of men the wrong way. Maybe she'd paused to deliver a lecture on the civilizing influence of ladies in saloons.

Maybe, Matt thought with mounting impatience, he should go downstairs and check on her.

Sophie finished serving the drinks and opened the door to leave. A drunken cowboy intercepted her as she stepped onto the landing. With a laugh, the cowboy hooked one arm around her waist and pinned her against the railing. The cowboy's hat fell to the floor as he tried to kiss her. He made lewd suggestions as he shoved his knee between her legs and reached under her petticoats to grab her buttocks. Sophie struggled in distress, clearly frightened.

Matt flew out of his seat without even thinking. Zeiger's owner allowed the girls to entertain customers in a more private setting upstairs—those girls who chose to. Sophie wasn't one of them.

Matt pulled the cowboy off Sophie. He grabbed a fistful of sweat-stained shirt and shoved the man backward against the railing until the drunkard's dusty boots left the floor. The cowboy teetered precariously on the railing, Matt's grip the only anchor that prevented him from falling fifteen feet, head first, onto the baccarat table below.

"All I have to do is let go," Matt said in a low, menacing tone.

Wide-eyed with surprise and growing fear, the cowboy

glanced over one shoulder as games on the main floor slowed to a halt and the heads of dozens of curious on-lookers turned in his direction.

All the saloon girls smiled up at Matt, their unofficial defender. Polly, from her perch on a customer's lap, saluted him with a blown kiss.

"You bastard," the cowboy snarled. "You'd best let me go." One hand reached for his gun.

"All right," Matt replied calmly.

He loosened his grip. The man started to slip back-ward. Forgetting about his gun, the cowboy clutched Matt's wrist with both hands.

"What did I do? What? Tell me, damn you!" he cried out.

"You forgot to ask the little lady whether or not she wanted your dirty, groping hands all over her."

"Hell, she's only a saloon girl."

"Wrong answer." Matt pushed him a little farther, until the railing rode lower on the man's back and gravity threatened to pull him over. The muscles in Matt's right arm strained with the effort of keeping the six-foot man from slipping free.

"Sorry, man. Sorry! I wasn't thinking."

"That much was obvious. Now, apologize to Sophie. And do it like you mean it."

"You're crazy, you know that?"

Matt sighed. His expression must have said everything, for additional threats weren't necessary.

"No, don't!" the other man choked out. "Okay, I'll do it. Just don't let me fall." He turned his head a cautious fraction to look at the red-haired girl. "I'm sorry that I . . . er, grabbed you. Won't happen again."

Sophie cast Matt a smile of gratitude and hurried away.

Matt knew he needn't worry about unwelcome advances continuing once Sophie reached the first floor. Local men would provide visitors with the essential facts: Matt Devereaux never tolerated rudeness to any woman, particularly women typically considered easy pickings.

When he was twenty-one, the madam of the most elite brothel in Albuquerque had hired him to protect her girls from overly rough customers. During those five years Matt had played confidant to the girls and was touched by their sad stories, learned to value the silver beneath their tarnished exteriors, and had been the appreciative recipient of everything they chose to teach him about women . . . everything.

Nate's heavy tread ascending the stairs sounded a mere moment before a feminine voice spoke.

"Is this man an example of the local riffraff you mentioned, Mr. Devereaux?"

The timbre of Ellie's voice threaded through Matt, sending sparks along his nerves and surprising him so much he almost dropped the cowboy.

"Not local, Miss Carlisle. The residents of Albuquerque have better manners. This one's an import." He hauled the sweating cowboy back to his feet and shoved him into Nate's waiting hands. "I'd say this one belongs on the street, Nate."

"Yes, sir," the bouncer replied. A grin softened his broad face. He dragged the cowboy to the stairs.

As they went down, a lean, bearded man in an olive-green shirt and brown leather vest squeezed past on his way up.

Matt turned to Ellie. Although her light gray gown qualified as conservative, modestly styled with a high neckline and black braid trim, she filled it out to perfection. A hat fashioned of gray velvet and black lace perched at a jaunty angle, holding her heavy blond hair in place atop her head.

A few loose tendrils trailed down her neck like caressing fingers. The sight captivated Matt. He wondered what it would be like to toy with that hair, to ease it aside and kiss the tender skin of her nape, to feel the answering shiver cascade through her sleek body.

Ellie shifted her cool gaze to his chest, where the jaguar talisman rested. A smile of anticipation brushed briefly across her lips—a smile that had everything to do with the talisman and nothing to do with the pleasure of his company. Matt's sensual fantasy vanished under a deluge of fresh annoyance.

"So, you finally made it." He checked his pocket watch. "I was beginning to think you'd changed your mind."

She crossed her arms. The fingers of her right hand tapped against her upper arm. "Thanks to your choice of rendezvous, I spent several minutes arguing with—"

"Hey there, Devereaux," interrupted the man who'd come up the stairs. He pointed in the direction where Nate and the cowboy had disappeared. "Did I miss all the excitement?"

Matt stretched out his hand. "Nothing worth mentioning." He schooled his expression as Ray Jones clasped his hand in a shake, hiding the profound dislike he felt for the man. "So you decided to accept my invitation. Glad you could make it."

"I always like a game with good stakes."

Matt smiled thinly. He had a special reason for including Ray Jones in the game, and had extended the invitation before his chance meeting with Ellie Carlisle.

Reliable sources pointed to Jones as the newest member of the Hayley gang. Jones hadn't been part of the group when they bushwhacked Matt, but that didn't diminish his usefulness now. He had participated in a recent train robbery down south, a hot job that had caused the gang to split up and go into hiding. One way or another, Matt would discover the time and place where the Hayleys intended to meet next.

The Hayleys had picked up Ray Jones to replace Carlos Fernandez, who had disappeared mysteriously two weeks ago. Matt thought of Fernandez languishing in jail even now, a secret known only to himself and the sheriff of Cerillos.

Fernandez was the first casualty of Matt's patient and systematic hunt for the men who had killed Angus. After Matt had buried his old partner and worked his way down from the mountains, he'd spent less than a week recovering before the restless urge for justice had driven him back on the trail. The purchase of a new horse and gear, a string of poker games, and a careful probing of the right people, and Matt had tracked Fernandez to the sleepy town northeast of Albuquerque. It hadn't been difficult to spot his quarry. The sight of Matt's custom-made saddle strapped to the back of Fernandez's buckskin gelding outside a saloon had been a dead giveaway.

He'd gotten the drop on Fernandez as the man left the saloon, without firing a shot. The blued-steel nose of Matt's Colt Peacemaker, pressed to the base of the outlaw's skull, had quickly convinced Fernandez to make the short trip down the street to the sheriff's office.

That little encounter also enabled Matt to regain his prized saddle and discover an essential fact: although Sam had beaten Angus for information and out of sheer sadistic pleasure, Clive, with his trademark impatience, had been the one to pull the trigger.

Ray's gaze slid to Ellie with the smoothness of a snake's underbelly. "And what have we here?"

She stopped drumming her fingers on her arm. Her eyes narrowed.

"Miss Carlisle, may I introduce Ray Jones," Matt filled in the awkward gap, wishing timing hadn't necessitated that he bring these two together. "Ray, this is Miss Ellie Carlisle."

"Mr. Jones," she acknowledged warily.

"Ma'am," Ray said, accompanying his low, suggestive tone with a sleazy smile.

Matt lightly clasped Ellie's elbow and turned her toward the private game room, using his body to block Ray's leer. He guided her through the door. The three men inside turned. Matt enjoyed the surprise that flickered across Seth Morgan's face when he spotted Ellie.

"I invited Miss Carlisle to join our game tonight, gentlemen. If any of you have a problem with that . . ." Matt left the last unfinished, implying that any man who disapproved could simply leave.

Seth approached immediately. He raised Ellie's hand, obliging Matt to release her elbow, and bowed. He kissed her knuckles. "I think Miss Carlisle's participation is a delightful idea."

Matt scowled. Trust Seth to overdo the charm to impress the lady.

And why the hell hadn't he thought of kissing her hand?

"A lady in a poker game?" sputtered George. Horizontal furrows formed across his high forehead.

"Miss Carlisle, this gracious gentleman," Matt said sardonically, "is George Dawson, the owner of Dawson's General Store. The fellow on the other side of the table is Thomas Pettigrew, founder of one of our local banks. And the rogue with the excessive fascination for hands is U.S. Marshal Seth Morgan."

Matt glanced pointedly at the way Seth retained possession of the lady's hand. Seth's mustache slanted, a sure sign of a teasing smile beneath his thick, dark blond hair.

"Gentlemen," Miss Carlisle acknowledged. She gently extricated her fingers from Seth's hand.

"Ma'am," George responded, though he still looked uneasy. "Regardless, Devereaux, I . . . well, I don't know about this. Maybe this isn't such a good idea."

"She's a Brit, George, looking for a little taste of the American West. You know how eccentric they can be," Matt joked, determined to defuse any further protests with light humor. .

Ellie glared at him, failing to find the humor in his remark.

George chuckled, however. "Oh, very well," he said grudgingly, then resumed his seat at the table. "What do you think, Thomas?"

The bank president shrugged. "As long as Miss Carlisle's money is legitimate American currency and not British pounds, I don't mind a pretty face and a charming smile to brighten the table." Thomas tugged a gold watch from his waistcoat pocket. "Let's get on with it, shall we?"

Ray Jones remained just inside the closed door, legs braced and arms crossed in a belligerent pose. "Well, maybe I don't like a woman in the game. It just ain't natural. I didn't bargain for this when I agreed to play."

Matt leveled a narrow-eyed gaze on the outlaw. It had taken a week to track down this lead to the Hayleys;

heaven only knew how long before he dug up another clue to their whereabouts. But if Jones decided to walk out, so be it. A delay wouldn't change the end result.

"Take it or leave it, Jones," Matt said. "We can manage without you."

Jones jutted his jaw and shifted his weight from one hip to the other. "Never known a *lady* to come waltzing into a saloon as if she belonged there," he muttered. "But I'll stay." He walked into the room and selected a chair.

Although Matt's hand itched to grab Jones by the collar and toss him out the second-story window, he decided to let the crude remark slide. This time.

Matt pulled out the chair to his right. "Here you are, Miss Carlisle."

After a brief pause, Ellie said decisively, "Thank you, but no. Since we are to be in competition with each other, I would feel more comfortable sitting across the table."

She moved to the opposite side and took the one remaining seat. The choice put George on her right and Ray Jones on her left. Sitting down, she placed her reticule—a large, rather lumpy black bag—in her lap.

Matt's knuckles whitened on the chair he held.

"Appears the lady doesn't trust having you too close, Matt," Seth said with a chuckle. "Can't say I blame her."

"Whatever suits her is fine with me," Matt lied, then took his seat.

Seth stroked his mustache and smiled. "My deal." With long, limber fingers, he shuffled the cards and dealt the first hand. "Five card draw. Deuces wild. Two dollars to get in the game. Ante up, gentlemen . . . and lady," he finished, with a wink that set Matt's teeth on edge.

Play continued for almost an hour, with no participant gaining a distinct advantage after several hands.

Matt watched Ellie with subtle intensity concealed behind a heavy-lidded, false expression of boredom. She played an honest, straightforward game. No bluffing. The lady didn't need to bluff to win her share of pots. She possessed the devil's own luck, a sharp intelligence at hanging on to the right cards, and the ability to maintain a bland expression that, to all but the most acute observer, concealed the tiny spark of excitement in her eyes when the cards turned in her favor.

Matt saw Ray dip his shoulder slightly and lean to his right.

Miss Carlisle flinched as Ray's groping hand found its mark. She glanced sharply at Jones, attempting to freeze him on the spot. She shifted her chair a few inches to the right to break the contact, but any more and she would be encroaching on George's space with a possible view of his cards.

Matt tensed. He wasn't sure what irritated him more—Ray Jones making passes at Ellie, or her silence. Why didn't she ask for help?

Play worked its way around the table. The gamblers tossed in their discards, received new cards, and placed their bets. The pile of greenbacks grew in the center. Seth won the hand. Matt's attention remained only half on the game.

During the next round, Ray cast Ellie a lewd sideways glance. He dipped his right shoulder again and reached for her leg.

A hot, sudden rush of anger swept through Matt. He was a heartbeat away from charging around the table, not caring that the action would sacrifice his best source of information.

The click of a revolver being cocked beat him to it.

Matt stilled, instantly alert. Ray froze. Hands moved

swiftly to holsters as Seth, George, and Thomas jerked upright and looked around uneasily for the source of the threat.

Ray looked pale.

Matt folded his cards and laid them face down on the table, his gaze intent on the lady.

She raised her reticule, her right hand still inside the bag. The outline of a large gun barrel distorted its shape. She aimed it directly at Ray's jaw. This was no small lady's derringer or pepperbox pistol, Matt noted with new interest. The length characterized a handgun of .42 caliber or better, comparable to the Colt Peacemaker he carried.

In a measured, icy tone, she said, "I am willing to tolerate a quick squeeze on the knee, Mr. Jones. In my travels, it would not be the first such attempt. But where your hand is wandering is absolutely unacceptable."

The other players relaxed, as they realized the threat was not directed at them. Chuckles sounded around the table.

"Bit off a little more than you can chew, Jones?" George taunted.

Ray's scowl deepened ominously. "Only a certain kind of woman comes into a saloon. That makes you fair game, sister," he snapped.

She responded, "A real lady—a woman of intelligence, education, and refinement—should have the freedom to go wherever she bloody well chooses, sir. And don't make the mistake of assuming I don't know how to use this."

Ray glared at her, then began shifting his gaze between her face and the gun. He was clearly at a loss for words. He didn't lack for embarrassed fury, however.

Matt settled back. "Nice bag the lady has there," he remarked, filling the tense silence. "Be a shame for her to blow a hole in the bottom of it."

"She's bluffing."

"Am I?" Ellie countered softly.

Matt sighed, bidding goodbye to his best opportunity yet to track down the Hayleys. He slid his gun from its holster and laid it on the table. "Whether she is bluffing or not, Jones, you can count on the fact that I'm not."

The corners of Ellie's full mouth turned down. "I have this under control, thank you. I don't need your assistance, Mr. Devereaux."

What was it about this confounded woman? She chose the most inopportune moments to assert her blasted independence. Matt countered sarcastically, "I'm just trying to prevent any problems that could delay our game."

"How very gallant of you," she shot back.

Matt scowled. How the hell did she manage to get under his skin so easily?

Ray shoved out of his chair, his face flaming. "You two are crazy, you know that?" he shouted. "Instead of arguing, you'd best think of how to protect yourselves when I come for you. Nobody threatens Ray Jones like this. You and me got unfinished business, sister."

On that parting shot, directed at Ellie with a feral expression, Jones swept up his money and stormed out of the room.

"Holy . . ." Thomas whispered, too stunned to finish the curse.

"Did he actually mean that?" George exclaimed.

"I'd say that's a safe bet," Matt said.

"How could you let a man like that join you in a friendly game of poker?" Ellie demanded, leaping to her feet. "That man seemed the perfect example of a—a—"

"Outlaw?" Seth interjected, grinning. "If we had hard proof of that, Miss Carlisle, Ray Jones would be locked in my jail right now. Problem is, the only thing we have against him is rumors."

"Until then, his money's just as good as anybody's. We're happy to relieve him of it," George said lightly. He gathered up the cards for the next deal.

Ellie remained standing, her palms pressed to the table. She looked at Matt with eyes like cold jade, making him fidget in his chair. He didn't like the sensation one damn bit.

He cocked one insolent eyebrow at her, a surefire method to break her unnerving silence. "Do you intend to continue or cash out of the game, Miss Carlisle?"

Delicate muscles flexed in her jaw. Slowly, she took her seat.

His small victory was short-lived. She proceeded to slowly and surely flay his temper by ignoring him for the remainder of the game.

Matt focused his full attention on winning after that. He refused each round of drinks. His friends tossed down a string of whiskeys during subsequent hands, growing bolder and more jovial in their attempts to charm the lady. Winning proved ridiculously easy with their attention so divided.

The short stacks of money before Ellie grew on occasion when she won a hand during the next two hours, but for the most part her supply steadily dwindled. In the end, she didn't stand a chance, because Matt was determined to win.

Finally, her stake was gone.

Seth, George, and Thomas spoke up almost in unison to offer her a loan. They lamented the possibility of being deprived of her company.

"Thank you for the kind offer, gentlemen, but I must refuse," she said gently, silencing their protests. "I have lost, decisively and fairly, and must call it a night. It was a pleasure to meet you all."

She rose with quiet dignity. All four chairs scraped back

as the men stood with her. She inclined her head toward Matt in a stiff but gracious nod of defeat. Then she turned, departing with squared shoulders and a graceful sway of her skirts.

George and Thomas muttered their disappointment and reclaimed their seats.

Matt stared at the closed door, frustration boiling inside him. She had lost her money fairly. The jaguar stone remained securely around his neck. So why did he feel guilty? And how would he gain her trust enough to discover what she knew about the stone?

"Well, Matt? Are you going to just stand there and let her go?" Seth prodded.

Matt quickly caught up his hat and coat. "Sort out what money is mine, Seth. I'll get it from you later. Good night, gentlemen."

"Well, of all the stupid, impulsive things to do," Thomas exclaimed. "I don't think she even likes you."

As Matt exited the room, he heard George say testily, "Go dig up a couple more players, Morgan. Hell, it's not even eleven o'clock. I'm not ready to quit playing yet."

Matt burst outside into the warm air of the New Mexico night. He looked for a slender figure in gray. She wasn't difficult to spot, heading down the boardwalk toward the Grand Hotel.

Matt maintained his distance as he followed. He remained alert, for even though Albuquerque was a great deal more civilized than a decade or two past, there still was occasional trouble.

Railroad Avenue was nearly deserted. The night's revelers were still crammed into the saloons and bawdy houses along the street. Ellie greeted the occasional stroller she passed, but otherwise her attention remained fixed on the boardwalk in front of her.

A dark figure appeared a block farther along her path. The man paused briefly, staying to the deep shadows cast by the electric street lamps, before slipping into an alley between the Western Union office and the two-story Fidelity Bank.

Ellies's pace didn't slow. She hadn't noticed the potential threat.

Matt swore.

He didn't care to approach a loaded gun with his tall frame silhouetted by the street lamps. Attacking from the pitch blackness of the rear would give him the element of surprise. Cutting around the nearest building, he raced behind several wood and brick structures. The soft dirt concealed the impact of his boots. He moved noiselessly into the alley.

The shadowy figure waited in a half-crouch at the opposite end. Just enough light filtered between the two brick buildings for Matt to distinguish an olive-green shirt and a leather vest.

He crept up behind Ray Jones and hooked his left arm around the man's neck. Jones managed only a grunt before Matt hauled him farther back from the street. The dark recesses swallowed them both. Jones's brief struggle faltered quickly as Matt restricted the flow of blood to his brain.

Ellie walked past the opening to the alley, her step crisp and confident, unaware of how close she'd come to disaster.

Matt eased his grip enough to prevent Ray from passing out. An unconscious man would be a disappointing source of information. Although not quite the way he'd envisioned it, this was the opportunity Matt had been waiting for.

He yanked out the outlaw's gun and tossed it aside.

Grabbing Jones by the shoulder, he spun him around and slammed him against a brick wall with a fistful of olive-green shirt clenched in one hand. Matt drew his own revolver and pressed the sight just beneath Ray's left cheekbone.

Ray coughed and wheezed as he rubbed his bruised throat.

"Son of a bitch, Dev . . . Devereaux," he croaked. "I'll get you for this."

"So you said earlier. I have yet to see it happen." Matt pressed the gun harder against Ray's face.

The man's eyes widened as the sensation of cold steel overrode the pain in his throat. He reared back abruptly, crushing his hat between his skull and the side of the bank.

"I'll make this short and sweet. Any refusal to answer my questions will make me angry. Anger gives me an itchy trigger finger. Am I clear so far?"

Ray nodded, moving his head as much as the Colt's barrel allowed.

"I know you're a member of the Hayley gang. Don't waste my time denying it."

"Yeah? So what if I am?" Ray retorted defiantly.

Matt drew back the hammer until it clicked with a satisfying, ominous sound. Ray swallowed hard. "I want to know which member of the gang rides a bay stallion. Fifteen and a half hands, black markings, black mane and tail, not a bit of white on him except a spot the size of a silver dollar on his right fetlock."

"Darby has him. Ben Darby. Clive said he wanted that horse real bad, but it was too small for him."

"Too good for him is more accurate. That stallion is Arabian blood, which accounts for his smaller size. Good breeding always tells. Clive Hayley is the perfect example of exaggerated size and poor breeding."

"He'd better not hear you say that."

"What about my Winchester rifle?" Matt said. "Can't miss it—carved walnut stock, engraved barrel, three mustangs inlaid with gold on the chamber."

Ray's mouth twisted in a sneer. "You're the one, ain't you? The one they bushwhacked in the mountains. That rifle was yours."

"Still is. Who has it?"

Ray's cynical expression suddenly disappeared, along with most of the color in his face.

Matt smiled sardonically, the answer to his question already clear. Ray's fear was a typical reaction to the meanest and most volatile member of the gang, a man whose temper and quick draw had carved a reputation up and down the Rio Grande valley. "Let me guess. Sam Hayley has it."

A quick jerk of Ray's head passed for a nod.

"You're supposed to meet back up with them. Where?"

"No way," Ray hedged, pulling back as if he hoped to melt into the wall. "I'm through with them Hayleys."

"You don't lie very well, Ray. When and where are they meeting up?"

"I can't tell you that! They'll kill me!"

"Well, they won't hear the source from me," Matt countered. "The Hayleys' killing you isn't a sure thing, but you can count on me pulling this trigger. Answer my question, or they'll spend a week scrubbing what's left of you off this wall."

Ray's knobby Adam's apple bobbed up and down. His voice emerged in a squeaky falsetto. "Santa Fe. Three days from now."

Matt stepped back. Grabbing Ray by the shoulder, he pulled the cringing outlaw away from the wall and shoved him toward the front end of the alley.

Ray stumbled several steps, then regained his balance and turned to demand, "Where are you takin' me?"

"Marshal Morgan's office. You're going to grow real familiar with the inside of one of his cells."

"Hey! There's no wanted posters on me," Ray whined. "You've got nothin' on me, no evidence at all."

"I do now. As a good, law-abiding citizen, I saw you stalking one Miss Ellie Carlisle with the intent to do bodily harm. Tsk, Ray. Careless of you."

"That's horse shit!"

"After threatening her in front of several witnesses at Zeiger's, too. Not very smart."

"You—"

"Name calling is not a smart way to keep me in a good mood. I'm the one with the gun, remember?" Matt's sarcastic tone turned icy as he said, "Now move."

"You'll pay for this, Devereaux. Clive and Sam won't just stand still and let you come after them."

"I'm not expecting them to," Matt responded darkly.

Chapter 5

H
E'D WON.

Ellie leaned against the iron railing of the third-floor veranda outside her hotel room. The grandfather clock in the lobby struck midnight, the rich yet mournful sounds drifting onto the street below. She'd spent two hours watching the nonstop activity surrounding the nearby saloons.

Her last shot at acquiring the jaguar stone had failed, and she'd forfeited almost all her money in the process.

She tugged the snake talisman from its hiding place beneath her bodice. She lifted the loop of ribbon over her head. Cradling the round stone in her palm, she rubbed her thumb over the raised design. The excitement of discovering another piece of the map had plummeted into a dull, hollow ache in her chest.

This couldn't be the end of it. There was too much at stake.

According to the desk clerk at the hotel, a man fitting Peter's description had passed through town almost two days before. Peter had maintained his head start on the trail. He'd even gained time on her, thanks to having *her* money to buy fresh mounts.

She held the talisman at eye level.

"Can Peter find Montezuma's treasure without you?" she mused, looking at the two-headed snake. "You're my only advantage, but alone you are not enough. According to the map, I must find all five talismans." Bitter regret and a sense of failure tightened her throat. In the last twenty-four hours she'd discovered another stone, touched it, come so close, only to watch a handsome, hard-hearted gambler take it beyond her reach.

Turning the talisman over, Ellie traced the etched line with a fingernail. She whispered to herself, "If Peter does find the treasure, he'll melt down every bit of it for the monetary value. Some of the greatest and most rare treasures of ancient times will be destroyed. All that history. All that beautiful art. Gone. I cannot allow that to happen."

A light flipped on in the corner room at the end of the veranda, capturing Ellie's attention. Matt Devereaux stepped into the center of the room, as if her thoughts had conjured him up. He tossed a pair of saddlebags onto an upholstered chair and went straight to the window.

Ellie feared he'd spotted her, but he only turned the latch and opened the glass pane. He then moved to the three other windows in the room and opened them. The warm night breeze swept through, billowing the curtains with each pass like a bold caress.

Relaxing, Ellie realized she stood in darkness while he was caught in the light. He couldn't see her. She could see him in mesmerizing detail.

It was the perfect opportunity to size up her nemesis, to search for a weakness, to uncover any way—however farfetched—to pressure him into negotiating for the jaguar stone again.

Matt pulled off his coat and threw it over the back of the chair. She'd been right about the breadth of his shoulders. The same lean, strong fingers that had shuffled the poker deck in a blur of cards now plucked at his black string tie and yanked it free of his collar. His vest flew onto the chair, the shiny satin fluttering down like a great black raven.

Anger radiated from every movement. Ellie stared, transfixed by the vitality emanating from him. She wondered briefly what frustration had inspired his fierce energy; certainly it was not due to her, for she wasn't in the habit of inspiring passion, of any kind, in men. Besides, he already had everything he wanted, and no reason to have anything more to do with her.

Ellie quickly rationalized her strange wave of regret—the rogue not only retained the jaguar talisman, he'd won the lion's share of her money as a bonus!

He jerked down his suspenders and left them dangling at his sides. Bending over the porcelain washbowl, he splashed water onto his face. Black trousers stretched over lean, muscular flanks.

Ellie took a step closer. Rogue or not, Matt Devereaux was a guilty pleasure to watch. He tugged his long white shirt free of his trousers. Limber fingers worked their way up the front, releasing each button to leave the shirt hanging open. The talisman nestled high on his chest, cushioned by a light covering of curly dark hair.

She looked down, catching a teasing glimpse of ridged muscles across a flat abdomen. He reached behind his neck with both hands. The gap in his shirt widened. A warm flush blossomed in Ellie's belly and spread out to every part of her body. Before she could question the strange, tingling heat, he lowered his arms. A heavy object dangled from his fingertips.

Ellie stiffened, her earlier alertness renewed tenfold.

He'd removed the talisman.

Abruptly, he moved out of sight. The light switched off, plunging the room into darkness.

Ellie's brows drew together in a frown. Where had he put the talisman? And did he intend to sleep with the windows . . . ?

She sucked in her breath as an idea took root.

SOMEDAY, ELLIE THOUGHT as she crept barefoot down the covered veranda, she would be able to put aside the bitter, stinging shame of this moment. Perhaps when she was a doddering old woman taking her grandchildren to the British Museum to see Montezuma's treasure. Hopefully, by then senility would have caused a variety of memories to dance out of reach, and she could finally free herself of the guilt over what she was about to do.

At three o'clock in the morning, most of the town had finally retired. Ellie prayed that the lingering rowdiness from the saloons down the street would draw any attention away from the stealthy figure on the third floor of the Grand Hotel. She'd donned the darkest clothes she owned, a pair of brown work trousers and a dark blue shirt. A large floppy hat, stuffed to capacity, concealed her blond hair.

Matt Devereaux had no right to the stone, she kept telling herself. He'd pushed her to this level of desperation by being so uncooperative. For goodness' sake, the man clung to the jaguar as a good luck charm, with no appreciation of its true value. Her destiny lay in uncovering its secret and sharing a wondrous, priceless discovery with the world.

All four windows of the corner room stood open to the night breeze. Ellie reached the nearest window and bent low to peer inside. Devereaux's commanding size filled the bed, shaping the bed linens into peaks like a small mountain range.

Oh, bloody hell, he was truly there, larger than life, a daunting barrier to her goal.

Ellie quickly pivoted away and pressed her back to the outer wall. She tilted her head back and squeezed her eyes shut. Her heart thundered, driven by fear, adrenaline, and guilt. The three interminable hours she'd waited for the man to fall asleep hadn't done much to bolster her courage.

She'd stooped to thievery in the name of archaeology. She had to claim that talisman or she would lose everything—her dreams, her freedom, her self-respect, and, most important, her ability to prevent that lying scoundrel Peter from reaching the treasure first. The preservation of an irreplaceable piece of history was at stake.

Ellie fingered the bills in her pocket, the last of her money. Despite his arrogance—despite being the most stubborn, difficult man she'd ever encountered—Devereaux deserved payment for the loss of his stone. It wasn't much, regrettably. Later, if . . . no, *when* she found the treasure, she would make certain he received further compensation. But from the safety of England, well beyond the impact of his steady brown eyes and lethally quick hands.

Ellie drew a deep, steadying breath. She lifted one leg carefully over the windowsill. Her bare foot touched the cool, smooth wood of the bedroom floor. Ever so slowly, she rested her weight on that leg, until she felt certain the floor wouldn't creak.

She bit down on her lower lip and ducked inside.

Moonlight slanted through the other windows of the corner room, casting everything in eerie shades of gray, as if she viewed the scene through a delicate silver veil. She paused, listening for the sound of his breathing. Though it was hard to detect, the slow, even cadence reassured her that he was indeed asleep.

She tiptoed over to the upholstered chair and patted down every inch of it and his discarded clothing, searching for the stone.

Nothing.

The bed sheets rustled. Ellie froze, battling a wild instinct to lunge for cover. Matt Devereaux possessed the alertness and instincts of a hawk. If he awoke, her only chance to escape notice was to blend in with the furniture.

He turned on his side. Ellie watched, fascinated, as the sheet shifted with his impossibly broad shoulders. One bronzed arm slipped out, locking the sheet close to his chest. Thick with muscle, even in repose, his arm formed a striking contrast to the pale gleam of the white sheet in the moonlight.

A shiver cascaded down Ellie's back. She attributed it to the sudden, horrifying thought that he might have tucked the stone under the mattress or pillow. *Please, please, please, not that.* Under no circumstance would she draw within arm's reach of that rogue. He was too dangerous, in a multitude of ways.

She waited for several minutes more. He didn't move again.

Finally, Ellie allowed the tension to ease from her shoulders. This wasn't so bad. She could do this. She scanned the room, seeking possible hiding places for the stone.

There was a small dresser against the opposite wall. Several personal items lay on the lace runner covering it.

Ellie tiptoed across the room.

As a child, she'd always been fascinated with the odd bits of masculinity her father left on his dresser, so different from the bottles, jars, and delicate things that decorated her mother's vanity. Ellie had frequently borrowed the earl's studs and cuff links and retreated to her room, playing with the fine pieces of gold, diamond, onyx, and other stones, even then envisioning herself as a great explorer and her booty as a sought-after treasure.

Devereaux's belongings brought back that mystery and wonder of the male domain. The scent of a light hair oil lingered on his comb. Loose coins were heaped in a pile, and a money clip held a thick fold of bills. His gold pocket watch shone softly in the moonlight.

He was either very careless—leaving in plain sight a wealth that would tempt an unscrupulous man to murder—or supremely confident that he could defend his possessions. Ellie harbored no doubt that the latter was true. A derringer rested on the dresser, but there was no sign of his revolver. Surely he kept it close at hand by the bed.

Devereaux's tie lay in a discarded coil. Ellie lifted the black ribbon . . . and suppressed a gasp of delight. The jaguar stone lay beneath it.

A triumphant smile spread across her face.

Ellie picked up the round talisman in both hands. The feel of the cool, ancient stone caused her heart to race with renewed excitement. There was nothing like it—the thrill of discovery, the eagerness for the hunt.

This vital piece of history was a significant step toward

her goal. She now had in her possession two of the talismans portrayed on the Aztec map, escalating her faith in the map's authenticity. Even Devereaux's revelation that he'd discovered the jaguar talisman in the Sangre de Cristo Mountains supported its validity, for the great Taos pueblo north of Santa Fe resembled the Indian dwelling that crowned the tomb map.

Her fingers moved eagerly over the jaguar image. Simultaneously she explored the reverse side of the stone, testing the piece as a whole, and taking particular note of the line cut across it.

Let's see you reach Montezuma's treasure before me now, Peter.

Ellie turned to make a hasty retreat. She was eager to return to the livery stable, pack her horse and mule, and get safely away.

Instead, she ran straight into a warm, living barrier.

Her first thought was resentment. How dare Devereaux move so silently, offering no warning he'd awakened and slipped out of bed? The second thought, instantly following the first, was of stunned horror. She tried to dart away. Powerful hands grasped her upper arms and held her fast.

"Going somewhere, Miss Carlisle?"

"Are you in the habit of sneaking up on people like that?" Ellie snapped.

She had no right to be mad at him, yet she was. Guilt lodged in her throat like a burr. Not only had he caught her in the act, she now stood nose to collarbone with an intimidating expanse of bare, undeniably male chest. He radiated warmth, like the heat from a sun-baked rock after the sun has set.

"Typically, no," Matt replied dryly. "Not in my own hotel room, anyway."

"Well, you nearly scared the life out of me."

"I might have done more than that, if I hadn't recognized you." He gave her a shake. "You little fool! Men in this country sleep with a revolver near at hand. I'm among those with a definite dislike for someone stealing my belongings."

Ellie opened her mouth, then closed it with a click of her teeth.

"What, no excuse? Can't that witty tongue of yours weave a clever tale to explain your presence in my room?" Matt taunted. With a snort, he added, "Hell, at least you didn't shoot me."

"Shoot you? Don't be ridiculous. I would never resort to such—" Ellie broke off, staring at a puckered scar on his right shoulder. More scar tissue stretched in a thick strip across his upper left arm, appearing shiny, smooth . . . recent.

"You've been shot before," she whispered.

"What of it?" he responded hotly.

Ellie looked down, succumbing to a strange sense of concern, to an urge to reassure herself that his chest wasn't marred by additional signs of violence.

She discovered more skin than she'd bargained for.

Jerking her head up quickly, Ellie stared wide-eyed into his grinning face. "You . . . you're—" she choked out.

"Yes?" he said when she couldn't finish. His brows rose in two daring, infuriating arches. "Go on. You were saying?"

"I . . . I refuse to say it. It wouldn't be—"

"Proper? Ladylike?"

Actually, *safe* was the word that had popped into her head, though Ellie couldn't understand why.

Without mercy or any appreciation for her embarrassment, he continued, "Still speechless? Let's see if I can help. Naked? Would that be the word you're avoiding?"

Like the plague, Ellie thought wildly. Her breath came roughly, responding to something that wasn't quite embarrassment, or guilt, or fear.

For goodness' sake, it wasn't as if she'd never seen a man in his altogether before. One didn't travel the world, or camp in the wilderness with more than three dozen native diggers, without catching an occasional glimpse of something male. But Matt Devereaux was different. From the top of his head down, he was more of, well . . . of everything a benevolent God and nature intended a man to be.

Physically, anyway. She wouldn't want to vouch for his character in a court of law.

Matt added, "Sorry if I've shocked your delicate British sensibilities. I prefer to sleep this way. I didn't bargain on company, sweetheart."

Ellie whipped her hands behind her back, afraid she would inadvertently touch some part of him she shouldn't. Actually, any part of him was dangerous, but some areas more so than others. When her hands met behind her back, she realized she still clutched the talisman in her fist.

His brows lowered. The teasing expression disappeared from his face. "You won't keep the stone from me that way."

Releasing her left arm abruptly, he reached around her. The warm flesh of his chest pressed against Ellie's chin. The taut, smooth muscle stretching from his neck to his shoulder dominated her range of vision. His hand brushed her bottom as he searched blindly for the talisman. Ellie sucked her breath in, bringing with it the scent of raw masculinity and sandalwood.

Quickly transferring the talisman to her left hand, Ellie stretched it out beyond his reach. He lunged in the other direction. She jerked the stone behind her back and switched hands, avoiding the quick strike of his powerful arms.

Drawing his head back, Matt looked down at her. "A little game of keep-away? Just how long do you think that will work?" The thrill of competition sparkled in his tawny eyes, and an audacious smile appeared on his face.

Ellie's eyes widened with alarm, and something more. An insane sense of anticipation grew in her body, like a charge building in the air just before a lightning strike.

Without warning, Matt wrapped an arm around her waist, pulled her hard against his body, and lifted her feet from the floor.

She let out a strangled yelp, startled by the tactic. He walked forward, holding her captive, until he pinned her between his hard body and the wall.

"What are you doing, Devereaux?" Ellie gasped.

"Settling this, right now."

"This is cheating. You're taking blatant advantage of your size."

"Actually, I'm not taking advantage of my size in the way I'd like to," he retorted, his voice rough. He removed her wide-brimmed hat and dropped it to the floor. Her hair tumbled down across her right shoulder. "I'm going to win this little skirmish, Miss Carlisle. You know it as well as I do. Give me the talisman."

"No!"

"Then tell me why the hell this thing is so important to you. What does it mean?"

She pressed her lips firmly together.

"What do you plan on doing with it?"

"I told you," she said through clenched teeth. "I am a collector, nothing more."

"I didn't know collectors resorted to theft," he said in a cynical tone. "I can see you're determined to do this the hard way."

Large, rugged hands slid slowly down her arms to where they joined behind her back. His hands engulfed hers. Breaths mingled. She felt the heavy drumming of his heart against her chest, though her heart beat as wildly as his.

Matt pried the talisman out of Ellie's fingers, then leaned back just enough to look down at her.

"Damn you, Devereaux. Why do you have to spoil everything? You have no use for the talisman. Why not let me have it? It is all I want. I swear."

His eyes narrowed suddenly. Anger flickered in their brown depths.

"That's all? There's nothing else here that interests you?"

"Nothing," she said, giving him the answer she believed he wanted.

His scowl deepened. "You claim to be a scientist, right? Then are you willing to put your theory to the test?"

"What do you mean?" she asked suspiciously.

"When a woman sneaks into a man's bedchamber at night, she typically has a little more than thievery in mind."

Outraged, she said, "I beg your—!"

Matt's mouth closed over hers, capturing her lips in mid-protest.

The kiss was hard and demanding, yet compelling in a way that banished any thought Ellie had of pulling away. Despite his anger and obvious strength, the kiss wasn't harsh. On the contrary, the firm, velvety texture of his lips worked a hypnotic spell.

Ellie grabbed his upper arms to steady herself—a mistake, as it proved. The awareness that had plagued her since she stepped into his room roared to full life, intensified by the feel of hard muscles against her palms. The sensual dance of his mouth fascinated her. Tentatively, she kissed him back, matching the shifting pressure of his lips.

Unexpected heat grew in the pit of her belly. A strange, languid warmth trickled through her muscles, stealing her strength and encouraging her to lean against the very thing that threatened her. Currents of pleasure reached out to hidden parts of her body, hinting at possibilities she had never before dreamed of. She savored the new sensations.

And feared them. They implied she had wanted this all along, secretly, without realizing it. But, no—that would suggest she found Devereaux desirable. She might feel a tingly pleasure in the silky texture of his mouth, but that was all. It certainly didn't mean she was capable of inspiring him with any greater emotion than a desire to punish and dominate.

He broke the contact, resting his forehead lightly against hers. His eyes were closed. A slight tremor, almost undetectable, passed through his large body. Just when Ellie was wondering about its significance, he drew back.

"Hellfire," he growled, irritable and frustrated.

Anger and frustration weren't exactly synonymous with passion, Ellie thought sadly. Point proven. Even in the intimacy of his hotel room, she could not inspire him with anything other than irritation. She was shocked to realize that she wanted to arouse his ardor.

"Time for you to go, sweetheart, before I do something I'll regret. You and I will deal with unfinished business tomorrow."

Grabbing her arm, Matt scooped up her hat from the floor. He marched her across the room to the window through which she had entered. Ellie offered no resistance, still dazed from the kiss. With a firm yet gentle nudge, he hastened her over the windowsill and out onto the wide veranda.

"Remember, Miss Carlisle, I have first rights to whatever this talisman leads to," Matt said through the window, issuing a parting challenge. He stood off to the side, lost in shadow. The hat sailed out and landed at her feet.

His words penetrated her bewilderment. "Now wait just a bloody—"

The window slid closed and was locked. Then the other windows clicked shut as Matt moved to each, sealing the room against further intrusion. Frustration and defeat swelled in Ellie's chest.

Devereaux stalked across the room to the bed. He stepped through a beam of moonlight. It highlighted his back from neck to heel, painting his broad shoulders, powerful thighs, and muscular buttocks the color of buffed silver. He merged with the darkness around the bed.

Heat flooded Ellie's cheeks. During those few stolen seconds she'd forgotten her fury and watched him with fascination.

Uttering a few choice words her father had always discouraged her from using, she hurried back to her window.

Safe in her room, she sank to the floor, drained of energy by the most bizarre, maddening encounter of her life. To make matters worse, there was that stunning kiss—from lips that were entirely too soft for a hard man like Devereaux.

She took refuge in her anger. Did he think he could chase her off so easily? Well, his calculated efforts had come too late. If only for a few moments, she had held the jaguar talisman in her hands.

Rubbing her fingertips together, Ellie remembered every detail of the stone, front and back, including the angle of the etched line. Scrambling to her feet with a spurt of energy, she switched on a light and searched quickly for paper and pencil.

Tomorrow, she swore as she sketched the design, she would leave town ahead of that arrogant gambler. She would hunt down the treasure while he frittered his time away haunting the poker tables and fleecing gullible cowboys and railroad workers out of their hard-earned money.

Her drawing of the talisman would suffice.

It had to. There was no way she would broach that man's domain again. If he caught her again, he might not stop at a kiss.

Ellie hugged her arms around her middle, bracing herself against the strange shiver that rippled through her.

Chapter 6

MATT DIDN'T WANT to think about that kiss.

Not anymore, anyway. He'd spent a restless night, torn between aggravation at Ellie's stubbornness and admiration of her daring. Memories of powder-soft skin and full lips tormented him. The soft paradise he'd discovered inspired dreams of a deeper penetration of her mouth.

His frustration was growing as he strode by Trimble's Livery at dawn. Then he spotted Ellie. She was preparing to leave, before he had a chance to gain more insight into the purpose of the jaguar stone.

Who was he kidding? Last night had clearly shown that she was too obstinate to share any information. Her next logical step was to head north toward the Sangre de Cristo Mountains.

Matt bit back a curse. Maybe he shouldn't have revealed the stone's origin. His only choice now was to follow her. Although he'd spent weeks hunting down the Hayleys to find justice for his old friend's murder, he'd also sworn to Angus he'd solve the mystery of the stone.

Ellie Carlisle offered his only lead. He couldn't allow her to slip through his fingers. Besides, her path would take him toward the Hayleys' scheduled rendezvous in Santa Fe two days hence.

Her horse and mule were tied to a hitching rail just outside the stable's open door. Ellie was securing several bundles of supplies to the mule's packsaddle. She had on the same brown trousers she had worn when she stole into his room the night before.

Daylight afforded Matt a much greater appreciation for the fit of those trousers. He'd seen women wear men's dungarees when practical needs overrode the dictates of fashion. They never fit right. Ellie's trousers, on the other hand, were obviously custom-made for a woman. Although they fit loosely, they couldn't conceal the slender yet shapely hips and legs that seemed to go on forever. A thick blond braid arrowed down her back over a simple white shirtwaist. The crown of her head disappeared beneath a floppy-brimmed brown leather hat.

Gone was the prim, sophisticated lady who'd graced Montezuma's Ball and the poker game. In her stead stood a woman who seemed to fit into the rough reality of this land, who'd abandoned traditional efforts to appear beautiful and instead looked quite . . . adorable.

Seth Morgan sat across the street from the livery, on the porch of his office. The vantage point provided a perfect view of Ellie's preparations. Seth leaned back comfortably, tilting his chair. His boots rested on the porch railing, crossed at the ankles. His hands cradled a steaming cup of coffee against his blue shirt.

Matt stalked up the steps to join the marshal.

Seth saluted Matt's arrival by raising the cup of coffee in a casual gesture. The dark brew smelled heavenly.

"Did something piss on your mood this morning,

Matt?" The coffee cup waved toward the livery stable. Seth's hazel eyes danced in amusement. "Or should I say . . . someone?"

"Maybe," Matt said gruffly, admitting nothing. He looked back at Ellie. She swung a saddle onto the pinto mare's back, then reached under its chest to grab the girth. The trousers tightened across a backside endowed with just the right amount of curve. "I can see there's good reason for your disgustingly cheerful attitude at this early hour."

"Have a seat," Seth offered. "Enjoy the view."

Matt pulled a chair around next to Seth's, sat down, and crossed his left ankle over his right knee. He rested his hands against the soft leather of his boot.

Ellie turned and caught sight of her audience across the wide street. She stilled for a few seconds, seeming uncertain what to do. Then she crossed her arms defiantly, turned, and entered the stable for another load.

Matt scowled. He'd been handily dismissed.

"What's happened to your sense of humor, my friend?" Seth asked. "I haven't seen you this ill-tempered since the Hayleys bushwhacked you."

Seth was the only man with whom Matt had shared news of the ambush, his plans to hunt down Angus's killers, and his promise to solve the mystery of the stone.

"I didn't get much sleep last night," Matt said evasively.

"I trust there was a blond-haired, green-eyed reason for it."

"Not in the way you're suggesting."

"Seems to me you bring out the worst in Miss Carlisle, if that helps you feel any better."

"And how, exactly, is that supposed to be a good thing?"

"Hey, at least she finds it impossible to ignore you.

Can't say that for the rest of the men in town. Their eyes come close to popping out of their heads when she walks by, but Miss Carlisle doesn't seem to notice."

"I have a disappointing explanation for you. She hates me."

"Now that's interesting. I wonder what brought that on. Couldn't be your charm, or possible lack of, because you're nearly as appealing to the ladies as I am. Or at least that's what I hear. Frankly, I can't see it." Seth took a sip of coffee to hide the smile twitching at the corners of his mouth.

"Very funny, Seth," Matt retorted dryly. "Miss Carlisle wants my cat stone, though she won't tell me why. That's why she joined the poker game last night, in hopes of winning it. She'll go to almost any length to get it. It's as simple as that."

Almost any length, Matt thought, vividly recalling her scent and her warmth in his darkened room. A twinge of lust shot through his loins. He pressed his thumbs hard into his calf muscle. Of the women he'd known, most would have offered themselves in payment for the talisman, especially a woman as obsessed as Ellie Carlisle. The thought of sex hadn't even entered her naïve British mind. Matt was glad. If she'd offered her body to him, he would have been sorely disappointed. She seemed a world apart from the soiled doves he'd spent five years of his life protecting.

"So Miss Carlisle apparently recognizes some significance in the piece and might be able to help solve its mystery. Sounds to me like the perfect opportunity for a partnership between the two of you."

"The lady appears determined to strike out on her own," Matt pointed out, inclining his head toward the stable.

Seth sighed with exaggeration. "Now that gives me a bit of a dilemma. I watched her pack her gear. The lady knows how to buy supplies and pack efficiently, I'll grant her that. Looks like she's done this before. Still, she needs protection, and I can't leave my duties in town to go with her."

"She seems handy enough with that gun, if you recall."

"Against a single idiot with wandering hands at a poker table, yes. You know how rough this country can be, Matt. Now, if I knew someone I trusted was keeping her in sight, I wouldn't need to make myself sick with worry."

Matt gave his friend a sidelong glance. "You're not very subtle."

"Should I be?" Seth took a long swallow of coffee. "Several men in town would volunteer to ride shotgun. Should I ask them?"

"Hell no."

"Exactly. You're the perfect choice. The white knight. The protector of women. The only one I can trust not to force his attentions on her."

"Hate to disappoint you, Seth, but she doesn't want me within a hundred yards of her."

"Aha!" Seth pointed a finger at Matt over the rim of his cup. "That was not a no. My bet is that you were already considering following her, before I said a damn thing."

Matt tugged the brim of his hat lower over his eyes.

"Yep, I thought so," the marshal said. "So you think she's hunting for whatever that stone leads to?"

"I'd say that's a safe bet."

"Then you and she are heading in the same direction, right? Sounds like a mutual goal to me."

"More like a competition. Winner takes all."

"Now that's the kind of situation I'd like to be in, especially with a woman who looks like that," Seth mused. He rolled the mug between his hands. "Tell you what, Matt ol' boy, you take over my duties for a couple of weeks, and I'll keep an eye on the lady."

"Not while I'm still breathing, Morgan."

Ellie emerged from the livery just then, her arms loaded with another bundle. She caught Matt's eye and sent him a glare that would have melted the snow on Mount Baldy. Matt's heart raced, responding to the challenge in her fiery green eyes. Never in his life had a woman inspired a sense of competition. Then again, he'd never encountered a woman as intelligent and resilient as this one. He felt like leaping from the chair and saddling his horse. But there was no sense in rushing until the general store opened and he could stock up on supplies. Her trail would be easy to pick up.

"No doubt it'll annoy her to know I'm hot on her heels," Matt muttered.

"A distinct possibility," Seth agreed with a chuckle. "Don't worry. I think Miss Carlisle will soon realize that working together is of benefit to you both. She needs you, Matt."

"Sure she does . . . for Angus's stone and my knowledge of where it came from," Matt said cynically.

Seth smiled. "A man has to start with something."

"I hope you choke on that stupid grin. Now, when did you intend to offer me some of that coffee?"

SIX BLISSFUL HOURS. Half a day of solitude and mounting anticipation for the hunt ahead—that's all the presumptuous gambler allowed Ellie before she glanced back and spotted him on the trail.

She abruptly reined in her mare. She glowered at Devereaux, who sat tall on his gray gelding and led a single pack mule a little more than a mile back.

She'd last seen Matt when she rode out of Albuquerque early that morning. He'd been lounging on Marshal Morgan's porch, enjoying a cup of steaming coffee, as if he hadn't a single interest beyond his next poker game. She should have known better.

Devereaux must have been following her for hours, but in this rugged country she seldom had a clear view of the back trail. She'd deliberately chosen a side route north through the Sandia Mountains, leery of the thieves who traditionally haunted well-traveled roads.

She couldn't allow him to continue. Under no circumstances would she let another man vandalize her archaeological find. Matt Devereaux could be as bad as Peter . . . or worse. It wasn't worth the risk.

She had to do everything in her power to get Devereaux to turn back. The fact that he seemed willing to keep his distance, for now, was not enough. She didn't have time to lead him on a wild goose chase until he grew tired of the game and abandoned the idea of using her to get to Montezuma's treasure. The situation demanded a more immediate, decisive measure.

A lump rose in Ellie's throat. Her life had deteriorated into a series of drastic measures, thanks to Peter's betrayal. She barely recognized this woman capable of lying to Mexican authorities, hiding out in the wilderness, and breaching the sanctity of a man's bedroom with thievery as her goal. Tears blurred her vision. They didn't spill over. She wouldn't let them. Although she hadn't sought trouble, she wouldn't shrink from it.

Half an hour later, the trail turned and dipped into a

narrow gorge. Walls of water-eroded limestone rose on either side, growing taller the farther she went.

Ellie rounded a bend in the rocky ravine. There she discovered the perfect spot.

ELLIE TIED HER horse and her mule to a stumpy tree. She pulled her rifle from its saddle boot and headed for an incline that led up the side of the gorge. Struggling against the steep slope, she climbed, carefully choosing her footing among the loose stones and brittle rock.

Reaching the top, she ran across the boulder-strewn ridge to a point overlooking an open area Matt would be forced to cross. She was perched a good thirty feet above the floor of the gorge.

She intended only to scare him. A couple of overhead shots should send any sensible person scurrying for safety. Then she would shout a warning that he'd best return to Albuquerque, or next time she wouldn't miss. That ought to knock a peg or two out of his arrogant superiority.

The image of Devereaux in retreat remained a gray blur in her mind. She grimaced. It was impossible to imagine him afraid of anything.

Okay, so it was unlikely she would frighten him. But she could, she thought resolutely, show him she wasn't worth the trouble.

She chose the best vantage point and lay flat. Sun-baked stone warmed her belly through her clothes as she waited. The rough surface pressed into her flesh and numbed her elbows as she cradled the rifle in a ready position.

She sighted down the barrel, aiming at a point well above an average rider's head. Then she nudged the sight up, adjusting for Devereaux's superior height.

Ellie's shoulders tensed as the clatter of hooves on stone became audible. Her hands steadied in preparation. She closed her left eye and aimed.

Devereaux's mount came into sight. Riderless. The mule followed on a lead secured to the gray gelding's saddle horn.

Ellie lowered the rifle and frowned. No, Devereaux couldn't have guessed—

Without warning, a broad-shouldered shadow fell across her rifle. She gasped and swung around, the gun still gripped tight in her hands.

A large, booted foot stomped on the barrel, forcing it against a boulder. The knuckles of Ellie's right hand rapped hard against the stone. The clang of metal echoed through the gorge.

"Ouch!" she yelped, jerking her hand away. She glared up at him. Her resentment bordered on hatred. She raised her hand and sucked tenderly on the skinned knuckles.

Matt bent and picked up her rifle. He straightened, cradling the weapon in his left arm. It simply wasn't fair for such a difficult man to be blessed with such powerful grace and a physique capable of blocking out the sun.

Then she noticed the Colt Peacemaker in his right hand. She gave him a satisfied little smile.

"I am flattered, Mr. Devereaux, that you consider me menacing enough to draw your revolver."

"Lady, you *are* dangerous," he growled. He flipped the Colt backward in a three-quarter spin and jammed it into its holster. "Reckless and hotheaded. You could have blown my damn head off."

"Hardly reckless. If I choose to blow your *damn* head off," Ellie retorted, "believe me, I will accomplish the task out of skill, not carelessness. And the idea grows more tempting by the moment."

He had the audacity to grin. Teeth flashed white in the shadowed bronze of his face. Ellie growled low in her throat. The last thing she wanted was for him to find her amusing. It infuriated her when men—and most recently, and particularly, this man—didn't take her seriously.

He extended a hand to help her up. She ignored it and climbed to her feet.

"Do you ever accept help from anybody?" he grumbled.

"Only rarely, and then only from people I trust." She brushed away clinging dirt with angry sweeps of her hands.

Matt sighed. He jerked his head to the side. "Come on. Let's go."

"Where?" Ellie asked suspiciously.

"Back to the horses. Unless you see some compelling reason to stay up here." Using her rifle, he pointed to the spot where she'd climbed out of the gorge. "After you, Miss Carlisle. Ladies first."

"Oh, spare me. You're just concerned I'll shove you from behind and push you over the edge. There's not a gentlemanly bone in your body."

A curtain seemed to fall across his face, wiping away all expression. Except for his eyes. Something dark stirred in them, causing golden flecks to glitter.

Uneasy with his cold stare, Ellie turned and started walking. He followed close behind. He moved quietly for a tall man, but every slight scrape of his boots against the stones triggered strange, tingling shivers of awareness between her shoulder blades.

Halfway to the path, she could no longer ignore her burning curiosity. "How did you know I was up there?"

"Other than the fact that turn in the gorge is named Ambush Point?"

Ellie squeezed her eyes shut for a moment. Humiliation could cause physical pain, she discovered, as a spasm constricted her throat. She enjoyed a brief fantasy of strangling Devereaux.

"Is it really?" she forced herself to say nonchalantly.

"Yep. Somewhat famous in these parts as the perfect spot to shoot virtuous, innocent folk minding their own business."

She shot him a look over her shoulder. "Not today it wasn't."

"Actually, I used that exact spot once myself to get the drop on three banditos who were tracking me."

"Did it work?"

"Yeah. It worked."

His hard tone did not invite further questions. They neared the top of the path.

"Can I have my rifle back now?"

"When I'm sure I won't get a bullet in the back for my trouble."

She spun to face him. "That's not fair," she exclaimed. "You know I wouldn't actually have shot you."

"Do I?" Locks of brown hair had tumbled over his forehead. His thick brows rose, catching and lifting the hair in a way that emphasized his look of incredulity.

"I only meant to scare you off. You have no right following me."

He pointed to the path, which dropped abruptly from the edge of the escarpment. "Down. And be careful."

Finding secure footing consumed all of Ellie's attention. They reached the floor of the gorge and approached her horse and mule. Matt emptied her rifle of bullets, then slid the gun into the saddle boot.

"Mount up. We're going back for my horse and mule,

then we'll travel on together. This time I intend to keep a close eye on you."

She mounted grudgingly. Matt walked alongside as they retraced her route. Ellie glanced down at the square, uncompromising jaw just visible beneath the brim of his hat. An idea slipped into her mind.

He was down there, and she was up here, and what if.

A daring, guilt-laden idea.

Think of the treasure, Ellie. Think of its safety.

She dug her heels into her mount's sides, calling on all the equestrian training her brother had provided over the years. The pinto mare surged forward. The lead rope snapped taut, causing the mule to break into a run. They quickly put a safe distance between her and Devereaux.

She raced the animals south down the gorge. The clatter of hooves echoed from the rock faces on either side. She expected a roar of outrage. She heard none. Ellie kept her eyes fixed forward, not daring to look back at Devereaux lest her courage falter.

Nearing his horse and mule, Ellie pulled her revolver from her saddlebag and raced at the hapless animals, shouting and firing the gun into the air. Devereaux's gelding whinnied in terror and bolted in the opposite direction, the mule in hot pursuit. She hoped they would get as far as Albuquerque before they stopped.

Ellie reined in, allowing her animals to catch their breath. Now came the hard part—heading back north with an angry, threatening, six-foot-two obstacle in the way. She would have to race right past him unless she wanted to go miles out of her way.

Besides, she wouldn't leave him stranded without water. She untied a spare full canteen from her saddle horn, then started her horse back down the gorge at an accelerating pace.

Matt stood in the center of the trail, in a particularly narrow spot between two boulders. With legs braced shoulder-width apart, arms folded, he appeared as unmovable as a pillar of granite.

Ellie's eyes widened in horror. Surely he wouldn't stand his ground? She would be forced to run him down.

At the last moment Matt leaped to the side behind one of the boulders. Ellie's horse and mule thundered over the spot where he'd stood. She dropped the extra canteen as they passed.

She twisted in the saddle and looked back. He was already on his feet, as quick and agile as a cat. He stood motionless in a cloud of settling dust, watching her flee.

A shudder of apprehension vibrated down Ellie's back.

She would have preferred that Devereaux shout at her, yell, curse, shake his fist—anything but that eerie silence.

She shook her head and concentrated on guiding her animals through the gorge. This was ridiculous! She needn't fear Devereaux's catching up with her now. It would take him hours to retrieve his animals. In the meantime, she would use every technique she knew for throwing a hunter off the trail.

Chapter 7

THE GORGE FLATTENED out. Ellie emerged into smoother country, broken only by craggy formations of granite, tumbled boulders, and clustered stands of trees.

She discovered a stream and reined her horse into the shallow water. The mule followed, braying in protest. They traced the streambed for nearly a mile, hiding their tracks, before Ellie led the animals back onto dry ground.

She glanced frequently over her shoulder. Although she chided herself for her nagging paranoia, she couldn't resist the urge to check the back trail.

Shadows stretched long on the ground, emphasizing the rugged beauty of the land. Ellie began watching for a sheltered place to camp. She started past a large cluster of trees and boulders on her right.

Without warning, Devereaux's voice erupted from the trees.

"That wasn't very nice, you know."

The pinto mare shied sideways at the unexpected explosion of sound. The sudden force jerked Ellie in the saddle, forcing her to drop the mule's lead rope.

Her left foot lost the stirrup. Grabbing the saddle horn, she hung on desperately as her backside slid halfway out of the saddle. She pulled the mare's nose around using one rein so the horse wouldn't bolt.

Matt rode out from behind the trees. He sat his horse in a relaxed pose, his wrists crossed over the saddle horn. He watched her idly, making no attempt to help as her mare snorted and pivoted in a tight circle.

Ellie gained strength from her mounting fury. She found the loose stirrup and shoved her foot into it. Pushing back into the saddle, she calmed the mare.

Her mouth thinned into a hard line as she faced Devereaux. If looks could only kill . . .

"You are a curse on my existence," she said sourly.

"You haven't exactly been all roses and sugar water yourself, Miss Carlisle."

They glared at each other, two equally stubborn wills clashing across eight feet of clear mountain air. Ellie's pride insisted she maintain eye contact and not back down in any way. But she realized that he'd somehow become dangerous on a personal level, not just as a potential threat to her goal.

She glanced down, taking in his powerful shoulders and thick forearms. Impossibly long thighs hugged his horse, causing muscles to bulge against the saddle. He reminded her of art created by ancient masters—lovingly crafted, rugged, made more beautiful by tiny, hard-to-discover imperfections.

The man didn't just fit into this land, he mastered it. Ellie envied his confidence, his abilities. Curiosity ate at her until she asked the inevitable question.

"How did you manage to get ahead of me?"

Devereaux gave her a wolfish grin. "Especially when the last time you saw me I was heading in the opposite direction on foot?"

A flush spread prickles of heat into Ellie's cheeks. "Yes," she agreed gruffly, refusing to apologize for spooking Devereaux's horse. He'd brought that on himself by following her.

"There's only one main trail through this part of the mountains. Sometimes it wraps back on itself to find the easiest route. Any man who grew up around here learns its shortcuts." He nudged his horse into motion. Leaning down, he scooped up her mule's lead and handed it to her. "We should reach Santa Fe sometime late tomorrow."

"I have no interest in traveling together," Ellie said firmly. "Have I not made that clear enough?"

"Abundantly so. But then, why are you assuming I'm listening to your wishes?"

Seeing genuine anger in his dark eyes, Ellie shivered. She had, without a doubt, pushed the man too far.

"Why can't you just leave me alone?"

"Because I never refuse a challenge. After you, ma'am."

Left with little choice, Ellie rode ahead. Matt Devereaux had issued a challenge of his own—more than one, in truth. He'd challenged her ingenuity, because, to be honest, she had run out of ideas on how to get rid of him. The man exhibited all the tenacity and patient determination of a boa constrictor. With that penetrating gaze and the incredible masculinity he wore like a mantle, he also challenged her willpower to treat him with complete indifference.

·   ·   ·

THEY SET UP camp under a sprawling oak beside a lovely stream. Dusk softened the surrounding colors to soothing shades of gray. A blazing fire cast a cheerful, dancing circle of light. The setting was idyllic and peaceful.

The atmosphere between the two travelers was anything but.

Ellie unsaddled her horse and mule, a duty she'd insisted on performing herself—despite Devereaux's offer to help after he'd finished his work with irksome speed and efficiency. He watched her now, and she sensed him even with her back turned. The awareness prickled across the nape of her neck and made her unusually clumsy.

Without warning, a twig snapped with a loud crack. Ellie spun around. She looked at Devereaux sitting on a low log next to the fire. With calm deliberation, he arranged the two broken halves of the twig side by side in one palm.

Now that he'd claimed her attention, he pushed his brown hat back on his forehead. His steady gaze made her feel like an insect pinned to a board for prolonged study.

"So tell me, Miss Carlisle, what does *your* stone look like?"

Despite the sudden leap in her heart rate, Ellie managed to school her expression. She fought the urge to place a protective hand over her chest where the snake talisman lay hidden beneath the high collar of her shirtwaist.

"What do you mean?"

"These long hours on the trail have provided me time to mull over a few things that have been bothering me." Matt toyed with the broken twig, drawing the halves through his long fingers. "Such as your stunned reaction the first time you saw my stone, as if you'd seen one like it before. Then there were the rather extreme measures you took in an attempt to acquire it."

"As I told you, I'm a collector of Indian artifacts."

The paired twigs snapped between his fingers again. Ellie winced. Matt's even tone and outward calm were a sham. A temper pushed to the edge simmered beneath the surface.

Although she couldn't blame him, neither was she about to let him intimidate her into spilling the whole truth. This was her secret, and she had every reason to keep it.

"That notion doesn't hold water any better than a sieve, lady. The stone obviously means more to you than a simple object to display in a glass case. Explain, if you can, why you recognized the significance of the line cut across the back of it. I saw your reaction when you turned the stone over at the ball."

Bloody hell, he noticed that. Ellie licked suddenly dry lips. She hesitated a fraction too long.

Matt's eyes narrowed. "You lied to me."

"I did not!"

He stood, unfolding his powerful torso and long legs. "You didn't admit to having a stone of your own." He tossed the twigs into the fire.

"How does that qualify as lying?"

"You withheld a pretty damn essential bit of information. In my book, that rates as lying."

"I'm not admitting anything of the kind."

"I haven't heard you deny it either."

Matt advanced toward her. Instinctively, Ellie recognized his patient, predatory grace as more dangerous than Peter's blustering fury. She told herself not to retreat. But one backward step turned into another, and then another, until her back pressed against the broad trunk of the oak tree. He stopped, just inches away, and braced his left hand against the rough bark beside her head.

Ellie lifted her chin, calling on her reserve of bravado. "Well, at least we agree to disagree. If you are so certain this other stone exists, then feel free to search my baggage," she said airily, waving one hand toward the stack of bundles she'd removed from her pack mule.

Matt watched her steadily, without even glancing at the bundles. "Waste of time. This thing means too much to you. No, you'd keep it safe. You wouldn't let it out of your sight."

"What are you implying?"

"That you wear your stone, just like I wear mine."

"And if I do?"

"You accused me of not being a gentleman." His voice dropped to a husky whisper. "You realize, of course, that if I were a complete scoundrel I wouldn't hesitate to unbutton your blouse and see what . . . treasures lie beneath."

Ellie's words of protest were stilled as the knuckles of his right hand touched her neck, tracing a slow path from her earlobe to the collar of her blouse. A strange river of sensation cascaded down her left shoulder and arm, all the way to her tingling fingertips. He folded down the collar, just enough to uncover the base of her throat.

"What have we here?" A hint of humor threaded through his deep, resonant voice. He slid one finger under the ribbon, causing her to catch her breath. "I wonder what's at the other end of this. Shall we see?" He caught a loop of satin around his finger.

The talisman shifted higher against Ellie's skin. She gasped. "I'll stab you if you dare try."

"With what?"

"The knife I keep in my boot."

"Knowing you, I believe you have one. But I also know you won't use it."

"What makes you so confident?"

"Because I won't give you cause. Despite your opinion to the contrary, Miss Carlisle, I am a gentleman. I've never forced a woman to do anything, and I never will." He released the ribbon and pushed away from the tree. "I want you to show me your talisman voluntarily. I'm patient. There will be plenty of opportunity for you to change your mind."

"What do you mean, plenty of opportunity?" she asked warily.

"Seems to me that the only practical solution to this damnable mess is a partnership."

The recent wound of humiliation caused by Peter opened again, leaving her feeling raw and vulnerable. Her voice trembled as she countered, "No. I'm not interested in a partnership. Under any circumstances."

"I might come in handy," Matt suggested wryly.

"If you mean for protection, I assure you that will not be necessary. My father and brother taught me to be quite proficient with weapons." Her gaze drifted to his powerful chest and legs. When she realized the involuntary direction of her thoughts, she flushed and said crudely, "You could prove useful if I needed something heavy moved, I suppose, but that is not sufficient reason for a partnership."

"Then try the fact that I know where to start the search. The Sangre de Cristos are vast. You may be sharp as a tack, Professor, and I'll admit you have plenty of grit, but how much time do you want to waste poking into dead ends?" He stalked to his bedroll and picked up his rifle. "I'm going hunting for dinner, dammit."

Ellie stared at him, dismayed by his astute recognition of the truth. He definitely had her trumped. Nevertheless, the tangled knot of fear inside her refused to let her take the risk again, refused to set herself up for betrayal. No, she could manage on her own; there was no need to shackle herself to Devereaux in a partnership fraught with complications.

The decision calmed her racing heart, allowing her to consider the rest of his words.

He had described her as sharp, with plenty of grit. No other man, beyond those in her immediate family, had verbally acknowledged her courage or her strength. Certainly her scientific peers had avoided endorsement of her achievements. Apparently, her fellow archaeologists considered it a direct threat to their manhood to acknowledge any woman as an intellectual equal.

Matt Devereaux, on the other hand, was very confident in his masculinity. He'd given her many compliments.

He'd also called her Professor.

Ellie smiled softly and blinked back silly tears. The nickname might have emerged from a rogue's temper, but she liked it.

THEY RODE INTO Santa Fe an hour past sunset the next day. The town was smaller than Albuquerque, Ellie discovered. Although less rowdy, Santa Fe boasted its fair share of gambling halls, brothels, and brightly lit saloons.

Devereaux rode his horse slightly ahead and to the right of Ellie's. His relaxed posture conveyed a natural confidence, an ease with the chaos and violence of western towns.

Light and shadow played across his shirt. His suspenders hugged the fabric close to his back, outlining strong shoulder blades and shifting muscles. His lean waist rocked with his horse's motion.

Ellie blinked, feeling suddenly muddled.

She would be so much more certain of her quest if she possessed the jaguar talisman. What if there was some trick to the way it worked, and her sketch of the piece alone would not suffice? But the stone was manacled to its stubborn owner, and she wasn't willing to court danger for the sake of convenience. If she believed she had the ability to judge men's characters . . . well, that would be a different story. But her failure to anticipate Peter's betrayal had proved her instincts couldn't be trusted. She needed a partnership like she needed a dagger at her throat.

Tomorrow she would find a way to slip away from Devereaux.

Just as they rode past another saloon, the sound of laughter swelled unexpectedly. Cheers rattled the windows. Someone fired two shots into the ceiling in celebration.

The raucous noise raked Ellie's nerves. Matt didn't even flinch. He was the calm in the center of the storm. She edged her mount closer to his. Just for good measure, she fingered the mother-of-pearl handle of the slender dagger hidden in her right boot.

They rode past two more buildings, and then, without warning, Matt reined his horse sharply to the right. He headed straight for a saloon with JACK'S BAR painted on a large sign above the door. More than two dozen horses were tied to hitching posts in front of a long porch.

"What is it?" Ellie asked. Exasperated by his unpredictable behavior, she prodded, "Really, Mr. Devereaux. Don't tell me you have a sudden craving for a drink."

He didn't answer. Instead, he kicked his right leg over his saddle and slid to the ground. He quickly tied his horse and mule to an open spot along a hitching post. Then he walked to another group of horses and slipped between a large buckskin and fine bay stallion. Soothing, murmured words drifted to Ellie over the merry sounds from the saloon.

"Devereaux?"

Ellie dismounted and secured her animals. She found Matt with his forehead pressed against the bay stallion's neck, his left arm looped over its withers, his right hand rubbing the horse's chest. The bay's ears turned back, listening to the same deep, resonant voice that sent little shivers up Ellie's arms.

Lowering its muscular neck, the stallion lipped the side of Devereaux's trousers. Ellie caught her breath. She recognized prime horseflesh when she saw it. But the tangled mane and gaunt ribs of the stallion indicated that it had been recently mistreated.

Devereaux glanced toward the saloon. Light from the nearest window caught him full on the face, highlighting a look of cold fury. Muscles bunched in his clenched jaw. Ellie took a step backward, even though she knew the look was not meant for her. Then, as if his behavior wasn't odd enough, he opened one of the saddlebags and thrust his hand inside, searching.

Ellie glanced up and down the street nervously. Luckily, most people were inside the saloons. Only a few wandered the boardwalks.

Moving closer, she whispered harshly, "Mr. Devereaux, what are you doing? This looks like stealing."

Matt withdrew his hand, only to probe the rolled blanket tied behind the cantle. "You needn't worry, Miss Carlisle. This has nothing to do with you."

"Of course it doesn't. I would never be involved in anything criminal," she snapped.

A sound between a snort and a laugh emerged from Matt's throat. "Where does breaking into my room in Albuquerque fit that definition?"

"That was different. That was for the sake of science."

"Nice try, lady." He moved to the stallion's left side and searched the other saddlebag. "Keep saying that enough and maybe you'll convince yourself."

Ellie winced. "Well, at least it was a matter just between the two of us. What you're doing now is quite public."

Matt reached for the saddle girth. He began pushing the leather tongue free of the buckle. "No one asked you to stick around and watch."

True. She should just leave him to his fate. "At least give me the jaguar talisman before the local constable tosses you in jail," Ellie said.

He stopped. He stared at her outthrust hand. "You never give up, do you?"

"Never."

"Let me see if I've got this straight. You're suggesting I give you the talisman for safekeeping, just in case I end up rotting in some dark, dingy, depressing jail cell?"

"It's the only intelligent thing to do." She wiggled her fingers, inviting him to place the stone in her palm.

"Your concern for my personal welfare is very flattering," Matt retorted dryly, "but I have no intention of giving the jaguar stone over to you." He turned back to his task with a vengeance, jerking the girth free of the buckle. "Some nagging instinct tells me I would only watch you disappear into the mountains and leave me behind."

Ellie pursed her lips. She hadn't thought that far ahead. The idea had some merit.

"I'm surprised you haven't attempted to have me thrown in jail on some pretext," he continued, "then beg some soft-hearted sheriff to let you have my stone."

Ellie smiled. "Do you think he would believe me?"

He paused to glare at her. "Oh no you don't. Don't even think about it."

"If I do, please recall it was your idea."

"It won't work. The sheriff of Santa Fe is a friend of mine. You're stuck with me."

He had an incredible knack for getting her ire up. Ellie stepped in nearer and said heatedly, "There is no 'with me,' stuck or otherwise. As I said, I refuse to accept a partnership of any kind."

"How could I forget?"

He turned toward her. That simple movement brought him closer than Ellie had anticipated. She stared at the open collar of his shirt.

"It's a pity you're so against the idea, Miss Carlisle, because a partnership makes sense. I have something you need, and you have something I need," he added in a husky tone.

Ellie looked up to his bronzed face. No retort came to mind. In fact, she was incapable of movement or thought . . . except to acknowledge that he was handsome in a rugged fashion beyond her experience. The resonance in his deep voice had also done something strange to her knees.

Two cowboys strode out of the saloon, their voices raised in a bawdy song, their spurs jingling. Ellie and Matt jerked apart, suddenly self-conscious.

Matt pulled the saddle and blanket off the stallion's back. He tucked the stirrups and used the girth to bind everything together in a tight bundle.

"I don't understand," Ellie said. "What could you possibly want with that man's belongings?"

"What I want, Miss Carlisle, is to see that the saddle and bags are returned to the son of a bitch who stole my horse. The stallion is mine, and I'm taking him back. Right now."

"This horse was stolen from you?"

"Yep." Matt grabbed the heavy western saddle by the horn and hitched it over his right shoulder.

"Shouldn't you let the constable deal with this?"

"Nope. This is one pleasure I refuse to share with anyone else."

Matt didn't hesitate in front of the saloon. He hit the swinging doors with the heel of his free hand. They swung inward, striking the adjoining walls with a loud crack of wood. He strode through like a gale-force wind.

Ellie caught the doors as they rebounded, just before they hit her in the chest. She shoved her way through, anxious not to lose sight of Devereaux—or rather, his talisman—in the crowded saloon.

The tinny tunes of a piano rose above the noisy crowd. Numerous tables bustled with gamblers playing various games. Over a dozen men were lined up along a huge bar, their elbows and drinks resting on a serving shelf of white marble. Six white pillars supported the tall bar back and heavy top of ornately carved mahogany. Three massive mirrors, each over five feet in length, reflected the revelers' images. A bullet puncture marred the surface of one mirror.

Matt headed straight for a round card table occupied by five men. He heaved the saddle over his shoulder and slammed it down onto the middle of the table. Poker chips bounced in every direction, and loose cards fell to the floor.

All the players except one leaped to their feet, swearing. The last man, wearing a faded black duster, stayed glued to his seat. He stared at Matt as if seeing a ghost.

"What's the matter, Darby?" Matt jeered. "Hadn't you heard I was back from the dead?"

Ben Darby reached for his gun. With a lightning-quick move of his hand, Matt drew his Colt first. Darby froze, the nose of his revolver still beneath the surface of the table. Ellie gasped at Matt's unexpected display of speed.

The men in the line of fire scrambled out of the way. Some of the other saloon patrons stopped to watch. Most of the gamblers glanced up without much interest, then went back to their games. Of course, Ellie thought, thoroughly fascinated—this kind of thing was commonplace in the American West.

"Go ahead," Matt said in a soft, menacing tone. "All I need is a reason to return the favor of bushwhacking me."

Darby's face took on an ashen hue.

Matt smiled grimly. "Just put your gun on the table and remove your gun belt. Then we'll settle this the right way . . . bare-knuckled."

"Sure. Why not," Darby agreed acidly.

Darby set his nickel-plated revolver on the table. He stood, yanked off his ankle-length black coat, then wrenched off his gun belt. Although at least four inches shorter than Matt, Darby was a short-necked, barrel-chested bull of a man with a scraggly dark beard and a mean snarl.

Matt slid his revolver into its holster and reached for the brass buckle at his hips.

Ellie watched in alarm. What was Devereaux doing, getting himself involved in a saloon brawl when the talisman could get lost in the fray? She started to push her way forward.

"Whoa there, miss," interrupted a deep voice. A solid man in a stained blue shirt and a tan cowboy hat stepped into Ellie's path. "You're not supposed to be in here."

Oh, no, Ellie thought in disgust. Not that stupid rule about women in saloons again.

"Nonsense," she challenged. "Why not?" She leaned sideways to peer around the man. Just then Darby jumped in, before Matt was free of his gun belt, and sucker punched him in the gut. Matt doubled over. He immediately straightened and delivered an uppercut to Darby's jaw.

The cowboy shifted, cutting off Ellie's view again. "Because women ain't allowed in here, that's why."

Ellie nodded toward a group of colorfully dressed saloon girls. "What about them?"

"Er—"

"I thought you said women aren't allowed?"

"Now, ma'am," he cajoled, his ears reddening. "You don't exactly fit in the same category as those women."

"How do you know that?" Ellie heard the sound of fists hitting flesh. Why wouldn't this idiot move out of the way? She was missing the fight.

"What's the problem, Joe?" asked another big man.

"I was just tellin' this little lady that women ain't allowed in Jack's Bar."

"And I was insisting I have as much right to stay as those other women," Ellie snapped. People clustered around the fight, cheering the combatants on. Everyone could see what was going on except her.

After exchanging a meaningful look, the men shook their heads.

"Come on," one said.

"Out you go, ma'am," confirmed the other.

They each took one of Ellie's elbows and escorted her firmly to the door. She craned her neck to look back over her shoulder.

"No, wait, you don't understand. I have to see—"

"Sorry, ma'am," the two men said in unison as they gently pushed her through the swinging doors.

Ellie spun around, prepared to continue arguing her point, but the doors swung closed. One of the gorillas stationed himself just inside the opening, circumventing her plan to sneak back in.

Heaven knew why, she didn't want to miss a moment of the fight. She should have been hoping that Matt Devereaux suffered a decisive defeat, enough to put him out of commission for a day or two so she could evade his persistent pursuit. Instead, not knowing who prevailed in the fight filled her with unease. She stood on tiptoe, straining to see over the doors.

Suddenly, a smarmy voice directly behind her said, "My, my, I wonder how disappointed Winston Carlisle would be to see his little girl captivated by a common brawl."

Chapter 8

ACOLD CHILL WASHED through Ellie from neck to toe. Her heels lowered to touch the boardwalk. Then the memory of melted gold and callous greed triggered a rush of hot anger.

She turned slowly. Several blistering words whipped through her mind, but none seemed adequate.

"Hello, Peter."

Her former fiancé climbed the two steps from the street, looking dapper in tan jodhpurs, black top boots, and a hunter-green coat. He didn't seem the worse for wear from the journey north, a realization that set Ellie's teeth on edge.

"I must confess, Elysia, I am surprised to see you here. Though I really should have guessed you would find some way to follow me. You always were bloody persistent."

"How typically arrogant of you, assuming I followed you at all. We just happen to be interested in the same destination," she said, her voice rising in righteous indignation. She stepped forward, fists clenched. "I for the purpose of archaeological discovery, and you for the purpose of pillaging, you low-life, scavenging—"

"Calm yourself, my dear."

She scowled. "Which reminds me. I believe you have something that belongs to me." She thrust out her hand. "The map rubbing, if you please."

Peter smiled in his charming and patronizing way. "I think not. You know the old adage—finders keepers."

"You've never honestly found anything in your life, Peter Wentworth. With three weeks to think about it, I've come to realize you've never put much effort into anything. You thrived on your father's money until your self-indulgence exceeded even his largesse. Then, when our marriage and my inheritance didn't materialize fast enough to suit you, you stole from me. As long as there is someone to provide for you, or do your dirty work, you never exert yourself to any extent."

A muscle twitched beneath Peter's right eye, confirming that her remarks had struck home. "I suppose you think you're bloody perfect?"

A lump rose in her throat. "I know my flaws only too well. But at least I'm not a manipulative scoundrel."

He lunged, catching her off guard. Ellie winced as his fingers dug into the tender flesh on the inside of her arm.

"Unfortunately, your presence here does present a problem," Peter snarled. "You see, I cannot allow you to beat me to that treasure."

She couldn't pull her arm free to reach the dagger in her boot. "What are you going to do?"

"I don't know yet. But I shall think of something, my dear."

Ellie struggled as Peter started to drag her away. His grip tightened even more. She shouted, but the uproar from the saloon drowned out her cries.

· · ·

MATT SMASHED HIS fist into Ben Darby's jaw, adding another bruise to the outlaw's growing collection. Darby staggered back, swaying as he glared at Matt with the one eye that wasn't swollen shut.

Matt's tongue slid between his teeth and lower lip, tasting blood. A deep breath sent a stabbing pain through his battered ribs. Darby fought dirty, and Matt had suffered his fair share of damage.

The crowd's shouts of encouragement merged into a jumble of noise. Matt ignored them. He only wanted answers, his horse, and the justice of sending Darby to the hangman's noose.

It was time to settle this. Grabbing Darby by the front of his shirt, Matt slammed him down onto a table. He pinned the outlaw with two hands fisted just below Darby's neck.

"Who shot me that day? Spill it, or I'll ram your head against this table so many times you'll forget which end you piss out of."

Darby groaned. He blinked slowly, struggling to maintain consciousness, then gasped, "It was Sam. He shot you."

Matt released him abruptly. "Every bruise and cut you're sporting is payback for the way you mistreated my stallion. Now you and I are taking a trip down to the sheriff's office."

A faint cry penetrated Matt's haze of anger. The voice was familiar.

Ellie?

He scanned the crowd. Most of the people were returning to their gambling now that the excitement was over. There was no sign of the British hellion. Matt scowled. Where the hell had she disappeared to now?

Perhaps that elusive, headstrong woman had taken advantage of the fight to slip away unnoticed. Had she grabbed another opportunity to gain a head start while he was getting pummeled?

The bitter suspicions failed to quiet his sudden sense of unease. Darby would have to wait. He released the outlaw with a shove.

Matt grabbed his gun belt and strode toward the main entrance. The crowd parted. He was halfway to the doors when the hairs on the back of his neck prickled. Matt pulled his revolver from its holster, cocked the hammer as he pivoted rapidly, and fired. Darby jerked his hand back just as the bullet struck his nickel-plated gun with a loud twang.

The gun spun off the table and hit the floor. Darby ran for the rear exit.

Matt caught a glimpse of tawny-gold hair beyond the double doors. Ellie stumbled, then steadied herself. A man he'd never seen before pulled her along.

Cursing, Matt sprinted across the room. Dammit, couldn't the woman stay out of trouble for two minutes? He'd spent weeks hunting Darby down. He shoved through the swinging doors.

"Hey!" he bellowed, standing on the boardwalk.

The pair froze, then turned.

Matt approached them, buckling on his gun belt as he went. Long strides quickly carried him to within six feet of the couple. The stranger maintained a tight hold on Ellie's upper arm.

Matt's brows dropped in a thunderous scowl. Something about that possessive grip really bothered him.

The man smiled. "Nothing to concern yourself about, old chap. The lady and I are longtime acquaintances. We were on our way to discuss a certain item she would very much like to see again. Is that not right, Ellie dear?"

Another Brit, Matt realized in frustration, recognizing the accent. Ellie didn't answer.

"Do you need help?" Matt asked.

Silence. She lifted her chin.

That stubborn tilt of her head gave Matt his answer. She was always at her most unreasonable when she needed help but wouldn't admit it. He drew his revolver and leveled it at the man's nose.

"Let her go. Now."

The stranger released her and raised his hands. Ellie moved to Matt's side, massaging her arm. Beneath her familiar angry expression, Matt thought he saw a tremor in her lower lip. He quelled a sudden urge to slip his free arm around her shoulders. Hell, wouldn't she bite his head off for that!

The Brit stared down the barrel of the Colt. "Ellie, if you want any chance to see that item again, you will tell this boorish Yank to put his gun away."

"I simply want you to give up what you stole," she countered. "It was never yours to begin with." Stepping forward, she pushed aside the lapels of his coat and began to search his pockets.

Matt's curiosity about this bizarre situation grew. Ellie was boldly digging through the man's pockets, searching for . . . what?

Apparently finding nothing there, she switched to patting down his linen shirt. "Where is it?" she demanded.

"Safely hidden away."

She stepped back.

"Did you find anything you liked, my dear?" he added with a smirk. He held open his coat as if inviting her to pat his chest again.

Matt didn't like the man's suggestive leer or his insinuations. "Do you want me to shoot him for you?" he growled, only half kidding.

"No!" She tugged on Matt's sleeve. "No, please, don't do that. It's really not that important."

Slowly, Matt lowered his gun arm. He wasn't sure he shared her dismissive opinion of this man. There was something in the stranger's keen eyes that reminded him of the sly patience of buzzards and coyotes.

"I promise you, Elysia, this is not the end of it," the Englishman said with a snarl as he walked away.

Ellie sighed heavily.

She looked up at Matt. Suddenly, she caught his chin between her thumb and forefinger and tilted his head toward a nearby street lamp.

"You're hurt!" she gasped. She released his chin to touch his swollen lip with a feather-light stroke.

"It's nothing," Matt said automatically. When she drew her hand away, he could have kicked himself for downplaying the severity of his split lip. Was it too late to gain sympathy with a dramatic little moan? He rather liked the feel of her fingers against his face.

"Of course it is something. Here, we have to doctor that. Come with me."

She grabbed his wrist and guided him back toward Jack's Bar. Matt followed, a little dazed. Maybe she had a tendency to adopt wounded birds and stray animals. He didn't know how else to explain her sudden interest in his welfare.

A man sauntered out of the saloon. Pulling a few coins from her pocket, Ellie purchased the half-empty bottle of whiskey he carried. With enough money now to buy a new bottle, he turned and reentered the saloon. Matt watched wryly. Ellie didn't seem to notice. She led the way to their horses and pulled a spare neck cloth from her saddlebag.

Matt thought she was going to moisten the fabric and dab at his lip. Instead, she tipped the bottle and poured straight whiskey over his lip, catching the overflow with the cloth held beneath his chin. It stung like hellfire.

"Ow!" he burst out, jumping back.

"Don't be a baby. The alcohol will clean it out."

"I know that! Damn, you could have warned me." He gingerly felt his throbbing lip.

"Stop touching it. You'll get dirt in it."

Although Matt grumbled under his breath, he obeyed. He eyed the whiskey-soaked cloth with suspicion, but this time she dabbed gently at his injury.

"He called you Elysia. Is that your full name?"

Ellie paused in her ministrations. "Yes. Now, will you hold still? I can't doctor your injury while you're talking."

"That's an unusual name. I've never heard it before."

"My mother gave me the name to please my father. His favorite periods of archaeological study were the Greek and Roman eras. In Greek mythology, the Elysian fields were where the great heroes were carried, body and soul, after they died in battle. There they could live forever in perfect happiness, free of worry and illness, surrounded by the beauty of lush nature and eternal sunshine."

"Paradise," Matt murmured.

"Supposedly. Actually, the name proved a deuced nuisance most of the time. The other children teased me." She raised the cloth in her fist, wielding it like a weapon. "I'm warning you, Devereaux—I long since grew intolerant of their mockery, so do not use my name as another means to goad me."

"I wouldn't dream of it . . . not when you might pour that whiskey over my lip again."

She eyed him warily for a moment, gauging his sincerity. Then, with a curt nod, she returned to doctoring his lip. "See that you don't," she added sternly.

Matt suppressed a smile. He thought the name beautiful, just as she was undeniably pleasing to the eye. He relaxed, taking the opportunity to study her face. The light shone over creamy skin and picked out golden highlights in her hair. Her eyes were an incredible green, enriched with the color and serenity of a high mountain meadow. Contentment began to work its way through his tense muscles and sore bones like warm sunshine.

She gnawed her lower lip in concentration. Matt's breathing deepened as he watched her. His heart accelerated, beating an insistent rhythm against his chest.

Ellie felt his warm breath brush across the back of her hand. The sensation triggered a shiver that raced up her arm. She became keenly aware of the masculine line of his lips. A day's beard roughened his square jaw. She took in his powerful neck, as well as shoulders so broad she felt fragile in comparison. She'd never been this close to a man who was so completely, undeniably male.

All at once, the contrast between his raw sensuality and her passionless existence was too great to bear. Ellie's lack of confidence in herself as a woman crashed in and pulled her away.

With a trembling hand, she quickly finished her task and stepped back.

"Why did you get involved in that fight?" Ellie asked to cover the sudden disappearance of her courage. "What was all that about?"

"A few weeks ago a local gang of thugs bushwhacked me."

" 'Bushwhacked'?"

"Ambushed—shot me from hiding, like damned cowards."

"Shot you?" she exclaimed, shocked. Her attention switched to his shirt and what lay beneath. Memories of that night in his room flooded back—her proximity to his bare chest, the battle marks she'd seen. Which scar resulted from that near brush with death?

"They obviously didn't succeed in killing me, but they did steal all my belongings." Matt moved to untie the bay stallion's reins.

Now Ellie understood his explosive reaction to finding the stallion in Santa Fe. "Including your horse."

"And my saddle, my clothes, my rifle." Unlooping the reins of the gray gelding and the mule, Matt turned the three animals and started walking toward the livery stable.

Ellie quickly untied her horse and mule and trailed after, impatient to hear the rest of the story. "Did they steal all your money?"

"Yes." He shrugged. "But money is easy enough to come by. It's certain other things—irreplaceable things— that I want back. They also killed a friend of mine, and for that I won't stop until each one is headed for the gallows."

She stared, astonished that he'd recently lived through such a nightmare. Then he turned to her with a face carved from stone.

"Now it's your turn to answer a few questions."

Ellie's sympathy evaporated like a rudely interrupted dream.

"Who the hell was that guy?"

A bigger problem than she'd originally thought, Ellie acknowledged inwardly. The encounter with Peter had shaken her. Greed sufficiently motivated him to be unpredictable, even potentially dangerous.

What if she couldn't manage without Devereaux's jaguar talisman? Alone, she was also unable to watch her back. She could choose to brave Peter's threat alone, or risk taking Devereaux on as a partner. Ellie only wished she could be certain Matt Devereaux was the lesser of two evils. Backed into a corner, however, she had to take that chance.

"Well?" Matt prompted, impatient with her silence.

At least she could pick and choose what to tell him. Cautiously, Ellie admitted, "His name is Peter Wentworth, Viscount Haverton."

"I mean, who is he to you? He seems to know you quite well."

She wrinkled her nose and made a face. "My fiancé."

"You're engaged?"

"Why are you shouting?"

"I'm not shouting, dammit. I just raised my voice. You keep throwing these little surprises at me."

"Although I fail to see what business it is of yours, Peter and I are no longer engaged. I terminated the arrangement—rather abruptly, in fact, when I called him a lying, thieving bastard and threw my ring in his face."

"So what is he doing here? Begging forgiveness and hoping for a reconciliation? He has a strange way of showing it."

Suspicion threaded through Devereaux's tone. Goosebumps rose on Ellie's skin. He didn't believe her. "Oh, that," she hedged.

"The truth . . . just for the sake of variety."

Ellie cringed, hating the lies, hating the need to weave secrets to protect her goal. She hated the way Matt saw through her deception even more. She needed to appease him with some degree of candor, but telling him the whole truth was out of the question. The personally humiliating part seemed less painful to share than the damage Peter had done to her career.

"Peter wished to marry me for my money. He is not very pleased at losing my inheritance."

"Inheritance?"

"If we married, he would have gained control of my dowry, plus a sizeable inheritance from my maternal grandmother that will come to me upon my marriage. Many English lords drive their estates into financial distress through poor management, then have to marry for money. Peter apparently hastened his predicament by frequenting the gaming hells of London."

They stopped at the entrance to the livery.

"And you got involved with this guy?" Matt asked incredulously.

Ellie crossed her arms tightly over her chest. "I know it appears poor judgment on my part, but Peter is an old friend of the family. I didn't find out until . . . until recently that he is in quite deep with the moneylenders."

"I think you need to work on your insight into human nature. Particularly men," he said dryly.

Matt turned and walked into the stable, calling for assistance. With his back turned, Ellie couldn't maintain her ire. She sagged inwardly. He'd only spoken the sad truth. She was a pathetic judge of men. "I know," she whispered to herself.

The horses and mules were led away by the stable boys. Matt gathered up her saddlebags as well as his own, plus both their rifles.

"Come on," he said gruffly, striding past her. "The hotel is this way."

Ellie followed, intent on forcing the necessary, dreaded words out of her dry throat. Her pride had never paid such a high price.

"Mr. Devereaux?"

"Yes?"

"I've been thinking."

"That's one of the things that scares me about you," he

said without slowing down. "When you get creative, trouble typically follows."

She wouldn't let his sarcasm get to her this time. He wasn't likely to cooperate if she lost her temper. "About this concept of a partnership . . ."

He stopped so abruptly that Ellie walked several steps farther before realizing he was no longer beside her. She turned to face him.

"Yes?" he coaxed, watching her with raised brows and an amused smile.

Ellie's fingernails dug into her palms. He knew. The rogue had already guessed what she meant to suggest, and he eagerly awaited her capitulation.

"Maybe we should consider working together," she muttered.

"You mean . . . partners?"

"Yes."

"Why?"

Ellie blinked. This was what he wanted, and now he balked? Her temper flared. "You were the one who suggested the idea!"

"Once. You refused."

"Well, that was then. I've changed my mind."

"When most women do that, it's just a minor aggravation. When you change your mind, it sends cold chills down my spine." He started up the steps to the hotel entrance.

No! He couldn't be spurning her offer. She hadn't laid her pride on the line only to have him step on it. Although she would never admit it, the more she thought about the vastness of these mountains and the potential dangers, the more daunted she felt. Devereaux's strength and experience in this country provided an advantage that would speed her search.

Ellie rushed up the stairs and jumped in front of Matt. He halted on the step just below hers. Their relative positions leveled their eyes.

"Aren't you being just a bit suspicious?" Ellie challenged. "I don't have much reason to trust you either."

"Touché. But there's still one problem."

"What is that?"

"You haven't told me what we're after."

Ellie's stomach sank. The man didn't miss a beat. That was the one thing she couldn't tell him. The only protection she had was to delay the revelation until the last possible moment. With the skills and power she'd seen in him, there was one thing Ellie knew instinctively—if Matt Devereaux decided to betray her, he'd make Peter seem an amateur in comparison.

Gravely, she said, "I . . . I can't explain that yet. But I shall tell you when the time is right."

She held her breath, searching his expressionless face for some reaction. He said nothing for several seconds. The word *please* rose in her throat, swelling until it threatened to choke her, but she couldn't make herself say it.

Matt frowned, resisting her unreasonable plea. She'd tried to rob him, scare him off, and leave him stranded—but she wouldn't share the one thing necessary to gain his trust. Nevertheless, Matt couldn't tear his attention away from the near desperation in her eyes. He knew she was overflowing with secrets, but there was nothing insincere about the emotions flickering across her face—a damn beautiful face, to make matters more complicated. How could she be tough as nails and so fragile at the same time? She needed protecting, dammit, especially as she refused to admit to any kind of need. Matt felt his resistance caving in.

"All right," he said gruffly. "Partners."

Her brilliant smile blinded him. She gave him a spontaneous kiss on the cheek, as light as a butterfly, then pivoted and darted into the hotel.

Matt stood frozen on the steps, his heart thudding like a bass drum.

"THAT SELFISH BITCH," Peter muttered furiously.

He swung at one of the posts holding up the porch roof of the general store, missing it deliberately. He was enraged, but he wasn't so far gone he would break his knuckles against a bloody post. His fist whizzed by the next post, and the next as he walked by.

As usual, Ellie was thinking only of herself. If only she'd kept things simple by marrying him according to their original schedule, instead of postponing the wedding date twice while she hared off to Greece, then to Peru on some crazy archaeological dig. Didn't she realize what those delays had cost him? How close he'd come to debtor's prison?

At least her arrival in Santa Fe confirmed that he'd come to the right place. This had better be the launching point in the search for Montezuma's treasure. He was tired of the lack of decent accommodations, the dirt streets, and the crude Yanks.

Speaking of which . . .

Peter scowled. Where had Ellie picked up the tall American with the tendency to play rescuer? She called him Devereaux. The man probably hung around hoping to bed that cold bluestocking. Wasn't Devereaux in for a big disappointment, Peter thought with spiteful relish Ellie Carlisle didn't have a passionate bone in her body.

Movement between two buildings caught his attention. A man emerged from the shadows, paused to look in both directions, then proceeded cautiously across the street. He passed under a street lamp, revealing several bruises and a swollen left eye.

Peter came instantly alert. Devereaux had sported a freshly split lip and a few bruises. Had this man been his opponent in the fight? Any enemy of Ellie's white knight could prove a valuable ally.

"Good evening," Peter greeted the man, moving to intercept him.

The man stopped in surprise, then glared at him. "What d'ya want?"

"Looks like you've had a bit of a fight, old chap. Would it perhaps have been in that saloon down the street, quaintly named Jack's Bar?"

"Yeah. So what of it?"

"Sporting a few bruises, I see."

"Yeah, well . . . you should see the other guy."

"Perhaps I have. Tall fellow, dark hair, cut lip, name of Devereaux?"

The man's expression turned nasty. "Yeah, that's Matt Devereaux all right. So what's your point?"

"What is his relationship with Miss Carlisle?"

"Who?"

"Hmm. Never mind." Peter folded his hands behind his back and rocked on his heels. "It would appear you and Mr. Devereaux are not on the best of terms."

"If that means I'd like to kill the bastard, you got that right."

Peter smiled. "Better and better. By the by, what is your name?"

"Depends on why you're askin'."

"I would like to hire you to do my—" Peter paused, thinking of the ugly accusations Ellie had hurled at him.

His smile broadened into a toothy grin. "To do my dirty work for me. It might involve killing Mr. Devereaux, if he should choose to get in my way. You would be extremely well compensated, I assure you."

"You mean paid? To kill Devereaux?"

"Indeed, if it should prove necessary."

"The name's Darby. Ben Darby. Where do I sign up?"

"You just did, old chap. Tell me, do you have any comrades who might be interested as well? I could use some additional assistance—men who wouldn't mind spending a few days in the mountains, perhaps a spot of digging, riding shotgun, that sort of thing. The pay could prove quite lucrative."

"Yeah, I have some friends who might take a likin' to the idea. They should be in town tomorrow."

"Excellent."

Chapter 9

I CAN'T BELIEVE I let you drag me up here when you won't even tell me why," Ellie grumbled as she struggled up the steep side of Table Top ridge.

She tested each foothold before entrusting her weight to the rocky slope. Matt was very mysterious about their destination, but he'd insisted on bringing her here after they'd made their way into the Sangre de Cristo Mountains and unpacked their supplies at Angus McFee's cabin.

"I thought you were an explorer," Matt countered as he climbed ahead. "Doesn't a true explorer thrive on venturing into the unknown?"

"Absolutely. But in this case, I would prefer to feel confident there is a purpose to this exercise. Why won't you describe to me what you've seen, so I can determine whether or not it is related to our expedition? Archaeologically speaking, that is. Time is precious, and I would prefer not to be toyed with at the whim of a . . . a—"

"Scoundrel?"

"I was going to say *amateur,* but since you insist, that

description is very apt as well." They were very close to the summit now.

Matt disappeared over the top. Turning around, he reached down, offering her a hand.

"Let me help you up," he said.

"I can manage, thank you."

"Take it," he growled. "It won't hurt you to accept help now and then, even from me."

"Oh, very well, as long as it is clear we are not dependent on each other." Ellie stretched up one arm.

"I wouldn't dream of saying such a thing. Grab my wrist."

She did. In turn, he locked his long fingers around her wrist in a secure grip.

Ellie expected him to steady her as she clambered up the last few feet. Instead, he lifted her straight up, leaving her dangling in space for a brief second before setting her feet gently on terra firma.

She stared at him for a moment, astonished by the display of strength. She could hardly be considered a petite woman, yet he'd lifted her as easily as a child. And she was the one breathing hard for some reason, not he.

The height offered a stunning vista in every direction. Bright light highlighted craggy mountain tops and dipped into the valleys as if trying to seek out their most hidden places. Tall evergreens stood on the slopes like dutiful soldiers. Ellie paused to take in scenery that could never be fully absorbed in a single glance.

To the east, a parallel ridge lay outlined against a cloudless sky of aquamarine. Huge natural sandstone formations, carved by aeons of wind and rain, jutted up along its crest.

"That ridge is kind of a landmark around here," Matt commented when he noticed the direction of her gaze.

"It's called Dragon's Bones, because the rock formations look like the skeletal spine of some huge beast. Beautiful, isn't it?"

"Yes, it is." The landscape of New Mexico was rugged and harsh, quite unlike the rolling green hills of England. But there was something about the stark beauty of this land that captivated her.

"Over here," Matt said briskly, leading the way toward a cluster of boulders.

Ellie followed. The neck-high rocks formed a semicircular alcove much like a shrine. They were out of place in this isolated setting, definitely man-made. Ellie's heart began to pound. Two long slabs of granite leaned against each other, forming a peaked roof over the top.

Matt pointed inside. "There. Tell me what you think, Professor."

Ellie bent over and peered inside. Matt watched over her shoulder. A flat slab of dark gray slate, about three feet across, rested atop a pedestal of stone like an altar. Images identical to those on the Aztec priest's map were etched into the stone in a straight row across the bottom. An intricately carved design filled the center.

This was it. This was the critical clue she'd been hoping to find, to guide her search where the tomb map left off.

The thrill of discovery burst through Ellie. She spun around. Spontaneously, she threw her arms around Matt's neck in a hug. It had been so very long since she'd had anyone to celebrate a victory with.

"You found it!" she said breathlessly.

Releasing him just as abruptly, she knelt before the slab and ran her palms reverently over the surface.

Several seconds ticked by before he spoke. He cleared his throat and said, "Okay, so I found it. I can see that it's a map of some sort. How the hell does it work?"

"It is a unique map. I've never seen anything like it before." She brushed her fingertips from left to right across the etched images that had become as familiar as her own reflection. "See these five designs?"

"Yes."

"They match the ones we are looking for—the jaguar, eagle, snake, monkey, and war god."

"What about the rest of it?" he asked, pointing to the design above the images.

Five round holes were carved into the slab, arranged like the points of a star. Four etched lines radiated out from each hole, forming a pentagon of lines across the center.

"These holes are just the right size for the talismans," she observed with mounting excitement.

"And the lines crisscross, intersecting in several different places," Matt said. "My guess is the lines etched into the backs of the talismans hold the key."

"Exactly! Without all five talismans placed in the correct holes, the casual observer would never be able to determine which lines to choose. The map is designed to fool anyone who doesn't understand how it works. Only one spot determined by these intersecting lines will lead us to the right location."

"The right location for what, Professor?"

"Though there is nothing here to indicate which stone goes in which hole," Ellie continued, avoiding his direct question. It was much too soon to trust Matt with the truth of their ultimate goal. She glanced up. "I would like to try them anyway. Give me your—"

She stopped in surprise. The jaguar talisman dangled from his right hand, still strung by its leather cord. He'd taken it from his neck even before she asked, volunteering the stone he'd previously guarded with such frustrating tenacity.

The round stone settled in her outstretched palm. The smooth back retained the warmth of his chest.

Matt pulled the leather string free of the hole. The cord traced a ticklish path across her palm. Disturbed by the sensation, Ellie turned away quickly—back to something she understood, something safe.

She turned the talisman over and placed it into the topmost hole. The stone settled into place, fitting snugly. Then again, it could fit just as well in any of the holes. Frustration undermined the excitement of this discovery.

"Now mine," Ellie whispered.

She reached behind her neck and grasped the ribbon. Her fingers fumbled blindly beneath her braid.

"Let me."

"I can—"

Matt insistently pushed her fingers aside, ignoring her protests, and began to work at the tight knot. "So this is Ellie Carlisle's famous talisman, the one she's refused to show me until now."

"There's a right time for everything," she replied defensively, expecting a rebuff.

He merely chuckled.

The heels of his palms rested lightly against her shoulders as he picked at the knot. His fingertips brushed the nape of her neck. She sucked in her breath.

That little gasp caused Matt's blood to run hot and hard. Was it just wishful thinking, or did he sense deep undercurrents beneath that prim exterior?

The knot came free.

Matt lifted the ribbon ends. He pulled the stone free of her high collar and dangled it beneath her chin. Ellie reached up suddenly and clutched the stone in a white-knuckled fist.

Anger and disappointment lanced through him. She still didn't trust him with her talisman—even after he'd led her to the map and willingly turned over his stone.

She tugged the ribbon free. Was the visible tremor in her hands a reaction to his touch, or was she simply overcome by the archaeological discovery? Matt wished to hell he knew.

She was about to place the talisman into the slab when she stopped unexpectedly. With a sigh, she held out her precious stone. "This is what the snake talisman looks like," she offered grudgingly.

Matt smiled; it was obviously hard for her to make that concession to their partnership. "A head at either end of the snake? Rather vicious-looking, isn't it?"

"All the figures are vicious-looking in some fashion. Even though the people who fashioned these were accomplished in science, art, and politics, their culture was deeply rooted in myth and sacrificial bloodshed."

Ellie turned back and fit the snake talisman into the next hole. The lines picked out by the two stones slanted off in different directions, never intersecting.

"This won't help us much," Matt commented dryly, "not until we determine the right order for placing the stones."

She responded, "For this map to mean anything, somewhere out in these mountains there have to be markers, positioned like the five points of this star, that correspond to each of the talismans. With each one we locate, we shall be that much closer to the solution."

Parchment crackled as she pulled a folded paper and a chunk of brown wax from her pocket. She opened the paper and carefully tore it in half. Retrieving the talismans, she placed each stone on a sheet and folded the paper over it.

"What are you doing now?"

"I am going to take a rubbing of each talisman, front and back, to preserve the images for safekeeping. It is a habit I've gotten into over the years."

Matt watched as she rubbed the wax lightly over the papers, using the texture of the carved stone beneath to reproduce the designs. She tucked the results back in her pocket and rose to her feet.

"We have another problem," Matt warned, though he hated to add to her frustration. "Even when we locate the first marker, this map doesn't tell us which direction to go from there."

"What do you mean?"

"Every map has a reference that relates it to the real world, typically an indication of true north."

Ellie frowned down at the slab. "This extra symbol must serve a purpose." She touched a shape cut into the slate above the top hole. Broad marks branched out from a central point in uneven widths, like a lady's open fan with some of the ribs broken. "It looks like a sunburst."

"I agree, but does it mean east or west?"

"I don't know . . . yet. But at least we can start where the jaguar stone was first discovered." She gave him an expectant look.

"This should prove interesting," Matt replied, thinking of the one important fact he'd neglected to tell her.

"Do be serious. It is imperative we find all the talismans and make careful note of their respective origins. Without them, we could be hunting aimlessly in this wilderness for years. Where did your friend find the jaguar?"

"Angus didn't get a chance to tell me before he died."

"Oh, dear," Ellie moaned, reaching out behind her. Her hand found a boulder. She sat down heavily.

"He did describe the marker, though. He said something about this same image carved into a cliff, and a place beneath it where he found the talisman."

Ellie leaped to her feet again, recovering from her disappointment with a buoyancy that amazed Matt. "At least that's proof the markers exist."

"What about yours?"

"What?"

"Where did you find the snake talisman?"

She looked into his eyes briefly, then looked away. "Mexico City."

"Mexico City?" Matt burst out. He scowled at the map. "I doubt the reference points on this thing reach all the way into central Mexico."

"No, no," Ellie said quickly. "At least, I don't believe so. Let's look at the facts. I found the snake talisman, along with the original map that led me here, buried in a tomb outside Mexico City. Someone involved in designing this map and the talismans, perhaps the man buried there, had returned to Mexico with the snake stone. But the snake remained there for over three hundred years. No one ever brought the set of talismans back together to solve the puzzle."

Matt crossed his arms. "Until you uncovered it at a grave site. So you think our man died before he could return."

"It seems the most plausible theory."

"Where does that leave us, Professor? These mountains have an awful lot of territory to cover."

Ellie gazed across the ridges of the Sangre de Cristo Mountains and the long, dense shadows cast by the setting sun. Matt was right. Without anything to pinpoint the start of their search, they would have to comb the terrain until they located the first marker.

Her only consolation was that Peter didn't have the advantage of these latest clues. On the other hand, he had an uncanny ability to sniff out gold. No doubt the Aztecs had hidden the treasure well, but three hundred years of wind, rain, and erosion could have left it exposed and vulnerable.

She wouldn't make the mistake of assuming she was ahead in this race.

MATT AND ELLIE returned to Angus's cabin.

As she started a meal, he led the pinto mare and his gray gelding into the barn. An eager neigh greeted him from one of the four stalls. The bay stallion thrust his head over the chest-high wall. He stretched out his long neck, nostrils flaring.

"Did you think we'd deserted you, Dakota?"

Matt eyed the stallion with satisfaction. A couple of days of easy travel and good quality grain had revived the sheen in the bay's coat. Another week or so of well-deserved care and Dakota should regain the weight lost under Darby's mistreatment.

After rubbing down the two saddle mounts, Matt measured some grain into his hat. He approached the stall. Dakota shifted restlessly in anticipation, blocking the door.

"Back up," Matt ordered softly. Dakota obeyed immediately, responding to the training Matt had given while raising the stallion from a colt. He poured the grain into a wooden trough.

As the stallion ate, Matt picked up a brush and worked over the bay's coat with long strokes. "Soon you'll be back in prime shape. Thankfully I got you back before that bastard Darby rode you into the ground." He rubbed the horse's neck. "Darby slipped through my fingers this time. It won't happen again. After I fulfill this promise to Angus, I'll be back on the Hayleys' trail."

Of course, that would also mean the end of his association with Ellie Carlisle. Matt frowned.

After dinner, he carried a chair onto the porch to watch night settle over the world like a velvet cloak. This was his favorite time, when a different set of sounds emerged to create nature's night music. Insects began to sing. Frogs croaked their chorus from the creek.

Bracing both feet against a post, Matt tilted the chair back. He folded his arms loosely over his chest and relaxed.

The mountains always soothed his soul. This isolated feeling was natural—unlike the loneliness that crept over him in a crowd, in the raucous atmosphere of a saloon, when he was surrounded by displaced people searching for some place to belong and a way to escape painful memories.

People like himself.

Ellie stepped onto the porch. Matt tensed. Other women he knew couldn't tolerate silence, feeling they had to fill it with chatter. But she just stood quietly near his left shoulder, sharing the close of the day. Did she also find solace in the dignity of the mountains?

The sound of her rhythmic breathing reached him. The subtle scent of woman and lilacs drifted on the breeze.

Matt tensed for an entirely different reason.

Slowly, he lowered his chair and rose to his feet. He stood next to her, inhaling her scent deeply. How did he go about charming his way past her bristling, porcupine exterior to coax a kiss?

Suddenly, a piercing, savage cry sounded in the distance.

Ellie looked up, confusion in her green eyes.

"Cougar or mountain lion, whichever you prefer to call it," Matt explained quietly. "It likely just made a kill." A primal shiver cascaded through him. After decades of being hunted, cougars were rare in this country. But he didn't need that logic to believe in the source of the sound. Some deeper instinct, some link established weeks before, whispered this was his cougar spirit guide, still thriving in these mountains. He probably wouldn't see the she-cat—a good thing, actually, because her survival depended on staying shy and elusive around man.

"I've heard something like it before," Ellie whispered, "when the jaguar hunts in the jungle. The sound always sent chills down my spine, yet there is a wonderful, stark beauty to it, don't you think?"

Her eyes glittered in the failing light.

How did she do that? How did she maintain a cool facade when such enthusiasm burned inside? The combination was dangerous, and the temptation to help her uncover that hidden passion was almost irresistible. Matt's eyes dropped to her lips. His rigid code of chivalry started to buckle under the weight of his growing hunger for her.

In a throaty voice he barely recognized as his own, Matt said, "You'd best go inside. Get some sleep. We're starting out early in the morning."

Ellie blinked, a little dazed.

Damn, he wanted to pull her into his arms and turn that tiny hint of confusion into a full-fledged upheaval of her prudish, safe world.

"Yes. Of course. Good night."

An hour passed before Matt felt safe to venture inside.

The sheet curtain they had rigged hung around her bed. Such a flimsy thing, really. But it might as well have been a tall white citadel behind a locked gate, for all the good it did him.

BY MIDAFTERNOON THE next day the weather had turned crisp and cool, heralding the onset of autumn. The aspens were starting to turn. Their leaves rattled lightly in the breeze.

Matt nudged the brim of his hat a little higher with his thumb. He watched the graceful rocking of Ellie's shoulders and waist as her horse picked its footing along the rocky slope. Typically in the lead, he wasn't afforded this appealing view very often. But an hour ago—showing tangible signs of frustration—the lady had insisted on riding in front.

As if their lack of success was his fault.

They'd searched for the markers, watching for any of the carved images from the map, but the mountains covered a lot of territory. So far they'd found nothing but trees, rocks, and small wild animals whose sudden, explosive bursts from cover threatened to spook the horses.

"It's a beautiful day, don't you think?" Matt commented, wondering if Ellie had even noticed the clear sky and the fresh scent of evergreens.

"Hmmm," was her only response. She rode on, studying the terrain on either side.

Matt rolled his eyes at her single-mindedness.

A flash of light halfway up the southern slope of a ridge caught his attention. Matt reined in his horse and studied the spot. Sunlight flickered off something shiny. A dark hole scarred the rock face above a series of grassy slopes and granite ledges.

Ellie twisted in the saddle, alert to his every move. "What is it?"

Matt inclined his head toward the ridge. "Something's up there. Looks like a cave."

She immediately dismounted.

"Don't get your hopes up, Professor. I don't think it's what we're looking for."

"Anything out of the ordinary is worth investigating." She started climbing the slope.

Matt dismounted with a sigh. This had the feel of an abandoned prospector's claim, nothing more. But there was no stopping the woman once she got her mind set on an idea. He thought he should let her make the wasted trip alone.

Then again, he didn't trust her to stay out of trouble. He secured the horses, then grabbed his rifle and followed.

Ellie zigzagged up the slope, navigating open stretches of grass. She worked her way around trees and ancient, tumbled rocks.

"There seems to be a path of sorts here," she called back.

"A path," Matt said to himself. "That's a stretch."

Despite Ellie's eagerness, Matt caught up before she reached the halfway point. The woman was a menace in those trousers. The fabric pulled snugly across her luscious backside as she climbed. The fact that she seemed totally unaware of her impact on his senses somehow made it worse.

"We're almost there," she said excitedly, looking up at a jagged rock ledge angling out from the slope. She dug the toe of her scuffed boot into the ground and pushed up.

Just as Ellie's head topped the ledge, her foot slipped.

With a little yelp, she slid back down. A cascade of dislodged gravel and dirt buried the toes of her boots. Matt caught another sound from above, almost undistinguishable from the noise of the pebbles.

A shot of adrenaline jolted through him.

Ellie, persistent as ever, was already finding another toehold. She pushed herself up.

Matt hooked his right arm around her waist. He jerked her down, spinning her toward him so they collided, chest to chest.

"What are you doing?" she cried indignantly.

He looked deep into her startled eyes. Her breasts crushed against his chest. Such spontaneous rescues definitely held a certain advantage, Matt decided.

"Excuse the language, ma'am, but I was saving your arse."

"What are you talking about?" She planted both hands against his shoulders and shoved. "Release me this instant."

"Stop struggling. You're likely to knock us both off the side of this mountain," he said sternly, keeping his arm locked about her waist. "Save the offended-maiden act until later."

"I beg your pardon?"

"Look up. Watch and learn."

His serious tone must have carried some weight, because she ceased her struggles. She followed the tip of his rifle as he lifted it above their heads with his left hand. The instant the sight rose above the ledge, a dark shape shot out. It knocked the barrel aside, then disappeared in a flash of movement.

Ellie gulped. "That was a . . . a—"

"Rattler. They seek out crevices in the rocks, perfect

hidey-holes for basking in the sun." He lowered the rifle. Brushing the back of one knuckle across her pale cheek, he said softly, "And he'd picked out this for a target . . . right here."

She licked her lips. "I saw rattlesnakes in Mexico. Desert ones."

"Yes'm, but this one's a timber rattler—bigger and meaner. I'm guessing this one's at least five feet," Matt drawled, keeping her talking. If she wanted to stay pressed against him all day, frozen with shock, that was just fine with him.

"You just . . . saved my life. Thank you," she whispered.

He gave her a slow wink. "Told you I might come in handy." The playful attitude concealed his tension as he wondered if her gratitude might take a more personal form. The thought of kissing her was approaching obsession.

Instead, she reacted in the way he should have anticipated. She drew back, shying away from the intimate and very improper pressure of their bodies—reverting to the proud British lady.

He quickly let her go. Fear was the last thing he wanted from her.

She looked up at the ledge again. All business, she asked briskly, "How do we get up there? Is there another way?"

"Yeah. Down."

"Surely you don't mean to give up? There could be something crucial to our search up there."

"I doubt it." He sighed. "All right. Stand back."

She moved behind him.

"Hand this to me when I say." He passed her the rifle. Choosing an angle where he could see onto the ledge, he climbed up at a safe distance.

"Can you see it?"

"Oh yes. I can see it," Matt said darkly. He had run across at least a hundred rattlers in his time—one couldn't grow up in the Southwest and avoid them. Even though he knew he was beyond striking distance, being this close to the thick, coiled body of a grayish brown rattler gave him the willies.

Its head shifted, turning toward the new threat with malevolent yellow eyes. The black tongue flicked out. It was a big one, all right. Old, too, with vertical bands of ten rattles whirring in fury.

"Okay," he said, reaching down. He didn't take his gaze off the rattler, not even for a second.

Ellie placed the rifle into his outstretched hand. Matt set his jaw, aimed the rifle, and fired.

The close-range shot blew the snake clean off the ledge. Ellie slapped her hands over her ears as the deafening report echoed through the mountains. The snake hit the ground a good twenty feet down the slope. It didn't move.

Just to be sure, Matt climbed down and shot off the rattler's head.

He returned to Ellie. "The path is clear, Professor. This time I go first."

"Really, that is not necessary. I know what to watch for now. I don't need to be pampered."

"It's not as if I offered to carry you, ma'am," he said. She was consistent, he gave her that, particularly when it came to refusing help of any kind. "Come on."

Matt commandeered the lead by taking shameless advantage of his size.

Ellie scrambled after him, grumbling under her breath. They soon reached their destination. A hole disfigured the rock face, true, but it could hardly be called a cave. No more than four feet deep, the depression had been crudely hacked out of the rock. A few remnants of human activity littered the ledge—a shattered bottle, a broken pick handle, an empty package of chewing tobacco.

Matt nudged the bottle with his toe. This was the source of the reflected light. He flipped a large piece of glass over. A label held the broken pieces together. Glen Loch Scots Whiskey—Angus's favorite brand. This site had been one of his old friend's prospecting spots.

Ellie looked around, her mouth compressed into a thin line. Her disappointment prodded Matt like an elbow in the ribs, until he felt compelled to speak.

"It was worth a try," he said awkwardly.

She nodded, the tendons in her graceful neck stretched taut.

"Let's keep looking. There's still some daylight left," he urged.

Her silence made him frown as they climbed down, retrieved the horses, and continued the search.

As twilight crept in, Matt spotted signs that caused him to rein in with a curse. He studied the ground.

"Did you find something?" Ellie rode up alongside.

"Not something I wanted to find." He pointed down. "Tracks. A day, maybe two days old. The ground is too rocky here to tell for certain, but it looks like four or five horses, with riders, and a couple of pack mules."

Ellie quickly glanced right and left. "Didn't you say these mountains tend to lure prospectors now and then? I'm sure it's nothing."

Matt watched her fingers worry the leather reins. She sure seemed nervous for someone who dismissed the signs as nothing.

"Maybe," he said. "Still, I don't like it." Especially when the two shots he'd fired could have alerted someone to their presence. He slid Ellie's rifle from its saddle boot and laid the weapon across her lap. "It always pays to stay alert in this country. I should know. The sun is going down. Time to head back to the cabin."

Chapter 10

ELLIE WAS KEEPING something from him, Matt thought with simmering frustration.

Something beyond her habitual and infuriating reluctance to reveal any information about the ultimate goal of their quest. This new withdrawal had started after their dead-end exploration of the prospecting site and the discovery of the tracks.

Her silence lasted all the way back to the cabin, throughout dinner as she picked at her food, and past the small necessities of cleaning up. Discouragement and worry hung over her like a dark cloud, snuffing out the vitality Matt was accustomed to.

After dinner, Ellie got down on her hands and knees and dug through Angus's secret supplies beneath the floorboards. When she sat back on her heels and lifted out a bottle of liquor, he regretted having shown her the cache.

Rising to her feet, she gathered up a clean tin cup and a blanket and headed for the cabin door.

Matt's brows snapped together. "Where are you going?"

"I'd like to be alone, if you don't mind," she replied with frigid dignity.

Not only did she still not trust him with a direct answer, she continued to maintain this colossal distance between them. He sought the only thing that consistently bridged the gap—antagonism.

Nodding at the bottle, he said, "Looks like you're not going out there completely alone. A little bourbon to keep you company? Not very intellectual, Professor."

She lifted her chin in that way that filled him with the urge to run his knuckles across her jaw and down the smooth, graceful column of her throat.

"It's Scots whiskey, actually," she retorted. "Your friend must have been a scholar and a gentleman, a man with good taste. Unlike some I could mention around here."

The door closed quietly behind her.

Matt closed his eyes and exhaled slowly. How did she do this to him—kindle this simmering rage that burned through his veins and went straight to his loins? Why did he let the infuriating woman get under his skin?

He walked to the window and lifted a corner of the faded curtain. Ellie carried an armload of firewood to the old campfire site in front of the house. She arranged the wood inside the stone circle, then went back for another load. Ten minutes later, she had the beginnings of a roaring blaze.

She sat on the ground, her expression melancholy, her back to one of the large logs scattered in a broken, outer circle around the fire. A generous amount of whiskey splashed into the tin cup. She tipped the cup to her mouth. Immediately, she bent over, coughing and wheezing. Matt couldn't resist a smile. The sophisticated little

Brit clearly wasn't accustomed to hard liquor. But she sat back, taking small sips, until her throat grew accustomed to the alcohol and her body relaxed.

She stared into the flames, giving every indication of intending to get mind-numbingly drunk.

Matt growled in irritation. Why was he watching Ellie do this to herself? It wasn't his responsibility if she wanted to get stinking drunk. He spun away from the window and snatched a deck of cards from his saddlebag. He sat at the table and searched for distraction in the shuffle of the cards.

After losing the fourth game of solitaire, Matt glanced at the window. Actually, his gaze had wandered to that window several times in the past hour.

Maybe he should check on her. Just in case.

Nudging the curtain aside, Matt looked out at a strange sight. The fire blazed, forming a circle that isolated Ellie from the blackness beyond. She stared deep into the flames.

She pulled her braid over one shoulder. Her fingers slowly undid the thick strands, until a waterfall of silky hair gleamed like pure gold in the firelight.

Matt's pulse quickened. He wondered how alcohol affected the wall she had built around herself. Would it tumble, releasing the passion trapped beneath?

Why did he indulge in this self-torment? Solitaire was safe . . . dull, but safe.

Five minutes later, he was still standing at the window. With an annoyed snort, he gave up the losing battle and went outside. He would prove she could trust him. He wouldn't take advantage of her the way men usually took advantage of women who were drunk.

She held the bottle propped on one outstretched thigh. Her right leg was bent, the half-empty cup held on her knee. He marveled that she could look pathetic but beautiful and endearing at the same time.

Matt stopped at her side. She turned her head to stare at the toes of his boots.

"I don't usually do this, you know," Ellie said clearly, with no sign of a slur in her words. A deep sadness echoed hollowly through her voice.

"I assumed as much." Matt folded his arms across his chest. "How long do you plan to keep this up?" he challenged.

"As long as I choose. I am entitled."

"Really. Entitled to what? The whole bottle?"

"That is not what I meant. But if I choose to finish it, then bloody hell, why not?" She saluted the fire with the bottle.

"You'll have one humdinger of a head in the morning."

She sighed heavily. "I know."

He couldn't stand seeing her like this. Although he had no right to know the source of her despair, he wanted her to tell him. He sat down and leaned back against another log. He stretched out his long legs, crossing them at the ankles, his booted feet a mere inch from Ellie's.

"Okay, if you didn't mean the whiskey," he probed, "then what are you entitled to?"

She made a grim attempt at a smile. "A serious bout of self-pity," she said morosely.

"Ah. That much I guessed. Will you bite my head off if I ask why?"

She swallowed hard. "I don't know where to look next."

Ripples of light cascaded through her loose blond hair. Matt ached to slide those silky locks between his fingers . . . over his lips . . . across his chest. . . .

"We'll get a fresh start tomorrow."

"But without knowing where to start, it's like looking for needles in a haystack." She stared into the rich amber liquid in the bottle. In a low whisper, she added, "Maybe I'm only fooling myself."

Her sad, hopeless tone sliced into Matt like a knife. Ellie Carlisle, resilient and determined, was capable of self-doubt. The revelation made her more human . . . and more desirable, Matt realized. He ached to draw her onto his lap. The way his lower body was responding, however, he wouldn't be able to stop at offering comfort.

"If you believe the markers are out there, so do I," he said huskily. "There is no easy way to find them. We'll just keep searching until we do."

"You don't understand, Matt," she exclaimed, shoving to her feet with a hint of her usual bravado. "Each day is so precious. We could wander around aimlessly for weeks, exhausting our horses and supplies. I don't have that kind of time."

Aha. Now they were getting to the heart of the matter. "You have some sort of deadline? This is the first time you've mentioned that to me."

The glass bottle clanked against the metal cup as she poured more liquor.

Matt pressed, "You've been real quiet since this afternoon. Does this have something to do with those tracks we ran across?"

The cup stopped halfway to her lips. "What would you understand about deadlines? You're a gambler, for goodness' sake. You're not bound by constraints, or responsibilities, or other people's expectations." She sighed. "I envy you that freedom."

Matt appreciated the benefits of his freedom, but he

was tempted to point out that a lack of responsibilities typically meant a lack of home, of family, of people who counted on you . . . or cared about you.

"You're avoiding my question, Professor, a skill you excel at. I asked you about the tracks," he persisted. He rose, eased the bottle from her hand, and set it aside. When he reached for the cup, however, she pulled it beyond his reach. He decided not to fight her for it.

"Tracks?"

"Yes. You know what I'm talking about."

She gave him a wide-eyed, innocent look. "Oh, those tracks. Why should they concern me?" She waved her free hand dismissively. The gesture threw her off balance.

Without thinking, Matt hooked his right arm around her waist, steadying her by pulling her hard against his body. Their bellies pressed together intimately. The urge to cup his hands over her bottom and grind his hips against hers hit low and intense. Before he gave in to temptation, he released her as if she were made of fire.

Ellie glared at him. "Do you find me repulsive when I'm foxed?"

Matt smiled. She was offended by the misguided notion that he found her repulsive, not that he had seduction in mind. Maybe there was hope of mutual passion yet. "Actually, I think you're adorable when you're drunk," he countered softly.

"Drunk?" She exhaled with exaggeration. "What a vulgar term. You may describe me as . . . as 'in my cups.'"

"Whatever you say, ma'am."

Ellie traced the rim of her tin cup with one finger, suddenly shy. "Did you just call me adorable?"

"I thought you might have missed that part." He watched for a sign that she was fishing for compliments.

Ellie surprised him by plopping back down, crossing her arms over her knees, and resting her chin on her forearms. She looked utterly dejected.

"Adorable sounds . . . well, quite wonderful. Unfortunately, that is not what I need."

The conversation was growing more bizarre by the moment. "So adorable simply won't do, huh?"

"It is not at all sufficient, I'm afraid. I need to be alluring, mysterious . . . beautiful," she said wistfully.

Matt's brows arched. "And you're not?"

She slanted him a hard look. "Don't be mean."

"I'm obviously missing something here." He sat down in his former spot. "Why do you need to be alluring?" *Sweet mercy, why don't you recognize that when you lower the barriers, you're alluring enough to drive any man to distraction?*

"I'm supposed to get married."

Her bald statement knocked the breath from his lungs. It took Matt a minute to recover. "I thought the engagement with Peter was off."

"It is. But unfortunately I must marry someone in the very near future. My ugly fate is there, like an ax hanging over my head."

"I gather you don't want to get married."

"Of course not. According to an agreement with my father, however, I must. And since I lost the fiancé I had, I suppose I'll have to go about finding another as soon as I get back to England." She sighed heavily. "What a bother."

"You've been on your own for a long time, haven't you, Professor?"

"Absolutely. I prefer it that way. The opportunities for archaeological discovery are endless. Why would I want to tie myself to a man whose aim is to chain me to his home as hostess, then keep me pregnant with his children while he rambles about smoking cigars, hunting, and gambling with his friends?"

Matt winced. He couldn't imagine snuffing out her vitality with such a limited existence. "Not all men are so self-indulgent."

"They are in my world. Unfortunately, marriage for a woman of my station is expected. Besides, I gave my word."

Matt thought of the women he'd protected at Madame Simone's bordello, the tears that had been shed on his shoulder, the bitterness that had turned most of the women into burned-out husks by their midtwenties. The three girls who'd turned to him for help when they found themselves pregnant were actually the lucky ones. Their despair—not even knowing the fathers of their children—had enabled him to coax them out of that life. Although they had been forced to rely on his financial support for years, they now lived independent, respectable lives.

There were worse ways a woman could sell herself than marriage, he knew.

"So you've never met a man who fulfilled and satisfied you with something archaeology can't offer?"

He expected her to scoff at his words. Instead, she whispered bleakly, "No. Never."

"No steamy kisses by moonlight that stole your breath away and weakened your knees? No sweet words of love?" Matt coaxed. Desire coiled into a hard knot of hunger in his loins. What would it feel like to be the man to guide her in discovering those buried riches of passion?

She stiffened. "Those are tempting notions to feed romantic fantasies, but they have little basis in real life."

"You've never known a man and woman who truly loved each other?"

"Well, yes." Her expression softened. She set down the tin cup. "My parents. My mother willingly left her life and friends to follow my father around the world. A great light went out of my father's life when she died."

"Then why do you assume you can't find the same——?"

She jumped to her feet. Swaying visibly, she said indignantly, "There are some people who simply are not destined to feel such emotions. Some people are simply too logical and levelheaded to get caught up in . . . well, you know."

"Desire? Passion?" he prompted with a touch of irony.

She narrowed her eyes. "I have yet to meet a man who inspires me with anything other than impatience."

If Matt had harbored any doubts before, this conversation had cleared them up entirely. Ellie Carlisle was a beautiful woman who'd never given herself to a man.

That fact pleased him much more than it should have.

Without warning, she flung her hands in the air and began to pace. "I just don't understand what men want!"

Matt watched the flex of her buttocks in those trousers, and the way her full breasts strained against the fabric of her shirt. "I could tell you what men want," he said hoarsely.

Ellie rounded on him. "You could?"

"It would be a little . . . complicated to explain."

"No, tell me, please. I really want to know. It's such a bloody nuisance the way men fear independent, forthright women. How do I attract a gentleman suitor, then not scare him off before he proposes?"

Matt considered the possibilites, the potential, of playing tutor. Maybe, in the process, he could help her discover the passion buried within. "It would be a lot more effective if I showed you . . . taught you."

She gasped with delight, as if experiencing a world-shattering revelation. "What a perfect notion! Teach me how to attract a gentleman husband. You are the ideal choice as instructor. Why, it's not as if we even like each other."

Matt smiled wolfishly. Ellie Carlisle had just thrown down the gauntlet. She didn't realize how eager he was to take up the challenge.

"It could be a very neutral arrangement," she added. "No complications. It's not as if you would . . ." She glared in her best prudish, indignant fashion. "You would not attempt to take advantage of my goodwill, would you?"

"Of course not." *Not until you want me to, sweetheart. I can be more of a gentleman than any of your British lords.* "As you just pointed out, we don't particularly like each other."

"Oh. Yes, of course." After a brief hesitation, she asked skeptically, "Why haven't you asked what you will get out of this arrangement?"

Matt schooled his expression. No doubt he'd raise suspicions if he looked like the cat that ate the canary. "Freedom from boredom will suit me just fine. It's a step up from playing solitaire each night."

"Well, all right. If you're sure. When do we start? Tomorrow?"

Ellie's cheeks flushed with color. Her eyes sparkled. She didn't rely on paint to enhance her beauty, or low necklines to capture a man's eye. There was no artifice in her.

Maybe she would benefit from these lessons, but he needed to have his head examined for placing such a strain on his self-control.

.   .   .

ELLIE WATCHED MATT unfold his powerful body with languid grace. She gulped nervously. She'd met any number of brawny men during archaeological digs, yet they all lacked in intelligence. And the suave men who populated the British aristocracy and the academic world didn't lack for intelligence, but their snobbery, affected manners, and pampered lifestyles spoiled the charm.

Matt Devereaux combined the best of both worlds—clever wit and the strength of elemental, unspoiled male—in a way that consistently scrambled her wits and left her jittery.

What had she just gotten herself into?

A smile hovered on his lips, drawing her gaze to his mouth. His lips were sinfully full and soft, yet their firm, sculpted lines only enhanced his masculinity.

Matt reached down and captured her right hand. The sudden warmth of his skin sent a little shock wave up Ellie's arm.

"What . . . what are you doing?" she asked breathlessly.

"You sounded eager to begin."

"Now? Tonight?"

"Why not? The first lesson is on flirting."

She groaned. "I'm utterly dismal at flirting. I cannot seem to grasp the concept at all. All those coy looks, fluttering eyelashes, and inane musings seem so foreign to me. Trying to act that way gives me a headache."

"Then don't act that way. Those tactics are for girls and debutantes. A real woman doesn't need to rely on anything other than her poise, her charm, and her wit."

"Truly? Dear heavens, what a relief."

"Now, pay attention. Think of me as a titled gentleman you're meeting for the first time at a ball. The hostess has just introduced me as Lord Terrwilliger. I'm attractive, wealthy, and rumored to be looking for a wife."

Ellie giggled. "Terrwilliger? Is that the best name you can come up with?"

"Laughing at a man's name is not the best way to get on his good side," Matt said sternly, trying not to smile.

Ellie's amusement vanished. "Of course not. Pardon me."

"After I kiss your hand, you smile and greet me. Make me feel as if I'm the most interesting man you've met tonight."

Bowing, Matt pressed warm lips to the back of her hand. Fire licked across Ellie's skin and dipped into her belly. She suppressed a gasp.

"Ellie, you're not supposed to clamp down on my fingers as if trying to break bone."

"Oh, dear. I'm sorry. I'm rather nervous."

"You needn't be. It's just me, remember? The partner you can barely tolerate."

Suddenly, that didn't seem like a reassurance at all.

"Let's try again." His lips touched her hand, lingering a fraction of a second longer this time.

Damn the liquor, Ellie thought wildly. She'd definitely consumed too much. That would explain this tingling sensation rushing through her body. It took her a disturbingly long time to come up with a logical retort.

"I ought to tell you that men typically do not touch their lips to a woman's hand. It is more of a symbolic gesture."

Matt looked up. "If a man finds you attractive, Ellie, he'll push tradition to its limits and actually kiss your hand. Now, once more, and this time try to charm me."

She tried to do as he asked, but the feel of his mouth was so distracting. Her words came out stiff and breathless.

"Put some warmth into it, Professor. Give me a smile and a look that says you're intrigued."

"But that is exactly what I don't know how to do!" she cried, frustrated more by her rattled nerves than her customary failure in the fine art of flirtation. "Most of the men are either too old, or too fat, or too primped and pampered, or too arrogant, or too—"

"And you want to marry one of them?" Matt asked incredulously.

"Would you please get the facts straight! I have no wish to marry. It is a matter of necessity."

"Then you'll have to learn to bluff."

"This is hardly the same as a game of poker." She tugged against his hold. "May I have my hand back now?"

"Not until you get the lesson right. Flirting *is* like bluffing in poker. You pretend to be in control, to have the upper hand when likely you don't, then use facial expressions and body language to fire repeated salvos until your opponent is convinced it's only a matter of time before he loses the game." He grinned wolfishly. "See the similarities?"

Ellie felt a startling resentment for all the gorgeous, desirable women he'd no doubt flirted with in the past. The feeling was so uncharacteristic that she swore to dispose of the remaining whiskey at the first opportunity.

"Don't try to make this more difficult than it is, Ellie. You're a beautiful, intelligent woman. If those British gents have any brains at all, they'll be falling all over themselves to be introduced to you."

Ellie stared at Matt in amazement. Beautiful? Her?

"If you don't find a man interesting, then fake it," Matt continued his instructions. "Think of something you particularly enjoy, or a juicy secret no one else knows."

"All right. I'll try." She would think of her most cherished dream—Montezuma's treasure, and her father's pride when she brought it home to England in triumph.

When Matt kissed her hand again, however, Ellie could only wonder if his chocolate-brown hair felt as silky as it looked. He thought she was beautiful! Elation swept through her.

"Good evening, sir," she responded, her voice dropping an octave. Her lips curved softly with a genuine secret—that the fire cast light and shadow across his face in a way that made him look more chiseled and handsome than ever. "I am pleased to make your acquaintance."

Matt stared at her for a moment. Something stirred in the depths of his dark eyes, causing Ellie to catch her breath. Then he released her hand rather abruptly and took a step back.

"Did I do something wrong?"

"Not at all." He raked one hand through his hair. "You catch on fast, Professor. That was a dramatic improvement."

"Really? I did it right?" She smiled with pleasure.

"Enough to give a man goosebumps," he said gruffly.

"Is that good?"

"In most circumstances, yes, it would be a damn good thing."

"Well, I suppose that wasn't so hard. What next?"

Massaging the back of his neck with one hand, Matt stared off into the darkness. "That's enough for tonight's lesson. We need to get some sleep if we're to get an early start in the morning. I'll draw some water to put out the fire."

He turned and strode toward the creek.

Ellie blinked in surprise.

First he insisted on conducting the lessons straight away. Then he cut them short without much explanation.

She just didn't understand the man.

WELL BEFORE DAWN, Matt deliberately banged the cast iron door of the potbellied stove. The clanging noise reverberated through the cabin.

"Time to get up, lazy bones," he called to Ellie, trying his best to sound annoyingly cheerful. "Another exciting day awaits us."

A sleepless night spent suffering the slow burn of unfulfilled desire tended to make a man cross. His student had acted on his flirting advice a little too well last night, giving him a warm look that ranked as the most innocently provocative glance he had ever experienced. The bitter knowledge that her husky purr hadn't been meant for him only added to his torment.

What secret thoughts had played through her mind when she gave him that look? Visions of artifacts and ancient bones? He had only himself to blame for suggesting she fake her way through flirting by thinking of something else.

One advantage of a toss-and-turn night, however, was the time it gave a man to think. The more he thought about the gaps in their understanding of the map, the more an elusive idea nipped at his heels—until a daring solution hit him an hour before dawn. The potential drove him from bed, filled with the need to reach Table Top by sunrise.

Ellie groaned behind the sheet curtain.

Matt worked the sink's pump handle vigorously, reveling in its stubborn squeak for the first time. "You know, I think I feel lucky today."

The frame of Ellie's narrow bed creaked as she turned over.

"Surely some fine Scots whiskey and a little morning-after regret isn't slowing down the gutsy Ellie Carlisle."

"Leave me alone, you bleeding sot."

"I thought sheltered British ladies weren't supposed to know words like that. I'm making coffee. Want some?"

"Why can't you just go away?" she moaned plaintively.

"I've been thinking about those tracks we found yesterday. Do you suppose those people could be seeking the same thing we are? For all I know, everyone in the damn territory knows what we're after except me." He banged the water-filled pot down on the stove. "Beats me how you can just lie there when those folks are likely getting a head start on us."

Ellie bolted out of bed.

She froze immediately. One hand grasped the hanging sheet for support, the other gripped her head. Although she kept the edge of the sheet curved around her, Matt saw one bare arm, a camisole strap, and a tantalizing bit of lace-edged cotton pantalets.

Despite bleary eyes, she looked utterly desirable with her tousled blond hair hanging over one shoulder. A tremor of desire shook Matt to the bone.

"I do believe I hate you," she croaked.

"I have a knack for arousing strong emotions in women, though hatred isn't typically one of them. I predict that soon, however, you shall come to adore me."

She managed to combine skepticism and anger in a single glare.

Matt merely grinned. He never cheated when gambling, but in this case he would take shameless advantage of an ace up his sleeve. Hopefully, his intuition was about to pay off handsomely.

Filling a tin cup with clear liquid, he walked over to Ellie. "Water?" he asked, holding out the cup.

She reached for it, leaning forward while attempting to keep the sheet wrapped around her lacy pantalets. The neckline of her chemise gaped just enough to reveal the creamy upper curves of her breasts and the shadowed valley between them.

Matt forced himself to step back to the stove. "I'll finish the coffee and make breakfast while you get dressed."

"But it's still dark out. What time is it?"

Matt made a show of pulling out his pocket watch, though he was well aware of the time. "A few minutes before five o'clock."

Her eyes widened. Her lips parted.

"There's something I want to show you," Matt said quickly, cutting her off. "Something I believe might help our search. We need to be there before the sun comes up or we'll miss it."

"This had better be worth it," she grumbled.

AN HOUR LATER, they'd finished the climb up Table Top. The sandstone formations along the crest of Dragon's Bones ridge stood out dramatically against a peach-colored sky.

"Exactly why are we here?" she demanded. Coffee, breakfast, and the invigorating climb had restored her spirit. She was back to her usual fighting form.

"Just watch. If anyone can appreciate this, you will."

The sun crested on the eastern horizon. Its golden light shone from behind the opposite ridge. As it climbed slowly, the sunlight angled through the sandstone formations, splitting into an uneven pattern of brilliant beams and contrasting shadows.

Like a lady's open fan with some of the ribs broken.

"The sunburst from the map!" Ellie immediately grasped its significance.

Matt felt a little awestruck himself. He hadn't really expected such dramatic results. Conditions had to be right for one to view the sunburst in its full glory—a clear day, the proper vantage point, and perfect timing. Even as they watched, the sun rose high enough that the beams slanted into a meaningless jumble of light and shadow. The critical clue returned to obscurity within minutes.

Ellie hid her face. He could just see the curve of one high cheekbone. There was no denying he'd hoped for another display of spontaneous gratitude. This time, if she threw her arms around him, he wasn't going to let her go.

Her silence made him uneasy. What could be wrong? How could she not be pleased?

"The sunburst symbol on the map represents east, Ellie," he pointed out. "Now we know in which direction to search."

"I know," she whispered. She sniffed. Her hand shifted to dash something from her cheek. Her attempt at subtlety failed.

Ah, hell, she was crying. Grasping her shoulders, Matt turned her gently to face him. When he ducked his head to examine her face, she pretended to discover something supremely fascinating on the ground. Feeling like a clumsy adolescent, he massaged her upper arms.

"Aren't you eager to start looking for the markers?"

"Yes, of course." She finally looked up, her eyes swimming with gratitude as well as unshed tears. Warmly, she said, "Thank you, Matt."

He struggled to control the sudden heat that rushed through his veins. He deserved some compensation for all he'd denied himself last night. His gaze fixed on her mouth.

He pulled her gently toward him. Her body was soft and pliant beneath his hands, her emotions open, trusting, and . . .

Exceedingly vulnerable.

Matt pressed his lips to her forehead instead of her luscious lips. It was the hardest damn thing he'd ever done.

Forcing his hands open, he released her. "Let's get started. We don't want to waste any daylight."

He turned away, not trusting himself to touch her again.

Chapter 11

WE'LL STOP HERE to water the horses," Matt said late that afternoon.

He swung his right leg over Dakota's back and dismounted. He stroked the bay stallion's neck, pleased that the horse had recovered so well.

"What a beautiful spot." Ellie reined the pinto mare to a halt. She scanned the deep river twisting between the adobe-colored walls of the narrow gorge. Stubby trees, thick brush, and scattered patches of grass crowded the spaces between the water and the rock cliffs. In front of them, the bare ground gradually sloped down to the crystal-clear river. To either side of the smooth riverbank, rocky ledges carved by aeons of flowing water jutted out over the river.

Ellie's appreciation for the beauty of the secluded spot brushed over Matt like a warm, soft rain.

"Did you know this was here, or do you just have the devil's own luck in finding places like this?"

"Both," he said. "I ran across it last year, though I don't come this way very often."

He led Dakota down the sloping bank toward the water. Halfway there, Matt took care to step around a suspicious mound of loose, pebbly dirt. The water lapped at the smooth bank of sticky clay soil. Dakota dipped his head and drank deeply. Muscles rippled up the horse's neck as he swallowed against the pull of gravity.

Ellie dismounted and followed with the pinto, though she hung back to let Dakota finish. The stallion had taken too much interest in the mare's scent during the day, and they'd wisely kept the horses apart.

Matt glanced back to where Ellie stood gazing with interest at the rock walls layered in colors of tan and rust.

"I wouldn't stand in that spot if I were you, Professor." Matt nodded toward the ground at her feet. "Ants."

Ellie looked down. Sure enough, red ants streamed across the toes of her boots. Several of the more aggressive ones headed up the brown leather, straight for her trouser legs. She yelped and jumped away from the mound, pulling the mare with her, then began slapping the ants away.

"Just stomp your feet, Ellie. They'll fall off."

She took his advice, walking in a tight circle, lifting her knees high and stomping her feet with vigor. Craning her neck from side to side, she checked the backs of her legs.

Matt watched her antics. Laughter burst from his chest. "Are you trying to stomp your way to China, woman?"

Spinning to face him, Ellie plunked her hands on her hips. "Why didn't you warn me sooner?" she asked furiously. "Oh, do stop laughing. This isn't in the least bit funny. Those nasty things came very close to getting inside my trousers."

Matt's laughter died abruptly as a surge of lust shot

through him. Her words triggered just the mental picture he was trying to avoid. Annoyed, he retorted, "Now that would have been interesting. If they did, how quick would you have yanked off those trousers and jumped into the river?"

A blush crept into her face. "Don't let your imagination dwell on the impossible, Devereaux."

Matt led Dakota up the embankment. He muttered to himself, "Too late, *querida*."

Once Dakota scented fresh grass, the stallion did the leading. He tugged insistently on the bridle until his black muzzle was buried in thick green near the base of a cliff. Matt turned his back to the brush camouflaging the foot of the rock wall.

He pretended to adjust the saddle girth as he watched Ellie. She squatted at the river's edge while the pinto drank. Her trousers pulled snug across her shapely bottom. She dipped her cream-colored bandana in the river, then opened the top few buttons of her blouse to dab cool water against her skin.

Matt swallowed hard. What he wouldn't give to be that bit of cloth, dribbling cool water across the tops of her breasts.

Suddenly Matt felt a strange draft circulating around his legs. His fingertips sensed the difference in temperature, several degrees cooler than the warm New Mexico afternoon. He turned, curious, then pushed his way through the brush. He discovered a wide, deep opening hidden at the base of the cliff.

"Did you find something?" Ellie called, eagle-eyed as usual.

"A cave."

"Really? Let me see."

He heard the excitement in her voice. This time, he

vowed, he wouldn't let her plunge dangerously into the unknown in that impetuous manner of hers . . . no matter how much he admired her courage.

"I'm bringing the lantern from my saddlebag," she called, coming closer.

"You are not going in," he announced when she stepped beside him.

"I beg your pardon? Who put you in charge?"

"I did. Just now."

"Under what—"

"Under the authority of pure size and brute strength. Give it up, Professor," he said, taking the lantern from her. "I'll always win when it comes to those traits."

"This is ridiculous. Just because you were born a man doesn't mean—" She jabbed a rigid index finger at his chest. It hit solid muscle, not fazing him one bit. She poked him again for good measure, with the same result. She looked at his neck, then his chest, finally shifting to take in the breadth of his shoulders. She swallowed hard. "Well, maybe not just any man. You are a bit . . . taller, and . . . broader, true, but. . . ." Her voice faded.

Matt's brows rose. Ellie was aware of him physically, aware enough to muddle her thoughts. And this time she didn't have the excuse of being drunk.

Matt couldn't help himself—he smiled. It proved a mistake.

Ellie stiffened and put on her best scholarly scowl. "Nevertheless, I am the archaeologist here. I've been in caves on several occasions. This time is no different."

"It is when I'm in charge."

"You needn't be worried about me. I can take care of myself."

"So I worry, perhaps needlessly. Even a scoundrel like

me has his weaknesses. You're not going in," he said irritably.

After lighting the lantern, Matt bent low and climbed down the tumbled rocks surrounding the opening. The last thing he heard before darkness swallowed him up was Ellie's quiet "Be careful!"

She'd whispered the words. No doubt her pride wouldn't let her freely admit she was concerned about his safety, too.

Matt smiled to himself. Slowly he was making progress in his campaign to break down her walls . . . one stubborn brick at a time.

THE SHORT TUNNEL widened into an open cavern so big the lantern light couldn't reach the far side. Matt immediately recognized the acidic odor of guano and the soft squeaking of bats. Once a man had explored bat caves, he never forgot that smell.

Matt followed the slope down into the center of the cavern. He lifted the lantern as high as he could reach. The ceiling moved with the stirring of hundreds of small brown bodies disturbed from their daily rest.

Matt studied them. On his previous visits to the river he hadn't noticed the cave or the bats, but then he'd never stayed to watch the night-hunting mammals swirl into the soft orange light of sunset. He never tired of watching bats. There was a place in southeastern New Mexico where he'd seen a flock of bats burst from their hiding place like a huge column of brown smoke, so numerous that their formation seemed to stretch from horizon to horizon. He couldn't understand why some people feared them.

Matt lowered the lantern and scanned the rest of the cavern. Underground seepage from the river formed a small lake off to one side, its surface like a polished black mirror. He walked the perimeter of the cave, avoiding the massive piles of bat droppings, as he searched for tunnels and any sign of carved images in the rock. There were none. The single, barren room formed the limits of the cave, interesting in its own way, but useless in their search.

A garbled noise drifted through the cavern, distorted by the vaulted ceiling. The bats shifted nervously.

It sounded vaguely like voices. Deep voices. Frowning, Matt drew his revolver and headed back to the entrance.

He climbed through the tunnel, shielding his face from the glaring sunshine until his eyes adjusted. He was just easing through the opening when something struck the rock near his shoulder. Splinters of stone stung his neck and jaw. The unmistakable report of a gunshot followed immediately, reverberating off the cliff walls.

Matt ducked back inside the cave—but not before he caught sight of Ellie's frightened eyes and the evil form of Clive Hayley standing beside her.

Swearing, Matt backed down the tunnel and into the vaulted cavern. The Hayley gang was back together—what was left of it, that is—and they'd managed to find him. Ellie was out there, a hostage . . . or worse. He was trapped in here with no way out, a single loaded six-gun, and enough cartridges in his belt to reload four times. Those bastards had the upper hand. All they had to do was threaten Ellie, and he would be forced to give himself up. He had to think of something fast. His mind worked furiously, seeking options in a seemingly impossible situation.

"Go after him, dammit! Both of you!" a deep voice yelled.

Shadows moved in the tunnel. Gunpowder flashed like

a tiny flare in the darkness, illuminating Darby's face for just an instant. The wild shot ricocheted, pinging off the rock walls twice before thudding into a mound of guano.

Several dozen bats dropped from the cavern ceiling and circled, evidently confused. The eerie flutter of their wings gave Matt the idea he had desperately sought.

Looking up, he whispered, "Sorry to interrupt your rest, but I need a diversion."

Aiming the Colt across the underground pool, where there would be no risk of hitting the animals, he fired three shots in rapid succession. Hundreds of bats exploded into motion. Their shrill cries filled the cavern. Matt covered his ears against the piercing noise. As he knew they would, the bats swarmed to the tunnel in a churning mass of beating wings. They preferred to shun the sunlight, but in the face of danger the small mammals were quick to use their only escape route.

Darby screamed, ducking and flailing his arms over his head. Matt recognized Sam's voice as the outlaw let loose a string of vile curses. Both men fled.

Matt holstered his gun and followed just behind the fleeing bats. He emerged into daylight.

Knowing he had to act quickly, Matt immediately tackled Darby to the ground. He then hauled Darby up, yanked the outlaw's six-shooter from its holster, and used the gun butt against the man's head. Darby dropped like a stone.

A bullet whizzed by, narrowly missing Matt's ear. He ducked. Pivoting, he fired back at Sam. The younger Hayley flung himself into the undergrowth, using the brush as cover.

Movement near the outlaws' horses caught Matt's attention. He swung his gun in that direction. The sight of Peter Wentworth, Ellie's ex-fiancé, ducking behind the four horses jarred through him. Why was Peter here with the Hayleys? There was obviously more going on here than the Hayleys' desire for revenge. But since the Brit's gun was still holstered, Matt ignored him for now.

Matt kept moving, otherwise Clive would find him an easy target. He dived forward in a shoulder roll as more shots erupted in his direction. He came out of the roll on one knee, a protective tree between him and Sam's last known position. He shifted his aim in Clive's direction.

A single heartbeat later, his finger loosened on the trigger. He lowered his gun arm.

Clive Hayley held Ellie with his left arm hooked around her throat, using her body as a shield. He pointed a revolver at her head with his right hand, and Matt could just see the butt of a spare gun in the outlaw's belt. A smug, tobacco-stained smile formed within Clive's full beard. His short, dark blond hair gleamed with the brassy color of fool's gold in the light of the setting sun.

Matt groaned. This was exactly the circumstance he'd feared most. Cowards like Clive always scrambled for whatever advantage they could find.

"Hiding behind a woman, Clive?"

"Works, don't it? Drop the gun, Devereaux, or she dies."

Fury at his own helplessness settled in Matt's gut like a lead weight. He was just about to let the gun slide from his fingers when Ellie suddenly drove one boot heel back onto her captor's knee.

Clive bellowed with rage and pain. His grip on her throat loosened. She bent her knees and dropped to the ground, exposing most of Clive's torso.

Clive's eyes flashed as he realized his vulnerability.

Matt raised the gun and fired.

Clive ducked to one side. The bullet only clipped the revolver and knocked it from his hand. Swearing foully, he ducked behind a boulder, then jerked the spare gun from his belt and returned fire.

Ellie crawled on her belly, stretching out desperately for Clive's lost gun. Matt knew he couldn't battle enemies coming from every side. He and Ellie might have a chance of getting out of this alive if only she could reach the gun before—

"Freeze, Devereaux!" Sam shouted.

Spinning on one heel, Matt stared down the lethal end of his own engraved Winchester rifle, the one the Hayleys had stolen when they bushwhacked him. That gun had a hair trigger, as he well knew.

He didn't move a muscle.

Darby stumbled to his feet. Blood dripped from the cut above his temple onto his black beard. He grabbed Ellie's hair in one beefy fist and her wrist in the other. Peter emerged from behind the horses and watched silently.

Sam grinned maliciously. Long blond hair stretched back from his lean, clean-shaven face in a trademark ponytail. "This time I won't miss. Now, drop the gun."

Matt let his revolver slide from his grasp. He braced himself, knowing the time between now and his death could be counted in seconds. Sam Hayley hesitated over pulling the trigger only because he was sadistic enough to want his victim to sweat before he chose to fire.

"No!" Ellie screamed.

Sam's grin broadened. He curved his finger around the trigger. Ellie fought against Darby's hold.

"Just shoot him, dammit," Clive snapped impatiently. He stepped out from his hiding place and scooped up his revolver.

Sam spit tobacco juice on the dirt. "Nah, this is too easy. I'm of a mind to see Devereaux die real slow, and real painful."

"You're always wanting slow and painful. What the hell is the matter with you? It takes too long. We're only here to get the woman and go."

The younger Hayley's eyes shifted between Matt and Clive. He pursed his lips, turning his hawklike expression petulant. "And you're always in such a friggin' hurry, brother! It spoils my fun. Why do you always get to decide?"

Matt exhaled slowly, still cautious not to move. Sam's alternative was likely worse, but at least it might give him time to find a way out of this mess.

"Because I'm the oldest," Clive countered nastily.

"So? You just hate Devereaux because he took all your money in San Miguel, then when you accused him of cheating in front of all those people, he got the drop on you before you could even draw."

"What about you? You said you had him dead in your sights last month."

"He moved at the last second. I offered to climb down the slope and make sure he was done for."

"I didn't think it was worth the wait. I trusted you to get him the first time. Some deadshot you are," Clive argued with a snort.

Peter looked at the two, growing increasingly annoyed. "I hired you for something other than a demonstration of sibling rivalry. Do make a decision, unless you would prefer I make it for you."

Clive glared at the Brit. Peter took an involuntary step backward.

Sullenly, Sam insisted, "You could at least listen to my idea."

Rolling his eyes, Clive said, "Shit. All right, but this better be good."

Sam flashed a quick grin, then spit another stream of brown liquid onto the dirt. "Let's stake Devereaux out by that ant bed Darby stumbled over after we rode in. A few hundred stings from those critters, plus the hot sun come sunrise tomorrow, and he'll bloat up like a week-old carcass."

Matt shuddered. Sam's idea was definitely the more sadistic of the two. Then again, if Clive had had his way, the shattered remains of Matt's chest would already be scattered across the riverbank.

Clive scratched his beard. "Maybe that's not such a bad idea."

"Can't we just kill him and get it over with?" Darby protested. Ellie kicked at him. Tightening his hold on her hair, the outlaw twisted her around until she faced away from him, her face tight with pain.

"Stop bellyaching, Darby," Clive snarled. The whining complaint seemed to spur him to a decision. He stepped closer to Matt with a smug smile. Without taking his eyes off Matt, he said, "Sam, go get some rawhide and cut us four stakes."

"I want to cut him after we stake him down, too. The smell of blood will attract the ants."

Matt paled, despite his rigid self-control. Clive noticed, for his satisfied expression deepened.

"Maybe. Just worry about sharpening those stakes for now."

Sam hurried off. Clive maintained his guard on Matt.

"What if I prefer you just shoot me?" Matt muttered, knowing Clive would do whatever he believed Matt most wanted to avoid.

"Not a chance, Devereaux."

"I figured as much."

"Don't put up a fuss while we tie you down, neither."
Clive moved his head in Ellie's direction. "Wouldn't want
to see the lady get hurt because you pissed me off."

"You're taking her with you, aren't you," he stated
coldly.

"That's what we came here for."

"Then why should I cooperate? You're going to hurt
her anyway, you son of a bitch."

Clive leaned closer, his words meant for Matt's ears
only. "But not right away. His snooty lordship over there
needs her for some reason, and he's offered to pay real
well. I'm of a mind to be patient for now. On the other
hand, if you put up a fight, I'll shoot that stupid Brit and
stake you down anyway with a couple of bullet holes
someplace that won't kill you too quick. Then I'll screw
the lady here on the ground, right next to you, where you
won't miss a single detail. I'm thinking it will take three,
maybe four times before I get my fill of something as
pretty as that filly."

Matt's breath hissed between his teeth.

Clive chuckled. "Yeah, I thought so. The thought of me
mounting her just eats you up inside, don't it? You can bet
she'll enjoy it, though. Women like what ol' Clive has to
offer."

"Like Joanie at Madame Simone's? Remember that,
Clive? Eight years ago. The first time we met. Joanie enjoyed it so much you had to beat her half senseless, even
after you paid for it. I remember pulling you off of her
mid-act, then showing you what it felt like to be bruised
like that. I would have gotten to you sooner if you hadn't
gagged her. That broken nose I gave you only made you
uglier."

Clive's revolver clicked menacingly as he thumbed
back the hammer. "You think you can provoke me into

shooting you now and saving you a slow, painful death, don't you? Well, it won't happen," the elder Hayley snarled. He glanced over to see Sam returning with four stakes and a coil of rawhide rope. "Strip down, Devereaux. We wouldn't want to deprive those hungry little ants any skin to nibble on. And don't forget what I said about the woman."

Knowing Clive meant every word, every threat, Matt unbuttoned his shirt. He watched Ellie's drawn, miserable face. Darby's rough handling enraged Matt, yet reinforced the need to cooperate. He peeled down his suspenders and took off his shirt, baring his torso and the jaguar talisman. He tossed the shirt aside.

"What are you doing to him?" Ellie demanded.

"Feeding him to the ants, sugar," Sam taunted as he pounded the first stake into the ground with the back of a small ax. He stepped gingerly around the ant mound, placing the stakes in a large rectangle. "Just be glad it's not you. You look so sweet these ants would just gobble you up."

"She's as tart as a lemon," Peter jeered. "Believe me."

Ellie gasped. "You can't do this. It's barbaric!"

Sam straightened after driving the last stake. "Yeah. That's why I like the idea." He walked over to Matt, his grin as crazed as the glitter in his eyes.

"Who's gonna stop us?" Darby gloated.

Ellie looked at the outlaws, her expression as disdainful and regal as a queen's. Matt felt a swell of pride for her courage, even if most of it did arise from pure orneriness.

"You're cowards, every one of you!" Ellie snapped.

"Shut up, woman," Clive ordered harshly.

Peter stepped forward. "What is that around the chap's neck?"

"This thing?" Sam snorted. "Looks like a worthless

chunk of rock to me." He slipped the flat of his blade beneath the jaguar talisman.

It took all of Matt's willpower to hold firm and not draw away as the cold steel skated across his chest. He expected the blade to turn at any point and slice deep into his flesh. With the looming threat of Sam's unpredictability, trying to defend the talisman took on a distant second place in importance.

"Perhaps it is worthless," Peter said with studied nonchalance. "A curious piece, nonetheless. I might as well take it, since he certainly will no longer have any need for it."

Shrugging, Sam sliced neatly through the leather string. He threw the talisman to Peter, who caught the stone, gave it a keen once over, and tucked it away in his pocket.

Ellie flinched.

A chill slid through Matt. How much of her distress was for his sake, and how much for the lost talisman?

"Darby, bind her wrists and hand her over to his lofty lordship there. Sam needs your help tying Devereaux."

Sam severed a twelve-foot section of rawhide and tossed it to Darby. "I cut you a little extra for a lead rope. That filly's got a lot of vinegar. Sure you can handle her?"

"Don't push me, Sam," Darby said sourly.

"Really?" Sam countered, laughing. "What're you gonna do about it?"

Darby's ears reddened at the taunt. Grumbling under his breath, he began tying Ellie.

"Strip down, Devereaux," Clive said nastily, waving the gun.

Matt's empty gun belt dropped to the dirt next to his revolver. He jerked off his knee-high boots and removed his trousers, dropping everything in a large pile. He stood there, only his hips covered by the thin cotton drawers he favored during hot weather.

Darby finished binding Ellie's wrists, then shoved her roughly into Peter's arms. She twisted around and looked back at Matt. He stood there nearly naked. She blushed. Matt couldn't help it—an answering flush rose into his neck and face.

"The drawers too," Clive said.

"Why? So the lady can see what she'll *really* be missing?" Matt countered, fighting to retain some dignity.

The taunt enraged Clive, as Matt intended. A beefy fist swung in an arc, catching Matt square in the jaw. Sparks exploded in his head. He hit the ground hard. Before he could rise, Sam and Darby grabbed his forearms and dragged him the few feet to the ant mound. They looped coarse rawhide around his wrists.

Pure, primal instinct screamed at Matt to fight back. A deeper reasoning reminded him of Clive's threat to rape Ellie. Cold logic suppressed his fear, for he didn't want to provoke Clive into pulling the trigger now and ending any possibility of freedom.

Sam and Darby pulled the ropes at his wrists and ankles taut, stretching him spread-eagled on the ground. Small rocks dug into his back and buttocks. Within seconds, the insects were crawling across his skin.

Sam squatted down next to him, Bowie knife in hand. Matt willed his attention to stay on Sam's face rather than the blade, infusing his expression with all the loathing he felt. Darby backed away until he was out of Matt's line of sight.

Testing the blade with his thumb, Sam said with relish, "Can I cut him now, Clive?"

"Yeah, whatever. Just be quick about it."

Ellie gasped, her face ashen. This kind of cruelty and

violence pushed well past the boundaries of her experience.

If Matt didn't figure out a way to get loose, she'd soon discover just how cruel the Hayleys could be on a very, very personal level.

Matt suppressed the wave of fury and fear that washed through him, burying it deep inside as a reserve of strength he would soon need. His one chance lay in Clive's characteristic lack of patience. It would take hours for the ant stings and sun to finish him off. He counted on Clive not bothering to wait it out, leaving Matt alone to die.

Sunlight winked off polished steel as Sam turned the blade.

"How about we start slow and easy?" the younger Hayley said in a low, excited whisper.

Matt held his breath as the knife descended.

Chapter 12

SAM DREW THE razor-sharp blade along the inside of Matt's bicep, making a shallow cut five inches long. Blood beaded along the hairline cut. It stung like hellfire. He repeated the process with surgical precision across the width of Matt's belly and down the outside of one thigh. Each time, Sam's breathing grew deeper and more ragged with anticipation.

Matt's clenched jaw began to ache. If this was Sam's idea of slow and easy, Matt didn't want to know where his tormentor intended this torture to go next.

Peter glanced at Clive and grimaced. "Bloody hell. Must he overdo it? I fail to see the purpose in this, or the benefit of causing Miss Carlisle to swoon," he complained, though his gray complexion showed that he was the one at risk of fainting.

"That's enough, Sam. You know I don't like to be kept waiting. You don't want the ants to finish Devereaux off too fast, neither."

Sam cursed under his breath and plunged the knife

into the center of the anthill. He gave it a violent twist, then yanked it out. Ants swarmed out of the mutilated mound in an angry red tide. Sam jumped back.

Tiny flicks of agony soon assaulted Matt from various parts of his body. The ants seemed especially attracted to the tender flesh of his sides, inner thighs, and, worst of all, his groin. He craved the ability to brush the ants away, to scratch the stinging welts. Not being able to move qualified as the most antagonizing torture of all.

Darby sauntered up, leading Dakota. The stallion stretched out his nose toward Matt.

"Hey, Devereaux," the outlaw taunted. "Looks like I'm the proud owner of this fine stallion once again."

The vindictive look in Darby's eyes indicated that this time he would ride him even harder, mistreating him until he broke Dakota's spirit . . . or the horse died.

Matt surged upward. The coarse rawhide dug into his wrists. Darby laughed and tugged on the stallion's forelock.

Dakota's ears flattened. The horse's upper lip twitched.

Matt settled back with a feeling of grim satisfaction. "Think again, asshole."

With a lightning-swift flex of his neck, Dakota lunged down and sank a vicious bite into the outlaw's thigh.

Darby screamed and dropped the reins. Dakota snorted, then pivoted on muscular haunches and galloped away. Loose reins and the black flag of his tail were the last things seen before he disappeared into the thick brush downriver.

"Nice going, idiot," Sam said snidely.

"That son of a bitch broke the skin!" Darby yelled. A circle of red spread out from the bite, staining his trousers.

"Wrap something around it," Clive snapped. "I'm tired of your whining."

"Should I go after the horse?" Sam offered.

Clive glanced irritably at the settling dust. "Naw, that stud is too damn much trouble. Forget it."

"HE WILL DIE, Peter," Ellie said hoarsely. Her throat ached with unshed tears and choking anger. "Have you really sunk so low that you can have a man's death on your conscience?"

"I am not the one doing the killing. As you may have noticed, my dear Elysia, your precious partner has gained a few enemies along the way."

"I think you should question your own taste in partners."

"Employees, if you please. Do get the terminology correct, will you?"

"Either way, I wonder what the Hayley brothers will do to *you* when you've done something to make them angry," she said with relish.

Peter licked his lips nervously. "I really do not give a damn what happens to this Devereaux chap, just as long as he is out of my way. All I care about is this and what it leads to." He reached into his coat pocket and tugged out a corner of the tomb map, revealing just enough for her to see.

Annoyed by the reminder of her carelessness, Ellie said sarcastically, "That map points only to the northern part of the New Mexico territory. You're already here. Where do you go now, O great preserver of ancient art?"

Peter scowled. "That is where you come in, Elysia. I cannot fathom why you would be here if you felt this was a useless exercise. No—you know something I do not, and your expertise is going to help me uncover the final clues."

"If I knew the secret, I would have found the site already. Do I look burdened down with artifacts to you?"

He squeezed her arm until she winced. "This new flippancy of yours is irritating, not to mention uncharacteristic. It must be the company you have been keeping," he finished with a sneer.

Ellie glanced at Matt's spread-eagled form. Even when staked helplessly to the ground, he still managed to appear defiant, confident, and capable.

"Perhaps it is," she said softly. Yet, Matt would die here. Her stomach clenched.

"There has to be more," Peter said, shaking her for emphasis. "This map leads to something, and you are going to help me find it."

She gaped at him. "Assist you after what you've done here? Assist you in ravaging another archaeological find? Are you completely mad? I will do no such thing!"

"Indeed you will, or I will turn you over to these rather sadistic Yanks and walk away. Now that you have seen what they are capable of, you might want to reconsider."

A cold chill sank into Ellie's bones.

"Yes, I thought so. I am your only source of protection now. Remember that."

She glared at him.

"And then there's this interesting little discovery," he added, pulling Matt's talisman from his pocket. The jaguar stone dangled at the end of the leather string, spinning slowly. "Fascinating, is it not, how this symbol matches one on the map? But that is only one of five. I wonder . . ."

Peter paused dramatically, his eyes focused on her neck. Ellie swallowed a groan. She hadn't buttoned her blouse after sponging her neck at the river. The ribbon and the top edge of her talisman were exposed.

He hooked one finger under the ribbon. A shudder of revulsion swept through her at his touch.

He lifted out the snake talisman. With her wrists tied, she could do nothing to prevent him. He moved the knot around and untied it. The ribbon slid free of her neck. Peter cradled the stone in his palm and eyed it greedily.

Numbly, Ellie watched her dreams shatter as both talismans disappeared into his pocket. He'd just taken her only advantage in hunting the treasure. But the talismans' importance faded. Matt was suffering. The real nightmare lay in the danger to his life.

"Tsk, Ellie, you have been keeping things from me," Peter said with a self-satisfied smile.

"It was purely intentional, I assure you."

The smile vanished. "Time to go." He pulled her over to where her pinto mare stood. "Get on the horse."

"No. I won't leave Matt," she said with conviction. "I cannot let you do this."

"You think you have a choice? Mount that horse, or I shall put you on it myself."

"Then I trust you plan to end up bruised, scratched, and in a significant amount of pain."

Peter didn't immediately follow through on his threat. Ellie counted on past knowledge that Peter preferred not to exert himself in any way. He watched her for several seconds with an icy, calculating perusal that made Ellie's heart pound uncomfortably.

"Why must you always complicate things?" Peter finally said. He turned to the pinto and tied the opposite end of Ellie's rope to the saddle horn. Then he mounted his sorrel gelding.

"What are you dong?" she asked uneasily.

"If you wish to fight, go right ahead. Let's see how your strength matches up against that of your horse."

"You intend to make me walk the whole way?"

"Walk?" He chuckled, disgustingly pleased with his joke. "Not bloody likely. You will only slow us down that way. You either mount now, or the horse drags you."

Ellie stared furiously at this man she'd known most of her life. Greed had stripped away his mask to expose something ugly and dangerous. She might have some chance against a man, but she couldn't hope to fight the strength of a horse. Fear knotted into a caustic lump beneath her breastbone.

Yet how could she live with herself if she left Matt here to die? Matt could have stayed in that cave and escaped all of this.

"You can go to the devil, Peter Wentworth."

"Very well, have it your way."

He dug his heels into his mount's ribs, urging both horses forward. They quickly accelerated into a trot. Ellie broke into a loping run. She desperately clasped her hands around the rope to prevent the pull from breaking her wrists. She struggled to hang on to her precious balance.

Then Peter kicked the horses into a canter, ripping away her last hope of matching the pace.

The sudden force yanked Ellie off her feet. Rocks and unyielding ground rushed to meet her.

The impact jarred her body. She rolled and tumbled, helpless to protect herself against the coarse brush and sharp, small rocks. Her clothes were her only protection. The pressure threatened to pull her arms from their sockets.

Without warning, everything stilled.

Peter had reined in the horses. Ellie bit the inside of

her cheek to keep from crying out as she lay face down in damp clay. Water soaked into her shirt and lapped at her right knee. Peter had dragged her full circle back to the river.

She turned her head, searching for a miracle. Her eyes fell on Matt. The cords in his neck stood out as he strained to hold his head up and watch her. The naked fury in his expression gave Ellie the strength to fight on.

Struggling to her feet, she jerked on the rope. It popped harmlessly against the saddle, emphasizing a helplessness that only fueled her wrath. The pinto turned its head, its brown eyes dilated and full of confusion and fear.

"You have looked better, my dear."

The metallic taste of blood mixed with dirt and rage in Ellie's mouth. "Don't you dare call me that ever again."

She stalked over to Peter, despite a limp. Her left knee, exposed through the shredded fabric of her trousers, stung fiercely from torn skin and embedded grit.

Ellie looked up at him. "Your father would drop dead of apoplexy to see what you've become. You're a coward and a bully, and I am ashamed to admit I was ever naïve enough to believe you would make a worthy husband." If she was willing to suffer, perhaps die for her principles, she would get her digs in while she could.

Peter's expression darkened. "You were too naïve to notice I never cared. Actually, my father will rejoice that I found a way to save our estates. Do not make the mistake of thinking I will tell him exactly where the money came from." With a brittle smile, he prodded, "Are you ready to mount now?"

Ellie spit at him, pushed well beyond ladylike behavior. She wanted to hit Peter's smug, smiling face, but he was too high on horseback. The measure of her respect for him splattered on his thigh.

Laughter erupted from the three outlaws. For the first time, Ellie realized the other men watched curiously, apparently eager to see how this insane scene played itself out.

Peter's mouth twisted with distaste and anger as he looked down at the bloody spittle on his tan jodhpurs. "How very refined of you, *my dear*. Shall we have another go at it?"

He drove his heels into his mount's ribs without hesitation. The rope snapped taut, pulling Ellie to the ground. Pounding hooves shook the ground and rolled across her senses in a haze of pain like thunder.

After what seemed an eternity, the nightmare stopped abruptly. Silence reigned as Peter sat waiting for her to quit, to acknowledge defeat. Damn him.

Ellie lay motionless. Pain radiated through her body in ribbons of fire. Her shoulders ached. Her hands burned from the coarse rope. She didn't want to open her eyes and acknowledge that there was no escape from Peter's malicious game.

"Ellie!"

The urgency in Matt's voice slashed through her. She lifted her head. He lay only a few feet away, his head turned toward her, desperation in his eyes.

She struggled up and shuffled closer on her knees and bound hands.

Ants crawled over him from the nest on the other side of his chest. She longed to brush away the wretched creatures, but Peter held the rope taut, preventing her hands from reaching out to Matt.

"Get on the damn horse," he said between his teeth.

His words thrust knife-deep, more painful than her external wounds. How could he ask her to do that, to live with his death on her conscience? "Matt, I can't—"

"Do it, Ellie."

"This is a stupid time to act like you're in charge." The sob in her throat spoiled her attempt at a reproachful tone.

"Woman, you'd argue with the angel guarding the pearly gates of heaven."

How could he joke at a time like this? "I can't even give them what they want," she whispered despairingly. "Peter wants me to solve the riddle of the map. How can I do that when I haven't even found the markers?"

"Those bastards don't know that. Besides, I'm sure we're on the right track. Stall . . . string them along as long as you can," he said with intensity.

"But you'll die if I leave you, Matt. Damn Peter. This is so bloody medieval."

"Watching *you* die now won't help me, Ellie. Survive, whatever it takes. Give me a reason to fight."

He offered hope when deliverance seemed impossible.

Ellie forgot the ants, the bruises, and the dirt. That his boundless vitality could be snuffed out so cruelly was beyond her comprehension. She wanted to apologize for her role in bringing him to this violent end, but words alone were pathetically inadequate.

For the first time in as long as she could remember, Ellie indulged in an urge that was purely instinctive. She leaned over and pressed her mouth to his.

Matt's lips softened, clinging and shaping to hers, defying the kiss to be brief. A ripple of sheer, tactile pleasure raced through Ellie.

The rope suddenly yanked tight. Ellie fell to her side, hitting the ground with a grunt.

"Enough of this maudlin crap," Peter snapped. "Mount up, Ellie. We are leaving."

"Go on," Matt whispered hoarsely.

A great internal weight dragged at Ellie's body as she climbed to her feet and walked to the mare. She mounted stiffly. Darby and the Hayley brothers mounted their horses as well.

"Let's go," Clive said.

"Can't we stay for just a little while?" Sam complained. "I want to watch him suffer."

Ellie closed her eyes and felt sick. She took deep breaths, fighting off nausea. She refused to give these men the satisfaction of seeing her lose her dignity.

"It'll take hours for him to die," Clive said. "What am I supposed to do while we wait? Twiddle my thumbs and watch you drool over your fun, little brother? Like hell. Show's over. Devereaux's a goner. His lordship here says the woman's the key to finding what we're looking for, and we've got less than an hour before sunset."

Ellie looked back at Matt as Peter led her away, until her partner was out of sight.

If only Matt hadn't been so stubborn, and skillful, and tenacious, she could have slipped away from Albuquerque without him following her. He wouldn't be dying now because of her crazy, selfish dream of a major archaeological find.

She thought of the sensual pressure of his lips and the way she'd suddenly longed to linger over that kiss.

Tears burned in her eyes.

THE SOUNDS OF horses receded. Matt strained against the stakes as the itching, stinging agony continued. He clenched his teeth, pulling with all his strength, but couldn't gain any leverage against the short ropes. Sam had done a thorough job of driving the stakes into the earth.

A silent roar of frustration built in his chest. He arched his back, pressing his shoulders and heels into the ground, straining to lift his body away from the tormenting invasion of the ants.

He had one advantage left, and he couldn't afford to waste it. If Clive or Sam heard him, and suspected he had any chance of escape. . . . With a patience beyond anything he thought he could endure, Matt waited. He shook his head vigorously to discourage ants from attacking the edges of his eyes. He snorted to prevent the tiny insects from climbing a ticklish path into his nose. There was nothing he could do to lessen the burning of fresh bites and the itch of old ones.

Finally, when he felt certain the Hayleys were well beyond earshot, he whistled for Dakota . . . and prayed. Perhaps his last chance depended on whether the stallion had stayed nearby.

Agile hoof beats vibrated through the ground like sweet music. With a low whinny, Dakota broke into the clearing. The stallion trotted up to Matt, almost stumbling over the loose reins that still trailed in the dirt, then came to an abrupt halt several feet away.

Using a calm, low voice that stretched his fortitude to the breaking point, Matt talked the stallion closer. Dakota advanced tentatively. When he stood over Matt, Dakota stretched out his long neck and blew warm air into his master's face.

"Whoa, boy. Don't move," Matt begged.

Matt strained at his bonds. He hooked the fingertips of his left hand around one of the trailing reins.

The stallion froze, then stood quietly. Years of time and training were paying off in a way Matt had never envisioned.

Matt slowly, painstakingly tugged the rein around the

taut rope once, then again. The rawhide ground into his wrist.

At last, he gripped the loose end of the rein in his fist. "Back up, Dakota. Back," he coaxed, willing away his growing desperation.

The stallion obeyed. The rein drew taut. The loop slid down the rawhide rope and lodged against the stake. Matt clutched the end of the rein to prevent it from unraveling. Dakota lifted his head, neck muscles flexing.

The stake tilted.

"Back!" Matt urged again.

The horse took another step, using his weight and strength against the resisting rein. Suddenly, the stake popped free.

"Whoa, boy!" Matt commanded. Pain shot through his shoulder. He let go of the rein. The leather unraveled limply.

With frantic speed, Matt reached across his chest and untied the rope from his other wrist. He sat up and yanked at the knots binding his ankles.

Within moments, he was free and sprinting for the river.

With a bellow of rage, he ran out onto the rock shelf and launched his body in a dive. He hit the water hard. Turning upstream, he stroked beneath the surface, washing off his tormentors and trying to outdistance the pain. The cool water drew some of the fire from his skin, but only enough to make it bearable.

Matt surfaced and flung back his head. He tried to resist the fierce urge to scratch. A long, ragged groan erupted from his lungs, continuing until his breath gave out. The sound echoed between the stone walls of the narrow canyon.

Standing in waist-high water, he scrubbed to remove

those resilient ants still clinging to his body hair. A sudden, violent thirst hit his throat like a blast of hot air. He sank lower into the cool mountain stream and drank deeply.

He desperately needed something to soothe his fiery skin, to draw out the heat and the poison of at least a couple of hundred stings.

Matt strode rapidly toward the shore. The powerful thrust of his legs kicked sheets of silvery water in the air. Just before the embankment he dropped to his hands and knees. He sank his fingers and toes into the cool, gooey bottom of the river bed. Thank God for the high clay content of New Mexico soil.

Cupping his hands, he scooped water onto the shore just beyond the edge of the river. He crawled forward, rapidly mixing water into the clay, until the resulting ooze was the consistency of wet putty.

Scooping up two dripping handfuls of the clay, he stood. He smeared the cold mud over his abused skin, spreading a thick layer over every inch he could reach—everywhere except the area between his shoulder blades. He bent frequently to replenish his supply. Working sticky fingers through his hair, he doctored the bites on his scalp. The hairline knife cuts along his leg, belly, and arms didn't sting too badly, as they'd already started to scab over. The evening breeze began to dry the clay coating even before he finished, covering him in a shell of pale gray.

He knew he looked like hell. How appropriate, he thought, since he felt as if he were walking through the fires of damnation.

Thirst crept up on Matt again as he worked, leaving him desperate for water. Avoiding the river so he wouldn't wash off the clay, he walked toward the grazing stallion. Matt looked longingly at the canteen tied to the saddle.

Before Matt took ten steps, Dakota began to back up.

Matt stopped. The stallion halted as well, shaking his head vigorously, turning his mane in a torrent of tumbling black hair. Matt moved forward again. Dakota retreated, stopping only when Matt paused. The horse demonstrated his distrust by pawing the ground.

"Am I that scary?" Matt croaked.

The stallion's ears pricked up, fully alert. Relaxing, Dakota walked forward, meeting Matt halfway. Matt caught the coarse-haired head before Dakota could press it against the tender skin of his chest. He rubbed the horse's muzzle gently.

"You needed my voice to reassure you it was me, eh?" He untied the canteen. "So the clay covers my scent. Good. The Hayleys' horses won't detect my approach and sound a warning."

Few things felt more heavenly than the cool, smooth water pouring down his parched throat.

Matt retrieved his discarded clothes and gun belt. As he slid his right leg into the trousers, he winced. Anything touching his skin now was torture. He preferred the cloth, however, to the harsh rub of saddle leather.

Matt eased the trousers on and buttoned them carefully. He left his chest bare. After donning stockings and boots, he refilled the canteen in the river, checked and reloaded his revolver, and slid the Colt into its holster.

He raised his left foot to the stirrup. He sucked in his breath as fabric rubbed across the raw ant bites. Gingerly, he mounted Dakota and took up the reins.

Matt didn't need to think what would happen to Ellie if he didn't get to her soon. He knew. He'd witnessed what savages like Clive and Sam Hayley could do to a woman. Peter would protect Ellie only as long as she was useful . . . and only as long as Clive let him.

Matt looked down at the fiery red welts beneath the clay. The dryness hit his throat once again.

Time was working against him in more ways than one. He had to get to Ellie before he succumbed to the mounting fever.

Chapter 13

WHICH WAY?" PETER demanded.

They'd ridden more than a mile from the river. Clive and Peter remained in the lead, Peter maintaining his grip on the pinto's reins. The other two men followed behind Ellie. An opportunity for escape seemed more distant than the moon.

The image of Matt, helpless and tortured, tormented Ellie every step of the way. Each degree the sun sank toward the horizon meant he was that much closer to death. Or could he already be——?

No, she wouldn't allow herself to think that way.

Especially not after that kiss.

Her situation wasn't much better than his. Whether or not she found the treasure, in the end they would kill her. They couldn't afford to let her live. She had to find some way to escape. Right now, ignoring Peter's question offered a small measure of defiance. She didn't count on the others taking exception to her silence.

A horse moved quickly alongside. Ellie tried to duck

out of the way, but she wasn't fast enough. A rough hand grabbed her hair and pulled back her head. She gasped and looked sideways into the hard gray eyes of Sam Hayley.

"The man asked you a question, missy. Answer him."

"Only after you let me go," she rasped.

"Now."

"No. I won't be treated this way. Besides, how can I think when you're yanking on my hair like a Neanderthal?"

Sam glowered. "What'd you call me? What the hell does that mean?"

He leaned closer. Whiskey-tainted breath wafted across her face. Ellie's stomach churned.

Peter spoke up. "Remove your hands from her. The woman is my property and an important means to an end. How can I get the information I need if she is injured?"

"Yeah, sure, you've done a damn fine job getting her to talk so far."

"Shit, Sam, this isn't getting us anywhere," Clive said after turning his horse. "She's too damn stubborn to answer when you piss her off. Do what he says."

"Are you getting soft on her?" Sam snapped. Nevertheless, he released Ellie.

Clive looked her up and down slowly, hungrily, his mouth tilted in a suggestive leer. "Soft ain't exactly the way I'd describe my interest in the little lady."

Darby chuckled. Sam snorted. Peter stiffened in the saddle and scowled, but didn't dare invite Hayley's wrath by saying anything more.

Ellie's throat was tight with dread. Suddenly eager to change the course of the conversation, she pointed north. *Stall . . . string them along,* Matt had advised.

"That way," she said. She intended to make their search as long, and difficult as possible.

As the light gave way to night, Clive called a stop. They made camp beneath some gnarled oak trees. After a supper of beans and biscuits, they tied Ellie's wrists again and secured the rope to a huge fallen tree limb blackened by lightning.

The moon began its nightly pilgrimage. The men set out their bedrolls, rolled a smoke, then fetched bottles of liquor from their saddlebags. They gathered on the ground for a game of poker. Even Peter joined the game, drinking brandy from a silver flask.

The sound of shuffling cards broke the quiet. Coins tossed onto the center blanket clinked together as they hit the pile. Liquor flowed as freely as the outrageous tales of daring, until the men's behavior deteriorated into a drinking contest and a series of crude male jokes.

Ellie watched them with cold, appraising eyes. They'd seized her rifle and revolver earlier, but thank goodness they hadn't considered searching her. The dagger remained secure in her boot. Her one hope lay in the men getting drunk enough to pass out. Then she could cut her bonds and slip away into the darkness. She waited, urgency clawing through her chest. If she tried before the time was right and failed, they would take the dagger and destroy her one slim chance.

In the meantime, she could doctor the scrapes from her earlier ordeal. They throbbed insistently, warning of infection if she didn't clean out the dirt soon.

Darby rose to fetch another bottle.

"I need some of that whiskey," Ellie said as he walked by.

The outlaw paused and gave her an odd half-smile. "You wantin' to party with us, little lady?"

Ellie lowered her brows. She despised the man and his lurid suggestion. "I'd rather allow that horse to drag me again."

Darby's smirk turned into a scowl. "Think you're too good for us, huh? Maybe we should show you that you ain't any different from any other whore in these parts."

"Actually, I'm sure every woman around here will be vastly disappointed that Dakota didn't bite a part of you about eight inches higher."

Clive chuckled, a low rumble that raised goose bumps on Ellie's forearms.

Darby reddened and started for her. "You bitch—"

"Darby!" Clive snapped, causing the other man to freeze. "Fun's over. You're taking first watch. Get out there."

"Aw, c'mon, Clive—"

"Just do it. And no more whiskey, neither."

Darby strapped on his gun belt and walked into the darkness, grumbling. Clive stared at Ellie with those cold, killer eyes. She forced herself to meet his gaze. From everything she'd witnessed, Clive Hayley despised weakness. Her only chance was to bluff her way through with a show of courage—which she felt certain would wither without her anger to sustain it.

Clive scratched his beard. "What do you need the whiskey for?"

"To cleanse my wounds. Unless, of course, you'd prefer they become infected so that I grow so ill I'm useless on this little trek through the wilderness."

The corners of Clive's mouth twitched. Ellie supposed that passed for a sense of humor. It sent a shiver down her spine. His lethal calm left her with no doubt that Clive was the most dangerous member of this lot of cutthroats—Darby's petulant temper and Sam's sadistic cruelty notwithstanding.

"Give her a bottle, Sam," he said gruffly, taking a swig from his own supply of whiskey.

The younger Hayley stepped up and handed Ellie a half-empty bottle of bourbon. "Anytime you get tired of that namby-pamby Brit, sweet thing, you just let me know."

Ellie looked up at Sam's lean face and the ponytail hanging over one shoulder. She suppressed a shudder. *Remember Matt's lessons on flirting,* she thought. *Remember what men want, and turn it against them. Bluff.*

She attempted a suggestive smile. Even though her mouth trembled, it seemed to work, for Sam's eyes darkened. He licked his lips.

"I'll certainly think about your offer. I do prefer strong men," Ellie suggested in a low voice. Bloody hell, did she sound as idiotic as she believed? What a horrible time to test her new skills at flirtation. "In the meantime, I'd hate to see you waste the chance for a few more drinks." She raised the bottle and took a tiny sip, though she pretended to take a gulp. She nodded toward his bottle.

Sam blinked. Suddenly, he seemed to remember the bottle in his own hand. He took a stiff, bracing swallow— just as Ellie had hoped. The more they all drank, the better.

"Yeah, sure," he agreed, glassy-eyed. He stepped back, nearly stumbling over a rock near the fire. Taking another swig of liquor, Sam settled back down at the game. He glanced at her frequently after that.

Ellie's nose wrinkled in revulsion.

After cleaning the deep scratches, she pretended to sleep. She cracked her lids occasionally, stealing a peek while she waited for the alcohol to serve its purpose.

Peter bowed out of the game first, curling up on his bedroll and falling asleep—but not before tying both talismans around his neck. Ellie ground her teeth in frustration. It was too dangerous to attempt to retrieve the Aztec stones during her escape. She would have to leave them in that scoundrel's possession and trust the rubbings she'd taken.

Sam and Clive continued playing for another half hour, bickering constantly, until they finally retreated to their bedrolls. A chorus of snores soon grated against the peaceful sounds of rustling leaves and the distant howls of wolves.

It was now or never.

Barely daring to breathe, Ellie slipped the dagger out of her boot and went to work.

THEIR TRAIL WAS easy to follow, even in the diminishing light. With no expectation of being followed, the Hayleys had made no effort to conceal their tracks.

A three-quarter moon eased above the horizon, duplicating the pale color of Matt's clay-coated skin. No doubt he looked like a ghost moving among the living. Fever throbbed through his body. The dryness baked his throat no matter how many swigs he took from the canteen. He kept telling himself he need last only long enough to rescue Ellie and escape.

Just as night closed in and he could track no longer, Matt caught a whiff of wood smoke and cheap tobacco on the air.

He remembered the cougar, his spirit guide. He needed the big cat's strength, her hunter's instinct, her stealth.

Matt opened his senses and breathed deeply. He clung to that faint smell of smoke, knowing the elusive clue now offered his only means of tracking Ellie in the darkness. He traced the scent until he spotted the glow of the Hayleys' campfire.

Leaving Dakota at a safe distance, he crept forward slowly, his mood grim. He was too weak to fight effectively, his reflexes slowed by fever and exhaustion. Nor did he hold out much hope of picking the outlaws off one by one. His only option was to steal Ellie quietly away and find some means to prevent the Hayleys from following and taking her from him again.

Another day would come for justice, and to see the Hayley gang brought before a judge and hanged for Angus's murder.

If he lived long enough to make it happen.

Matt waited until they slept. He remained motionless, allowing no sound to reveal his presence. The lack of activity aggravated his awareness of the persistent itching beneath the clay, driving him half mad with a quiet frenzy.

Two hours passed before the camp grew quiet. A lone man stood on guard beyond reach of the firelight. Matt recognized the bull-like physique.

He stalked Darby, creeping up behind him. With a calculated lunge, Matt hooked his right arm around the man's neck. Just as swiftly, he intercepted Darby's grab for his gun. Matt pulled the revolver from the holster and thrust it into the back of his own waistband.

"I've returned from hell, Darby," Matt whispered menacingly into the man's ear. "Just when you thought you'd gotten rid of me for sure."

Darby twisted his head to the side, just enough for a close-up view of Matt's gray, ghostly visage. His eyes widened in terror. His mouth opened, but before he could shout, Matt tightened his grip. The outlaw struggled, hastening the inevitable end. Within seconds the lack of blood to his brain caused Darby to black out.

Matt carefully lowered Darby to the ground. He removed the outlaw's suspenders and used them to bind the unconscious man's wrists and ankles together. Darby's bandanna served as a gag.

Matt closed in on the camp site, as silent as a wraith. Moonlight glinted off the blade of the Bowie knife in his hand.

THE ROPE BINDING Ellie's wrists fell away. Gripping the hilt of her dagger, she eyed the four men's saddles.

Her greatest challenge was to keep Peter and the Hayleys from following her. Otherwise, her efforts to rescue Matt would be cut off quickly and mercilessly.

Peter and Clive used their saddles as pillows; Sam had set his tack off to the side. Darby's lay in a heap near his empty blankets. The girths curled limply from beneath each saddle.

Heart pounding, she crawled forward on hands and knees, praying that Darby's attention was focused away from the camp. She hadn't heard a sound from the sentry in a while. Maybe, if her luck held, he'd fallen asleep on the job.

Careful not to jingle any harness, Ellie set to work. The sharp dagger cut through the well-oiled leather girths with some difficulty. The chirping of crickets masked the slight hiss of the cutting blade. Blessedly, her captors remained undisturbed in their drunken slumber. The damage rendered the saddles useless.

As she finished Sam's saddle, Ellie's attention was drawn to the intricately carved mahogany butt of the Winchester rifle in his boot. A surge of possessive fury flared through her. That was Matt's rifle—the engraved prize the Hayleys had stolen from him. Slowly, cautiously, she slid the rifle from the boot, vowing to return it to its owner.

With one last angry glance at Peter—a look filled with regret over losing the talismans—she rose and backed away.

Just as she turned toward the horses, she paused, her attention caught briefly by an unusual sight. The unwashed skillet and coffeepot sat high on a stack of supplies, just beyond the fire's flickering light. The skillet was propped on its side. How odd. She could have sworn Darby had left the pots near the fire after dinner.

Shrugging off the insignificant detail, Ellie crept toward the horses. She clutched the rifle in one hand and her dagger in the other. She eased alongside the pinto and murmured soothing sounds. Setting the rifle down, she reached for the mare's bridle.

Suddenly, she spotted movement out of the corner of her eye. A surreal, moonlit shape separated itself from the night.

A hand imprisoned her mouth from behind, cutting off her involuntary cry. An arm clamped around her waist like a steel band. It pulled her back against a solid wall of muscle. Ellie reacted with an immediate rush of battle-readiness. She gripped the hilt of the dagger, poised to stab it deep into the man's thigh.

She never struck. A deep recognition overrode her instinctive self-defense.

"Don't scream. It's me," a deep, raspy voice whispered close to her ear.

Elation swept through Ellie. Matt! He was here. Alive. Free!

And he'd come after her. Tears pricked at her eyes.

She nodded eagerly.

The moment he released her, she spun about and flung her arms around Matt's waist. He sucked his breath between his teeth.

The ant bites. It would be agony for anything to touch his skin. How could she have let excitement overcome her like that?

"I'm so sorry," she whispered, trying to pull back. "I forgot for a—"

His arms swept around her, capturing her with gentle insistence against his chest. Ellie's senses heightened, making her keenly aware of the excited pounding of their hearts, of feeling safe even in the midst of the enemy's camp.

Her cheek encountered a strange, crispy crust rather than the smooth skin of his chest. Her throat tightened. Sweet heaven, had the insects' venom done that much damage? She pulled away. He let her go.

"What is this?" she croaked, barely audible.

"A layer of clay to draw out the poison."

Ellie sagged with relief. "Of course. How clever."

Grasping her elbow, Matt whispered into her ear, "Come on. We'll have to leave your saddle. Can't risk the noise. Can you ride bareback?"

Ellie nodded. The warm brush of his breath curled inside her ear, triggering a shower of sparks beneath her skin. It seemed a strange reaction, but this was hardly the time to analyze her emotions.

Matt bent to retrieve the gun. His head jerked up the instant he recognized his prized rifle. His brows arched in silent inquiry, sending an array of tiny cracks through the dry clay on his forehead. Ellie smiled—half at his surprised pleasure and half at the bizarre gray mask smeared across his face and encrusted through his swept-back hair. He looked endearing, gorgeous, and quite ridiculous. She'd never seen a more wonderful, welcome sight.

With a nod and a smile, he handed her the rifle.

He bridled the pinto mare and led her away from the

camp. Ellie followed silently, though a barrage of questions burned in her mind. She cradled the Winchester in her arms, absurdly pleased that he entrusted her with its care.

They reached Dakota.

"What about the talismans?" he asked.

"Peter strung them around his neck. I couldn't. . . ." Her voice faltered. Ellie was ashamed that she'd failed to retrieve such important clues in their quest.

Matt nodded with grim understanding. "It's all right. Maybe they've served their purpose. If we do need them, we'll just have to get them back."

His gritty determination lifted Ellie's spirits.

A shout of warning sounded from the camp.

Fear jolted through Ellie. If Clive and Sam caught them now, that would be the end of it.

"Damn!" Matt interlaced his fingers. She slipped her left foot into his cupped hands and swung onto the pinto's back.

"At least it won't be that easy for them to follow us."

"It sure as hell won't."

"I cut through the girth straps," Ellie offered.

Simultaneously, Matt said, "I cut through the horses' hobbles."

They paused, each digesting the other's revelation. Then they grinned.

"I didn't realize you had such a head for sabotage, Professor. Give me the rifle." Ellie handed it down to him. "Watch. Maybe you can add this little technique to your bag of tricks," Matt added mysteriously.

He turned toward the camp, which was lit by the fire's glow. Cocking a bullet into the chamber, he raised the rifle to his shoulder, took a few seconds to aim, then fired.

The coffeepot somersaulted off the stack of supplies,

accompanied by a raucous clang of metal. The camp erupted into chaos.

"Son of a bitch!" shouted Sam.

Clive bellowed, "Devereaux, that's you, isn't it! Shit, you've got more lives than a damn—"

Matt fired again in answer. The skillet leaped into the air. The ringing noise reverberated through the night.

Whinnying in terror, the outlaws' horses and mules bolted. Their hooves pounded away into the darkness. Additional shouts and curses sounded as the men gave chase.

"It'll be a long time before they can try following us."

"That was amazing," Ellie whispered, realizing Matt had positioned the skillet and coffeepot for just that purpose. "Where did you learn such marksmanship?"

He frowned. "When I was a teenager, from men I wish I'd never met."

Ellie was disappointed in his gruff, noncommittal answer. After the shared nightmare of this day, she had thought there might be a chance for trust to grow between them.

"Where can we go so the Hayleys won't find us?" she asked.

"Back to the river. They won't expect us to return to the same place. If they do track us, they'll have to pass through that bottleneck in the gorge first. It's safer there than out in the open."

"All right. That makes sense."

Matt looked up at her solemnly. "Besides, I need fresh clay. Most of this has flaked off." He hesitated several seconds, then added, "Can you find the spot?"

"I think so. But surely you know the way better than I."

With a grim smile, he handed her the Winchester. "Here, you'd better hang on to this."

"Matt? What is wrong?" she asked uneasily as he moved to Dakota's side.

He didn't answer. It took the fearless, powerful man—who'd endured so much to rescue her—three tries to mount his horse. He settled gingerly into the saddle. Swaying slightly, he gathered up the reins.

Suspicion lanced through Ellie. Nudging the pinto with her heels, she quickly moved alongside Dakota. She reached for Matt's face.

He tucked his chin.

"Don't you dare pull away."

"You're a mite too accustomed to giving orders, ma'am."

"It is something I excel at," she retorted.

Despite his wry criticism, he didn't move when she touched her knuckles to his cheek. He watched her with a dark, unfathomable gaze. As she traced her thumb up the bold line of his jaw, his look intensified until his eyes were like coals in the night. A shiver fluttered wildly just beneath Ellie's ribs. She slid her fingers into the hair behind his ear.

She gasped.

Matt was burning with fever.

"You should have told me!"

"Why? What difference would it have made?" He turned Dakota sharply and headed into the night.

Men and their stupid pride, Ellie thought irritably. She followed, filled with concern.

MATT LASTED ALMOST an hour, even at the brisk pace they set. Moonlight illuminated the land sufficiently to keep the horses at a slow canter.

Ellie watched him carefully every step of the way. The moment he began to sag in the saddle, she dug her heels into the mare's ribs and shot forward. She grabbed Dakota's bridle, pulling the stallion to a stop.

Matt jerked his chin up. He blinked, reorienting himself. "I'll make it," he said gruffly.

"Certainly. Right into the ground, you'll make it," she scolded. Fear tightened her throat, and she felt every frantic beat of her heart. What if he was dying? If only he had a wound she could treat, some tangible way she could take away his pain.

"You've got a better idea?"

"Actually, yes. I'm going to ride with you. It will be infinitely easier for me to keep you in the saddle than to try to heave your big body back up there if you fall on your arse."

He tried to scowl at her, but the weight of his eyelids prevented any effort to look intimidating.

"And I don't want to hear a word of protest." Ellie dismounted and tied the mare's reins to Dakota's saddle. "Shift behind the cantle, so you can ride at my back. That way you can hold on to me."

"I get to put my arms around your waist?"

"That is the general idea."

"You won't get any argument from me." His mouth kicked up at one corner. "How tight do I get to hold on?"

Ellie blushed. Was Matt . . . ? No, he couldn't be. This was not a lesson. Men reserved real flirtation for women they found attractive. "Only as tight as you need to keep from falling."

"I like it when you leave things open to interpretation."

He shrugged his boots free of the stirrups, so Ellie could shorten them. She hitched each side up six inches. Much of Matt's height was in his long thighs—those same thighs that were at eye level right now, rippling with muscle as he shifted back onto Dakota's rump.

Ellie swallowed, awed at his blatant masculinity.

Did Matt see her as more than a partner? A friend, perhaps? Could he possibly find her interesting as a woman? Ellie winced at the sharp pang that spread through her chest. No—she wouldn't allow herself to indulge in such thoughts. She wouldn't get her hopes up, only to suffer once again the crushing humiliation of a man labeling her a passionless ice princess whose only appeal lay in her money.

Shoving the toe of her boot into the left stirrup, Ellie maneuvered her right leg across the saddle and slid into place in front of Matt.

He wrapped his arms around her loosely, shocking her with the intimacy of their solid warmth across her belly. His chest rested lightly against her back.

Ellie held her breath. His broad shoulders engulfed her. The arms wrapped about her waist were thick with muscle. How could he feel like a bloody suit of armor when he was so weak?

His cheek brushed her ear. Then he nuzzled his face against her neck.

"Damn, your hair smells good."

His deep voice started a tremor that resonated to Ellie's bones. She tried to draw in breath and sigh it out at the same time. To cover her confusion, she said, "You can . . . uh . . . lean against me—if you need to, that is. It's all right."

"No. I might hurt you."

"I'm not as fragile as I look."

"I've noticed. But I'm heavier than I look. Believe me, you don't want to support my weight all the way back."

"I don't mind. Truly."

"Well, I do," he countered gruffly. "Stop trying to be strong all the time, Ellie. You need someone to take care of you for a change. Sorry I'm doing such a lousy job of it."

How could he say that? Regardless of his motives—despite the fact that he could barely stand—Matt had risked his life to come after her. Not since her youth, and the loving security of her father and brother, had she considered a man in a protective role. The reason was simple— she'd never met a man who could infuse her life and her work with more skill and savvy than she could muster herself.

Until now. Until an arrogant rogue gambler who merited that kind of respect.

Softly, Ellie said, "No, you're not doing a lousy job at all."

At first she thought he hadn't heard her. Then he shifted his arms, drawing her the slightest bit closer . . . but not in an obvious or suggestive way. Sparks danced across her skin just the same. She longed to lean back, to curve into his body and cherish his strength. The longing spiraled deeper, centering in her woman's core like a gnawing hunger.

The truth flashed through Ellie's mind like the vivid white of a lightning bolt. This was desire—this wonderful, elusive excitement. She wasn't hopelessly cold and passionless after all.

The joy of discovery buoyed her spirits until she felt like floating.

Reality brought her crashing down again. Matt had

come after her. But why? Because he was a white knight beneath that rugged exterior? She couldn't allow herself to succumb to wishful thinking. More likely, he'd rescued her because he couldn't continue the quest for the treasure alone.

Chapter 14

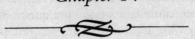

THE VISION CAME to Matt somewhere between sleep and wakefulness, in an otherworldly realm of half-dreams.

The cougar emerged from the sunlit wall of rock like an apparition, though her sleek muscles and twitching tail seemed real enough. Her eyes glittered like gold. She watched Matt solemnly at first. Then she snarled, baring white fangs. Her image blurred unexpectedly, mixing like brown and gold paint swirled together on an artist's palette, then reshaped into the jaguar symbol on the talisman.

In the blink of an eye the image returned to his cougar spirit guide, leading him down to the river. He smelled the rich, earthy scents of wet soil and lush plant growth. A canoe appeared on the embankment. The cougar stepped into the canoe. Matt followed. They floated downstream.

The gentle, rocking current took them beneath a stand of willowy trees. Soft, dangling limbs swayed hypnotically in the breeze. Without warning, the peaceful scene shattered as five warriors attacked, each dressed in jaguar skins and wearing a hideous mask. Their war lances were decorated with exotic feathers. The long, slender lance points—fashioned of a strange green metal—punctured his skin. The color held some significance. Why green? Matt searched his mind for the answer. Just as he turned to his spirit guide, the canoe ran aground against a sandbar. The cougar leaped from the boat, splashed through the shallows, and disappeared.

"Matt? We're here."

Matt opened his eyes. The rocking motion of the horse had stopped. They were on the riverbank. Moonlight glossed the water with a silver sheen. Three stakes and the mutilated ant mound gave mute testimony to his earlier battle.

Matt dismounted after Ellie. It took all his willpower to keep his legs from buckling as he touched the ground.

"Are you all right?" she asked.

He nodded. Ellie moved away, not recognizing the lie for what it was. He felt disoriented after the vision. Was he going mad, or had the fever pulled him into a spiritual realm? According to his grandmother, many of the great instructive visions given to the Navajo came during bouts of illness or following serious injury.

Lush trees, green lances, warriors clad in jaguar skins, and cougars that could walk through rock walls . . . What did it signify?

Matt remembered his past, the events that had stained his late teen years with blood and shame. Hell, what was he thinking? Dreams and visions were sacred. With his past, who was he to think he deserved insight from a higher realm? He, who was only one-quarter Navajo, who had never been taught their ways as a child, who had turned his back on them as a teen and suffered disastrous consequences?

Yet he couldn't shake the feeling that something important was left undone. Secrets danced just beyond his reach.

Matt glanced at Ellie. She had tied the horses and was now gathering wood for a fire. When he was certain she wasn't watching, he stripped off his boots and trousers and waded waist-deep into the river. His arms felt like lead weights as he washed off the old clay in preparation for a fresh coat.

Ellie wouldn't have dared the small comfort of a fire except that Matt needed warmth. She used only dry wood, to minimize smoke, and counted on the steep walls of the gorge to hide the light.

Water splashed as Matt bathed. Ellie's head seemed to turn of its own volition . . . just a quick peek to make sure he was all right.

Dawn lightened the sky, painting Matt's torso in velvety shades of gray and palest peach. The quick glance she'd intended stretched into a lingering perusal. The clay sluiced down his chest, rivulets streaming over his lean muscles. The sensual awareness she'd felt earlier danced in her belly like a flock of butterflies.

Gradually Matt's movements slowed, until his arms hung limp at his sides. His eyelids drooped.

The sensual fantasy evaporated.

"Matt? Are you all right?"

His head started to roll on his shoulders. He swayed.

"Matt!" Ellie shouted. Although the water was only waist high, he would drown if he lost consciousness.

Yanking off her boots, she lunged into the river and splashed through the shallows. She ducked under Matt's left arm just as he began to sink toward the glassy surface of the river.

Blinking down at her, he said in a rough, deep voice, "Rushing to my rescue, Professor? Does this mean you've taken a fancy to me?"

"Do not flatter yourself, sir." Ellie's scolding tone concealed her fear. Didn't he know when to take things seriously? Grabbing his wrist and holding his arm across her shoulders, she added, "Drowning is simply not an option when I'm in charge. I don't give a fig how bossy you think I am."

He sighed. "I'm sorry about this."

"Don't you dare apologize. This whole mess is my fault for getting you involved. I should never have let you follow me from Albuquerque."

"I don't mean to sound cocksure, Professor, but you didn't have much of a choice." He gave her a teasing smile.

Something tugged at Ellie's heart. She quickly looked away. With Matt's arm draped across her shoulders, Ellie started toward shore. She fought to maintain her balance against his weight and the persistent tug of the current.

"Wait." He stopped abruptly.

"What is it?"

"Those trees." He pointed at a sandbar that jutted out from a curve in the river. Long limbs swayed gracefully in the light breeze. "They're willow trees."

"That is interesting, Matt." Ellie started to the embankment again, wondering why such an inconsequential detail had caught his attention.

"No," he maintained. Spearing the fingers of his right hand into his hair, Matt pressed the heel of his palm against his forehead. "Damn, what is the answer? Must think. Willow leaves are slender . . . pointed . . . shaped like the head of a lance. And they're green."

"Yes, leaves typically are green," Ellie responded, humoring Matt even though fear constricted her throat. He was hallucinating. She had to find a way to bring his fever down. She tugged on his arm. He didn't budge. How was she to move a six-foot-two mountain of a man if he chose not to cooperate?

"Just like in my vision," he murmured. "The cougar, the warriors . . . the green lances. They're symbolic of something."

Tears burned in Ellie's eyes. She was losing him. "Please, Matt, we can't stand here in the middle of the river. You'll get chilled."

Suddenly he relaxed his furrowed brow. He tilted back his head and laughed.

Ellie stared at him, aghast.

"Sweet heaven, I'd forgotten," Matt said to the sky. The tendons in his neck corded as he tucked his chin and grinned down at her. "When I was eight, I was stung by a scorpion. My grandmother boiled me some tea from willow tree bark to control the fever and bring down the inflammation. She was Navajo, well versed in the healing arts."

Ellie exhaled in a rush. His ramblings about cougars and warriors made no sense, but if this herbal remedy could work . . . Despite sudden hope, doubt nagged at her. "Are you sure you can trust this memory? What if it's a hallucination and the bark is actually poisonous?"

"It's the real thing. Trust me."

Something in his solemn expression calmed Ellie. He seemed so confident. "All right. How do I prepare the tea?"

"There's a small pot in my saddlebag. Cut some bark, peel off the rough outer layer, then boil the rest for thirty minutes or so. I'm not sure of the exact time. I only remember the liquid was dark brown and tasted like the bottom of someone's boot."

She smiled reluctantly. "Let's get you out of here first."

Matt didn't move. "Ellie," he said in an odd tone.

"What is wrong now?"

"The water's already down to my hips. Any lower, and you won't be able to salvage your modesty."

"Oh." Hot color rushed to her cheeks. Memories of moonlit skin and sleek muscles that night in his hotel room swam through her mind.

"I can manage on my own from here. Thanks."

"I'll just . . . in that case, maybe I should go make the tea."

"Good idea," he agreed. He lowered his head. His forehead briefly touched her hair before he stepped aside.

Ellie scooted away. If he'd meant to fluster her, he'd succeeded admirably. She pushed to shore, taking care not to turn around, just in case he wasn't decent—just in case she humiliated herself by being unable to look away.

After setting water to boil, Ellie pulled out her dagger and hurried downriver to the willow trees. When she returned with the bark, Matt had finished the new coating of clay on his legs and was starting on his arms. The blanket wrapped around his hips concealed his thighs but left his chest bare. Ellie swallowed hard. She wasn't sure the blanket was an adequate solution.

After trimming the bark and dropping it into the boiling water, she paused to watch him. Admittedly, the clay seemed to be doing its job. The ant bites across Matt's clean chest had lost most of their angry color.

He squatted to gather more clay, and turned his back in her direction. Ellie gasped. Vivid red blisters were scattered across the area between his shoulder blades.

"Oh, Matt, your poor back."

He lurched to his feet, staggering slightly as he spun to face her. "I couldn't reach it earlier to spread the clay," he said defensively.

Why was he so tense? There was nothing to be embarrassed about. She walked up to him. "Perhaps I can help."

He clenched his jaw. "I can manage."

Ellie rolled her eyes. She would never fathom the self-destructive capacity of a man's pride. "Well, I suppose you could roll in the mud like a pig and hope the clay sticks to your back."

"Very funny," he said. "There's no need, really. I've been enough of a bother already."

"And you were scolding me about being stubborn and not accepting help? Don't be such a goose. Now, will you turn around, or must I force you?"

"Force me?" His eyebrows arched.

"In your weakened condition, it is entirely possible I might prevail," she retorted playfully.

Her teasing failed to elicit his usual smile. His somber expression only deepened. "Ellie, I really don't think you want to see this."

"Nonsense. I have seen and treated more serious wounds before."

"Who said anything about wounds?" He turned slowly, adding in a dark tone, "All right. But don't say I didn't warn you."

Ellie couldn't suppress a cry of dismay. Beneath the swollen ant bites were long, thin scars crisscrossing Matt's back. Her family had protested the mistreatment of diggers by native foremen often enough for her to recognize whip scars when she saw them. These were old, deeply embedded in Matt's muscles, so faint that one had to be close to notice them.

What kind of monster would inflict such punishment? "Who did this to you?"

"It's a long story," he said gruffly.

"Does it look like I'm leaving anytime soon?"

"Maybe you should, now that you've discovered what kind of man your partner is."

"What? That you were unable to protect yourself against someone's wanton cruelty?" she exclaimed furiously, angered further by his self-castigation. "How can you think me so shallow?"

"That's not what I—"

"Please, spare me the extremes of male pride. These scars are old. This must have happened when you were quite young."

"Fifteen."

Ellie's anger cooled abruptly. Fifteen? She remembered her brother, Derek, at that age—rebellious, temperamental, struggling to discover his path to manhood. Those years in a young man's life were difficult enough without living a nightmare of torture. Tears blurred her vision. She brushed her fingertips gently across his shoulderblade, tracing a sign of old pain. Matt sucked in his breath. Ellie pulled her hand away, fearing she'd hurt him, physically or emotionally, or both.

"What happened, Matt?" she whispered.

He turned around slowly to face her. "Have you ever heard of Comancheros?"

"No."

"Years ago they were a constant threat, but since then Mexican soldiers have pretty much hunted them down and wiped them out. Their bands drew men who thrived on violence—rogue Comanches who refused to stay on the reservations, army deserters, Mexican outlaws, mestizos and other half-breeds."

"Men like the Hayleys?"

"Often worse, if you can believe that." He clasped her shoulders.

Ellie was silent, frozen by the intensity radiating from his tense body and stark expression. She was aware of him on every level—from the strong thumbs that massaged her shoulders to the breadth of his muscular chest, with its light covering of curly brown hair.

"The Comancheros were animals, and they hated and distrusted everything, including each other. But they were willing to band together to steal and terrorize the helpless. They usually raided in Mexico, though now and then they would cross over into American territories. Kidnapping and selling people as slaves was one of their specialties." His grip tightened almost painfully on her shoulders. "A band of thirteen men attacked the mission orphanage where I lived. They killed Father Mendoza and the other Catholic priests, then took all the older children. Not only did the Comancheros show no respect for God's house, they murdered the gentle, unarmed men who had helped to raise and educate me."

"How horrible," she whispered with sympathy. His hands relaxed.

"They sold the other children as slaves. I was the strongest, so they kept me for themselves. If I didn't obey their orders, the choice was to be whipped or shot."

Ellie cringed. Standing close to him, within the circle of his embrace, she began to sense what it must have cost him to live under the subjugation of evil men. "I assume you were too stubborn and proud to willingly do as they asked."

He almost smiled. "Noticed that about me, have you? Yes, I rebelled, until I questioned my wisdom at inviting their punishment. After that I learned to bluff, concealing my hatred and every other emotion behind a blank mask. I obeyed, but just barely. To my surprise, they gradually came to respect me for standing up to them. They taught me to shoot and fight with a knife. But I was still a slave. If I tried to escape, they wouldn't have hesitated to shoot me in the back."

"But you got away eventually. How?"

Suddenly his expression turned cold. "I escaped." He released her shoulders.

His explanation ended with that one gruff statement. Ellie sensed he didn't intend to elaborate, and she didn't want to pry further into his memories. It touched her that he had revealed so much of the painful episode in his mysterious past.

Ellie searched awkwardly for something to say. What words could possibly be adequate? Softly, she said, "I'm sorry you had to live through that, Matt. At least the experience strengthened you, made you more capable, more of what you are today."

He watched her silently for several moments. Dark emotions stirred in his brown eyes, filling her with a powerful urge to help him.

Ellie attempted a smile. "So, how do I make the clay?"

"Mix just enough water to make it the consistency of wet putty. It needs to stick." He turned his back to her.

She crouched and dug trembling hands into the ground. The cold clay slithered between her fingers. She kneaded it to the right consistency. Gathering two handfuls, she glanced up from her work.

Her gaze locked on a pair of thick, muscular calves, then drifted up over the outline of his firm buttocks beneath the blanket, his lean waist, the flare of his no longer perfect back. Matt was flawed. Oddly that made him more human, more intriguing. He had endured unspeakable pain and humiliation at the hands of the Comancheros, yet he'd emerged with a gentleness and sense of humor that blatantly defied his violent past.

That overwhelming rush of excitement swept through Ellie again . . . but with a difference. She was no longer the affection-starved heiress toying with the new discovery of desire. This was much more elemental, more intense, like the rumble of thunder echoing through mountains.

She stood and began to smooth her palms over Matt's shoulders, spreading a thin layer of clay, keenly aware of the powerful combination of flesh, sinew, and muscle. Her touch lightened over raw ant bites and old scars. There was something very sensual about the slide of the clay over his skin. Rhythmic tingles cascaded down her back and into her legs. Ellie finished by running a wet hand down the length of Matt's spine.

He groaned.

She froze, jolted out of her sensual daze. "Am I hurting you?"

"Not like you think. Don't stop now."

"But I'm finished. I've covered your entire back. You can reach the rest."

Matt sighed heavily. "I'm weakening fast, Ellie. Bending over to collect the clay makes me dizzy."

"I could mix it and put it in your hands."

He turned to face her, shaking his head. "I don't think that will be enough."

"What can I do?"

He lifted one hand toward his chest. It fell away limply. "My chest. I don't think I can manage it. Could you . . . ?" he hinted hopefully. His brown eyes—

Sparkled with mischief.

Ellie bit the inside of her lip. The rogue. His teasing attempts at helplessness dispelled the horror of his memory. She decided to join him in the game.

She cocked her head and said saucily, "A few minutes ago you were moaning about being too much of a bother."

"That was before I discovered your talent at this kind of thing. You have gifted hands, Professor."

Ellie scooped up two huge clumps of clay. She held her palms up before him.

"These hands?" she asked sweetly. Before he could respond, she pressed both masses of gooey clay onto his chest. The excess squeezed between her fingers.

He looked down at the slippery mess she held against his chest. Chunks of clay slid free and plopped on the ground. He smiled. "Yes, those hands. Heavenly hands. Doctor my wounds, sweet angel."

The deep, velvety sound of Matt's voice threaded through Ellie like a caress. He was the angel—a dark angel with locks of wet sable hair tumbling across his forehead, whose hypnotizing eyes promised mysterious pleasures that broke all her rules, self-imposed and otherwise.

"That would be terribly . . . wanton . . . of me," Ellie managed to whisper as his strong fingers curved around her arms.

"Even to aid an invalid? I was the strong one before; now I'm relying on you to help me." He tightened his grip and eased her closer.

"You're the least helpless man I've ever met," she said breathlessly.

"You'd be surprised. Like now. I'm telling myself what a mistake it would be to kiss you, but I feel helpless to stop myself."

Amazement shot through Ellie. Matt wanted to kiss her?

"Tell me you don't want this, Ellie." He lowered his head slowly, then stopped, hovering for several heartbeats. Her lips tingled as his breath brushed across them. "Say no, and I'll stop."

"No—I mean, I don't want you to stop. I . . . I want you to kiss me."

Matt's lips captured hers. A shock wave swept from Ellie's throat to her toes. His mouth moved gently over hers at first, then more insistently. Each movement was a caress, soothing yet demanding at the same time, filling her with an explosive sense of excitement and anticipation.

Her hands slid up his chest and over his shoulders. Matt released her arms and pulled her hard against him. For some reason, she still didn't feel close enough. A low whimper of need escaped her throat.

Matt abruptly broke the kiss.

He set her back at arm's length, then looked down between them. Clay stained the front of her blouse. The heat in his eyes suddenly faded, giving way to a distant, bleak expression that left her with a sinking feeling in the pit of her stomach.

"You should have stopped me, Ellie," he said softly. "Now you're dirty."

Who cares? Just kiss me again. "I don't even like this old blouse."

He brushed his knuckles lightly along her jaw. A stray piece of clay left a cold, wet streak. "Damn. I only made it worse."

"I don't mind."

"You should. I can manage the rest myself. Thanks."

The moment had slipped away. Ellie Carlisle the archaeologist could read journals in French, Spanish, and middle English, decipher old maps, and carefully resurrect treasures from the earth. Ellie Carlisle the woman was at a loss as to how to retrieve the magic of that kiss. What had she done wrong? The obvious answer sliced deep into her heart.

How naïve she'd been to think desire automatically worked both ways. One had to inspire passion as well as feel it. She looked away as tears welled in her eyes.

Matt turned away to hide the prominent evidence of his arousal beneath the blanket as well as the pain of self-denial in his face.

The clay on Ellie's blouse and face had hit him with an ugly reminder that she was a lady—pristine, innocent, and decent—while he was . . . what? A randy bastard taking advantage of a woman in his care, for one thing. A man stained by the degradation of having been a slave . . . and an outlaw.

Long ago—when he'd stood over the bodies of two women murdered by the Comancheros, and had looked around at the burning village and the carnage he'd been unable to stop—he had pledged to protect women. Ellie was particularly special. She deserved someone better than a gambler with a sordid past.

No matter how much Matt tried to compensate for the ghastly experiences of his youth, they were a blot on his soul that could never be removed.

DAWN PAINTED A river of gold across the horizon as Ellie handed Matt the cooled tea. The rising sun tinted the feathery clouds a soft peach.

Matt drained the brown liquid from the tin cup.

"More, please," he said, grimacing. "If I remember right, I should drink some every thirty minutes or so until the fever breaks."

"I shall keep track of the time for you." She pointed to a blanket she'd spread on the smooth part of the beach, well away from the ant mound. "Now, lie down before you collapse."

He wanted to tease her about being bossy again. Even more, he wanted to kiss her prim mouth. Had she really responded to him so sweetly earlier, or was that more wishful thinking?

Matt lowered himself gingerly onto the blanket. His body seemed to wilt of its own accord, relaxing completely as he acknowledged his exhaustion. His eyelids drooped as he watched a wide beam of sunlight slant over the eastern wall of the gorge. It illuminated the opposite rock face until it glowed.

Matt's eyes flew open. He lifted his head. There it was—the sunlit wall of rock, the one he'd seen in his vision! The portal for his cougar spirit guide.

"Ellie," he called, pushing to his feet.

"You're supposed to be resting," she scolded.

"We need to investigate that wall of rock."

"Really," she said dryly, crossing her arms. "Why?"

"Just humor me."

Throwing up her hands in mock defeat, she strode toward the wall, muttering something about stubborn Yanks. The dry, chest-high brush crackled as she shoved her way through. She stomped down some dead bushes for good measure.

Matt followed warily. Despite his premonition, he froze when Ellie pushed the brush away from the rock face.

A chill shuddered through Matt, as if he'd walked across a grave.

"The jaguar marker," Ellie said breathlessly. "It was here all along, right under our noses."

She traced her finger over the jaguar etched into the rock. It was identical to the image on the talisman. She plunged her hand into a deep shelf cut in the stone beneath the design. She pulled out an abandoned bird's nest.

"There is a niche here carved for the talisman. Matt, this is it!" Her voice rose with excitement. "This is where Angus discovered the jaguar stone!"

Matt understood the willow tree and the green lances in his vision—they were symbols to resurrect a memory of a healing technique. But this was different. This wasn't based on memory. He was certain he'd never seen that carved symbol before; it had been buried by time and the camouflage of nature.

Ellie spun to face him, her face glowing with victory. "You found it! How did you know it was here?"

A shiver trickled down Matt's spine. "Your guess is as good as mine, Professor."

"WHAT THE BLOODY hell do we do now?" Ellie whispered just before sunset.

Rather than answer immediately, Matt went down on his left knee beneath the concealing shelter of the trees. He managed the movement smoothly, without too much discomfort. The willow bark tea, combined with the clay, had worked wonders. His fever was gone. Most of the ant bites had receded. The worst ones Ellie could see below the rolled-up sleeves of his shirt had started to scab over.

He rested the Winchester across his raised right knee.

Ellie felt his hand tug on her wrist. She squatted next to him.

From their hiding place, they watched the four familiar horses tied to the rail of Angus McFee's front porch. A chorus of crashes and shouts sounded from inside the cabin. A gunshot rang out. Something shattered. Ellie winced as the firewood box smashed through one window and tumbled across the porch.

Matt showed no reaction to the destruction of the cabin and their belongings. Ellie glanced at his rigid face. Now she understood why he'd left the horses on the other side of the trees and insisted on such caution as they approached.

"You suspected the Hayleys would be here, didn't you?"

"I thought they might think of this place first, trying to track us down, yes."

"Why? How do they even know about this place?"

"They were here before, when they killed Angus," he said in a grim tone. Using the rifle as a brace, he pushed to his feet. "You can say goodbye to our supplies. Right now they're either destroying or stealing everything they can lay their hands on."

"What do we do now?"

"We go back to Santa Fe and buy more supplies."

Not bloody likely, Ellie thought. She'd emptied her bank account to buy the supplies that now provided the Hayleys with such malicious enjoyment. How could she possibly explain to Matt that she no longer had the money to hold up her end of their partnership?

The delay would also cost them dearly in the race for the prize. Now that Peter had the talismans, he stood an improved chance of tracking down Montezuma's treasure.

"This is the worst possible time to leave," Ellie argued. "Now that we've discovered the jaguar marker, we have a starting point to locate the others. I have experience living off the land, Matt. I know how to survive on less."

"Food is not our only problem. We can't manage without more ammunition. Not now," he said darkly.

Chapter 15

ELLIE STEPPED OUT of the cooling bath water and reached for a thick towel. They'd been forced to return to Santa Fe, and Matt had booked rooms at the Crystal Palace, the only hotel in town to offer a hot, private bath brought to a guest's room.

Tendrils of hair escaped the mass piled atop her head and clung to her damp, flushed skin. She toweled herself dry and sighed with contentment. She might as well enjoy this one luxury tonight. First thing tomorrow, she and Matt had to buy supplies and return to the Sangre de Cristo Mountains as quickly as possible.

As soon as she figured out some way to pay for the supplies, that is.

She opened the trunk she had left behind in Santa Fe. Thank goodness she had decided to store it at the hotel, for the trunk contained the only clothing she possessed other than what she'd worn when they rode into town.

She had just donned a chemise and drawers when she

heard a knock. Tying the belt of an ankle-length linen robe, she opened the door.

Matt stood in the hallway, dressed in a clean version of his customary open-collared white shirt, brown trousers, suspenders, and knee-high boots. His wet brown hair was brushed back close to his head, sleek and shiny and curling at his nape. A close shave had lightened the perpetual shadow across his jaw. The clean, fresh scent of soap couldn't conceal the pleasant male musk that wrapped around him like a mantle.

Matt's gaze dropped, traveling slowly down her thinly clad body. As it rose again, so did Ellie's temperature, and a blush warmed her cheeks.

"You've bathed," he commented with an appreciative smile. Bracing his right arm against the doorjamb over their heads, he leaned forward.

"So have you," Ellie murmured, at a loss for anything more intelligent to say. His large body filled the doorway and overpowered her senses.

"Is everything all right with the room?"

"Yes, thank you. It is lovely. I shall find a way to repay—"

He shushed her by pressing his left index finger to her lips. "There's no need." He looked at her mouth. His finger lightly traced the shape of her lips, then drew away.

The intimacy astonished Ellie. Why had he done that? After their aborted kiss at the river two days ago, and his moody silence since, she'd struggled to accept the humbling fact that he didn't find her desirable. Could he possibly find her attractive after all . . . perhaps just a little?

"Are you hungry?"

"For what?" she said without thinking, her attention on the smooth texture and sculpted edges of his lips.

"Food, Professor."

Ellie suspected that the blossoming emptiness low in her belly had nothing to do with the need for food. "Maybe."

"There's a nice dining room downstairs. We can eat there later this evening, say eight o'clock? That will give you almost two hours to get ready. Then I'll show you around town, so you'll know where to find everything you need during your stay."

"My stay? What do you mean? We are leaving early tomorrow."

"I'll be heading back out to the mountains by myself. You're staying here."

She stiffened. "I beg your pardon?"

"The Hayleys will be gunning for me, and I don't want you caught in the middle. Peter won't be satisfied until you reveal what you know—and that puts you doubly at risk. I don't like the odds, so I've booked this room for you for the next two weeks."

"I'm fully cognizant of the danger, Matt Devereaux. Whether I risk it or not is my choice."

"Not anymore, it isn't. Not when I feel responsible for your safety," he insisted. "If I haven't found all the talisman markers within two weeks, I'll return. It's the only sensible, safe thing to do."

"I didn't sacrifice everything and come this far to be sensible." She crossed her arms tightly, resisting the urge to soften at his show of concern. "Do you have any idea how completely high-handed you are being?"

"Yes. I'm being a complete ass."

"How very accurate. But if you think to distract or disarm me with such a candid reply, think again."

He scowled. "Your safety is more important than your ambitions, Ellie."

He truly didn't intend to budge. Ellie seethed with frustration. First the outlaws, then the loss of the last supplies she could afford, and now this. The barriers on her quest were escalating at an alarming rate. Furiously, she emphasized, "This is my discovery, my dream. I simply will not be left out of it. It is my responsibility to protect the treasure."

Matt leaned closer, until his warm breath brushed down her cheek and set her senses on full, tingling alert. "That's the first time you've referred to our goal as a treasure, Ellie, though after bearing witness to your obsession, the term hardly surprises me. Why don't you tell me what, exactly, we're after?"

Ellie compressed her lips into a thin line, appalled that a set of broad shoulders and a deep, vibrant voice could so muddle her thoughts. She'd always intended to reveal the truth to him, but in her own time, not like this. Her anger had sabotaged her.

"I see," Matt said in a flat, cold tone when she didn't answer immediately. He pushed away from the doorjamb, straightening. "You don't trust me. You think I'll take the treasure for myself, don't you?"

Although he didn't add, *Even after all we've been through together,* the words hung between them, raw and accusing. Ellie wanted to trust him. Desperately. But with so much at stake—and with a humiliating history that gave her every good reason to doubt her judgment in men—how could she trust anyone but herself?

"I have my reasons for being cautious."

"Apparently not cautious enough, if you're willing to go back out there and face known killers."

"Being forewarned is forearmed, so to speak. I've excavated in secret before, concealing my activities from grave robbers and thieves. I believe it is worth the risk. You cannot force me to stay here."

"Planning to bolt the moment my back is turned, Professor?"

"It's the only sensible, *courageous* thing to do."

Matt's expression hardened as she twisted his words and threw them back in his face. "Let's not forget the local sheriff is a friend. If you try to leave town, I'll seriously consider asking him to lock you in his damn jail."

Ellie lifted her chin. "Then I'll just have to use those techniques you showed me for flirting with a man and charm my way out."

Matt grabbed the doorknob. She took a wary step back, keeping a safe margin between herself and his scowling visage.

The pictures on the wall rattled as he slammed the door.

Ellie pressed her ear to the still-vibrating wood. His footsteps receded down the hall.

She'd scored a victory in this skirmish, but what did Matt plan next? How seriously would he pursue stopping her from renewing her search? And which was her greater fear—that he would exclude her from her own discovery, or that once they found the treasure he would disappear from her life?

TEN MINUTES LATER Ellie jumped as the hardwood floor creaked just outside her room. A muttered curse identified her visitor. She opened the door.

Matt sat on the floor in the hallway, adjacent to her door, with his back against her wall. His left leg spanned the hallway. The shotgun propped against his bent right leg gave mute testimony to his purpose.

"I do not need a guard, sir."

"I'll be the judge of that," he said gruffly, without giving her a glance.

"Is your purpose to keep me in this room, or to keep the Hayleys out?"

"Both."

"Surely you don't intend to stay out here all night!"

"You're welcome to try and move me."

Easy enough for him to say, when he knew it was impossible for her to shift a hundred ninety pounds of solid bone and muscle. "What about dinner? I thought you said we were going down to dinner at eight o'clock?" Ellie demanded, throwing out a mock challenge. Actually, within thirty seconds of his earlier stormy exit she'd abandoned hope that he ever wanted to speak to her again.

"I've arranged for your dinner to be brought to your room instead."

Ellie huffed in frustration and closed the door with a snap.

Impossible man! She paced the room, steaming. The weight of her damp, heavy hair loosened several pins. Half of it tumbled free. With an exclamation, she dislodged the remaining pins until the golden mass hung free about her shoulders.

Matt deserved whatever discomfort he found on that hard floor in the hours ahead.

Then again, he might grow chilled. Stopping abruptly, she glared at the door. Despite Matt's arrogance, she knew he hadn't fully recovered from his ordeal with the ants. What if his fever returned?

Opening the door again, Ellie said irritably, "Since you refuse to listen to reason, may I at least offer you a pillow and blanket from the bed?"

He glanced up, then looked away just as quickly. "No, dammit."

Ellie nearly slammed the door, but the rigidity of his profile gave her pause. Her brother, Derek, erected a similar wall around himself every time something threatened his manly pride or exposed a vulnerability in his emotions. Could she possibly have wounded Matt's pride, even his feelings, by refusing to trust him with her secret?

"There is a very valid reason why I find it so difficult to trust you," she ventured, "and it has nothing to do with you personally."

He took a soft cloth from his shirt pocket and began to polish the steel-gray barrels of the shotgun. "I'm listening."

You could have fooled me, Ellie thought, her irritation fueled by the way he devoted his concentration to the task. Nevertheless, it seemed worth offering him an explanation if it cleared the air between them.

Taking a deep breath, she admitted, "A little more than a month ago Peter joined me on my dig in Mexico City. I thought I could trust him. Instead, he stole every artifact I'd recovered. He melted down the gold pieces into ingots, robbed me of the map I discovered in the tomb, and left me stranded."

"And have I given you any reason to think I'm like him?"

An unfamiliar emotion swelled in her chest and thickened her throat. Softly, she responded, "No."

"Then give me the details this time, Ellie." He opened the shotgun and slid a shell into each chamber. "Tell me what this treasure is that we're hunting."

He'd proven she could trust him with her life, but what about a fortune in gold and jewels potentially beyond his wildest imaginings? History was peppered with stories of supposedly honorable men succumbing to the allure of gold. Yet a growing part of her wanted to tell him.

The shotgun snapped closed with a loud, metallic click.

Ellie jumped. With a sinking feeling in the pit of her stomach, she realized she'd hesitated because she still wasn't prepared to share her greatest vulnerability.

"I shall tell you, Matt. Soon," she promised in a rush. "You have my word."

"When? The moment before Peter and the Hayleys start breathing down our necks? In fact, maybe I should just ask Peter. Odd, isn't it, that your ex-fiancé knows more than I do?"

His sarcasm pricked at her conscience. On the defensive, she retorted, "Certainly not now, in this open hallway. I don't need someone overhearing and providing more competition than we have already."

"Well, you'd better decide soon, before I leave in the morning." He set the shotgun aside. His smoldering gaze rose to meet hers. "My search will be more efficient if I know what I'm looking for. And don't give me that stubborn look. Try to leave this hotel without me, and you won't get ten feet before I toss you over my shoulder and haul you back to this room."

"Oh, really?" she replied defiantly. "And then what?"

He looked down.

Belatedly, Ellie remembered her loose hair. The tie of her robe had also loosened during her prowling of the room. The front gaped, revealing her delicate, lace-edged chemise and the upper swells of her breasts.

"After I have you at my mercy, you mean?" he said huskily, looking up to meet her eyes.

"You are delusional, Devereaux." She tried to cling to

righteous anger, truly she did, but the dark promise in his eyes made her feel like melted wax.

"Just to make sure you have a safe landing, I'll toss you on your bed. The problem is, once I see you lying on that bed, I'm not sure I'll be able to walk away."

"Oh."

"I suggest you back away and close that door, Ellie, before this goes any further."

She couldn't move. She didn't want to break the spell, the novelty, the strangely compelling allure of his lion-hungry gaze. Excitement coiled in her chest, shot fireworks through her belly, and rained sparks down the backs of her legs.

"What if I choose to leave it open?" she whispered.

"This isn't a game."

"I never said it was."

Matt lifted his hand tentatively, waiting for signs of retreat. When she stood her ground, he slowly gathered in a fistful of her robe. His fingertips brushed her belly through the soft cotton.

Ellie inhaled raggedly.

He pulled gently, steadily on the robe. Ellie sank to her knees in the open doorway.

MATT WATCHED ELLIE come to him, willingly, her intense gaze fixed on his face in anticipation. Her hair hung on either side of her face like curtains of gold. His body quickened, immediately recognizing his fantasy.

He slid his hand behind her ear, cupping her head. The silky warmth of her hair between his fingers caused his breath to catch. She was all heat and soft, sensuous woman, and he wanted her so badly he ached.

He tilted her head at the perfect angle to receive the

caress of his mouth. Her lips were as velvety and clinging as he remembered. But it wasn't enough. He wanted to claim and cherish her, dominate her until her doubts faded into oblivion, get so close she could no longer maintain the wall between them.

He brushed his thumb against the corner of her mouth. The moment her lips parted, he penetrated with his tongue. She pulled back slightly in surprise. Matt reassured her, showing her how good it could be between them, with long, sensual sweeps of his tongue. He explored every part of that moist, fragrant paradise, until his manhood hardened insistently with the need for a deeper penetration.

She relaxed, pressing closer. Damn, what a time for her to trust him, Matt thought wildly. Her delicate little tongue became bolder, sparring and tangling with his, until he could feel every throbbing beat of his heart.

She broke the kiss. She rested her forehead against his. Her breath panted across his cheeks and caused his sensitized lips to tingle. The lush curves of her breasts pushed against him as her chest rose and fell rapidly. He suppressed a groan.

"Maybe . . . we should get out of this hallway," she said. "Just in case someone comes along."

Matt rose immediately, grateful for the excuse to get her into the privacy of her room. He leaned the shotgun against the wall just inside her door. Then he caught her up in his arms. She slid her arms around his neck with confidence, a gesture that ignited a possessive wave of heat in him. He would prove she could trust him with everything, he vowed, including her precious secret.

He carried her into the room, kicked the door shut, and switched off the light.

Slowly, he lowered her onto the bed. She kept her arms

locked around his neck. It was as good an excuse as any not to back away, not to listen to the lingering doubts losing volume and credibility in his mind. Bracing his hands on either side of her head, he kissed her again, long and caressingly, until they were both short of breath.

She needed to tell him to stop. He couldn't do it on his own this time, when her scent ignited a fire in him and the pink satin ribbons down the front of her chemise tempted his fingers until they itched. If she invited him to make love to her, he would be lost.

"Ellie, you don't really want this," he said huskily.

She unlocked her hands, freeing his neck, only to hold him more firmly in place by running her fingers through his hair. Her touch sent a shiver down his spine. She smiled tenderly. He held back a growl of aching need. She was not helping matters.

"All my life I've thought myself passionless, cold," she murmured, "that only archaeology could inspire any deeper feeling."

He let out a ragged chuckle. "How can that be true, woman? There's so much passion in you, it burns me."

A look of wonder crossed her face. He sobered, fascinated by her expression.

"But it is true, Matt. I scoffed at passion, not realizing how it could be. I've never felt this way before." She stroked his hair again. "Only with you."

Only with me. Matt closed his eyes, aching with tenderness and the hot desire to bury himself inside her. Her innocent passion was seducing him, not the other way around.

She urged him down for another kiss.

"Wait. My boots. Let me take them off," he said, hesitating for the wrong reasons. He felt himself caving in.

He sat on the edge of the bed. Her hands explored his

back, caressing, stealing most of his strength as he struggled to remove his knee-high boots. Finally, he yanked the second one off. He turned quickly, impatient to kiss her again. She shifted over, making room for him on the bed. Feeling humbled by her acceptance, Matt eased his big body beside hers.

When she opened her mouth to him this time, his roving hand couldn't resist the temptation to seek her breast. Her breath caught in her throat when he touched her intimately through her chemise. He cupped the lush fullness, massaging gently. When he brushed his thumb across her nipple, she moaned and arched toward him.

A shudder rippled through him. The ache in his loins intensified.

Her hands sought him in turn, sliding up to curve over his chest. His muscles flexed in reaction. She gathered his shirt into her fists, crushing the fabric. Matt moved back, desperate to feel her hands against his bare skin. He pulled off his suspenders, leaving them dangling at his sides. His hands flew down the front of his shirt, undoing buttons as fast as he could manage.

He leaned down to her again, his shirt open. Her lips curved in an appreciative smile. Her hands slid inside his shirt. As she smoothed her warm palms over his taut belly, she grew bolder, as if every ridge of muscle held a special fascination. A sensual shudder shook Matt to the bone.

He kissed her again, whispering roughly, "I want to touch you in the same way, Ellie." His fingers went to the satin ribbons securing the front of her chemise. She tensed. Her hands shifted instinctively to block his access. "Let me," he said. She lowered her hands.

But she didn't relax completely. She watched him, wary and expectant. He freed the little bows and parted the chemise, baring her breasts to his hungry gaze.

"I knew you'd be beautiful—perfect," he whispered reverently.

Tears sparkled in Ellie's eyes, humbling him further with her vulnerability. It didn't matter to her that he'd been a slave and had allowed men to beat him. But she didn't know the rest about his time with the Comancheros. She didn't know what else he'd done.

She was unbelievably warm and passionate. He wanted to see her reach that supreme height, then tumble over the edge. The idea of bringing her to climax suddenly became an obsession. He would give her that gift, he vowed, without taking her virginity.

Her hands threaded into his hair as he lowered to her breast. She gasped as he kissed the inner curve of the silky mound, then worked his way in toward the taut, pink crest. Then he took her into his mouth, teasing the pebbled nipple with his tongue. She moaned.

His mouth sought hers again in a deep kiss. His palm flattened over her belly. He traced a circular pattern, timing the seductive massage with the stroking of his tongue, coaxing her acceptance. Her kisses grew frantic as he slipped his hand inside her drawers. Her tongue moved harder, faster against his own, until his heart thundered. He curled his hand over her woman's mound.

She gasped.

Matt's breath quickened when he felt the moist heat of her arousal. She was wet, ready for him. His finger slid between her sleek petals and stroked over the center of her passion. Her hips tilted up. Her fingernails dug into his shoulders.

Matt stopped kissing her, devoting his complete attention to her most intimate part. She writhed, moving in time with the stroke of his finger. Sweat broke out on his forehead and trickled down his back. He'd never felt such overwhelming desire before, such a riveting need to join with a woman's sweet fire. The torment of not giving in to that urge frayed his nerves.

He denied his body, but not her pleasure. He slid his middle finger into her tight sheath. She moaned. The sound sank velvet claws into his loins. He stroked his finger into her slick heat, at the same time caressing her outside with his thumb. Her breath reached a frantic pace, surrounding him and drawing him into an awareness of every tiny shudder of her body. Passion ran deeper, hotter in her than he'd ever suspected.

She cried out suddenly. Her body arched in the sweetest reaction he'd ever been privileged to share. Her satiny sheath tightened with her climax, clutching at his finger with rippling spasms. Matt clenched his teeth and buried his face against her neck.

Slowly, he withdrew his finger, struggling not to seek out the sleek opening with his rigid manhood. She sighed. The scent of her passion—on her body, on his hand—drove him half mad.

Matt rolled onto his back and pulled her into his arms. Her head settled in the curve of his shoulder.

"Matt?" she whispered. "You're so tense. Is something wrong?"

"Ssh. Everything's fine. You just sleep. I know you're worn out."

"If . . . if you're sure," she responded hesitantly. Her fingers teased the hair on his chest.

Damn, she pushed his restraint to the limit. In a husky voice, he said. "I'm sure."

"Matt? Please don't make me stay in Santa Fe. I can't let you face the Hayleys alone. Promise me."

Her soft, sleepy plea sank deep into his conscience, undermining his resistance in a way that no strident argument could have managed. She was actually worried about his safety. Protecting the treasure was not her only motivation for insisting on returning to the mountains. Although he doubted she trusted him completely, he had to accept the fact that this was also her expedition, her dream. Besides, the more he thought of it, the more he preferred the idea of keeping her under his watchful eye.

"I promise. Now hush and go to sleep."

Within seconds she slipped into a deep slumber. Her gentle breath stirred the hair on his chest. Her hand rested warm and delicate against his ribs.

A strange contentment threaded through Matt, despite the bittersweet agony of unfulfilled desire. In fact, holding her felt too right—a realization that disturbed him deeply. Ellie deserved better than a man with a tainted past.

He held her for more than an hour. Even before the knock sounded at her door, Matt detected the succulent scents of roast beef and fine red wine. Eight o'clock. The hotel was delivering dinner as he'd requested. His stomach growled, reminding him that neither he nor Ellie had eaten since breakfast.

Matt jumped up. If anyone saw him in her hotel room, in such a compromising position, she would be exposed to gossip. Although she wouldn't be in Santa Fe long, it infuriated him to think of people destroying her reputation. On the other hand, if he didn't answer the door, the servant would take her dinner away and she would wake later, as famished as he was now.

There was a middle ground. Matt held his breath until the servant moved away. He would leave her room in secret, go downstairs, and reorder dinner. He knew he should leave anyway. If she woke, all soft and supple in his arms, he knew he couldn't stop himself from taking her.

He eased out from beneath Ellie and gently lowered

her head to the pillow. She sighed softly in her sleep. Her full lips were pouted. Desire sent flames through him. He'd helped her discover the passion beneath her prickly exterior, but he'd been the one burned by it.

She'd even extracted a promise from him in the heat of the moment, a promise that should have been against his better judgment.

He reached for his boots.

ELLIE STEPPED DOWN from the boardwalk to cross the street to the bank. She took care to lift her hem free of the dust. She needed to protect the stylish gray walking dress with black braid trim. It was the last day gown she possessed—possibly the last she would own for a very long time to come.

The rumble of hooves and wheels suddenly filled her ears. Someone shouted. The angry warning stopped her from being run over by a passing wagon. Ellie stepped back, shaken. Her lack of concentration shocked her more than the near collision. Her thoughts had been a mass of tingling memories and raging doubts since she'd awakened last night to the mouth-watering scent of roast beef . . . and the sight of an empty bed.

She had yet to see Matt this morning. Had he slipped away last night to spare her embarrassment? Or was he well on his way back into the Sangre de Cristo Mountains?

She winced, feeling uncertain and exposed. What did he think of her, now that she'd allowed him to touch her so intimately? If only he'd been there when she woke, to hold her and reassure her that their relationship had changed only for the better.

Hadn't Matt promised her last night he would take her

with him, or was that just wishful thinking on her part? Her memories of last night were a blur, overwhelming her with images of tenderness, whispered words, and unexpected pleasure. She wanted to trust him. But raw emotions plagued her, resurrecting past hurts. Renewed doubts hinted she might be the victim of one of the oldest tricks of mankind—seduction for the sake of wealth.

Which made it all the more important to secure her own source of funds. That was assuming, of course, her father had responded to the telegram she'd sent from Albuquerque over a week ago. Squaring her shoulders, Ellie forced her attention to the present and crossed to the opposite boardwalk.

The bank's interior had a somber, traditional appearance, with counters and wainscoting of a dark, polished wood. The scent of lemon oil hovered in the air, accompanied by dust motes dancing in beams of sunlight slanting through the narrow windows. Floor-to-ceiling pillars topped with carved Italian designs lined either side of the lobby.

The main door closed behind Ellie, cutting off the bustling noise from the street. She stepped up to the counter. The young clerk looked up, then suddenly sat up straighter and squared his shoulders.

"Good morning, ma'am. How may I help you?"

Ellie smiled. She nervously pulled at the fingers of her gloves, gradually removing the soft leather. "Good day. I need to see if a deposit has recently been wired to me."

She gave the clerk her name. The silence seemed interminable while he checked the bank's records. Ellie gnawed the inside of her lip.

"No, ma'am. I'm sorry, but there has been no deposit or account created."

"I see. Thank you." Her father had not wired any additional funds. Perhaps her telegraph from Albuquerque hadn't reached him.

What was she to do for money now?

She'd just turned away when the clerk added, "Oh, I nearly forgot! There's a telegram that arrived for you several days ago, Miss Carlisle. The telegraph operator said the sender requested it be held for you here at the bank."

Ellie eyed the note with misgiving. She reached out, grasping the envelope between her fingers. A cloud passed in front of the sun at the same moment, casting a gloom throughout the bank. What an apropos portent of doom, she thought grimly as she opened the envelope.

Chapter 16

HER FATHER'S WORDS were succinct and painfully clear:

You gave me your word. Stop. Come home now. Stop. Escort on his way in fortnight or less from Galveston. Stop.

Anger pricked deeply, stirring Ellie's shame. Her father had given her freedom for years. He'd shown faith in her independence and judgment until recently. Why, suddenly, was it so essential she return home? Bloody hell, why couldn't he offer his support just a little longer? She thought of defying him, of seeking out another source of funds, but Winston Carlisle had chosen exactly the right way to introduce his ultimatum.

You gave me your word.

She slapped her gloves against the counter's edge. Unable to face the clerk's blatant curiosity, she turned away and crushed the paper in her fist. If only she'd been able to describe her goal clearly in her telegram, her father might have relented. But even a vague mention of Montezuma's treasure could have risked the telegraph operator tipping off every fortune hunter in the area. Nor could she have told her father that the man he'd long expected her to marry was an utter scoundrel.

The last part of the message struck a particularly discordant note. An escort? What did Father mean by that? Whom could he have contacted? Galveston, Texas, was close enough to reach her easily in less than two weeks. And the message was dated almost a week ago. Dear heavens, she had relied heavily on having more time.

More time to hunt for the precious artifacts.

More time with Matt.

She needed to talk to him right away.

Ellie turned quickly toward the door, then froze in recollection. A lump swelled rapidly in her throat. She had no idea where Matt was or even if he was still in town.

The door to the bank manager's office opened. Ellie eased back into the shadow behind a pillar, ashamed lest anyone witness the tears along her eyelashes.

A petite blond woman in a rose-colored gown stepped out of the office. She was a beautiful creature with china-blue eyes and curly hair caught up beneath a beribboned straw bonnet. A large man with bushy side-whiskers followed her, his rounded paunch dividing the lapels of his dark gray suit. A small boy with brown hair, about ten years old, escaped the stuffy confines of the office and darted past them into the lobby.

The woman smiled at the man. "Thank you, Mr. Ballard. I've enjoyed doing business with your bank over the years."

Mr. Ballard hooked his thumbs in his vest pockets and rocked on his heels. "I am happy for your good fortune, Mrs. Conway, but must admit to a touch of sorrow that you are withdrawing your funds."

"My son and I will be starting for California this

morning. We're both very excited about our new plans, though of course we will miss Santa Fe."

"Best of luck to you, ma'am."

Mrs. Conway walked into the lobby. "Ethan?" she called. "Where are you? It's time to go. The stage will be leaving soon. I thought you were anxious to get to Albuquerque and catch the train!"

Just then the bank door opened. Matt stepped through.

Ellie's heart jumped at the sight of his handsome face. He was still here! His masculine grace dominated the lobby, triggering a memory that dipped below her belly and weakened her knees. She hesitated, feeling woefully unprepared to greet a man with whom she'd shared such intimacy.

"Matthew!" Mrs. Conway cried out before Ellie could move.

Smiling radiantly, the woman flung herself straight at Matt's chest.

He wrapped his arms around her, holding her close.

Ellie retreated behind the pillar.

"Rhonda, there you are," Matt said. "I just heard—"

The woman clasped his face between her hands, cutting off his words by pulling him down for a kiss.

The sight of Matt kissing another woman felt to Ellie like a dagger thrust. The intensity of it caught her off guard. Slipping deeper into the shadow, she struggled to control her pounding heart. The memory of the first time she saw Matt, in Albuquerque with two beautiful women on his arm, twisted the knife deeper. He had a past before she arrived—no doubt filled with women—and his affairs would continue long after she returned home. How naïve she'd been to assume she was the only one in his life!

"That was a thank you, Matthew, for all you've done for Ethan and me," Rhonda said in a husky tone. "I'm about to withdraw the four thousand dollars I've saved, most of it money you've given me over the years. We are using it to move to California."

The boy reappeared then, sidling up next to his mother. Ellie's stunned gaze shifted between Matt and Ethan, noting the same square chin, the similar brown eyes and hair. The resemblance wasn't strong, but the boy could be Matt's son. If not, why had Matt invested so much financial support in this woman?

The patterns of light and dark in the lobby began to swirl together. Ellie braced a hand against the pillar to steady herself.

Matt grasped Rhonda's shoulders and set her back at arm's length. He grinned. "So you're finally going. That takes a lot of courage. I'm proud of you."

"I couldn't have done it without your help."

"Yes, you could. I hope you'll be happy."

"I'll miss you," Rhonda said softly.

Ellie glared at them. Irrational anger burned like a white flame. Was this what jealousy felt like?

Matt chose precisely that moment to look up. His eyes instantly met hers. Ellie lifted her chin and glowered at him, determined never to let him see the hurt she felt.

"Damn," Matt said. "Ethan, take your mother over to the teller's window. She needs to finish her business at the bank."

"Yes, sir."

Rhonda turned, following the direction of Matt's intense gaze. Her brows rose when she saw Ellie. She took her son's hand and quickly crossed the lobby.

Ellie's body felt as rigid as an iron pikestaff as she made a straight course for the door. Matt refused to acknowledge her cold-shouldered hint—infuriating, arrogant man that he was. He stepped directly into her path.

"Ellie. That was not what it seems."

"It doesn't matter what it is. Your business is your own. It does not concern me in the slightest." Ellie was pleased with her self-control despite the slight quaver in her voice.

She seemed only to aggravate his temper. "Rhonda is just an old friend."

"An old friend to whom you have given thousands of dollars over the years? How very generous of you."

"You're twisting this around. Let me explain."

"There is no need, I assure you." She tried to push past him. He grabbed her elbow, bringing her to a stop.

"Well, you're damn well going to listen anyway."

"Were you and she lovers?" Ellie whispered fiercely.

"What the hell kind of question is that?"

"One you are reluctant to answer, apparently. Which is an answer unto itself. Release my elbow at once," she demanded, tugging on her arm to no avail. Tears threatened. She was filled with a sudden, inexplicable feeling of despair.

"We are going to your hotel room so we can have some privacy."

"Thank you, but no. Last night was mildly entertaining and . . . educational, but I have no desire for a repeat performance."

Matt's eyes narrowed to dark slits. "I was only suggesting we talk, Ellie."

"Regardless, I do not want that kind of privacy with you ever again. Now, if you please, I have important business to attend to."

"Not until we've talked. I'm not going to let you stew over this—not any more than you have already, dammit— and blow it out of proportion. You can accompany me in a civilized fashion, or you can come kicking and screaming, entertaining the fine folks of Santa Fe. Either way is fine with me. Choose."

He meant every hard-bitten word. Despite their low tones, the intensity of the conversation hadn't escaped the other bank patrons. Curious stares turned their way. Rhonda watched, her expression solemn. Ellie squirmed inside with embarrassment. The attention didn't even faze Matt.

Gathering together the last vestiges of her dignity, she replied, "Very well, I'll go—since you choose to be unreasonable about it."

"I'm at my best when I'm unreasonable," he retorted.

She pulled her elbow from his slackening grip, then led the way across the street to the hotel. A silent, frowning Matt followed close behind. When they had closed the door to her room, she turned around.

"I cannot fathom what you could say to possibly make any difference."

"Try not to be so open-minded, Ellie," he snapped.

She looked at him with righteous indignation. What reason did he have to be so angry?

He started to pace. "All right, I'll tell you about Rhonda and me. I really don't have the right to reveal her past when she's worked so hard to put it behind her and build a decent life, so first you have to promise not to repeat a word of what I say here." He stopped and pinned her with a hard stare.

"Very well, I promise."

He seemed satisfied. The pacing resumed. "After I . . . escaped from the Comancheros, I met Angus McFee. He took me on as a partner, gave me a new start, taught me everything he knew about people and poker. We were together four years. Then someone he loved died tragically.

He lost all interest in gambling, and cut me loose. I still hadn't developed my own skills at cards well enough. Most of the games weren't going my way. A woman in Albuquerque named Simone offered me a job protecting the girls in her house from drunks and sons of bitches who felt they had the right to hurt women." He paused, glaring at her defiantly. "Simone was the madam of the most elite brothel in the New Mexico territory. Though most of the people in your world would look down their aristocratic noses at such women, most of them were good girls. Rhonda was one of them."

Ellie was startled by his revelation. That beautiful woman had sold herself as a whore? Ellie immediately felt ashamed of herself. She had traveled in many poor areas of the world and seen the pattern repeated. Who was she to judge how desperate women chose to survive when they fell on hard times?

Matt accepted her silence and went on. "Rhonda got pregnant. She never knew who the father was. She could have given the baby away, but she wanted to keep him. It changed her whole attitude. She decided to quit the business. She had to leave Albuquerque, change her name, and lie about being a widow. It was tough at first, but she managed."

"With your help," Ellie said softly. Her anger unraveled at the seams.

"Yes, dammit," he snapped, assuming she was condemning him. "And if that doesn't make you mad enough, there were two other girls in the same situation who I've helped over the years. But how can I expect you to understand? You would never have let yourself descend to a life like that."

"How can you be so sure?"

"Because you're too proud."

"Pride is not always a positive trait."

"It is when it protects you and gives you a fighting spirit. You're stronger than Rhonda, and smarter. Whatever it took, you would have found a way. You would never have relied on the solution she chose, or on being dependent on someone else."

Renewed shame sliced through Ellie. "I depend on my father's money. Look at me!" she cried in frustration. "I haven't kept my bargain with my father, haven't returned to England to marry, and he is cutting me off without a farthing. Now I am out of funds, helpless to buy supplies or pay for my own hotel room."

"I'll pay the hotel bill, and buy the supplies."

She squared her shoulders, angry with herself now instead of him. "I'm not one of your charity cases, Matt Devereaux."

"That's a low blow, Ellie."

"I'm sorry. You're right, that wasn't fair. I hate being dependent on someone else."

Matt stepped forward and grasped her shoulders. His expression held a new intensity. "With your resourcefulness, you can find a way to make money here. Then you could stay and hunt artifacts to your heart's content. You wouldn't need to return to England."

Sadly, she admitted, "There is more to it than that. My family is counting on me. I gave my word."

"To marry well."

"Yes."

"And how does last night, and what happened between us, fit into your plans to marry someone else, Ellie?" he asked harshly.

She paled. "I . . . I don't know."

"Perhaps I'm the charity case," he said, his voice laced with frustration and bitterness.

He strode from the room.

ELLIE LEFT THE hotel thirty minutes later, her emotions under control after she'd had a chance to think. She was looking for Matt, to find some way to mend the rift in their relationship. He was anything but a charity case. He was her temptation, the man who inspired her passion. She couldn't get last night out of her mind. Perhaps she was wrong to have allowed him such liberties, but she wasn't sorry. On the contrary, she would cherish the memory for the rest of her life.

A red stagecoach was parked in front of the Wells Fargo office. People milled around, waiting for the scheduled departure. Ellie stepped around the coach and came face to face with Rhonda Conway.

Rhonda watched as her luggage was strapped to the coach roof. Ethan stood at her side.

Ellie stopped. The two women eyed each other warily.

"You're the woman from the bank," Rhonda ventured. "Matt's friend."

"Yes. My name is Ellie Carlisle." She offered a smile and her hand.

Rhonda relaxed slightly. "Nice to meet you. You're not from around here, are you?"

"No, I'm from England."

"That explains the accent."

"Yes." Ellie looked at the coach. "It appears you have a long trip ahead of you. I would like to visit California myself someday. I trust you will be happy."

"Thank you. I've been corresponding with a man

there. We're to be married. I hope you and Matthew will be happy together, as well."

Ellie was surprised. "I beg your pardon?"

"I couldn't help but notice—you know, at the bank— that you and Matt are real close."

Cursing the blush that filled her cheeks, she responded, "What makes you say that?"

Rhonda chuckled. "The way he looked at you, all possessive like. I've never seen Matthew lose his cool with a woman before, neither." Then she shrugged, apparently not noticing how Ellie stared, dumbstruck. "Anyway, I couldn't help but notice I caused a problem between the two of you. You don't need to be jealous of me, you know. Matthew and I are just friends."

"Please," Ellie said awkwardly, embarrassed by her earlier suspicions, "don't feel you need to tell me any more."

"No, really. I owe him so much. If he hasn't told you about me already, tell him I said it was okay." She paused, studying Ellie's face, then added sadly, "I have to admit, I've often wished Matthew would look at me the way he looks at you."

"What way is that?"

"Like he'd enjoy nothing better than to strangle you."

Ellie smiled. "I think he has come close a few times. I'm at a loss as to how that is a good thing, however."

"Honey, passion is passion, no matter what form it takes. If you're smart, you'll latch on to that and not let go."

The stage driver called for all passengers to board. Ethan leaped around in excitement. Smiling indulgently at her son, Rhonda bade an astonished Ellie goodbye and climbed into the coach.

· · ·

"MATT, THERE YOU are. Been looking all over for you."

"Hi there, Nathan," Matt greeted the tall, lanky telegraph operator. He tightened another strap, securing the
bundle of supplies to the mule's pack saddle. Nodding
toward the stable and adjacent general store, he added,
"It's not as if I've been hiding. I've been right here off and
on most of the day."

"Shoot," the other man drawled, dragging out the
word. He scratched his narrow chin. "I thought for sure
I'd find you in one of the saloons."

"Nope. Had enough poker to last me for a while."

Nathan looked doubtful. "Okay, if you say so. Here," he
added, holding out a folded sheet of paper. "Got a telegraph for you from Seth Morgan in Albuquerque."

Unease trickled down Matt's spine. It wasn't Seth's cus-
tom to telegraph unless he had a damn good reason. Had
Ray Jones escaped?

Matt took the paper and opened it. He had barely
started reading when Nathan edged closer.

"Couldn't quite figure out the marshal's meaning
when I took it down. Sounds serious, though," the telegraph operator hinted, apparently eager for a little gossip.
"Something about Mexican soldiers."

The uneasy feeling solidified into a cold knot in Matt's
stomach. His first thought was that the soldiers had finally
tracked him down. Then reality returned, and he shook
himself mentally. Sixteen years had passed since that
nightmare in Mexico. As far as he knew, every
Comanchero responsible for that crime had long since
been captured and hanged. His own role was lost in obscurity.

Then he read the message and discovered an entirely
different problem.

He folded the paper and tucked it into his pocket.

"Thanks for bringing this to me, Nathan. I'll take care of it. Now, I don't mean to be rude, but I need to get back to packing my supplies."

"Er, well, glad to oblige," Nathan muttered. "You sure there's nothing I can do to help?"

"Positive. I appreciate the offer, though."

Nathan glanced back as he departed. The smile Matt plastered on his face was for the benefit of the telegraph operator. Beneath the mask, fury mounted.

Seth's message warned that a certain "mutual acquaintance" was possibly up to her graceful neck in trouble. A Mexican captain named Enrique Salazar had arrived that morning with a squad of six soldiers. The description of their quarry fit Ellie to perfection. Since women as beautiful as Ellie Carlisle never passed unnoticed, the soldiers were already on their way to Santa Fe, guided by the curious folks of Albuquerque who vividly remembered the mysterious blond stranger.

The captain had also politely requested that Seth's jail be made available to hold a woman prisoner when they stopped overnight on their way back to Mexico City.

What the blazing hell had Ellie gotten herself mixed up in?

She still didn't trust him. Not enough. He longed to wring her lovely, troublesome neck. He ached to claim her mouth in a passionate kiss, then enter her in a total possession that would leave no doubt total trust was destined between them.

Matt jerked on the strap. The mule grunted.

Swearing under his breath, he loosened the strap to a comfortable level. Then he put the mule in a stall, next to their readied horses, and headed for the hotel to gather his personal belongings. Ellie should still be there, sorting through her trunk and picking out necessities for the trail.

What other essential facts was Ellie keeping from him? Matt winced, admitting there was one crucial fact about his past that he also kept concealed.

Whatever offense this Enrique Salazar believed Ellie had committed, genuine or otherwise, the soldiers intended to take her back to some hellhole that passed as a Mexican jail.

Well, they couldn't have her, Matt thought fiercely. Certainly not until he had some straight answers right from her secret-hugging, proud, luscious lips. Not afterward, either, if he had anything to say about it.

He never gave up what was his.

ELLIE SWUNG ONTO the pinto's back, settling into the saddle with a grin lighting her beautiful face. She looked eager and stunningly vibrant.

Matt clenched his teeth.

She had been very pleasant to him as they finished their preparations to leave . . . charming, even. He'd returned her efforts at conversation with curt, monosyllabic replies. His relief that she believed him about Rhonda was overshadowed by his simmering fury over the warning in Seth's telegram. Ellie's cache of secrets was growing. He didn't feel like being pleasant, dammit. The fact that she ranked him among every other untrustworthy man of her acquaintance ate at his pride like acid.

"We are going to find it this time, Matt," Ellie said excitedly. "I just know it. I feel good about this trip."

He grunted in reply.

Her fresh face and sparkling green eyes could have fooled a saint. And he was certainly no saint, considering the way his randy imagination dwelled on all kinds of interesting ways to seduce her secrets out of her. She was either completely innocent of any wrongdoing or a consummate liar.

He mounted Dakota. They started out of town with two fully laden mules in tow. Although Ellie's expression darkened every time she looked at the packs, he didn't begrudge paying for the supplies. The cache of gold Angus had left him had swelled an already healthy bank account.

When the bustle of Santa Fe lay behind, Matt took advantage of the privacy he'd been waiting for. "We're full-fledged partners now, right?" he asked.

"Absolutely."

"Then don't you think it's high time you filled me in on the facts?"

"Yes, of course." She glanced at him, then looked away, as if what she was about to say was either awkward or painful.

Matt waited to hear why Mexican soldiers were on her trail.

"I have decided to tell you about the treasure."

Matt was taken aback. After Seth's telegram, he had shoved their usual point of contention to the back of his mind.

"Unfortunately, I don't have anything foolproof to go on, just legend and some scattered historical facts. The treasure we are after is Aztec in origin. Montezuma's treasure, to be exact. After Cortés and the conquistadores attacked the Aztec nation and ransacked their wealth, a select group of priests decided to empty what remained of the treasury and take it north for safekeeping. It required over three hundred bearers to carry it all. Then it disappeared from historical record. No one knows for sure what happened to it. But everything I've discovered so far points to the Sangre de Cristo Mountains as the hiding place."

She turned to him with a smile.

"And that's it?" Matt countered gruffly. Although he felt a definite measure of satisfaction that she'd finally confided their goal, it was no longer enough.

Her smile wavered. "Of course. What else would there be?"

"So you've told me everything now. There aren't any critical facts you've left out?"

Her delicate brows rose. She shook her head. "No. I've told you everything that is important."

Matt frowned. Everything that is *important*. That left a lot open to interpretation. He had to admire her for finding such a smooth way to hold back. "No unfinished business you haven't taken care of?"

She suddenly looked away, avoiding his eyes. "Nothing that has to do with our search. Are you quite finished with the inquisition?"

"Yes. We have a long ride ahead of us before we reach Angus's cabin and see whether it's fit to live in."

I'm finished for now, he added to himself, *until I see whether you're willing to confide in me on your own.* He wondered how patient he could be before wringing the truth out of her.

If Enrique Salazar proved persistent, and a good tracker, he might not have much time to find out.

Chapter 17

S HE SHOULDN'T READ extra meaning in Matt's actions, Ellie reminded herself again and again.

After a day on the trail, staring at his broad shoulders and back, however, the argument rang a note as discordant as a hammer striking tin. What had she done to drive him away? Was he still angry over their argument about Rhonda, or was this something else altogether? He'd been gruff and unresponsive to her efforts to be nice, and she had yet to find the nerve to discuss something as tenuous as their relationship.

Matt's attitude had changed abruptly upon leaving Santa Fe—just after he'd asked those odd questions that seemed vague on the surface yet tainted with insinuation underneath.

There aren't any critical facts you've left out?

How could he possibly know about the escort her father was sending to drag her back to England? She'd crushed the depressing telegram into a tight little ball and packed it away.

She had no intention of telling Matt. The escort might never find them, and there was no sense in both of them constantly looking over their shoulders. Nor did she want to spoil the time they had left together. Matt had already proven very touchy about the subject of her future marriage.

There was so much more now at stake than the disappointment of coming up just short of the treasure. The promise she'd given her father would take her away from Matt and put an ocean between them. How much would it matter to him when they were forced to say goodbye? Matt was so independent, such a part of the free spirit of this land . . . and he had yet to say anything about wanting her to stay.

Not that she could, of course. She'd given her word. Her father, who had given her so much, wanted only this one thing from her in return.

Her father's threat of an escort was the only important detail related to their quest that she'd neglected to tell Matt.

Well, there was that debacle in Mexico City. But since there was nothing she could do to restore the artifacts Peter had destroyed, she had resolutely left that painful incident behind when she crossed the border. She felt certain Capitán Salazar wouldn't follow her onto American territory, where he had no jurisdiction. At some point she would find a way to make restitution to the Mexican people.

They rode deep into the mountains. Bittersweet thoughts dampened Ellie's enthusiasm. They found Angus's cabin habitable—though just barely, after the Hayleys' destructive spree. They straightened up the place, then unpacked the supplies and left the mules in the corral.

Using the location of the jaguar marker as a starting

point, Matt capitalized on his knowledge of the mountains and mapped out a search plan. When they set out, he rode with his rifle held across his thighs. Thankfully, they didn't run across any further sign of Peter and the Hayley gang.

It took them just half a day to find the second marker.

An ancient, gnarled oak nearly obscured the eagle design etched into the rock. As before, the Aztecs had carved out a narrow shelf below the symbol.

Ellie cleaned debris from the foot-deep hole. Slipping her hand inside, she touched the past. The ancient talisman lay in its niche. Excitement swept through her as she pulled out the prize. All her life she'd believed that nothing could match the exultation of uncovering history's most guarded secrets.

How naïve she had been. Now she knew the one thing that felt better than the thrill of discovery—making love to Matt.

She faced him and held out her hand. The stone eagle talisman lay nestled in her palm.

"Congratulations, Professor."

The hard, unyielding expression on his face gave way to a tender smile. He actually looked proud of her. Ellie's heart rate jumped. On impulse, she untied the white ribbon from the end of her braid and threaded the strip of satin through the hole in the stone. Apparently each of the stones possessed a similar hole, though it seemed odd to her that the Aztecs would design necklaces as pieces of a treasure map.

Stepping forward, she slid her arms around Matt's neck. His scent teased her nostrils. The strong line of his jaw molded impressively into a powerful neck and shoulders. She felt delicate in comparison. Without thinking, Ellie leaned closer.

He caught her waist in his large hands. "What are you doing?" His voice emerged an octave lower than normal. He cleared his throat.

"I am tying this around your neck."

"You trust me with it?"

"Yes. I know it will be safe in your care." *Just as I am,* she wanted to add, but pride stilled her tongue.

He opened his hands, fanning his fingers lower across her hips. The heat of his palms penetrated thick fabric, sinking into her flesh and curling tendrils of desire low into her belly. Ellie fumbled with the knot. His masculinity never failed to overwhelm her. When she finally managed to secure the ribbon, her hands moved to his shoulders.

His breathing deepened. His hands curved over her buttocks, squeezing gently as he pulled her closer.

Their bodies met, touching from shoulder to thigh. The electric contact sent sparks along Ellie's nerves. She felt wildly alive in a way she had never experienced prior to Matt's stormy entrance into her life. His lips sought hers, soft yet firm, enticing her thoughts to jump ahead to bare skin and stroking hands. His tongue slid boldly into her yielding mouth, advancing then retreating in a way that sent ribbons of fire into her woman's mound. She tried to capture his tongue, hold it by curling her own around his, but that proved as elusive as his mood.

He broke the kiss and drew back slowly. She sensed a reluctance, but the hard, measuring look of the past two days had returned to his eyes. He let her go.

"Let's keep moving. Now that we know the locations of the eagle and jaguar markers, I can better gauge distance and direction."

Ellie nodded. Although he withheld something significant, she was willing to accept the steaming kiss as progress. At least he wasn't indifferent to her.

As Matt predicted, it was comparatively easy to find the next marker later that same day. Another rock face boasted the dual-headed snake design. Although the niche below it was empty, as expected, of the talisman, which had journeyed back to Mexico over three hundred years ago, the location of the marker was critical in pinpointing the position of Montezuma's treasure.

It was also a sobering reminder that Peter held two of the talismans.

The next morning, the search for the monkey led them to a cluster of boulders. Matt and Ellie couldn't find any sign of the marker until they climbed up into the formation. Inside they discovered the hidden image, carved on the inner wall of a huge rock. A two-foot-long lizard lay sunning itself on the hollowed-out shelf, its black and yellow striped neck vivid above the deep green body. The reptile scampered away as they approached.

Ellie reached inside the shelf, only to find nothing there. The monkey talisman was missing. Matt saved her from a surge of panic by spotting the talisman lodged between two rocks, where it could have fallen yesterday or three hundred years ago.

The war god proved the most challenging. They combed the estimated area three times on horseback before deciding to trace a ribbonlike stream to its source. Set back in a rocky crevice, alongside a small pool, they found the scowling visage of the war god etched into a smooth wall of granite. The Aztecs had treated this marker with special reverence. No shelf scarred the stone below the carved image. Instead, a square altar, fashioned of stacked rocks, graced the base. Matt and Ellie discovered the talisman buried within the altar.

The sun was just reaching its zenith in a vivid, cloudless blue sky when they returned to Table Top ridge with their hard-won booty. Ellie's hands shook as she laid the three new talismans in a row across the bottom of the map. She pulled out the rubbings of the snake and the jaguar. She carefully tore each piece of folded paper into the proper size.

She drew a deep breath. "All right, we're ready to see if this map works."

"It will. Have faith."

Matt's confident tone helped steady her nerves.

"The eagle was the easternmost marker, so it should go here." She placed the eagle talisman face down in the top hole below the sunburst.

"Right. Then clockwise, based on the relative locations of the markers, you have the jaguar, snake, monkey, and war god." Each time Matt named a symbol, he pointed to the corresponding point on the star diagram. Ellie followed his lead, positioning the talismans in their respective holes.

The lines across the backs slanted off in haphazard directions, converging at four separate points in a way that made no sense.

"Something's wrong," Matt said with a scowl. "They don't intersect at a common point."

"But this has to be right!" Ellie cried. "We've laid them out just as we found them positioned in the mountains." Disappointment built inside her.

Matt studied the map. "Are you sure you positioned all the talismans upright?"

"Yes, quite certain."

"Then maybe that's not how they're supposed to go."

His words generated a spark of hope. "You mean, rotate each stone? But how do we know which direction, and how much?"

"If these damn lines would just match up, only four stones would be needed to form a pair of intersecting lines, not five. Why the extra stone?" His mouth compressed into a hard line, accentuating the stubble darkening his square jaw. "Have you noticed how all the stone images are animals, except this one?" he asked, tapping the stone in the upper left point of the star. "This fellow here is the odd man."

"The war god! Of course!" Ellie exclaimed. "Before I left for Mexico, I read the chronicles of a Franciscan friar who traveled to New Spain soon after the initial Spanish conquest. The books were wonderfully detailed accounts of Aztec culture. The war god was the chief deity in the Aztec religion, the main god to whom the priests sacrificed prisoners by cutting their hearts out."

"Number one god for bloodletting, eh? I'd say that sounds significant," Matt countered wryly. "All right. Let's say he's the key. Then what?"

"The other stones would . . . well, bow to him, I suppose. Perhaps they would point to him in some fashion. But two of the symbols face in the opposite direction." Ellie gasped. Her eyes widened. "The holes! I thought it strange that holes were drilled through each stone. What if the holes weren't for wearing the stones around the neck? What if—?"

She rotated the four animal images—two stones and two rubbings—until the holes pointed toward the war god talisman. The grooves etched across the backs lined up perfectly, picking out two lines that intersected at a single point. Ellie squealed with excitement. A huge grin lit her face.

Matt laughed, a deep, rich sound of satisfaction. Then his gaze locked with hers. "We make a good team, don't we?"

"Yes," she whispered. "Yes, we do."

Ellie broke eye contact, suddenly distressed by the poignancy of the moment. Their partnership was bittersweet, for soon it would be over.

"Can you tell where this is?" she asked Matt.

"Devil's Ravine stretches through that area. This will be challenging."

When they reached the ravine, Ellie immediately saw the reason for Matt's comment. Steep walls, some nearly forty feet high, twisted and curved between two mountain ridges. Caves dotted the rock faces. The area certainly seemed the perfect choice for concealing a treasure. Unfortunately, each of the caves had to be explored.

Most were shallow and quickly dismissed, but Matt and Ellie lost half of the afternoon examining almost two dozen caves. Each proved a crushing disappointment. Ellie's frustration mounted. Until they rounded the next curve in the ravine.

Five very familiar images were carved high into the cliff face, side by side, directly over the looming entrance to a cave.

Ellie stared, astonished. Her excitement was tempered by doubt. This was not what she'd expected, after the effort they had expended in solving the complex puzzle.

"I don't like this." Matt shook his head. "This is just too obvious. It doesn't fit the profile of men who were intelligent and secretive enough to create that map."

"I agree. But we should explore it anyway."

Reluctantly, Matt agreed.

They dismounted and tied their horses. After lighting two lanterns packed in their saddlebags, they worked their way into the tunnel, beyond the reach of sunlight.

Matt followed close on Ellie's heels, keeping a

protective eye on her every movement. The tunnel was high enough that he didn't need to duck his head, for a change. The passageway widened, then narrowed, then widened again, following a pattern common to naturally formed caves. Nothing seemed out of the ordinary, until he detected the odor of kerosene.

"Hold up a minute, Ellie."

He turned aside to investigate the smell. His lantern picked up the reflected gleam of metal and glass against one wall. The sharp end of a pickax was jammed into a rocky crevice. Its handle was snapped in two. A discarded lantern lay shattered on the stone floor.

"We're not the first ones here," Matt said gravely.

She added the light from her lantern to the strange scene. She groaned when she spotted the modern items. "Oh, no! How long ago?"

He nudged the lantern with the toe of his boot. "You can still smell the spilled kerosene. The ax handle is white and fresh where it broke. A day or two, three at the most."

"Peter," Ellie hissed. "It must be. He would have recognized the symbols outside."

"There's no way to know for sure, but Clive and Sam have lived in this territory for over ten years. They know these mountains nearly as well as I do. They could easily have stumbled across this cave with three extra days to search. I don't think they found what they were looking for, though."

"How can you tell?"

Matt set his lantern aside and crouched down next to the damaged items. "Someone jammed this pickax into the wall. As for this lantern," he added, turning it so the light shone fully on a puckered hole in its metal base, "it died of a gunshot wound."

"Somebody shot a lantern?" she asked, incredulous.

"This is a bullet hole, all right. Looks like someone had a fit of temper and impatience. Does the description fit anyone we know?" he asked dryly.

"The Hayleys."

"Clive or Sam, take your pick."

"Nevertheless, we should explore the cave. I might very well spot something Peter missed." Without waiting, she lifted her lantern and walked deeper into the darkness. She moved her head from side to side, examining the walls.

Suddenly, her lantern's circle of light disappeared. There was a precipice in the cave floor. Blackness loomed beyond.

"Ellie, look out!" Matt shouted. He sprang forward, grabbed Ellie around the legs, and tackled her to the ground. She hit with a loud grunt.

The lantern fell from her grip. It rolled forward another foot, then tumbled over the edge. The sounds of glass shattering and metal striking stone echoed faintly from a long distance below. Matt and Ellie looked at each other, breathing hard with the knowledge of a narrowly averted disaster.

"Woman, would you please watch where you're going?" he croaked. "You damn near stopped my heart."

"I think my heart *has* stopped," Ellie responded with a squeak in her voice.

Still on their bellies, they crawled forward to peer into the abyss. The blackness was so thick it looked solid.

"I suppose it would be too much to hope that Peter and the Hayleys fell in there," Ellie said.

Matt's crack of laughter bounced off the cave walls and echoed in the chasm below. "Unfortunately, I don't think we can count on it."

She looked at him in dismay. "Did I really just say that?"

"You sure did." His teeth gleamed white in the darkness.

"Oh, heavens, I'm growing as bloodthirsty as the Aztecs."

"You're entitled. Besides, it's not as if you planned to push them in." He added with a wink, "Leave that to me."

Matt rose and, offering his hand, helped Ellie to her feet.

"Come on. We'll check out the rest of the cave so you'll be satisfied, but I don't think we're going to find anything. Stay close to me as we go around this hole. We only have the one lantern now."

Matt's prediction proved correct. Nothing in the cave indicated that the Aztecs had ever concealed a treasure here. He and Ellie retreated to the opening. Shielding their eyes from the bright sunlight, they stared at the five carvings.

"Those designs aren't here by chance," Matt commented in frustration. "They must be another clue."

"How curious—the jaguar and eagle are backwards compared to the designs on the map."

"They sure are."

They looked up at the same time. Brown eyes and green eyes widened in revelation as Matt and Ellie faced each other and said simultaneously, "They're all looking the same way!"

Matt laughed. The thrill of the hunt had grown steadily for the past few days, until the excitement building beneath his stoic exterior rivaled Ellie's outward enthusiasm. He was beginning to see why she pursued archaeology with such intensity.

"They're pointing toward that cliff," he stated with confidence.

She scanned the thirty-foot wall on the opposite side

of the ravine. The upper half of the cliff was sheared away, forming a slope of dirt and gravel that extended out from the bottom half at a thirty-degree angle. "It looks like the upper part eroded and crumbled away."

"Either that, or someone deliberately dislodged the dirt and loose shale above to cover something at the bottom."

Ellie sucked in her breath. "There is a large indentation high in the slope where the soil has sunk in."

"Now this fits the Aztec pattern," Matt said, "all twists and turns and teasing mysteries."

He removed his shovel and pickax from Dakota's saddle, then climbed up the slope and started digging. Ellie put on leather gloves, grabbed her shovel, and joined him. They moved dirt and loose rock aside, working through a foot and a half of earth, not knowing what to expect.

They didn't anticipate a wall of rock.

"Dammit." Matt jammed the shovel deep into the ground.

Ellie leaned closer. She brushed loose dirt away from the surface with her gloved hands, uncovering what appeared to be a seam between two large rocks. A few scraggly strings of dry grass stuck out. Digging one finger into the seam, Ellie pulled out a piece of compacted dirt. She held it up.

Matt took the chunk and crumbled it between his thumb and fingers. Dried grass floated away in the breeze. "Adobe. It can be used to make bricks or serve as mortar."

"Clear away more dirt," Ellie said excitedly.

They shoveled vigorously, gradually revealing a four-foot-square section of manmade barrier. The well-matched stones, most more than a foot across, were joined together tightly by narrow, adobe-packed seams.

Matt leaned on his shovel. "Someone went to an awful lot of trouble to build a wall here. There must be something worthwhile on the other side."

She grinned. "Well, hurry then. Let's break through."

"Stand back." Bracing one leg downhill and the other up, Matt drove the narrow point of the pickax into a seam. Although nearly as tough as the surrounding rock, the adobe slowly chipped, loosening a large stone. When he felt it wobble, Matt pounded the pick against the rock itself.

Without warning, the stone dropped free. It crashed to a point out of sight, several feet below. The impact reverberated with a hollow, echoing sound.

Black emptiness gaped from the opposite side of the hole. Musty, humid air swept out to greet them.

Ellie looked at him, her eyes alight like a child's Fourth of July sparkler.

"We found it, Matt."

SWEAT TRICKLED DOWN Matt's back and glistened over his broad shoulders. Every time he swung the pickax, muscles flexed and rippled in intricate harmony.

Ellie watched, mesmerized by each movement, as Matt worked to open a hole large enough for them to enter the cave. She'd never known a man could be so beautiful. She could have stared at him for hours—though she was still annoyed with him for setting her aside to stand guard.

She shifted on the rock that served as a seat, vainly seeking a comfortable position. Her rifle lay across her knees. Her attention should be fixed on the surrounding terrain. She should have been looking for any sign of danger, but she couldn't help herself. Her attention frequently drifted back to Matt's powerful body—the body that had touched her soul, the hands that had stroked her with passionate gentleness.

Ellie shivered with remembered delight and renewed need.

Forcing herself to turn away, she scrutinized the rocky ravine with its sharp turns and steep walls. Matt was right. They were vulnerable here. Only scattered boulders and a small stand of trees twenty feet away provided any cover.

The sound of the pickax striking rock echoed rhythmically through the ravine. Matt had refused to let her explore inside until he cleared an opening at least three feet square, large enough for them to freely move in and out with their equipment.

Another stone fell free, enlarging the hole. Not long now.

Anticipation raced through her. This could be it—the significant historical find she craved, the victory she desperately needed to sustain her through the years ahead.

And she and Matt had found it together. She might never have solved the puzzle without his insight working hand-in-hand with her experience. How was it they worked so well together? What sparked this magic between them, what triggered the instantaneous rushes of desire and enabled their thoughts to match so closely? Ellie shied away from putting a name to it, for her promise would carry her back to England all too soon.

She concentrated instead on her duty as guard. Her ears stayed tuned for any sound that didn't belong. She searched for any movement or flash of color foreign to the purely natural landscape. Nothing seemed out of place.

An instinct suddenly told her otherwise. The hairs on the back of her neck prickled.

Someone was watching her. How could that be? No man, mounted or on foot, could have approached without her seeing in this rocky ravine. Ellie whipped around, dreading she would encounter Sam Hayley's wicked grin.

Something unexpected, yet equally dangerous, stared back at her from beneath the trees.

She might not have spotted it at all, if not for the lazy twitching of its long tail. Tawny fur blended almost perfectly with the sandy soil. The black markings on its face and tufted ears enhanced the camouflage effect.

A cougar. A wild predator.

Ellie froze, holding her breath. She was being stalked, like prey.

She breathed again slowly. She was afraid to move at all lest she invite an attack.

"Ellie, what's wrong?"

Matt's question broke her frozen grip of terror. She jerked the rifle to her shoulder and sighted down the barrel. The cougar stood, its watchful expression transforming into a hissing snarl.

"No!" Matt roared just as Ellie pulled the trigger.

His shout upset her aim, pulling the shot wide. Nevertheless, she hit her target. The bullet cut through fur and gouged a red streak along the cougar's shoulder. It yowled in pain and fury. Undergrowth snapped as the big cat spun and bolted away. It disappeared up the ravine.

"What the hell have you done?" Matt demanded, standing right behind her. He grabbed the warm rifle from her hands. With long, vigorous strides, he quickly reached the animal's hiding place. He squatted down and examined the spot.

Ellie followed. Cold sweat prickled across her skin. "A cougar was stalking us. I shot it. I'm so sorry for the noise,

Matt. I know it might lead the Hayleys to our location, but what else could I do?"

Matt touched the ground. When he pulled his hand back, a drop of blood slid between his thumb and forefinger. He hung his head and closed his eyes.

"What's wrong?" Ellie demanded, confused by his behavior. "Are you worried the cat will become more aggressive now it is wounded?"

Matt rose, his mouth set in a grim line. "The cougar wasn't stalking us, Ellie. She was watching over me."

Ellie was taken aback. "What the bloody hell are you talking about?"

A predator-like ferocity of Matt's own flashed in his brown eyes. Gripping both their rifles in one hand, he clasped her upper arm. He turned her toward the horses. The reason for his anger mystified her.

"Let go of my arm."

"Am I hurting you?"

"No, but it's not exactly comfortable."

"You'll survive." He released her when they reached the horses. "Mount up."

Stubbornly, she turned and faced him, hands on hips. "Where are we going?"

"To track the cat."

"Why? The cougar will leave us alone now. We don't have to kill it."

The play of muscles in his face startled Ellie. For pity's sake, she'd saved them from being mauled.

"I don't want to kill her, dammit. I want to help her. Somehow I have to undo the damage you've done."

"Are you mad? That is a wounded predator out there. Surely you realize how dangerous it can be?"

He leaned the rifles against a nearby boulder with a

calm that reassured Ellie—for an instant. Then he turned, facing her with passion in his eyes. "I don't care. I'll risk it. That cougar saved my life, and I won't stand by and just let her die. Even though you only winged her, she might not be able to hunt. She could starve to death, along with the kittens she must have given birth to by now."

"You are not making sense. How could a wild cougar have saved your life?"

"Don't ask me to explain how or why, because it's a mystery to me, too. I only know that when the Hayleys bushwhacked me, I was wounded and stranded in these mountains. I came very close to dying from thirst and loss of blood. That supposedly vicious animal protected me. She led me to water. She shared her kill with me."

"Why didn't you tell me this before?" Ellie whispered.

"Would you have believed me?"

"Perhaps. I believe you now."

"You don't think I'm a raving lunatic?"

"I would call you incredibly lucky, definitely. Blessed would be an even more apt description. But hardly insane."

He moved to slide the rifles into the saddle boots. "Either way, I'm going to do what I can to help her."

The significance of his actions sank in, leaving Ellie cold. "Matt, you . . . you can't leave now. We're so close. The cave, the treasure—"

"Will have to wait," he interrupted. "For me, at least."

She gaped. The greatest triumph of her life potentially lay hidden in that cave, exposed to the outside world for the first time in three hundred years. It was vulnerable and all too accessible—especially now that her touchy trigger finger had provided Peter and the Hayleys an intriguing sound to follow.

Matt mounted his horse and paused, watching her. He

neither demanded nor cajoled, though he was impatient to begin tracking the wounded cat. Ellie admired his loyalty, his sense of responsibility to a wild animal that had saved his life. Suddenly she wished she could inspire that kind of loyalty.

She owed Matt for everything he'd suffered and tolerated to help in her quest. This was critically important to him. He could have dug his heels into Dakota's sides and galloped off, but he waited. The fact that he wanted her along touched Ellie deeply.

With one last, longing look at the dark opening to the cave, she untied her mare.

Matt nodded stiffly, his only acknowledgment of her decision to accompany him. Ellie winced at the anger hardening his face. She'd disappointed him yet again, succeeding only in driving him farther away. Emotion clawed at her throat, but she choked back the tears.

If the cougar died, would he ever forgive her?

Chapter 18

MATT BENT LOW to the ground. He lifted a brittle brown leaf and tilted it. The drop of blood traced an undulating path over the dry surface and dripped off the side. They were closing in on the wounded cougar.

"Can you still read the trail? She hasn't eluded us, has she?" Ellie asked from horseback.

The anxious note in her voice pricked at Matt's conscience. She was truly distressed over what had happened. The silent treatment he'd given her wasn't helping. But he no longer blamed her for shooting his spirit guide.

He blamed himself.

If he had shared his earlier experiences with the cougar, Ellie would have been forewarned, perhaps even prepared for the shock of seeing the big cat. But he had held back because she still withheld a significant portion of her trust. Secrets loomed between them like a stone wall.

Why was a Mexican officer tracking her? Although he

shouldn't expect it, he still wanted Ellie to share every detail of her life, her thoughts, her dreams . . . and her fears.

"She's heading that way," Matt said, nodding toward another large copse. The cougar had led them a merry chase through every rocky pass and wooded area she could find.

"If she is weakening, we should catch up with her soon."

"No."

"No?"

"She's leading us the wrong way." Matt glanced over his shoulder in the direction of the beautiful valley the cougar had shared with him months before.

"How can you tell?"

"She's heading in the opposite direction from her favorite spot, her safe haven."

"Perhaps she is afraid of becoming trapped."

"No. She's leading us away from her kittens," Matt concluded. He swung into his saddle, certain now of his theory. "We're wasting our time trying to catch up with the mother, and only succeeding in pushing her to more blood loss and collapse. Come on," he said, reining the stallion around. "I'm not going to leave those kits unprotected. We're going to find them and wait for mama to come to us."

"If she comes," Ellie said gravely.

"She'll make it," Matt said through clenched teeth.

ELLIE FOLLOWED MATT to a small valley between two mountain peaks. She gazed over the peaceful setting.

Water flowed down from one peak and collected in a pond. Edged by tall reeds, the pond was a mirror for the blue sky. Only the V-shaped ripples from paddling ducks disturbed the pond's glassy surface. On the opposite side of the valley floor, just before a stand of aspens at the base of a ridge, scattered rocks and fallen trees lay haphazardly.

"Look!" Ellie gripped Matt's arm.

He followed her pointing finger to where a sleek, tawny ghost slipped through the yellowing grass.

"How did she get here before us?" she asked.

He watched the cougar. After a few seconds, he said with soft vehemence, "Son of a bitch."

"What's wrong?"

"That's not her. That cat is lighter in color, not to mention a good deal larger. It must be a male. Damn. This is where she brought me before. I thought for sure—"

The cougar changed its stance, lowering its head and shoulders. It moved forward slowly, drawing close to the cluster of rocks and logs.

"What is it doing?" Ellie asked.

"Stalking some—"

Matt froze. Without warning, he pulled out his rifle and kicked Dakota into a run across the meadow. He shouted as he cocked the rifle. Then he fired four shots in rapid succession in the general direction of the male cougar. Knowing the deadly accuracy of Matt's aim, Ellie knew he wasn't attempting to hit the animal, only to scare it away. But why?

The big cat pivoted sharply and bolted. It disappeared into the forest at the valley's far end.

"Bloody hell!" Ellie exclaimed, hurrying to catch up.

When she reached Matt's side, he had returned the rifle to its boot. He continued to ride forward. Ellie followed.

"I suppose it would be too much to ask what brought on that spurt of lunacy?"

"I don't know. Some instinct just told me to stop him."

"What are we looking for now?"

"His prey."

Ellie couldn't deny her curiosity about what the cougar had been stalking so intently. They tied the horses near the rocks and fallen trees. As Matt worked his way to the right, Ellie picked her way to the left. She looked for anything out of the ordinary.

For some reason, a log nestled deep in the grass caught her attention. Ellie paused. Undergrowth crept up the opposite side of the log. Overhanging trees created a mottled pattern of vivid sunlight and velvety shade.

She stared, questioning her interest and common sense, when suddenly her perspective shifted.

A trio of alert little faces came abruptly into focus, so well camouflaged they seemed invisible until her conscious mind allowed her other senses to take over.

Ellie caught her breath.

Three spotted cougar kittens looked up at her.

ADORABLE DIDN'T BEGIN to describe the cougar kittens.

Dark spots scattered over their fluffy coats, creating a remarkable camouflage. Their faces had a concealing pattern of dark fur and black markings on either side of their noses that looked like handlebar mustaches. They looked so soft, cute, and comical that Ellie had to force herself to remember that they would grow to more than one hundred pounds each and possess the predatory skill to pull down an adult deer.

Ellie stood still. Now what? Matt was almost thirty feet away.

"Matt!" she whispered urgently. The kittens' whiskers twitched in surprise, but they didn't move.

He quickly worked his way to her side.

"There," she said softly, nodding toward the log.

"Well, I'll be damned."

"What do we do with them?"

"If their mother doesn't return within half a day, we'll bring them food. I don't know if they can eat meat yet, but we have no other option." He glanced at her. "And we curb any urge to interfere with them. That means no touching, petting, or cuddling, Ellie—no matter how adorable they are."

"I wasn't thinking anything of the sort."

"Yes you were."

"Whatever gave you such an idea?"

"The expression on your face." He lifted one hand to catch her chin in the crook of his finger. He smiled indulgently. "You look all soft and protective-like."

Ellie swallowed hard. "If you are referring to motherly instincts, I have none."

"Are you so sure?"

His smile grew warmer, making a score of butterflies flutter through her stomach. It was the first sign of approval he'd offered since she shot the cougar.

His splayed fingers slid into her hair, while his thumb stroked across her cheekbone. The hungry look in his eyes ignited a shiver that moved with exquisite, tormenting slowness from the nape of Ellie's neck to her toes. She wanted his forgiveness but would gladly settle for a kiss to start.

His mouth lowered. His warm breath caressed her lips.

A rustle of grass distracted them. They turned their heads.

The kittens were gone.

Ellie gasped. "Oh, no!"

"Don't worry. They won't go far."

A pang of renewed guilt shot through Ellie. Tears pricked her eyes. "I am so sorry I shot their mother, Matt. I just—"

"Ssh," he said, briefly touching a finger to her lips. "Anyone would have instinctively done the same thing. I realized that after I cooled off. There is something terrifying in confronting a wild creature you know is capable of killing you with one swipe of its paw." His mouth slanted. "I almost shot her myself the first time I saw her."

"I'll never forgive myself if the kittens die."

"Their mother will be back soon. We'll stay here in the meantime to protect them, just in case the male cougar returns."

Her eyes widened in disbelief. "You don't mean he was—"

"Yes, I do. That male was stalking the kittens."

"But they are just babies!"

"Cougars are very territorial. That rogue male knows damn well these kits will grow up to compete for food— females, too, if any of them are male. He'll gladly get rid of them before they get that far. It's very likely they aren't his, either, and he knows it."

Ellie gazed at the surrounding trees and rocks . . . and all the possible hiding places. "I wonder where they are."

"Nearby. We'll make camp across the meadow."

Ellie closed her eyes. Thoughts of the treasure at risk and delays they could ill afford caused her stomach to ache. But the image of those three wary faces remained branded in her memory. Matt was right—this was more important right now. They couldn't abandon those help-less cougar kittens.

Montezuma's treasure had been undisturbed for more

than three hundred years. She could curb her impatience and wait a little longer, couldn't she?

But would the treasure wait for her?

Peter was still out there, determined to pirate her discovery, and she and Matt had made it easy for him. All Peter had to do was stumble across the exposed cave opening, and everything she'd fought so hard to attain would be gone.

"I WILL LET you be smug about being right, just this once."

"Can I gloat about it, too?" Matt teased.

"Very amusing." Ellie cast a sidelong glance at Matt's profile as he stood beside her at the campsite. "I'm simply relieved she made it back safely."

The female cougar crossed the meadow along the far side. She showed definite signs of a limp. Otherwise, she looked reassuringly fit.

An immense burden suddenly lifted from Ellie's shoulders. Despite Matt's profession of forgiveness earlier in the morning, she had feared the mother cougar would never arrive.

She could see now how Matt distinguished between the two cougars. This cat was smaller, more lithe, and had a darker coat.

The cougar's ivory fangs gleamed as she opened her mouth in a series of short, staccato yowls. She sounded almost like a barking dog.

"I thought cougars would roar or growl—something like African lions," Ellie exclaimed.

"I've heard a cougar roar from a distance. It's more like a low, guttural scream than any roar you'd expect."

The kittens came tumbling out of their hiding place,

falling over one another in the rush to respond to their mother's call. The cougar sniffed each one thoroughly, then bestowed several vigorous licks of greeting that knocked her young off their feet. They batted playfully at their mother's face with their front paws.

Matt reached for his rifle. "She'll need to eat to make milk and keep up her strength. I'm going to see what I can scare up for dinner."

THE KITTENS TUMBLED and played most of the afternoon, learning hunting skills by stalking one another and pouncing on their mother's twitching tail. The cougar turned her young over and cleaned them with her tongue, until they lay limp and contented across her paws.

From a respectful distance, Ellie watched with awe, deciding this was one of the most fascinating experiences of her life.

The mother cougar suddenly began to pace. Her abrupt screech sent the kittens scurrying for cover.

Ellie clutched her rifle. Had the male cougar returned? The apprehension eased from her shoulders a moment later as Matt rode into sight. A young mule deer buck lay strapped behind Dakota's saddle.

Ellie met him as he rode up. Dismounting, he untied the ropes securing the carcass and pulled the deer to the ground.

"Do you think she will eat something that is not her own kill?"

"She's accepted something from me before. I'm hoping the instinct to feed her kittens will conquer any doubts."

Looping one end of the rope around the buck's antlers and the other end around his shoulder, Matt dragged the offering across the meadow. The big cat watched his every movement with keen interest. Just as he neared the fallen trees, the cougar lowered her head and stretched out her body. She broke into a low, swift attack . . . straight for Matt.

Ellie's heart surged to her throat.

"Matt! Look out!"

He let go of the rope and stepped aside. The big cat pounced on the deer. Ellie's initial relief instantly gave way to a feeling of foolishness.

The cougar sank her fangs into the dead buck's neck and dragged the heavy carcass to a nearby spot. Then she called the kittens to share the meal.

Matt returned to the camp. He and Ellie sat side by side in the thick grass, watching nature's ritual.

"Thank you for showing this to me," she murmured.

Matt plucked a foot-long strand of grass and ran it through his fingers. "Even through we're neglecting our own hunt and risking the treasure?"

Ellie remembered her initial resistance. "I've been very single-minded, haven't I?"

"You have a right to be. It's your dream. Besides, single-mindedness can be a good thing. It's pushed you decisively within sight of your goal, when most people spend their whole lives getting nowhere by hesitating."

"Still, I'm glad I didn't miss this."

Matt lay on his side, propped up on his left elbow. He looked up at her solemnly. The long blade of grass twirled between his right thumb and forefinger. "I wouldn't have shared it with anyone else."

"Really?"

"Have I ever lied to you?"

Not that I know of, she wanted to respond. Her heart wouldn't let her. It thudded in her chest instead.

Matt ran the narrow end of the grass blade down the

side of her neck, across her collarbone, and brushed it against her throat. A shiver raced through Ellie's chest, turning every breath into a fire-edged reminder of his muscular body and the passion they'd shared in Santa Fe.

"That tickles," she whispered. So much for clever repartee and lessons on flirtation.

"Good." A smile widened his sensuous mouth. He trailed the stalk up under her chin and across her lips.

Ellie licked her tingling lips and pressed them together.

He dipped the grass into the shadowed cleavage exposed by the open collar of her blouse. He twirled it so the curled end tickled the inner curves of her breasts. Her nipples tightened almost painfully.

Every thought fractured into a hundred fragments with his teasing touch.

He tossed the blade aside. Curling one hand around her neck, he lowered her gently into the grass. He slid closer, pressing the length of his body against hers. Ellie's bones melted in the warm sunshine and the heat of desire in his eyes.

"I can be pretty single-minded myself, you know," he murmured. He pulled her collar aside and nibbled at the sensitive skin along the curve of her shoulder.

Excitement shimmered through Ellie. She worked trembling hands down his shirt, undoing the buttons, until she pressed her palms against his bare chest. "Make love to me, Matt. Now."

Her words opened a floodgate. Gone was the seductive tease. Matt once again became the intent, ardent lover.

He rapidly undid the buttons on her blouse. He spread the front open to reveal her corset of ivory watered silk with embroidered flowers. Ellie blushed.

He bent his head. Warm lips caressed the upper curves of her breasts.

A delicate shudder rippled through her. His fingers released the metal fasteners down the front of the corset. Ellie held her breath in anticipation. Then the garment parted and only the thin, clinging silk chemise beneath separated him from her heated flesh. He urged her to sit up, then helped her slip free of the blouse and corset. In one swift move, he peeled the chemise over her head.

Before she knew what he was doing, Matt slipped around to sit close behind her. He encouraged her to lean into him, until her back pressed against the hard muscles and crisp hair of his chest. The contact made her quiver with excitement. When his warm hands cradled her breasts, Ellie felt as if she were sinking into a soft, sensual paradise.

He caressed her flesh and teased her nipples with masterful strokes of his fingers. She whispered his name. Her head fell back against his shoulder. Fire licked deep into her belly, finding a connection between her breasts and the pulsing emptiness lower down.

His right hand moved over the smooth skin of her stomach. Ellie tensed with a strange mixture of eagerness and fear. She gripped his thighs on either side. Then his hand curved over her woman's mound and pressed into the crotch of her trousers. Ellie's body jerked in response. Matt's throaty groan vibrated against her back, creating a wild tingle across her skin.

His left hand gently kneaded her breast while his right stroked that sensitive place between her legs. Heat washed into her lower body and dampened her trousers. Ellie writhed, seeking a closeness the fabric denied.

Wave after wave of fire licked up her body and sent sparks tingling down the backs of her legs. This time, she thought wildly, she would fully explore the rare passion between them. This time she would have all of him. The gnawing hunger inside her demanded nothing less.

His fingers moved to the waist of her trousers.

A sudden rush of frustration jerked Ellie from the fantasy. Pivoting quickly, she shoved Matt in the chest. He fell back in the grass, eyes wide with surprise. Ellie straddled his thighs.

"You intend to deny your own pleasure again, don't you?"

Something flickered through the passionate intensity in his eyes. "It's better that way. Believe me." He reached for her shoulders, saying seductively, "It gives me all the pleasure I need to watch you."

She scooted back beyond easy reach of his hands to sit just above his knees. "Better for whom?" Deep inside, Ellie knew what she wanted. Despite feeling wanton, she reached for the buttons on his trousers. "You might be willing to deny yourself, but don't you dare deny me. This is what I want."

He gasped as her knuckles brushed the hard ridge of his manhood through the fabric. His hands clamped around her wrists.

"What about your future plans?" he demanded roughly.

He didn't have to mention the word *marriage*. It hung in the air between them. The reminder of her father's plans caused desperation to thread through Ellie, only adding to her determination. "I don't care. No man has ever made me feel the way you do, Matt. I'm not going through the rest of my life regretting I missed this one chance at passion."

His hands dropped away from her wrists. "You'd better not feel this way with another man," he growled.

"Never," she whispered, meaning it like a sacred vow.

With every button she unfastened, Matt tensed a little more, until his hard, erect manhood came free.

"I want only you . . . all of you this time," Ellie whispered.

This part of him was as powerful and masculine as the rest. She stroked her fingers along satiny skin. His pulse throbbed against her fingertips, filling Ellie with amazement and trepidation at the same time. How was he ever to fit inside her? She curled her palm around his staff and squeezed gently. A shudder rippled through Matt's big body. The proof of his vulnerability reassured her, dispelling her fears.

Matt helped her remove her trousers with a new measure of urgency. Then he pulled her up to straddle his hips once again. His hard ridge pressed against her sensitive heat. She shivered.

"Can it work this way, with you beneath me?" she asked, amazed and a little doubtful.

"Oh, yes, *querida*."

Ellie's breath caught. He'd called her *beloved*. Was the endearment born in the heat of the moment, or did it hold a deeper meaning? Then he grasped her hips and pushed into her slowly, shattering any thought beyond the stunning fullness that dominated her senses. He hesitated when he reached the barrier of her maidenhood.

"I don't want to hurt you," he said hoarsely.

"Don't stop now," she begged.

He surged up. Ellie went rigid as a sharp, stinging pain lanced through her belly.

Matt lay still, buried deep inside her body. He stroked her thighs, her belly, and her breasts, until she relaxed.

"Does it still hurt?" he asked. He shifted gently.

She gasped as velvety fingers of pleasure spread throughout her lower body. "No. Not now."

"Good, because I don't think I can hold back any longer."

He started to move, pressing deeper until Ellie felt him touch her core. Clasping her hips, he pushed her up, withdrawing until he almost pulled free of her body. Her sheath clenched around his manhood, protesting the loss of the exquisite fullness. She braced herself against his chest, cherishing the feel of lean, taut muscles.

With his hands as guides, he showed her the rhythm, encouraging her to move in counterpoint. The deep stroking sent tendrils of flame throughout her body, leaving her weak and invigorated at the same time.

Matt moved faster, his own ecstasy reflected in the corded tendons of his neck and the feverish intensity of his gaze. Ellie matched him eagerly, thrilled and humbled that she inspired such passion in him. Pressure built inside her like a tempest, coiling tighter until her whole world focused on the place where their bodies met and throbbed. She recognized the spiraling sensation from before, but this was so much deeper and richer—enhanced by sharing every sensation with him, entangled with his body as if one.

The climax broke over Ellie, startling her with its white-hot intensity. Her body arched like a bow. Ecstasy washed through her in wave after pulsing wave. The aftershocks continued with the deep stroking of his manhood, still inside her. She wanted to collapse, but the pleasure wouldn't release her.

Muscles tightened in Matt's face. Suddenly he stiffened and let out a guttural shout. He pressed deeper into her than ever before. Finally, he relaxed.

She fell against his chest. His arms came around her, stroking her back. She felt safe, cherished, and complete.

This ecstasy came from fully discovering herself as a woman in Matt's embrace.

This deep contentment came from being in love, Ellie realized with a start.

Everything about their lovemaking felt so beautiful and right, well beyond physical passion. Matt had inspired strong emotions from the moment they'd met—first anger, then frustration, then passion. He'd earned her admiration and respect with his intelligence and ready wit. But somewhere along the way it had become so much more.

She loved him.

Remembering her oath to her father, Ellie's throat tightened. She turned her head so he wouldn't detect the stray tear.

Heaven help her, she didn't know how Matt could be a part of her future . . . or if he even wanted to be.

Chapter 19

THE SETTING SUN cast long shadows into the valley the next day when the mother cougar stood, her body rigid except for the twitching end of her tail.

Ellie rose from her spot by the fire, immediately forgetting the duck she was roasting. She shivered with apprehension. Bloody hell. Of all the times for Matt to be out hunting again. . . .

She reached for her rifle. Fat dripped into the fire, hissing, causing her to jump as she followed the direction of the cougar's fixed gaze.

A low, sleek body parted the waves of tall grass. A flash of golden fur confirmed Ellie's worst fears.

The male was back.

With the rifle slung across her back, Ellie raced to within a hundred feet of the female. She climbed a tree, primarily for safety but also to get a better view. She found a low, sturdy limb just as the male trotted into the clearing.

Striding confidently, he approached the female, then

slowed and began to circle her. The female snarled and crouched.

He persisted, rubbing against her several times in passing, obviously with mating on his mind. The mother cougar apparently knew the male posed a grave threat to her kittens. She hissed and flattened her ears, then swiped at him with bared claws. The blow caught him on the haunch, drawing blood.

Abruptly, the game changed. The two cats faced each other, ears back and teeth bared hideously. Suddenly the scene exploded into a flurry of twisting bodies, flashing paws, and feline screams. Just as quickly they broke apart. Flecks of fresh blood glistened in the sunlight on both animals.

The female, a good forty pounds lighter and disadvantaged by her wound, didn't stand a chance. Terror for the mother and her babies swept through Ellie, leaving her body ice cold.

Taking aim, she whispered fervently, "Just go away. I don't want to have to kill you." But neither could she wait until the two clashed again. If she hesitated, her only opportunity for a clear shot might be lost.

The male gathered his powerful body for a strike.

Ellie held her breath and pulled the trigger.

The cougar jerked in midleap, then somersaulted through the air. He hit the ground and lay still.

He'd been so beautiful.

Her hands opened limply as a terrible pressure built in her chest. The rifle dropped. Numbed, she climbed down the tree after it, half sliding and falling to the ground. Her legs buckled the moment her feet touched down.

Ellie fell to her knees, curled over until her forehead brushed the swaying grass, and sobbed. She'd been forced to destroy one magnificent creature to save another. She cried until a pair of strong hands curled around her shoulders.

Turning, Ellie buried herself in Matt's embrace. He sat on the ground and cradled her close to his chest. Not since her teen years, when she'd sought solace in her father's arms, had she allowed a man to witness such vulnerability. Matt stroked her back as her tears soaked the shoulder of his blue shirt.

"Better?" he asked when her sobs began to diminish.

Ellie nodded into his shoulder. She clutched his shirt, afraid to let him go and take with him the warmth and strength that was becoming more and more integral to her happiness.

"Those kittens and their mother are damn lucky you're such a good shot."

"Maybe . . . maybe I should have fired in the air to scare him off, as you did the first time."

"If that rogue came back once, he would again. You did what you had to do," Matt said as he drew back. He paused, then added decisively, "I'm sure the family will be fine without us now. We'll head out tomorrow morning."

Ellie frowned. "Are you sure?"

He grinned. "We can come back and check on them in a few days if it will make you feel better."

Ellie lifted her chin. "Yes. I'd like that. And don't you dare try to deny the idea appeals to you for your own reasons, Matt Devereaux."

"You're starting to read me too well," he said with an enigmatic look.

Chapter 20

ELLIE DROPPED TO her knees beside the opening of the cave, unmindful of the dust clinging to her brown trousers. She ran her hands over the dirt and gravel surrounding the hole.

"No sign of footprints," she concluded breathlessly. "I don't think anyone has been here while we were away, thank heavens. Here," she added, thrusting out her hand to the side, "give me the lantern."

Matt put their one remaining lantern carefully in her hand, shaping her fingers around the handle so she wouldn't burn herself in the midst of her excitement. His body responded to her zeal. He wanted to capture that energy, to immerse himself in the center of her passion again until she forgot about the treasure and everything else beyond their joined bodies and feverish desire.

She lowered the lantern through the hole, then thrust her head and shoulders in after it. Half expecting her to tumble headfirst into the cave, Matt grabbed the waistband of her trousers. He rolled his eyes.

"I'm all right, really. You can let go now." Her muffled words were immediately followed by a ghostly echo.

Matt eyed the tight stretch of fabric over her derriere. He grinned wolfishly. "That's all right. I'll just hang on to make sure you're safe." Unable to resist, he tickled her tailbone.

Ellie yelped. "Stop that, Matt!"

"Don't you like it?"

"No. Yes. I don't know! This is not the right time. I'm losing my sense of balance."

"Maybe it's because the blood is rushing to your head."

"That's not the only place where my blood is rushing."

Matt grinned with satisfaction. "Don't worry about falling. I've got you."

"That's not the problem. You are destroying my concentration."

"I believe I have the perfect cure."

Her long pause fed his imagination. She was definitely thinking about his proposal. Finally, she answered softly, "That's not a fair question, Matt. I just got started here."

Matt sighed. She was right. They'd struggled through one obstacle after another to reach this point. The treasure might lie within reach now, awaiting the first human presence in over three hundred years.

"All right," he agreed. "I'll back off if you will."

"What is that supposed to mean? I'm not the one with my hand inside your trousers."

Matt sucked in his breath as another rush of heat flooded his body. Whether in the role of innocent or temptress, she made it damn difficult to stick to business. "I need you to back out of the hole, Ellie. I'm going into the cave first."

Her soft tone vanished. The echoes intensified as she shouted, "Like hell you are! I'm the archaeologist here."

"And I'm the one with the revolver. We don't know what's in there. I'm going to check it out first."

"No, you . . . you can't. Let go of me. I'll be fine." She reached deeper into the darkness, pulling against his hold.

"Ellie," he said tightly. "I'm not going to steal your thunder by discovering the treasure first. Neither am I going to let you fling yourself into something stupid with your usual impulsiveness. Now come out or I'll lift you out."

"Wait! I think I see something. I only need to stretch the lantern a little bit."

She screeched—half in surprise, half in terror—and abruptly backed out of the hole. She collided with Matt. They both slid down ten feet of gravel to the base of the slope. The extinguished lantern rolled down next to them. Shaking his head, Matt set the lantern upright to avoid spilling any of the precious kerosene.

Ellie lay half sprawled across his chest. Bracing her forearms against his ribs, she shoved up on her elbows. She blew loose tendrils of hair away from her eyes.

"What the hell was that about?" Matt asked.

Her eyes widened until the whites shone. She shuddered, the vibration passing into his body. Matt groaned. He couldn't get yesterday out of his mind. Making love to her had only heightened the fever in his blood, not quenched it.

"Skulls," she croaked. "I saw human skulls."

Matt sobered instantly. He pulled her up with him, then set her lightly on her feet. "Come on." Few things scared Ellie. Nor was she one to be fanciful. He retrieved the lantern and relit it.

As they climbed back up the slope, she muttered, "This is embarrassing. It's not as if I've never seen human skulls before. Actually, I've seen quite a few in past expeditions. But this caught me by surprise. It looked as if—"

"What?" he prompted.

"As if they were watching me. The eyes seemed to gleam and flash, as if angry at my intrusion."

"Hmmmn," Matt answered. Her story piqued his interest. Now he didn't have to bow to her expertise as an archaeologist. He could lead rather than follow. Dealing with bogeymen was his specialty.

He knelt and reached deep into the hole. Despite Ellie's warning, the sight exposed by the lantern's glow gave him a jolt of surprise.

A small pyramid of human skulls, facing outward and stacked five levels high, stood on the cave floor. Several pairs of eyes flashed in varying shades of yellow.

Matt grimaced at the macabre sight. The ghoulish pyramid was no doubt a warning to any intruders to turn back.

"Well?" Ellie called out.

"You were right about the dead being angry."

"You see it too? The eyes shine?"

Matt stood, facing her. Cocking one eyebrow, he teased, "Don't tell me that beneath your logical, scientific exterior is a woman prone to superstitious beliefs?"

She huffed and plunked her hands on her hips. "Of course not. It is just . . . bizarre, that's all."

Matt smiled. She was adorable and endearing when she tried to hide any weakness. It made him want to protect her all the more.

"The skull's eyes must be a trick done with quartz, or perhaps gemstones," he offered. "They didn't shine until the light hit them just right."

"Of course! There is always a logical explanation for

everything. See—nothing to fear." Stepping to the edge, she looked at him expectantly. "Here, lower me down."

He gave her a slow warning look. That's all it took.

Ellie threw up her hands. "Oh, very well. If you are going to be pigheaded about this, then you go first. But don't you dare go beyond the area under the hole unless I'm with you."

"Yes, ma'am. Whatever you say, ma'am."

Matt lowered himself into the hole. There was an additional drop of about two feet before he landed on a smooth stone floor.

Sunlight slanted through the opening, striking the floor like a bright golden lance. Filtered light brushed the dark gray walls and illuminated the entrance. A deeper blackness swallowed the light at the far end, indicating a tunnel that stretched deeper into the earth.

The stillness emanating from the tunnel reminded Matt of the silence of a tomb. A cold chill traced a shivery path down his spine. He experienced an awareness similar to the sensation he felt when his cougar spirit guide was nearby, except this was unpleasant. He curled one hand over the butt of his revolver.

The morbid pyramid of skulls was not the only source of gloom. Sorrow and death also whispered to him from the depths of the tunnel. That he got any impression at all from something he couldn't touch made him damn uneasy. First the cougar and the strange link between them, now this. Where was this heightened awareness coming from? Some part of his Navajo heritage? He didn't like the sensation of cold, skeletal fingers on the back of his neck one damn bit.

A faint scent teased his nostrils—the odor of decay. He hoped it wouldn't lead to any additional human remains.

"Well?" Ellie called down. "Can I come down now?"

Her voice, so full of energy and eagerness, washed over him like sunlight and dispelled the gloom. They had work to do. Whatever remained hidden in this depressing place deserved to see the light of day—or have a decent burial.

Ellie lowered herself through the opening, providing a delectable view of long legs and a curvaceous bottom. Matt grasped her waist and lowered her slowly, making certain her body rubbed against the length of his own. When her feet touched down, he held her for a moment longer, his heart pounding. Then he breathed deeply, cherishing the fresh smell of woman, lilac soap, and vibrant life. He released her and offered an encouraging smile.

She flushed a becoming color. Her chest rose and fell rapidly. She opened her mouth, failed to find adequate words, and closed it again with a click of her teeth.

Pride filled Matt. He'd managed to leave Ellie Carlisle speechless.

Ellie approached the skull pyramid. The light picked up a golden reflection in each eye. "You were right, Matt. There are semipolished topaz gemstones suspended in the eye sockets, each one about the size of the end of my thumb." She leaned closer. "Magnificent."

"Do you want them?"

"The topaz stones? No. I think these poor souls have been denied their rest enough. We'll leave them undisturbed."

"Do you see any Aztec symbols?"

She looked around at the unadorned cavern walls. Fresh excitement infused her voice as she answered, "No, but we must be in the right place."

"I agree with you there," Matt muttered darkly, remembering the sensation of sorrow and death.

She eyed the black tunnel suspiciously. "This cavern may branch off several times. How do we find our way back?"

He pulled a chunk of soft white limestone from his pocket. "Old cave explorer's trick. Periodically, I'll draw an arrow pointing the way out."

Her grin gleamed white in the dim light. "Perfect. Shall we go, then?"

"Yeah, but I'm leading the way. No arguments."

Ellie followed so closely he could feel the warmth of her breath between his shoulder blades.

The tunnel curved to the left, then the right, offering nothing remarkable until they'd traveled nearly a hundred feet into the mountain. The musty odor of decay intensified.

The left wall of the tunnel abruptly dipped out of sight. At first Matt thought it was a branch tunnel, until the lantern light seeped into the recess and revealed a deep, bowl-shaped niche in the wall.

A natural niche that had been converted into an altar.

Startled, Matt and Ellie froze.

For several moments, all they could do was stare. Ellie's expression showed excitement and wonder. Matt was too stunned to move. Although he'd listened to her stories and caught her fervor for the hunt, deep inside he'd doubted that they would find anything significant.

Ellie broke the silence by whispering hoarsely, "We are definitely in the right place."

A variety of objects leaned against the walls, lay stacked on the floor, and cluttered the natural stone shelves of the niche. Icons, jewelry, and other items of precious metals sat alongside less extraordinary pottery vessels and bits and pieces. Gold objects were scattered throughout the collection, but the bulk of the cache appeared to be natural materials in an advanced state of decay.

Feathers were tied in bundles, their brittle gray shapes retaining just a hint of their former color and glory. Stacks of fabric sagged under the weight of dust and rot. The decaying items were arranged with obvious care, given as much a place of honor as the pieces of gold and other precious metals.

"This doesn't make sense," Matt muttered. "Why would they haul this stuff all the way from Mexico on their backs?"

"Most of these items were as good as money in the Aztec culture and used for barter or trade," Ellie said reverently. She carefully picked a shriveled black pellet from a carved stone bowl. "These are cacao beans, prized in making a drink of bitter chocolate. And these exotic feathers were esteemed for adorning warriors' costumes and priests' robes. The feathers must have been incredibly beautiful at one time. How sad. Think of all the vibrant colors—scarlet, green, yellow—lost to age and decay." Wistfully, she touched a fingernail to a large parrot feather. A section of it crumbled.

Matt wiped the dust away from one shelf, uncovering a row of slender shapes in shades of ivory, brown, and black. "Take a look at this. These look like quills from a large bird." A small, tarnished silver plug capped each one.

Ellie picked one up from the end of the row. Removing the cap, she turned the quill upside down. White, sparkling granules poured into her palm in a steady stream. She sniffed the small pile.

"Salt," she announced. "Always a valuable commodity in a culture without a ready supply. How ingenious, the way they used these hollowed-out quills for storage. Light and portable. These at least are well preserved."

"I wish we could say the same for this other stuff." Matt nodded toward a pile of disintegrating fabric that had once been a neatly folded stack of colorful blankets.

"The humidity trapped in when the cave was sealed has done a great deal of damage." Lifting a corner of each pile, Ellie named the contents as she examined the less deteriorated portions. "Woven fabrics, blankets, jaguar skins, and straw mats." Edges crumbled at her touch. A musty, stale odor filled the niche.

Matt coughed. "Let's leave those undisturbed."

"I knew the Aztecs valued such items highly, but I didn't think . . ." Her voice faded away on a note of profound sadness.

"That things unable to withstand the test of time would comprise a large portion of Montezuma's fabled treasure?" Matt finished for her.

Ellie nodded. Tears shone in her eyes.

Matt felt her sadness. "That certainly lowers the collection's value. I'm sorry, Ellie."

"I used to wish for the glamour of gold and jewels," Ellie admitted. "After all, fabled wealth is what museum visitors flock to see. But these poignant reminders have touched me much more personally. They show the Aztecs' love of color, the salt they needed to feed their children, the clever ways they stored things, the blankets they needed to keep warm." She ran her fingertips over the row of quills. "I feel closer to the people, somehow."

"Then you found what you came here for."

"Maybe I have," she whispered.

Surprisingly, frustration and anger flicked at Matt like a whip. Ellie had reached her objective. Beyond this she had no logical reason to stay in New Mexico . . . to stay with him. That unavoidable conclusion disturbed him more than he had ever thought possible. It was too damn soon to give her up. Yet, he had no right to hold her. Especially not with his past, which he was sure would disgust her.

"If only there was a way to save these," Ellie murmured. "But everything is so badly decayed. The items simply cannot be moved without destroying them."

Why did it turn him inside out every time she grew sad or distressed? "There's still the pieces of metal, stone, and pottery. You can pack those and ship them home."

"Yes, that's true."

"Let's see what's in these." Hoping to distract her from her unhappy thoughts, he indicated a trio of small gourds.

She sighed. "Very well." Ellie handed one gourd to Matt, then picked up another and opened it.

At first she tried peering into the mouth of the gourd, but the neck was too narrow. She tipped it slightly. A grayish brown sand poured into her palm. "More salt, not nearly as well preserved." She tossed it away and wiped her hand against her trousers.

"Now, this *is* curious," Matt said mysteriously. Raising the gourd to his ear, he shook it. A sound like rolling pebbles cut through the silence. He grinned. "It rattles. I wonder what it could be." A sudden eagerness in Ellie's expression rewarded his efforts to dispel her gloom.

"Well, don't keep me in suspense. Open it."

He tipped the gourd. Six rough, blue-green stones rolled out.

"Turquoise," she whispered excitedly. "I've never seen unfinished stones this big. What's in the other gourd?"

Matt reached for the last of the three. His eyebrows shot up. "It's heavy." Tipping it over, he poured out a little of the contents. Gold dust glittered, reflecting the lantern light in flashes of white fire and rainbow colors.

"Oh," she said flatly. "That's not very interesting."

Matt suppressed a laugh. Ellie was the only woman of his acquaintance who found gold dull, just because it wasn't art and steeped in historical significance.

Ellie turned toward the opening to the niche. "We

must go back for my notebook. Everything must be documented. So much of this will never see the light of day."

"Ellie."

"What?"

"There's more cave to explore," Matt reminded her, amused. Single-mindedness was one of her most endearing, albeit frustrating, qualities.

"Oh! Yes, of course! Well, come on then. Don't dawdle."

Chapter 21

MATT FOLLOWED, PRAYING they would find more. Ellie had pinned all her hopes on the treasure.

"From the placement of the artifacts," she explained as they continued along the main tunnel, "it is apparent the Aztecs didn't expect to leave the treasure here long. They must have intended to return quickly and restore all of this to its rightful place in Tenochtitlán. Perhaps continued trouble with the Spaniards prevented them."

"Look there."

Matt pointed ahead to another dark recess in the wall. This one opened into a side passage, which they followed for a short distance before it dead-ended. The abrupt end of the tunnel formed another altar, with a similarly arranged mixture of beautiful, pristine artifacts and crumbling ruin.

Ellie lightly touched several objects with loving care.

Matt remained silent, unsure of what to say. This was what she'd hoped to find. Then again, it wasn't.

They searched for another hour, finding eleven

additional small rooms or niches containing similar mixes of items. Although the quantity of artifacts was impressive, only a small percentage was salvageable.

Ellie gazed at the last altar. "That is everything, isn't it," she stated quietly.

"Yes. That's the extent of the cave."

She released a long sigh. "I always thought there would be more. The legend evidently exaggerated."

"Legends typically do. Are you disappointed?"

"No, just a bit melancholy. The Aztecs tried to salvage what Hernan Cortés and his soldiers didn't steal, but perhaps there wasn't much left. These are the things they considered worth saving."

Picking up an item from a shelf, Ellie blew the dust away. Matt stepped closer. She held a dagger unlike any he'd ever seen. The hilt was formed of hammered gold, the blade of a hard black stone that had been chipped and shaped until it was almost smooth.

Ellie continued pensively, "Over three hundred bearers were sacrificed to the Aztec gods, their hearts cut from their chests with an obsidian blade like this one. That way no one could carry the tale of the treasure's location."

Pulling out a handkerchief, Ellie polished the blade. She held it up. The glossy volcanic stone reflected the lantern light.

"On the other hand, what we have discovered is an archaeologist's dream. I estimate over four hundred artifacts of stone, metal, or pottery, all in pristine condition. And I don't have to painstakingly dig them from the dirt," she concluded. Her smile sparkled with renewed enthusiasm. "I need my notebook from my saddlebags."

She started back down the tunnel, a spring in her step. The Aztec culture fascinated her. She'd come to terms with their history of violence and bloodshed, Matt realized.

He wondered if she could be so forgiving of the dark episode in his past.

ELLIE CHATTED FREELY as they emerged from the cave, making plans for the best way to excavate the treasure.

Suddenly, a deep instinct drew Matt's attention to the top of the western cliff. The late-afternoon sun shone brutally, forcing him to shield his eyes.

The cougar sat atop the cliff, watching him, silhouetted by the sun so her coat glowed like antique gold. She'd temporarily left her kittens to seek him out. Why? Matt felt a familiar shiver down his spine.

She stood abruptly and trotted to the left along the cliff's edge. As Matt's gaze followed her, a sudden flash of light snared his attention. He reacted from experience and an aptitude for survival.

"Ellie, look out!" he shouted, tackling her to the ground. He shielded her with his body. Within the space of a single heartbeat, a bullet zinged off a nearby rock, sending shards of stone flying into the air.

The light had reflected from the barrel of a sniper's rifle. The cougar had alerted him to danger. His spirit guide had saved both their lives this time.

Matt grabbed Ellie's arm as they both jumped up. Another shot ricocheted off the ground where they'd just been. They sprinted for the base of the cliff, hoping to throw off the angle of the sniper's next shot. Matt pulled his revolver and fired back several times to cover their flight.

As they ran, the cougar's snarl reverberated through the

canyon. She charged the sniper, half hidden among the rocks. Matt's heart surged into his throat. Would the gunman turn the rifle on the mother cat?

The man's head jerked up. The wide brim of his hat no longer concealed his face. Matt instantly recognized Ben Darby.

Springing to his feet, Darby retreated from the cougar, scrambling back in terror. He fumbled to bring the rifle in line. A scream burst from his throat at the sight of a hundred pounds of bared teeth and hissing fury rushing directly at him.

At the last second the cougar veered away, breaking off her attack. She disappeared beyond the rim of the cliff.

The outlaw took another step back, apparently too dazed to notice a different danger. The loose edge of the cliff crumbled beneath his boot. The rim gave way.

Arms flailing, Darby tumbled back into open space. The sickening sound of bone hitting rock reached Matt. Ellie's grip tightened on his hand.

"How did she know he was a threat to us?" Ellie exclaimed.

"I'm not sure, but I believe animals have a greater capacity for sensing evil than we do." He tugged on her hand. "Come on. The Hayley brothers won't be far behind."

Pounding hoof beats immediately followed his words. Clive and Sam rode around the nearest bend in the ravine, guns drawn. Peter was close on their heels.

It was too late to reach the shelter of the cave. Matt spun around to face his attackers, not wanting to end his life with a bullet in the back.

They passed the spot where the sniper had fallen. Clive spared a glance at Darby's bloody body, then rode on, his face impassive.

Matt pulled Ellie behind him, ignoring her protests. He stood tense and prepared for battle, cursing the fact that the gunfight with Darby had exhausted all his bullets except one. He kept his gun lowered, knowing that to raise it would invite the Hayleys to open fire immediately.

The thought of Ellie raped and murdered filled Matt with seething rage and gut-wrenching fear. Although he'd sworn an oath long ago to lay down his life for any woman in danger, with Ellie that protectiveness took on a ferocity as essential as his next breath.

The three men reined in their horses not ten feet away. Matt knew that even with his wits, his fists, and the Bowie knife at his belt to supplement the single bullet, he didn't match up well against three revolvers.

Peter's attention was divided, at least. Peter stared at the hole in the earth, his jaw slack, his eyes glazed.

"Now ain't this cozy," Clive drawled.

Ellie tried to slip out from behind. Matt gripped her arm, holding her in place. Leaving her vulnerable would only hand the outlaws another advantage.

Leaning on his saddle horn, Clive waved the nose of his revolver toward Matt's chest. "You know, Devereaux, if I shoot you enough times, at least one of those bullets will cut through your body and hit the woman. I don't see why you waste your time protecting her."

"You wouldn't, Clive. That's one of many differences between you and me."

"Yeah, you're stupid and I'm not." His thumb caressed the hammer of his revolver. Then, with a grin, he cocked the gun.

"No," Ellie whispered in a choked voice. She didn't move, however, understanding that any distraction would spoil Matt's only chance of taking action.

The walnut grip of Matt's Colt felt smooth and cool in

his hand. Even though he might succeed in killing Clive first, exhausting his only bullet, the victory would be short-lived. Sam would instantly cut him down. But what choice did he have?

Matt's muscles tensed, prepared to raise the gun and—

Sam's voice broke in. Matt froze.

"Dammit, Clive," Sam said nastily. "Devereaux's gotten away from me twice. Nobody does that to me. I want to kill him."

"Sometimes you're a real pain in the ass, you know that?"

"You promised me," Sam retorted.

Clive snorted with impatience and holstered his gun. "Suit yourself, little brother. But make it quick, or I'll shoot you both. And this time, make sure he's dead."

Peter finally spoke up. He pointed to the opening of the cave. In a voice trembling with excitement, he asked, "Is that it? Did you find it?"

"You are an overwhelming example of a lower form of life, Peter Wentworth," Ellie snapped.

"I suppose I should not begrudge your having the last word, Elysia," he countered smugly. "After all, it is quite evident now who has won this race."

"Only by cheating."

"You never could tolerate losing."

"Go on in," Ellie taunted. "I dare you. See what you can find . . . if you can get past the skeletons and the traps, you bastard."

"Skeletons? Traps? Surely you jest." He pursed his lips nervously.

Ellie spoke with the voice of doom. "That's not even the half of it. There are also spiders. Big ones. And open pits that I suspect are bottomless."

Her stubborn, spitfire courage amazed Matt. He squeezed her hand. "That's enough, Ellie."

"But he will destroy everything," she hissed.

The pain in her voice made Matt's heart tighten. The treasure meant more to her than the wealth and fame he had once suspected her of courting. Its discovery touched her very deeply. She wanted to protect the treasure. He wished desperately he could make it all right for her.

"We have bigger things to worry about right now."

She nodded.

Glaring at Clive, Matt said forcefully, "You don't have any reason to hurt Ellie. Just me."

Clive glanced at the cave opening. "Looks like I don't have any reason to keep her around, neither. Not anymore." He spit tobacco juice. "But a pretty thing like that might prove useful for something. I'll give it some thought after you're gone, Devereaux."

The leer on Clive's face made Matt's skin crawl. It apparently had the same effect on Ellie, for her fingers dug into his forearm behind his back.

Sam dismounted. He took off his gun belt and hung it across his saddle. Then he drew his knife—the one he'd used to torture Matt when they staked him at the ant hill.

"Come on, gambler man," Sam goaded, weaving the knife through the air. Sunlight rippled along the polished steel blade. "I'm going to prove who's the best."

Matt pressed the gun into Ellie's hand. He whispered, "There's only one shot left. Don't waste it."

"Matt," she choked as he moved away, her voice thick with emotion.

If he died today, at least he had the satisfaction of knowing he mattered to her. Thank heavens she didn't try to hold him back or shed tears. He didn't think he could concentrate on the fight ahead if she cried.

His Bowie knife slid smoothly from its sheath. The horn handle balanced in his hand. This was the one benefit of his time with the Comancheros—a man didn't survive in their company unless he could prove his skill with a knife.

A strange calmness flowed through Matt's body. His world focused in on Sam Hayley and the blades.

Sam grinned malevolently. "I've been looking forward to this." He started to circle, searching for a weakness.

Matt swore he wouldn't find one. "You always were a lot of talk and little action, Sam."

The outlaw lunged. Matt twisted smoothly. The blade passed a few inches from his belly. He countered with a cut across his attacker's arm.

Air hissed between Sam's tobacco-stained teeth. "Shit! You'll pay for that."

They circled, taking each other's measure. Once more, Sam initiated the attack. Matt parried and struck in a countermove to drive him back.

Again and again knives flashed, cutting and slashing, reflecting sunlight in a macabre dance. Blade struck blade with a grating of metal. Muscles strained as the combatants sought to throw each other off balance. When they broke apart, the wet sheen of blood marred a razor-sharp edge. Usually it was the same blade that came back triumphantly stained.

Sam grew more frenzied every time Matt's knife scored a cut while his did not. The outlaw flung himself into the fight like a lumbering bull. Matt conserved his energy. Not a movement was wasted, not an opportunity lost.

Sam started to exhale in hard gusts. His ponytail clung to the sweat dripping down his neck.

"You're fading," Matt challenged softly.

"Like hell I am."

Matt lunged, leaving a deep gash across Sam's ribs.

"I never lose, Devereaux," the younger Hayley snarled.

Wrenching back, Sam shoved his free hand into his right boot and withdrew a double-shot derringer. He took aim. His finger tightened around the trigger.

"No!" Ellie screamed.

She lifted Matt's Colt and fired.

The bullet's impact flung Sam onto his back. A red stain blossomed across his shirt. His last breath rattled from his shattered chest.

Matt whipped around, his heart thundering in his ears. Ellie had just sacrificed her only shot . . . and she'd used it on Clive's brother.

"You bitch!" Fury turned Clive's face a mottled red. He leveled his gun at her forehead.

Ellie flung herself to the side in a futile attempt to avoid the deadly end of the revolver. Matt rushed forward, though he knew he could never reach Clive in time to—

A single gunshot cracked through the ravine.

A bellow of rage and denial built in Matt's throat . . . then stopped as Ellie rose to her feet, unharmed.

Clive pitched forward off his horse and hit the ground. A red hole appeared between his shoulder blades.

Matt and Ellie turned to look at the top of the cliff.

A tall, dark-haired man sat astride a sorrel gelding. A thin curl of smoke wafted from the revolver in his hand. The epaulets of his uniform sat squarely on his broad shoulders.

Peter, who up to this point had been a silent spectator, spurred his horse and quickly disappeared around the bend in the ravine.

Ellie stared up at the uniformed man. Her relieved expression changed into one of stunned dismay. Matt immediately suspected the identity of the newcomer. The irony of this man saving Ellie's life rose like bile in his throat.

Enrique Salazar offered a mock salute. "Señorita Carlisle, we meet again."

Chapter 22

SIX SOLDIERS CAME up from behind the Mexican captain, three on each side. Matt held himself rigidly. Adrenaline still pumped through his system, keeping him poised for battle. Without the intervention of this man, Ellie would be dead, yet the arrival of the soldiers composed a new threat.

"Bloody hell," Ellie whispered.

Salazar raised his gun again and pointed it at them. "I think you should wait there while my men come down. You will do this, no?"

"Like we have a choice," Matt muttered.

A quick order sent the soldiers searching for a path down into the ravine, while Salazar maintained his position and his guard. Matt and Ellie took the warning seriously, not moving.

"Sorry about the hombre," Salazar called down. "But I do not think he was a friend. He was about to shoot a woman, who is also my prisoner. This I could not allow."

Ellie cleared her throat. "If you will just come down here, Capitán Salazar, I can explain everything."

His teeth flashed in his dark beard. "Yes. I am sure you will try. But this will not change the fact that some very valuable artifacts belonging to my country are missing."

Matt crossed his arms and glared at her. "You told me Peter stole the artifacts. You didn't bother to mention that the Mexican authorities knew about it and were after you."

Ellie snapped, "It was something I preferred to forget."

The soldiers reached the floor of the ravine and took over guarding Matt and Ellie. Salazar began his own descent.

"The capitán's job was to make sure the Mexican government received the artifacts," Ellie explained. "How could I explain they were gone, destroyed? I had to sneak out of Mexico City to avoid arrest. I always knew Salazar was a persistent man, but I never thought he would follow me all the way here, into American territory."

"Well, lucky for us he did."

She looked at him, startled. Realization dawned quickly in her green eyes. "Salazar saved my life."

"Yes, he did. Clive was too far away for me to reach him in time, Ellie." Gruffly, Matt added, "Why didn't you tell me?"

"When I left Mexico, I put that ugly incident behind me and focused on reaching Montezuma's treasure before Peter could."

"I wish you'd trusted me with the story before we left Santa Fe."

She gasped. "That's when you asked me those odd questions about critical facts and things left undone. How did you know?"

"Seth sent a telegram from Albuquerque, warning me Salazar was looking for you."

Her fists settled on her hips. Her eyes narrowed. "And you didn't think to pass a warning on to me? You thought I would appreciate the surprise?"

Matt realized he'd withheld something she had a right to know. He'd been too preoccupied with his own anger. "I was hoping you'd tell me first."

"How could I share something that wasn't even on my mind?"

"I dropped some heavy hints," he grumbled.

"Oh, hints. I should have guessed." Throwing her hands in the air, she exclaimed heatedly, "Of all the stupid, proud things to do—"

"Why didn't you trust me?" Matt cut in, letting his frustration show.

Ellie hesitated. She lowered her hands and met his gaze with regret. "It was also rather embarrassing that I, a dedicated archaeologist, was accused of stealing antiquities. Sharing that part of my past left me feeling . . . vulnerable. And don't try to claim that I know everything about your past, Matt Devereaux," she challenged.

Shame cut through him like a hot knife. She was certainly right about that.

"Children," interjected a deep voice. "Are you finished arguing?"

Startled, they turned. Salazar sat his sorrel gelding just five feet away. Matt got his first close look at Enrique Salazar. A thin scar marred the man's face, starting above the left cheekbone and dipping into the beard. His eyes were an unusual, striking shade of light gray.

Recognition hit Matt like a lightning bolt. The memory reared, ugly and vivid—a scene of violence, gunfire, and screams, and an enraged, grieving teenage boy with the desire for vengeance in his vivid gray eyes and a knife in his hand. The Comanchero had laughed as he cut the

Mexican youth's cheek with his saber. Then the bandito had pulled his gun to finish the boy off. Matt remembered his sudden rage as he'd witnessed the scene from across the village square.

He'd fired his gun without thinking, consumed with hatred for the Comancheros who had dragged him into that hell. The satisfaction of killing one of the men who'd enslaved him was immediately followed by the cold, stark realization that escape was no longer a dream, but an urgent necessity. Either flee or die for killing one of their own.

A horse's snort wrenched Matt back to the present, leaving him in a cold sweat. He'd hoped to put that nightmare behind him forever, but it seemed inevitable that his past catch up with him.

Salazar frowned. "You look familiar to me, muchacho. We have met before, no?"

Matt schooled his expression, calling on all his experience at bluffing to return a neutral gaze. "I don't think so."

He knew his face had changed significantly from the lean appearance of a seventeen-year-old. In addition, he no longer wore a beard. Salazar too had changed noticeably. Without the scar and the strange gray eyes, Matt wouldn't have recognized him.

The Mexican officer's stare narrowed, seeking the elusive memory Matt didn't want him to find. But first he needed to focus on the danger to Ellie.

"You're after the wrong person, Capitán," Matt said. "That coward who just rode out of here is the one who stole your artifacts, not Ellie. His name is Peter Wentworth."

Salazar's brows arched as he looked at Ellie. "And why should I believe this?"

"Because it is true. It grieves me to tell you, but Peter

melted down all the artifacts. By the time I found out, he had already destroyed every piece and disappeared with the gold."

"So you are saying you fled Mexico City because you could not restore the artifacts to us?"

Ellie nodded.

After considering for a moment, Salazar countered, "Even if this is true, you agreed to take responsibility for the tomb, did you not?"

Swallowing hard, Ellie squared her shoulders. "I did."

"If one of my men accidentally shot an innocent villager, would I not be responsible as his senior officer?"

They stared at each other. Matt sensed a change in Ellie—a flash of guilt, a hint of acceptance.

"I always sensed you were a man of integrity, Capitán," she said softly. "Now I know for sure." Leaving Matt's side, she stepped to the sorrel gelding.

"What the hell are you doing?" Matt growled.

She turned to him, her eyes tortured but her expression calm. "I am ultimately responsible, Matt. I've known that all along. Perhaps I should go back to Mexico and face the consequences."

"There are no consequences, dammit. Your only crime was in trusting the wrong person."

"Salazar saved my life. Am I supposed to ignore that?" She glanced longingly at the cave. "Take care of that for me, will you? Don't let Peter get to it."

"This is crazy," Matt said through clenched teeth. "You're not going anywhere." He stepped forward. Immediately, six rifles pointed directly at his chest.

"Promise not to hurt him!" Ellie demanded of Salazar.

"As long as he does not attempt to kill one of my men. At the moment, he looks as if he might try to do so with his hands alone."

"Promise me you won't try anything, Matt," she pleaded. "It would destroy me to see you die."

Even if he could have found an adequate answer, he couldn't force a sound past the sudden lump in his throat.

She thrust her wrists toward Salazar.

He smiled briefly. "I do not intend to shackle you, señorita."

"Oh." She lowered her hands. "Well, that is a relief."

"Ellie, we'll find a way out of this," Matt said.

She mounted her horse. "No, this is my problem. I have to solve it on my own. Besides, it is safer for you this way. You shouldn't be involved or take any more risks on my behalf."

"Now, what to do with you?" Salazar muttered, eyeing Matt thoughtfully.

"Put me on my horse and send me on my way?"

Salazar shook his head. "For you, that would not be enough. You will try to follow, no?" He barked a series of orders to his men in Spanish.

Matt understood every word. He swore under his breath.

The six soldiers dismounted. Two held their rifles on Matt, while the four others headed for a flat slab of rock broken from the wall of the ravine.

"Forgive me, muchacho, but I see no other choice. I cannot allow you to follow us and attempt to regain the señorita. I will leave your belongings here, and I will make sure the sheriff in Santa Fe knows of your location," he added as the two armed men forced Matt back to the mouth of the cave. "They will come and release you."

Matt's attention flew to Ellie. A tight knot formed beneath his breastbone at the sight of her.

"You swear to that?" Ellie demanded of Salazar.

"I swear."

She nodded, apparently satisfied that the capitán was a man of his word.

Two fat tears rolled down her cheeks as she turned to face Matt. "Goodbye. I didn't think it would—" Her voice broke.

That it would end like this. Matt realized he hadn't really believed it would end at all. He couldn't imagine a future without her.

"Ellie," he whispered fiercely. He knew all too well the bottomless pits called Mexican jails, where a man could disappear for years. How much more vulnerable would a woman be?

Matt lowered himself into the cave, two rifles still trained on him at point-blank range. The four other men dragged the large, flat rock up the slope. Grunting under the weight, they levered it into position.

"Salazar!" Matt roared as the stone slid into place, cutting off all but thin slivers of light.

Chapter 23

MATT PUT HIS shoulder against the stone and shoved with all his strength. He had just detected a slight movement when his feet slipped. He crashed to the floor.

Swearing, he rose and started climbing to the blocked opening. The cave wall offered few footholds. One way or another, however, he was going to move that damn stone. Every minute he delayed meant Salazar was getting farther away with Ellie.

Just as he repositioned his shoulder, the dangling end of a rope slipped through the narrow opening on one side.

"Pass it around the stone," a muffled voice called out.

Although suspicious, Matt decided he could deal with unpleasant surprises later. Right now, the critical thing was to move that slab of rock. He shoved the end of the rope up through the crack of sunlight on the opposite side. He heard a shout. A horse whinnied. Moments later the stone slid free.

Brilliant sunlight cut through the cloud of dust. Matt shielded his eyes. He recognized Peter.

Light glinted off the nickel-plated revolver in the Brit's hand. "In a bit of a sticky wicket there, aren't you, Devereaux?" Peter called down snidely.

Matt eyed him like a bug he would dearly love to squash. "You missed all the excitement," he retorted.

"Is that what you call this barbaric display?" Peter cast a meaningful look at the dead bodies in the ravine. "I ought to thank you for disposing of the Hayley gang for me. They really were proving a deuced bother."

"If you really want to thank me, make sure Ellie doesn't take the blame for your crime."

"Surely you are not suggesting I should confess to that boorish Mexican captain?"

"No, actually. I don't expect that of you." Matt crossed his arms, despite the gun pointed at his face. "That would take courage, and you don't have a single noble bone in your body, Wentworth."

Anger flashed in Peter's eyes and reflected in the curl of his lip. "You should be more concerned for your own fate at the moment. I find myself without any labor to carry the treasure down the mountains. You just volunteered, Devereaux."

The gun trembled in Peter's rigid hand, giving Matt a new respect for the danger he faced. Although Peter had a profound distaste for violence, his mental stability was in serious doubt.

Matt's way out was to appeal to the man's most fundamental motivation.

"Don't you want to see it?" he coaxed.

Peter eyed the dark tunnel behind Matt. "Bring it out to me," he ordered.

"What's to prevent me from staying in there? And how are you to know if I bring out everything, or leave the best pieces behind?"

"Bollocks," Peter hissed. "Do not toy with me."

"This is hardly a game, not with that kind of fortune."

Peter licked his lips. "How much gold is there?"

"Like nothing you've ever seen—pieces so pure you can press your fingernail into the soft metal, each one an object of art. Embedded jewels wink at you in the lantern light."

Peter swore again. "Very well. Back up then. I am coming down. You had better not try anything."

Matt backed up. He half smiled in anticipation.

"Show me," Peter insisted when he reached the cave floor.

Matt picked up the lantern he and Ellie had left in the cave. Moving quickly and confidently, he led the way. The lantern pushed back the darkness, encasing the two men—and the gun between them—in its light.

They quickly reached the first altar niche. From the sudden reddening of his face, it was evident Peter's first glance revealed nothing more to him than the grayish mass of decaying objects.

"What the bloody hell is this garbage?" Peter snarled. He kicked a stack of rotted blankets. A cloud of dust and brittle fibers rose. A small pot fell to the floor and shattered.

"Look closer," Matt countered softly. He shifted the lantern to shine directly on the hoarded treasures.

The dust began to settle. Gold gleamed on the shelves. Something flashed among the shards of the broken pot, winking up in vibrant shades of green. A heavy gold ring with a large, square emerald lay in the wreckage.

The air rushed out of Peter's lungs. His eyes glazed over. He bent to scoop up the ring.

It was the opportunity Matt had been waiting for.

In a lightning-quick move, he grabbed the barrel of the nickel-plated gun and jerked it from Peter's grasp. A right cross flattened his rival on the cave floor.

Matt planted his boot in the center of Peter's chest, pinning him down. He derived a great deal of satisfaction from pointing the revolver straight down the Brit's line of sight.

"I really ought to shoot you, you gutless son of a bitch."

"But you will not, Devereaux," Peter croaked. "You are not a killer."

Shame and guilt washed over Matt in icy waves. The memories of the Comanchero raid twisted in his belly like a knife. Innocent villagers had died horrible deaths all around him that day. It didn't matter that he'd fired over their heads deliberately. He'd been helpless to stop the slaughter.

Matt cocked the revolver. In a hoarse whisper, he challenged, "How can you be so sure?"

Peter stared. For a change, the man seemed incapable of a clever, cynical response.

Disgust filled Matt. He removed his foot. "Get up."

Peter scrambled to his feet. "There is no need for us to fight, Devereaux. This alone is a small fortune, but surely there is more?"

"Oh, yes. Quite a bit more."

"There, you see? We can split the treasure and become rich men." His eyes gleamed. "Beyond our wildest dreams."

Matt shook his head. "You really are lower than a snake's underbelly, you know that?"

"This is more money than you will see in a lifetime," Peter said sourly.

"I've never really needed more than the efforts my

own two hands could provide. And right now, all I care about is getting Ellie back safely."

"Give this up for that frigid little bitch? Are you mad?"

Gravely, Matt answered, "No. I'm more sane than I've ever been."

"You are a fool, Devereaux. Now what?"

"First, you're going to give me those talismans you stole. They may have served their purpose, but they mean a great deal to Ellie. Hand them over."

Peter snatched the two stones from a pocket and threw them at Matt. The ribbon and the leather string were entangled, causing the talismans to twirl around each other like a bola. Matt neatly snagged the central knot of the strings in midair. The stones spun around his hand and clicked together. He dropped them inside an empty vase on one of the stone shelves.

"I'll just leave them here so Ellie can retrieve them when she comes back. Now, we're going to catch up with Capitán Salazar and his men."

"Why? We have few weapons and little chance of besting seven men."

"I plan to avoid a gunfight at all costs. Ellie might get hit in the crossfire."

"Then what? Do you have some semblance of a plan in that provincial Yank head of yours?"

"You mentioned a confession."

Peter blanched. "You think Salazar will believe me? How naïve of you. The man already has his prize," he argued with a new measure of desperation in his tone. "What makes you think he will take me in exchange?"

"One way or another," Matt said darkly, "Enrique Salazar is going to release Ellie."

. . .

MATT EMERGED FROM the cave to discover that the soldiers had left his horse, as Salazar promised. None of his belongings had been touched. He quickly retrieved his rifle and revolver and reloaded them. He tucked Peter's gun into his waistband for added insurance.

"Mount up," he ordered the sulking Brit. "And don't push my patience any further than you have already."

They took off at a canter along the soldiers' trail. Matt stayed to the rear, always with a clear shot at Peter's rigid back.

Sooner than Matt expected, they caught up with the Mexicans. He forced Peter to circle around, then they cut through the trees and emerged onto the trail directly in the path of the soldiers.

Two soldiers shouted a warning. The whole company reined in their horses. Ellie's expression was a mixture of relief and anger at Matt's interference. He'd expected no less.

"Very clever, Señor Devereaux," Salazar conceded. "I congratulate you on your escape."

"I brought you something in trade," Matt said gruffly.

"Ah, yes, now I remember Señor Wentworth. A very arrogant man. He was not well liked in Mexico City."

"I say now—" Peter started to protest.

"A fair exchange," Matt continued. "The real culprit for Miss Carlisle."

"I am sorry, but there is no proof of the señorita's claim that Señor Wentworth destroyed the artifacts. Even if this is so, she is still responsible for the loss. I cannot agree to your trade."

"I told you," Peter crowed.

"Shut up, Wentworth."

Matt clenched his teeth, his frustration growing. He

couldn't allow Ellie to go with Salazar. He'd spent two years of his youth running and hiding with Comancheros in Mexico, and he knew how easily someone could disappear. The chances that he would find her once she crossed the border were slim to none. But how could he prevent it? He couldn't start a gunfight and count on her to come out unscathed.

Ellie had shown the courage to surrender herself and face the consequences of her poor judgment. His haunting mistake years ago eclipsed her error. If anyone deserved punishment, it was he.

It was time to stop running from his past.

"You thought you recognized me earlier, Salazar," Matt offered darkly. "You must have been right, because I sure as hell recognized you."

The officer's eyes narrowed.

"Remember? Fifteen years ago . . . your village . . . a Comanchero raid?" Matt pressed. "One of the bandits on horseback cut your cheek with his saber. He almost shot you."

The capitán's hand moved to the gun in his holster. Growing anger transformed his calm expression.

"Matt, what is going on?" Ellie asked nervously.

He ignored her, concentrating instead on his adversary. "I'd heard rumors that every Comanchero involved in the raid was hunted down over the next two years, tried, and hanged. Impressive. Did you do that yourself, or did you have help?"

"Only someone who was there would know such things."

"Picture me younger, with long hair tied back, and the kind of scraggly beard grown by a man not yet eighteen."

"Sí, I remember you now. I saw you as the smoke cleared. You turned your horse and rode in the opposite direction of the retreating Comancheros. Did you lose your way, gringo?"

"Now is your chance for justice to come full circle. Let Ellie go," Matt persisted, ignoring the taunt. "Take Peter in exchange. I offer myself as a bonus, as long as I have your word I'll receive a fair trial where I can speak my peace. No lynch mob."

Salazar pulled his gun. "What makes you think I will not kill you now?"

"Ellie has faith in you as a man of integrity, and I have faith in her judgment in men."

Shock overrode the confusion in Ellie's face. Considering her pattern of dismal judgment in men, he'd made the one pronouncement sure to surprise her. But he meant every word.

Ellie protested, "This can't be right, Capitán. What is Matt accused of?"

"Fifteen years ago a band of drunken Comancheros rode into my village, señorita. The people were tired of being bullied by these banditos. They tried to fight back. It was a mistake they all regretted. Many women were raped before they were murdered, including my mother and sister. By the time the shooting stopped, almost everyone in the village was dead. I was spared because the Comanchero who tried to kill me was shot down himself in the crossfire." Pointing an accusing finger at Matt, Salazar said furiously, "He was there."

"Matt?"

Her voice and eyes begged him to deny it. He couldn't. His throat felt as if he'd swallowed a handful of sand.

"I was there, Ellie," he admitted roughly. "People died all around me. I didn't do anything to stop it."

Horror dawned in her eyes. Her reaction didn't surprise Matt. His own did. He felt like he'd just been kicked in the teeth. He'd lost Ellie's respect and regard, and their demise left an emptiness inside him. He closed his eyes for a moment, wishing he could retract the words, but there was nothing he could do to take back what had happened.

Matt opened his eyes, but he still couldn't bring himself to look at her. "Do we have an agreement, Salazar? She goes free?"

"Yes, it is agreed. You have my word."

Matt nodded. He nudged Dakota forward. Four soldiers surrounded him. One took his revolver, rifle, and knife.

"Go, Ellie."

"I . . . I can't." She barely managed to choke out the words. "It wasn't supposed to be like this."

"Don't waste the chance, Ellie. If you don't go now, he'll take all three of us back to Mexico. Then what will happen to your discovery?"

"Here now," Peter protested as another soldier rode forward to grasp his horse's reins. "You apparently have what you really want, Salazar. There is no need for me to tag along."

Ignoring him, Salazar signaled his men to move out with the two prisoners. He turned to Ellie one last time.

"Good luck to you, señorita. I admire your courage. I shall speak to *el Presidente* on your behalf."

Ellie watched them ride away, too stunned to react. The story horrified her. All those people dead—women and children. But as the initial shock wore off she found herself less and less able to believe that Matt had been part of the killing . . . no matter what he said.

What, exactly, had he said? Her mind worked furiously,

recalling his bitter words: *People died all around me. I didn't do anything to stop it.*

Never, not once, had he confessed to killing any of the villagers. He'd expressed a painful regret instead. And his face . . . She knew Matt intimately enough to identify the anguish in his eyes, as well as a deep self-condemnation for being unable to stop the killing.

She remembered his heart-wrenching tale about being enslaved by the Comancheros. They had forced him to go on the raid. What could a seventeen-year-old boy have done to stop the slaughter? But knowing the man now, and the extreme demands he placed on himself, she had no doubt that he held himself responsible.

One of the banditos on horseback cut your cheek with his saber. He almost shot you, Matt had told Salazar.

Ellie gasped. Matt had seen it happen. Was the bullet that saved young Salazar the result of random crossfire, as the Mexican officer assumed, or had Matt fired the shot?

You turned your horse and rode in the opposite direction of the retreating Comancheros.

That must have been when he'd fled from the Comancheros' tyranny! Matt had condemned himself for taking advantage of the chaos to finally make good his escape. As if a seventeen-year-old could stand up to drunken, vicious outlaws, Ellie thought with fierce protectiveness.

He might have been there, forced to ride with the Comancheros, but he hadn't participated in the brutality. She believed in his innocence with sudden, piercing certainty. If he had tried to fight back, he would have died, and she would never have had the opportunity to know him.

To love him.

But how to stop the soldiers from taking Matt back to Mexico? How could she make Salazar listen to reason and see the truth, even through eyes glazed by an old desire for vengeance? She had nothing to offer in exchange that would interest Salazar in the least.

Or did she?

Her heart thundered with a surge of hope. She turned the pinto and galloped back along the trail.

THE SIGHT OF TWO riders on the way back to the cave caught Ellie by surprise. Relief filled her, however, when she recognized one of them as Seth Morgan.

She rode toward the men, knowing she could count on help from Matt's best friend. The identity of the other man remained a mystery until he tilted back his broad-brimmed hat.

"Derek!" Ellie exclaimed. She reined in her horse, stunned to see the familiar golden-blond hair, blue eyes, and handsome features of her brother. "Is it really you?"

He gave her a lopsided grin. "None other."

"Hello, Marshal Morgan."

"Ma'am," Seth acknowledged, tipping his hat.

Nudging the mare forward, Ellie gave Derek a quick hug. "What are you doing—?"

Realization dawned suddenly. Her smile sank like a stone, replaced with a look of suspicion. She pulled back.

"Father sent you, didn't he? You are the escort from Galveston."

"So much for warmhearted greetings," Derek said in a deep voice. "I volunteered, Ellie. It was either that or watch Father send someone with no respect for your feelings in the matter. I have had my own recent experience with Father's ultimatums."

"Well, all of that has to wait," she said heatedly. "I have something infinitely more important that requires your assistance. Both of you."

"Where's Matt?" Seth asked suspiciously.

"That is what I've been trying to tell you. The Mexican soldiers arrested him. They are taking him back to Mexico."

"Son of a bitch," Seth said.

"This would be the man you have been alone with for over two weeks?" Derek interjected, his voice filled with righteous indignation. "I say good riddance to him, then."

Ellie glared at Derek, then at Seth.

"I've been filling him in on the basics," Seth confessed.

"Obviously," she said dryly. "Really, Derek, I don't have time for you to play protective older brother. I love Matt, and you're going to help me rescue him."

Derek's sandy brows arched incredulously.

"Now, Seth," Ellie continued, taking charge, "they are taking the long way down out of the mountains. Matt showed me a shortcut on our way in. If we hurry, we can intercept them before they get too far." She scanned their gear, then added hastily, "We can use your mules and the two we had to leave behind, as well as the Hayleys' horses—"

"The Hayleys!" Seth exclaimed, reaching for his gun.

"Don't worry, they're dead," Ellie said impatiently. "But we have to hurry if we are to save Matt. Come on!" she finished, urging her horse into a gallop.

"Hey! Aren't you heading the wrong way?" Seth called out.

"No!" she shouted over her shoulder. "Now hurry!"

Derek exchanged a curious look with Seth and shrugged.

"She always was impulsive," Derek muttered.

The two men kicked their horses into a run.

Chapter 24

THIS GROWS TEDIOUS, Señorita Carlisle. Can you two not decide who is to stay and who is to go free?" Salazar snapped three hours later when Ellie, Derek, and Seth caught up with the soldiers.

The squad of men sat their horses in a semicircle behind their captain, closely guarding the prisoners, guns drawn. Antagonism crackled in the air as they stared at the cocked revolvers in Seth's and Derek's hands.

Straightening, Ellie said clearly, "We both go free— Matt Devereaux and I."

"I say, what about—?"

Cutting off Peter's protest, Salazar interjected, "A bold suggestion. However, I will not give Señor Devereaux up so easily." He shifted his gun higher on his thigh. Nodding toward Derek and Seth, Salazar asked, "Is our standoff to end in gunfire?"

"I won't allow anyone else to be injured because of me, much less die. I'm here to offer you an alternative."

He snorted. "You are a very brave woman, but as you have seen, this is one thing I will not bargain for."

"I guarantee you will find my suggestion very interesting," she said emphatically.

"Ellie," Matt said in a low, warning tone, "what the hell are you up to?"

"I know what I'm doing, Matt." His answering look reflected his doubts. "Trust me," she added softly, meeting his eyes. After a moment's hesitation, he nodded. The sudden warmth in his eyes sent a thrill fluttering through her stomach.

Ellie forged ahead. With her heart in her throat, she coaxed, "Are you not the least bit curious, Capitán?"

"Sí, a wise man always has room for curiosity. I will listen to your proposal. But I must warn you—there is nothing you could offer that would appeal to me."

"That remains to be seen. Now, how much do you trust your men? Are they absolutely faithful to you?"

"To the death."

"Nevertheless, this is something only you should see for now. I suggest you have them back away until we complete our business."

Salazar's black mustache slanted with his skeptical expression. "That would put me at a disadvantage, no?"

"I am not suggesting your men move beyond pistol range. Marshal Morgan and Derek will also put their guns away."

Seth holstered his revolver. Derek followed suit.

"You are all quite mad, do you realize that?" Peter declared. "Derek, I cannot believe you are listening to your sister."

"Ellie told me how you betrayed her, Peter," Derek countered. "At least that farce put an end to your engagement. I never did believe you deserved her."

Ellie glanced at her brother, startled by his show of support. So many years had passed since they spent any time together, she'd assumed Derek had grown indifferent.

Salazar barked orders at his men. Although the soldiers grumbled, they obeyed, moving back out of earshot, taking Peter with them. They left Matt astride his stallion in the open area between themselves and Salazar.

"Very well, Señorita Carlisle. What do you offer that could possibly interest me?"

"This, Capitán," she said softly, pulling her best bargaining chip from her saddle bag. She held out a jaguar war mask of enamel and gold.

Matt tilted his head back and groaned. "Ellie, not that. Don't do this."

Salazar's stunned expression quickly reverted to a scowl. "Do you think me a man who takes bribes, señorita?"

"No, I do not. I believe you are a man who loves his country. That is why I offer you all of this, Capitán Salazar, not for yourself but for Mexico and her people." She motioned Derek forward with his mule, then lifted the cover of one of the hastily stuffed packs. Gold glinted in the sunlight.

"Madre de Dios," Salazar whispered in awe.

"Montezuma's treasure, Capitán, the legendary artifacts the Aztecs spirited away from the conquistadores. It is a significant part of your history, your heritage. It has been hidden here for three centuries."

"You found this—you and Señor Devereaux?"

"Yes, on American territory. It is mine by right of discovery. I am willing to give it to you, in exchange for Matt, only because I trust you to see it safely home to Mexico. I believe you will protect the collection until it can be placed in a museum for all to see."

In a voice laced with regret, Salazar stated, "Señorita Carlisle, I cannot guarantee the treasure's safety, nor that it will remain intact. Mine is a poor country. The people, they are forever fighting one war or another. Mexico's government is corrupt much of the time. The pieces may slowly disappear, used to buy food or shelter or even ammunition."

"I understand that, sir, and it causes me distress to think of it. But these pieces whisper to me of human sacrifice and tradition, of inspired art, of a complex heritage only the descendants of the Aztecs can truly appreciate. I have come to realize this treasure belongs to Mexico and her people, not in London. I only pray that the best pieces will be preserved for all to see in a museum, or that one way or another, they will be used to benefit your people."

"Your proposal is very tempting."

"I ask only that you release Matt and never seek to arrest him again."

Salazar sighed heavily. "I cannot, Señorita. Señor Devereaux must go back to Mexico to pay for his crime. You heard what he has done. Horror was in your eyes."

"The story shocked me, I will admit. I may not know Matt Devereaux's past, but I know the man," she said fervently. "He simply is not capable of such wanton cruelty. When I recovered enough to stop and think, I realized I'd only heard your side of the story."

"He did not disagree with anything I said."

"He deliberately refused to defend himself so you would release me and take him instead," Ellie countered.

Matt interrupted gravely, "I was part of that raid. I've already admitted it." His voice softened as he added, "This is your dream, Ellie. Don't give it up."

"It *was* my dream. It's been replaced by something more important now." She looked at him, her heart in her eyes.

Hope flared in his expression for an instant, but then he shook his head.

"Did you kill any of the villagers?" Ellie insisted.

His face tightened, reflecting the force of suppressed emotions. He remained silent, unable to get past his self-condemnation. He clung to his stupid role of martyr with all his typical tenacity.

There was only one way around Matt's stubbornness and Salazar's assumption of his guilt.

Urging her horse forward, she grasped Dakota's reins and turned the stallion until Matt's back was to Salazar. The sight of Matt's bound wrists made her shudder. It was an ugly omen of things to come if her gamble failed.

She didn't ask Matt for permission. He wouldn't have granted it, of course. But she needed to shock Salazar into listening. She pulled out her knife and cut Matt's shirt open from collar to tail, exposing his bare back—complete with whip scars. She ignored Matt's muttered curse.

"Yes, Capitán, those are whip scars," she confirmed, responding to Salazar's stunned expression. "Surely you are aware the Comancheros were known for taking slaves. Willing participants typically do not sport signs of torture."

"Explain yourself, Señorita," Salazar demanded.

"I believe Matt is the one who deserves to explain himself." She reined Dakota back around, then gave Matt a pleading look. "I believe in your innocence, Matt. Describe what really happened that day."

He searched her face hungrily. At first he hesitated—a few tension-filled moments that made Ellie want to scream. Finally he spoke, his voice hoarse. He didn't take his gaze from Ellie's face.

"I was fifteen when they took me. They made me a slave, then beat me when I resisted. I found more subtle ways to defy them, which began to amuse them, then finally earned their respect. I was with the Comancheros almost two years when they asked me to ride as one of them."

Salazar watched Matt intently. Ellie prayed that the story was having the desired effect—and that the capitán truly valued the truth above all else, as she believed.

Matt's tone was bitter. "Saying no wasn't an option. If I refused, they would have shot me in the back without blinking."

Matt looked at Salazar. "When the shooting started in your village, everything quickly turned to chaos. I couldn't stop the killing. So I hid, hoping the Comancheros would think I died in the fighting, so I could slip away afterwards a free man. When the shooting stopped and they were gone, I came out of hiding. There were dead men all around me . . . but that wasn't the worst of it. It was the sight of the murdered women that made me vomit on the street." His jaw hardened. "So I knelt by the body of a woman and swore. I swore I would always protect women, that I would never willingly stand by while one was abused again."

Salazar's expression remained rigid, unreadable. "You are saying you shot none of the villagers? You expect me to believe this?"

Muscles twitched beneath Matt's eyes. "I fired over the villagers' heads, until the Comancheros lost sight of me in the fight. If I had not fired at all, they would have shot me."

Doubt still darkened the other man's face. Fear snaked through Ellie's stomach. Matt's life depended on her gamble paying off. Quickly she pointed out, "Capitán, Matt described how he first saw you when the Comanchero cut your cheek and pulled his gun to shoot you. Surely you don't believe it was mere random chance that the man was gunned down before he could kill you? Tell him how you shot that Comanchero, Matt."

Matt's jaw remained set. "Yes, I shot him. Hell, I had no choice but to run after that."

"Tell me where the Comanchero was hit," Salazar challenged, anger still threaded through his voice. "Only the man who killed him would know this."

"In the throat," Matt rasped. "Not that I meant to hit him there. I aimed for his chest, but he moved at the last second."

Salazar muttered a fervent oath. Then he demanded, "Why would you grieve for my people, for the women? You did not even know them."

Matt looked directly at him and snapped, "I didn't have to know your people to feel sorrow for wasted lives. But if you must know, I grieved just as much for myself, for the loss of my innocence, for the fact that I would carry their deaths on my conscience because I was helpless to stop the slaughter."

The two men glared at each other, the pain of raw memories flashing between them like heat lightning.

"They would have killed you if you tried to stop it," Ellie ventured softly. "You were only seventeen years old, Matt."

For several minutes, the only sound was the squeak of saddle leather as everyone shifted restlessly, awaiting Salazar's verdict.

"For fifteen years of my life, I have prayed that I would find you. You were the last."

"So you found me. Let's get on with it." Matt's patience was exhausted, his pride clearly wounded.

"Let me finish," Salazar said irritably. "I always wondered why that Comanchero was shot down the moment before he pulled the trigger."

Matt eyed the Mexican officer warily.

Salazar sighed. "It would appear I have wasted many years on hatred when my vengeance was already complete."

"You believe him?" Ellie asked eagerly. Her heart thundered in her ears.

"Yes, but I very much hope to never see him again. I will take your generous offer, Señorita Carlisle, and return this to its rightful home in Mexico." He signaled his men forward to take the lead ropes of the mules laden with treasure.

They were letting Matt go.

Suddenly faint with relief and exhaustion, Ellie started to sway. Matt and Derek urged their horses forward at the same instant. Derek reached her first. He grasped her arm to steady her.

The two most important men in her life stared at each other across her horse's neck.

"Ellie, who the hell is this guy?" Matt growled.

She smiled, relieved to finally have a problem easy to solve. "Don't you see the family resemblance? Meet my elder brother, Derek Carlisle."

Matt's brows rose. Derek scowled. They still stared at each other.

"Elysia, what about me?" Peter called out as the soldiers started to lead him away. "You cannot let them take me. Think of our families, our reputations! What will your father say?"

Derek answered for her, "Actually, Peter, considering what you have done, I think Father shall say it is a bloody good thing you are beyond his reach, otherwise he would horsewhip you himself."

"You always were a cheeky bastard, Derek."

Her brother grinned. "Yes, always."

Peter swore viciously.

A sense of guilt and responsibility prompted Ellie to say, "We shall tell your father of your whereabouts, Peter. No doubt he will buy the freedom of his only son and heir."

"Adios, Señorita Carlisle." Salazar tipped his hat. "To my regret, we shall likely never cross paths again."

Ellie felt a sadness beyond the loss of the treasure. Men with Enrique Salazar's integrity and devotion were rare. "Vaya con Dios, Capitán."

"Vaya con Dios. I wish you a safe return to England."

Chapter 25

SUNSET CAME QUICKLY. The four set up camp.

Matt was grateful for the darkness; he could ease the rigid control he'd maintained over his expression. As Seth and Ellie picked through the supplies and started a meal, Matt walked a short distance from the camp. It wasn't as if anyone had burdened him with questions or conversation since they'd parted company from Salazar and his men. On the contrary, no one had said a word. He just needed some solitude to sort through the thoughts and questions threatening to tear him apart.

Ellie had given up Montezuma's treasure for him—her dream, the goal that had driven her to surmount every obstacle. Why? Gratitude for what he'd sacrificed to protect her and the treasure? Something more?

He sat on a flat-topped boulder. Locking his hands around his bent knees, he looked up. Stars brightened the black bowl of the sky with flickering pinpoints of light. The moon had yet to rise.

She had believed him. He would remember her spirited defense of his role in the Comanchero raid for the rest of his life. It had helped him confront the past and acknowledge the cold yet forgivable reality of his helplessness that day. He would always regret that he couldn't have done more to help the villagers, but his own death would have served no purpose.

Matt's emotions swung wildly between elation at Ellie's trust and frustrated fury because her quest had ended unrewarded. He had wanted her to have Montezuma's treasure so badly he could taste it.

There was only one explanation for this fierce protectiveness that gnawed at his insides, this desire to place her happiness above his own. Despite knowing he didn't really deserve her, he loved Ellie, and would continue to do so until his last breath. He couldn't imagine a future without her.

The soft tread of boots warned him he was no longer alone. Ellie's brother stood beside him, his head also tilted back to watch the stars. Matt's mouth twisted in a cynical smile. The moment of reckoning was here. But that suited him just fine. He had his own compelling reasons to talk to Derek Carlisle.

He decided to aim straight for the center of the target.

"I want to marry your sister, Carlisle."

The intervening silence challenged Matt's patience to its limit.

"Does she wish to marry you?" Derek finally asked in a hard, unforgiving tone.

"I haven't asked her yet. I prefer to approach her knowing I have the support of her family."

"I believe it is more customary to gain a father's blessing."

"Well, her father isn't here. You are." Matt stood, slowly unfolding long limbs stiff with tension. He faced Derek, eye to eye. "And considering that he made her promise to return home and marry some lord or other, I'm hoping my odds might be better with you."

"Ellie has reached her majority. She no longer requires permission to wed. If she chooses to accept you, I cannot stand in her way."

Muscles tightened in Matt's jaw. "But you'd like to, wouldn't you?"

In a voice that shook with resentment, Derek challenged, "You certainly didn't wait to ask for my blessing before you bedded her."

Matt winced at Derek's bald statement, but he responded strongly, "If that was all I wanted from her, I would be long gone by now. And don't expect me to say I regret it, because I don't."

"Is that meant to convince me?"

"Not that alone. I can support her quite comfortably."

"In the style and society she is accustomed to?"

A flush climbed up Matt's neck. He was grateful that the darkness hid his reaction. He felt increasingly defensive. "I can't promise that, but if she's so keen on your aristocratic society back in England, why has she spent the last few years avoiding it?"

"Because she is independent, headstrong, and hasn't always known exactly what she wants," Derek snapped back. "But that doesn't change the fact that she is the daughter of an earl. Certain responsibilities, as well as certain privileges, come with the position. It is bred into the blood."

"Well, I can offer her something your high society can't," Matt growled. "I can allow her to continue pursuing what she loves most—archaeology."

The other man watched him silently for several moments. "And what about a home? Children?"

The question jarred Matt like a blow to the skull. He'd

been so caught up in protecting Ellie, in sharing her passion, that he hadn't thought ahead to the prospect of kids. "I'd love to have children. If she doesn't want them, however, I'm willing to accept that."

"Can you offer them stability? Can you provide the love of a large family—grandparents, aunts, uncles, and cousins who aren't an ocean away? Can you duplicate the support of Ellie's family and friends?"

Matt stiffened. Anger knotted in his chest because he had no argument to offer.

A family was the one thing beyond his ability to give Ellie—and the one thing he had profoundly felt lacking for most of his life. He knew only too well how it felt to lose loved ones, to be bereft of family, alone and adrift in the world. He wanted her to be truly happy—but could she be, cut off from those she loved? Derek had made it quite clear that her family wouldn't accept him into their aristocratic fold.

The fresh doubt reinforced his nagging fears, bringing them to the surface. He had come to terms with his past, and found forgiveness in Ellie's trust, but that didn't change the fact that they were from vastly different worlds. No matter how much he wanted to shelter her, he was a no-account gambler, a man without a home.

He didn't need Derek to say the words. Matt knew that if he truly loved Ellie, he wouldn't ask her to make that sacrifice.

ELLIE WAITED FOR more than two hours for Matt to return to camp. Several times she started to search for him, only to stop and convince herself he needed the time alone. Finally, she lost the battle against exhaustion. She slept until dawn kissed the sky.

The first sight to meet her eyes was Matt saddling Dakota. Seth was cooking breakfast.

A sense of uneasiness spread through her. With her heart beating loudly in her chest, she rose and asked the marshal, "Is Matt leaving?"

Seth scowled. "Yes. There's no accounting for that man's stubbornness. I'll be going with him. Got business I have to attend to. Now that you have your brother to look after you, Matt and I'll be leaving right after breakfast."

"But . . . I don't understand." She hadn't expected Matt to leave so quickly. She'd thought, now that the danger was past, they would have time together.

"You and me both, ma'am."

Ellie smoothed her rumpled clothes and rebraided her hair. She took Matt his breakfast.

"I brought you a plate," she said breathlessly.

"Thanks." He avoided her eyes. Nodding toward his bedroll, he added, "Just set it down there."

Ellie did as he suggested, taking those few precious seconds to revise what she'd planned to say. She hadn't expected him to be so aloof, and that made her uncertain of the best way to convince him she should stay. Until she was sure of his feelings, she decided, a neutral approach would be best.

"I've been thinking about staying in New Mexico for a while," she ventured. "The land is harsh, yet extraordinarily beautiful."

He finished cinching the saddle. Sliding his rifle into the boot, he said idly, "What about your promise to your father?"

His words triggered a chill in her heart. Didn't he care? She wanted to tell him she would defy her father in only one respect—by marrying where she wished, whom she wished. But Matt had never asked her to marry him—never indicated his feelings went beyond cherishing her and treasuring the passion and adventure they'd shared. To introduce the idea of marriage would come perilously close to begging. Her pride rebelled. She wanted Matt desperately, but only if he felt the same.

"I haven't forgotten," she said huskily. "I was just hoping it could be fulfilled a little differently."

He turned to her then, his voice low and sincere. "You have more integrity than anyone I've ever known, Ellie Carlisle. Your family needs you. You'd never forgive yourself if you broke that oath."

He was urging her to leave. Her hope that he might love her withered.

"No, I suppose not," she whispered.

MATT AND SETH were riding away from camp when Matt suddenly paused, reining in Dakota. He twisted in the saddle and looked at Ellie silently, his expression unreadable.

It was the longest minute of Ellie's life. She lifted her chin and struggled to control her emotions. She wouldn't cry until he was gone . . . until she could find a moment of privacy. Her throat convulsed.

Then Matt turned and rode away.

"Are you coming home with me now?" Derek asked softly, breaking the silence.

"Yes, of course. That is what you came here for, isn't it? To take me home to the staid, restricted life you've done your utmost to escape," she said bitterly.

A muscle twitched under his eye. "Ellie, I'm not going to force you to go with me. If you want to stay, just say so. But I cannot guarantee Father won't send someone else after you."

"Where else would I go?" she countered morosely. "Montezuma's treasure is gone. There is nothing left for me here. Can we—" Her voice caught on a sob. Ellie bit the inside of her lip to still its sudden trembling. "May we leave now?"

"ARE YOU SURE you don't want to come back to Albuquerque with me?" Seth prodded. "There might be something worth your while passing through town real soon. There's a certain amount of predictability in being the major train stop in the territory."

The two men sat their horses at the point where the trail split, one path heading southwest toward Santa Fe and the other heading north.

Matt ignored Seth's heavy hint. He didn't want to risk seeing Ellie again. If he did, he might abandon the last of his good sense and do something desperate and unforgivably selfish—like kidnap her. If only she'd argued with him to stay, and offered reassurances to overcome his tormented doubts. He knew he shouldn't expect those reassurances, yet he needed them just the same. Unless she loved him, he had no right to ask her to make the sacrifices required for them to stay together. She'd never said anything about loving him.

Right now, he needed someplace peaceful and isolated to lick his wounds.

"No," Matt answered dully, looking north. "I'm going to stay in the mountains for a while."

"Sounds lonely," the marshal commented.

Matt winced.

Mercifully, Seth changed the subject. "Well, it's time for me to collect the Hayleys' bodies and take them in for burial." He grimaced. "I hate that part of the job."

"At least they won't be causing any more trouble."

"There is that." Nonchalantly, Seth added, "They had quite a hefty reward on their heads, you know."

"Give it to Ellie," Matt said gruffly.

"I already offered. She refused, rather strongly."

"Well, I don't want the money either."

"It could pay for a voyage to England."

Matt's eyes narrowed. "You're treading where you don't belong, Morgan."

"Just a thought."

"Then maybe you should avoid thinking altogether."

Seth snorted. "Hell, if there was ever such a stubborn, blind—" He gathered up his reins. "I'll see the money is deposited in your account. Just in case."

He wheeled his horse and trotted away.

"Dammit, Seth," Matt called after him, "I said I don't want the money."

"Then maybe you should figure out what you do want, my friend," Seth shouted over his shoulder. "As soon as you finish feeling sorry for yourself out here, come to Albuquerque and pay me a visit."

MATT WATCHED AS the cougar kittens frolicked across the meadow. They tumbled over one another in a mock fight, their attempts at growls more amusing than ferocious.

Not even the hint of a smile cracked the granitelike expression on his face. The pain of losing Ellie penetrated too deep, swallowing the pleasure he'd hoped to find in the kittens' antics, swallowing joy of any kind.

Thank you for sharing this with me, she'd said.

Matt dropped his head in his hands. Pain lanced through his chest, stealing his breath. He'd been lonely most of his life, but nothing like the last three days. His future stretched before him, cold and empty.

I shouldn't have let her go.

The thought slipped in for the hundredth time. Of course he should have, his logic instantly countered, it was better for her this way. She deserved so much more than he could offer.

Driven by a restlessness he couldn't control, Matt left the valley that afternoon. He had to find a place where memories of Ellie didn't reign, where he didn't hear her sultry voice, or smell her lilac soap, or remember the way their bodies had lain entwined, spent with passion.

Before he realized what he was doing, he found himself at the base of Table Top ridge. Grimly, he looked up, acknowledging why he'd come here. He wouldn't be satisfied until he pursued a quest of his own. He climbed to the top and retrieved the three talismans still in the map. He wrapped the stones together in a handkerchief.

But the talismans were only the beginning of the dream that had thrown him and Ellie together. He suddenly felt driven to follow it to its conclusion. Descending from the ridge, he mounted Dakota and followed another familiar route.

The depths of the cave revealed the scene of a lovingly yet quickly ransacked treasure trove. Despite her haste, Ellie had carefully picked through the artifacts to remove the pieces of value. Confronted with the visible evidence, Matt felt all the more humbled by the sacrifice she'd made to save him.

At first glance, only the decaying natural matter remained of the treasure. He explored further, carefully sorting through ancient items with a reverence he'd learned from Ellie. At the far end of the cave, hidden within some pottery, he discovered two overlooked items—a sculpture of a two-headed snake covered in turquoise and mother-of-pearl and a sacrificial obsidian blade with a hilt studded with jade and gold.

A shiver coursed through him. In his hands rested the last remnants of their quest together, artifacts that meant the world to Ellie and proved her search hadn't been totally in vain.

He couldn't let her leave for England without these precious pieces of history.

Matt tilted back his head. A groan slipped between his clenched teeth as he finally acknowledged his true purpose in coming here. He'd sought out the cave one last time to collect any remaining artifacts for Ellie, but not to send them to her. He was searching for an excuse to see her one last time.

Along with these special gifts, he would offer his heart.

If she refused him then, he would at least have the satisfaction of seeing her board her brother's yacht with these priceless mementos of her quest.

Driven by a renewed sense of urgency, Matt rode Dakota down from the Sangre de Cristo Mountains and on to Albuquerque, where he boarded the train east for Texas.

Ellie had several days' head start. With her brother's ship at their disposal, they could sail for England at any time.

Matt prayed he wouldn't be too late.

Chapter 26

ELLIE AND DEREK entered through the side door of the Tremont Hotel as they returned from an evening at Galveston's Grand Opera House.

"I apologize for not enjoying the opera more, Derek. It really was quite well done. Thank you for taking me."

He patted her hand where it rested in the crook of his arm. "Think nothing of it, little sister. I am simply pleased you went with me at all, rather than continuing to mope in your hotel room. It hurts me to see you like that."

Ellie felt fresh sorrow at the truth of his words.

"You really care for him, don't you?" Derek asked softly.

Her fingers flexed against the fine black material of his evening coat. "Yes. More than I can say." She didn't expect her open wounds to heal in just a week's time, but she hoped that soon she would discover a way to go on with her life.

They neared the point where the side hallway joined the rotunda lobby with its Corinthian columns and Italian marble floors. The sound of raised voices at the main desk caught Ellie's attention.

"I am sorry, sir, but we set a certain standard when it comes to hotel guests."

"I've proven I can pay. Are you saying my money isn't good enough?"

Ellie's breath froze as she recognized that deep, arrogant voice. Her fingers dug into Derek's arm as a tremor of disbelief and dawning excitement curled through her.

"Money is not the problem, sir. Frankly, it's your . . . er, appearance."

"There was no train scheduled beyond San Antonio. I had to ride the rest of the way on horseback, and I was in a hurry. How the hell do you expect me to look?"

"I sympathize with your situation. Nevertheless—"

Ellie heard the clerk squeak in surprise. She released Derek's arm and hurried across the lobby. Her brother followed at his leisure, an odd smile tugging at the corners of his mouth.

A very dirty, disheveled Matt held a fistful of the clerk's shirt in his powerful hand. He had pulled the hapless, wide-eyed fellow halfway across the counter.

"How do you like this close-up view of my trail dirt?" Matt growled in that familiar, sarcastic tone Ellie had missed so dreadfully. "Notice also the handmade silk shirt and embroidered vest beneath the grime, my friend, which should be right in keeping with your elite clientele's elegant form of dress."

"Uh, yes, Mr. Devereaux, that is a very nice shirt. However—"

"First, I need a room and a bath so I can clean up. After that, I want to leave a message for Miss Elysia Carlisle."

"I shall save you the trouble of delivering that message, Mr. Cassidy," Ellie offered softly.

366   *Kristen Kyle*

Matt froze, still holding the poor clerk sprawled across the counter. Matt gave her a hungry, passionate look that shot flames of desire to the tips of Ellie's toes. She felt giddy, lighthearted, and . . . cautious. He had come after her, but why? She couldn't let herself jump to conclusions.

A trembling smile touched her lips. "Matt, I believe you can let Mr. Cassidy go now."

Looking sheepish, Matt released the clerk.

"Mr. Cassidy, my brother and I will vouch for Mr. Devereaux. You do have a suitable room for him, I trust?" she coaxed with a charming smile.

"Yes, Miss Carlisle. Certainly. Number 36." He handed Matt a key with a sigh of relief.

They stepped away from the counter.

"Are you sure you don't want me to clean up first?" Matt muttered with a hint of embarrassment. "I'm not exactly pleasant to look at right now."

"I think you look perfect," Ellie whispered. He looked as if reaching her in Galveston had been his only goal for days—beyond comfort, beyond sleep. She'd never seen a more handsome or welcome sight.

Matt smiled in a way that made her fingers ache to stroke his lips. It took all of her willpower to keep her hands folded against the front of her sapphire-blue evening gown. She wouldn't let her hopes spiral out of control.

"I believe we've been in this situation before, though the roles were reversed," Matt teased.

The fact that he remembered pleased her. "The hotel in Albuquerque, when we first met."

He looked up and spotted Derek over her shoulder. Her brother watched intently from where he'd stopped on the opposite side of the lobby. Matt scowled.

Carpetbag in hand, Matt steered Ellie aside to a group of chairs beneath the rotunda's curved balcony. A large potted palm spread an umbrella of green fronds at their backs. He invited her to sit, then took the chair at her side.

"I brought you something."

He opened the carpetbag and pulled out three bundles wrapped in white cloth. He placed one in her lap. With a boyish grin, he urged, "Open it."

She unfolded the cloth. The three talismans from the map stared up at her. She'd forgotten all about them when she left New Mexico, her only focus on the pain of believing she would never see Matt again. Her throat tightened. Lightly, lovingly, she traced her fingertips over the familiar designs. Regaining possession of the stones didn't mean nearly as much as Matt's efforts, however.

The second bundle appeared next to the first, only half visible through sudden tears. Spreading aside the cloth, she discovered the snake and jaguar stones.

She looked up at Matt, startled. "The talismans Peter stole—you took them back from him. When?"

"When he tried to steal the treasure, and failed. I left them for you in the cave, thinking you would find them. You must have missed them."

"I was in a bit of a hurry."

His expression altered subtly. He set the talismans aside and handed her the third bundle. His rapt attention as she unwrapped the cloth caused Ellie's hands to tremble slightly. He was awaiting her reaction, but to what?

Her astonishment couldn't have been greater as she uncovered the turquoise and mother-of-pearl sculpture of a two-headed snake, as well as the finest obsidian blade she had ever seen. The pieces were exquisite examples of Aztec art.

"You overlooked these in the cave, thankfully," he said tenderly. "Now you have something to show for all your efforts."

She stared at the beautiful artifacts. At one time, their discovery would have meant everything to her. How dramatically her life and priorities had changed in the past few weeks! Her interest in the pieces suddenly waned. She raised her eyes to Matt's face.

"Is this why you came all this way, to give these to me? Was that the only reason?" If he said yes, Ellie swore, she would burst into tears or throttle him. Either one seemed a viable response to the turmoil in her heart.

He watched her for a moment, his gaze deep and searching. Then he shook his head. "No, I came because I had to see you. I've been miserable without you, Ellie. I can't accept your leaving without a fight."

"Why would you fight for me?" she asked in a throaty whisper.

His large hands curled over hers, warm and strong. The thrill of his touch—a touch Ellie had feared she'd lost forever—coursed through her with all the thundering power of a mountain waterfall.

"Because I love you," Matt answered softly.

Her heart skipped a beat, then pounded wildly with joy.

"I want you to stay here," he added with fierce determination. "I want you to marry me. Will you defy your father? Can you tolerate a scoundrel for a husband?"

The anxious expression on his face as he awaited her answer softened Ellie's heart even more. "I'll brave anything, as long as you are my scoundrel." She lifted one of his hands and pressed it to her cheek. "I love you, Matt Devereaux."

She thought he would devour her with the passionate, possessive hunger in his eyes.

The sound of footsteps fractured the mood. Derek strode up to them, his expression stern.

Matt carefully returned the artifacts to the bag. Then he rose, drawing Ellie up beside him. Despite the dirt, he held her close to his side with his arm secure about her shoulders. Ellie didn't mind at all.

"You may not like it, Carlisle," Matt said, confronting her brother, "but I intend to marry your sister."

"You think so?"

"Damn right I do." Matt's voice had dropped to a low rumble. "I asked her, and she said yes. I'd still prefer your permission, though. How can I prove I deserve her?"

Derek smiled. Humor unexpectedly lightened his blue eyes. "You just did, Devereaux. You came after her. I only needed to be certain that you love her." He turned toward the grand staircase. Pausing briefly, Derek said over his shoulder, "Though it took you long enough. If I had to watch her pine away for you much longer, I was going to come after you myself."

Chapter 27

MAYBE I SHOULD go," Ellie insisted two days later as she gripped Derek's hands. "I should face Father myself."

"You are twenty-seven years old, Ellie, past your majority. It's not as if you require his permission to marry."

"Still, I gave him my word."

"And you have honored it. As of this morning, you are married. That is all Father really wanted all along, to see you settled and happy with a man who will cherish you, and who deserves your respect."

"You're certain Father will be pleased with my choice of husband?" she asked uneasily.

Derek glanced over her shoulder at Matt, who stood several feet back on the dock to give brother and sister a private goodbye. The crisp sea breeze along the waterfront ruffled Matt's brown hair. His arms were crossed over his broad chest, his booted feet braced shoulder-width apart in the stance of a proud, noble man.

"Quite certain," Derek said with confidence. "You

know one of the main reasons Father pursued archaeology was to escape his boredom with his social class. He frequently complained the women were insipid creatures and the men vapid sportsmen who hadn't a thought beyond grouse hunting and their latest wager. I've always considered it a tremendous paradox that he encouraged you to marry one of them." He blew out a breath of disgust. "Thank goodness you didn't."

Ellie looked back at her husband. Pure male energy radiated from Matt. She still found it difficult to fathom that he was actually hers. They'd rushed the wedding, ostensibly so that Derek could give her away before he left, but their underlying impatience had been a lot more basic.

A ripple of desire left her body tingling. "Matt is anything but vapid," she said proudly.

"I think Father and Matt will get along famously when you come visit in a few months—when they are not butting two equally stubborn heads, that is. Give the old man grandchildren, Ellie, and he will swear your headstrong husband was his personal choice."

She blushed.

Derek chuckled. "Actually, I think it one of the great ironic justices of life that Winston Carlisle will end up with a rogue adventurer as a son-in-law."

"Perhaps that will not come as such a surprise. He already has one as a son."

"Me?" her brother exclaimed, arching his brows in innocence. "I am merely a staid, unexciting man of science."

She watched as Derek boarded his yacht, the *Pharaoh's Gold*, bound for England. Sorrow threaded through her at his departure. It had been so good to see her brother again, to know that she could still count on his support, and that the deep affection between them had not diminished over time or distance.

A solid warmth seeped into her back. With confidence, Ellie leaned back against Matt's chest. His arms came around her waist. Ellie folded her arms over his, locking herself within his secure embrace. They watched silently as the sails were hoisted on the *Pharaoh's Gold* and the sleek schooner eased out into the Gulf.

Then Matt tilted her head and gave her a long, searing kiss. "Are you ready to go back to the hotel and start our honeymoon, *querida*?"

"No," she said quietly, turning to slip her arms around his neck, "I'm ready to start the rest of our lives together."

Chapter 28

MATT SNUGGLED ELLIE closer against his side. Contentment washed over him like warm summer rain. Her breath caressed his shoulder. Her left thigh curved over his legs and settled against his loins. Matt felt his manhood stir. So much for feeling sated after a round of passionate lovemaking. He would never get enough of loving her.

A fresh, salt-scented breeze billowed the curtains in their fourth-floor hotel room. Late-afternoon sunlight filtered through the gauze, bathing the room in a soft white glow. Right now he desired nothing more than the feel of cool sheets at his back and the warm, supple presence of the woman he loved at his side.

Her left hand lay against the center of his chest. Matt reached down and toyed with the band of gold on her finger.

"I can't believe that after all the magnificent works of art you've seen, you chose this simple band."

"I prefer it. I don't need anything ornate to remind me that I love you . . . that I am yours."

"Always," Matt whispered fervently, "as I belong to you." He pulled her closer.

He expected Ellie to fall asleep quickly, replete from lovemaking. She didn't. He sensed ideas and plans churning in her quick-witted mind. Matt smiled indulgently.

"So, tell me what we're going after next."

Ellie lifted her head. Her green eyes sparkled. "Well, I've been studying the history of the pirate Jean Lafitte. He was supposedly one of the most successful and wealthy pirates of all time. And he lived right here in Galveston!" She propped herself up on one elbow, unable to contain her eagerness for the hunt. "There is evidence that Lafitte buried some of his booty near here. Just think of the historical significance of the things he must have stolen from the treasure ships of Spain!"

"Okay, okay." Matt chuckled at her enthusiasm. "I get the picture. All of it sounds good to me."

"You've caught the fever, haven't you?" she asked with smug satisfaction.

"And what fever would that be?"

"For archaeology."

"Really? That's a mighty fancy term for glorified treasure hunting."

She punched him lightly in the side. He grunted and clutched his ribs in mock pain.

Catching her thick blond braid, Matt wrapped it around his hand, shortening it to draw her closer. He untied the ribbon at the end and tossed it aside. The strip of white satin fluttered to the floor like angel's wings. As he spread her hair in a thick curtain of gold, he murmured huskily, "I'm actually concentrating on a much more consuming obsession right now." He stroked her cheek. "You are the fire in my blood, *querida*. I love you."

She smiled, her eyes filled with adoration in a way that still amazed and humbled him. Her palm slid over his taut stomach and paused over one hip. Matt sucked in his breath.

"I think it only fair to warn you, husband, there is no cure for that particular type of fever. I should know."

"Then I suppose we shall just have to burn together," he murmured, pulling her down to claim the soft paradise of her mouth.

About the Author

Kristen Kyle has always been a die-hard romantic. Although roses and dinner by candlelight are nice, what really ignites her imagination are stories packed with action, conflict, a headstrong heroine, a dark and dangerous hero, and, most of all, passion and love. Her goal is to provide the reader with a page-turner of a story. Kristen shares her home in a suburb of Dallas, Texas, with her two sons, both to-die-for heroes in the making.

Visit Kristen's web page at www.KristenKyle.com for the latest news, contest information, writing tips, and more, or send e-mail via Kristen@KristenKyle.com.

Bestselling Historical Women's Fiction

❏AMANDA QUICK❏

___28354-5 SEDUCTION . . . . .$6.99/$9.99 Canada

___28932-2 SCANDAL . . . .$6.99/$9.99

___28594-7 SURRENDER . . . .$6.99/$9.99

___29325-7 RENDEZVOUS . . . .$6.99/$9.99

___29315-X RECKLESS . . . .$6.99/$9.99

___29316-8 RAVISHED . . . .$6.99/$9.99

___29317-6 DANGEROUS . . . .$6.99/$9.99

___56506-0 DECEPTION . . . .$6.99/$9.99

___56153-7 DESIRE . . . .$6.99/$9.99

___56940-6 MISTRESS . . . .$6.99/$9.99

___57159-1 MYSTIQUE . . . .$6.99/$9.99

___57190-7 MISCHIEF . . . .$6.99/$8.99

___57407-8 AFFAIR . . . .$6.99/$8.99

___57409-4 WITH THIS RING . . . .$6.99/$9.99

❏IRIS JOHANSEN❏

___29871-2 LAST BRIDGE HOME . . . .$5.99/$8.99

___29604-3 THE GOLDEN BARBARIAN . . . .$6.99/$8.99

___29244-7 REAP THE WIND . . . .$6.99/$9.99

___29032-0 STORM WINDS . . . .$6.99/$8.99

Ask for these books at your local bookstore or use this page to order.

Please send me the books I have checked above. I am enclosing $_____ (add $2.50 to cover postage and handling). Send check or money order, no cash or C.O.D.'s, please.

Name _____

Address _____

City/State/Zip _____

Send order to: Bantam Books, Dept. FN, 400 Hahn Road, Westminster, MD 21157
Allow four to six weeks for delivery.

Prices and availability subject to change without notice.   FN 16 1/01

Bestselling Historical Women's Fiction

□IRIS JOHANSEN□

___28855-5 THE WIND DANCER ....$6.99/$9.99

___29968-9 THE TIGER PRINCE ....$6.99/$8.99

___29944-1 THE MAGNIFICENT ROGUE ..$6.99/$8.99

___29945-X BELOVED SCOUNDREL ....$6.99/$8.99

___29946-8 MIDNIGHT WARRIOR ....$6.99/$8.99

___29947-6 DARK RIDER ....$6.99/$8.99

___56990-2 LION'S BRIDE ....$6.99/$8.99

___56991-0 THE UGLY DUCKLING ....$6.99/$8.99

___57181-8 LONG AFTER MIDNIGHT .....$6.99/$8.99

___57998-3 AND THEN YOU DIE ....$6.99/$8.99

___57802-2 THE FACE OF DECEPTION ....$6.99/$9.99

□TERESA MEDEIROS□

___29407-5 HEATHER AND VELVET ....$5.99/$7.50

___29409-1 ONCE AN ANGEL ....$5.99/$7.99

___29408-3 A WHISPER OF ROSES ....$5.99/$7.99

___56332-7 THIEF OF HEARTS ....$5.99/$7.99

___56333-5 FAIREST OF THEM ALL ......$5.99/$7.50

___56334-3 BREATH OF MAGIC ....$5.99/$7.99

___57623-2 SHADOWS AND LACE ....$5.99/$7.99

___57500-7 TOUCH OF ENCHANTMENT. . $5.99/$7.99

___57501-5 NOBODY'S DARLING ....$5.99/$7.99

___57502-3 CHARMING THE PRINCE ....$5.99/$8.99

- -

Ask for these books at your local bookstore or use this page to order.

Please send me the books I have checked above. I am enclosing $_____ (add $2.50 to cover postage and handling). Send check or money order, no cash or C.O.D.'s, please.

Name _____

Address _____

City/State/Zip _____

Send order to: Bantam Books, Dept. FN 16, 400 Hahn Road, Westminster, MD 21157

Allow four to six weeks for delivery. Prices and availability subject to change without notice.